50
STRANGE AND ASTONISHING TALES

50 STRANGE AND ASTONISHING TALES

RUPA

Published by
Rupa Publications India Pvt. Ltd 2023
7/16, Ansari Road, Daryaganj
New Delhi 110002

Sales Centres:

Prayagraj Bengaluru Chennai
Hyderabad Jaipur Kathmandu
Kolkata Mumbai

Edition copyright © Rupa Publications India Pvt. Ltd 2023

All rights reserved.
No part of this publication may be reproduced, transmitted, or stored in a retrieval system, in any form or by any means, electronic, mechanical, photocopying, recording or otherwise, without the prior permission of the publisher.

P-ISBN: 978-93-5702-244-6
E-ISBN: 978-93-5702-248-6

First impression 2023

10 9 8 7 6 5 4 3 2 1

Printed in India

This book is sold subject to the condition that it shall not, by way of trade or otherwise, be lent, resold, hired out, or otherwise circulated, without the publisher's prior consent, in any form of binding or cover other than that in which it is published.

CONTENTS

Introduction	9
1. A Corner in Lightning *George Griffith*	11
2. A Man with Two Lives *Ambrose Bierce*	25
3. A Thousand Deaths *Jack London*	28
4. A Wife Manufactured to Order *Alice W. Fuller*	40
5. An Express of the Future *Michel Verne*	50
6. The Brink of Infinity *Stanley G. Weinbaum*	55
7. Christmas 200,000 B.C. *Stanley Waterloo*	69
8. Dr. Heidegger's Experiment *Nathaniel Hawthorne*	76
9. Finis *Frank L. Pollock*	88
10. From the "London Times" of 1904 *Mark Twain*	101
11. Graph *Stanley G. Weinbaum*	114
12. Here Lies *Howard Wandrei*	118

13.	In the Avu Observatory *H.G. Wells*	124
14.	In the Court of the Dragon *Robert W. Chambers*	133
15.	In the Year Ten Thousand *William Harben*	143
16.	The Incredible Aliens *William Bender Jr.*	152
17.	Mesmeric Revelation *Edgar Allan Poe*	163
18.	Moxon's Master *Ambrose Bierce*	176
19.	Mr. Brisher's Treasure *H.G. Wells*	188
20.	Roger Dodsworth: The Reanimated Englishman *Mary Wollstonecraft Shelley*	200
21.	Selling Point *Norman Arkawy*	211
22.	The Cage *J.D. Beresford*	218
23.	The Case of Mr. Helmer *Robert W. Chambers*	222
24.	The Clock that Went Backward *Edward Page Mitchell*	233
25.	The Conquest of the Earth by the Moon *Washington Irving*	250
26.	The Conversation of Eiros and Charmion *Edgar Allan Poe*	259

27. In the Year 2889 *Jules Verne and Michel Verne*	267
28. The End of the World *Eugène Mouton*	285
29. The Facts in the Case of M. Valdemar *Edgar Allan Poe*	295
30. The Flying Head *A. Hyatt Verrill*	307
31. The Flying Man *H.G. Wells*	320
32. The Triumphs of a Taxidermist *H.G. Wells*	328
33. The Inside of the Earth *Edward Page Mitchell*	333
34. The Man in the Machine *J.D. Beresford*	343
35. The Man in the Moon *L. Frank Baum*	347
36. The Man with the Strange Head *Miles J. Breuer*	353
37. The Man Without a Body *Edward Page Mitchell*	365
38. The Misanthrope *J.D. Beresford*	374
39. The Monarch of Dreams *Thomas Wentworth Higginson*	385
40. The Monster of Lake LaMetrie *Wardon Allan Curtis*	398

41. The Pool of the Stone God — 414
  Abraham Merritt
42. The Rocket of 1955 — 418
  C.M. Kornbluth
43. The Scientific Ape — 420
  Robert Louis Stevenson
44. The Star — 424
  H.G. Wells
45. The Stolen Bacillus — 437
  H.G. Wells
46. The Stone Cat — 445
  Miles J. Breuer
47. The Unparalleled Invasion — 456
  Jack London
48. The Voice in the Night — 472
  William Hope Hodgson
49. Venus and the Comet — 488
  Robert Duncan Milne
50. What Was It? A Mystery — 498
  Fitz-James O'Brien

INTRODUCTION

Among the stories we read, the ones that enthral us the most are those that question our beliefs and leave us wondering and reeling about what happened and how. In the centuries gone by, these would take the shape of either mythology or fairy tales. But in our contemporary world of scientific principles and material reality, the supernatural and the extraordinary find new and often wondrous ways to exist in the form of science fiction and speculative fiction.

Speculative and science fiction expands our received understanding of scientific concepts, much in the same way a fairy tale expands and goes beyond our received understanding of the real world. While such narratives do make for some interesting and escapist visions, they do often tell us more about our contemporaneity and the moment and places that we inhabit. By examining and questioning objects and ideas in the far reaches of space, or events in the distant future, these stories tell us about ourselves—how we define what it means to be human, how life works, and the idiosyncrasies of our lives, by stretching the very definition of the normal and the everyday.

This anthology of fifty stories navigate the length and breadth of the realms of speculative fiction, exploring ideas of time travel, space exploration, invasion, defeating death, and more. Our hope is that these stories, while serving as an introduction to the genres of science and speculative fiction, will also encourage a deeper understanding of the context behind these tales, and afford a window to the reader into how conceptions of the self and the other existed in the Victorian era and the early 20th century.

These stories have been selected for their historical importance, as well as the renown of their authors, such as H.G. Wells, Washington Irving, the Vernes, Miles J. Breuer, and Ambrose Bierce, among others. So dive into these wondrous and terrifying tales, and confront the odd, the curious, and the outlandish.

Happy Reading!

A CORNER IN LIGHTNING

George Griffith

They had been dining for once in a way tête-à-tête, and she—that is to say, Mrs. Sidney Calvert, a bride of eighteen months' standing—was half lying, half sitting in the depths of a big, cosy, saddle-bag armchair on one side of a bright fire of mixed wood and coal that was burning in one of the most improved imitations of the mediaeval fireplace. Her feet—very pretty little feet they were, too, and very daintily shod—were crossed, and poised on the heel of the right one at the corner of the black marble curb.

Dinner was over. The coffee service and the liqueur case were on the table, and Mr. Sidney Calvert, a well set-up young fellow of about thirty, with a handsome, good-humoured face which a close observer would have found curiously marred by a chilly glitter in the eyes and a hardness that was something more than firmness about the mouth, was walking up and down on the opposite side of the table smoking a cigarette.

Mrs. Calvert had just emptied her coffee cup, and as she put it down on a little three-legged console table by her side, she looked round at her husband and said:

"Really, Sid, I must say that I can't see why you should do it. Of course it's a very splendid scheme and all that sort of thing, but, surely you, one of the richest men in London, are rich enough to do without it. I'm sure it's wrong, too. What should we think if somebody managed to bottle up the atmosphere and made us pay for every breath we drew? Besides, there must surely be a good deal of risk in deliberately disturbing the economy of Nature in such a way. How are you going to get to the Pole, too, to put up your works?"

"Well," he said, stopping for a moment in his walk and looking thoughtfully at the lighted end of his cigarette, "in the first place, as to the geography, I must remind you that the Magnetic Pole is not the North Pole. It is in Boothia Land, British North America, some 1500 miles south of the North Pole. Then, as to the risk, of course one can't do big things like this without taking a certain amount of it; but still, I think it will be mostly other people that will have to take it in this case.

"Their risk, you see, will come in when they find that cables and telephones and telegraphs won't work, and that no amount of steam-engine grinding can get up a respectable amount of electric light—when in short, all the electric plant of the world loses its value, and can't be set going without buying supplies from the Magnetic Polar Storage Company, or, in other words, from your humble servant and the few friends that he will be graciously pleased to let in on the ground floor. But that is a risk that they can easily overcome by just paying for it. Besides, there's no reason why we shouldn't improve the quality of the commodity. 'Our Extra Special Refined Lightning!' 'Our Triple Concentrated Essence of Electric Fluid' and 'Competent Thunder-Storms delivered at the Shortest Notice' would look very nice in advertisements, wouldn't they?"

"Don't you think that's rather a frivolous way of talking about a scheme which might end in ruining one of the most important industries in the world?" she said, laughing in spite of herself at the idea of delivering thunder-storms like pounds of butter or skeins of Berlin wool.

"Well, I'm afraid I can't argue that point with you because, you see, you will keep looking at me while you talk, and that isn't fair. Anyhow I'm equally sure that it would be quite impossible to run any business and make money out of it on the lines of the

Sermon on the Mount. But, come, here's a convenient digression for both of us. That's the Professor, I expect."

"Shall I go?" she said, taking her feet off the fender.

"Certainly not, unless you wish to," he said; "or unless you think the scientific details are going to bore you."

"Oh, no, they won't do that," she said. "The Professor has such a perfectly charming way of putting them; and, besides, I want to know all that I can about it."

"Professor Kenyon, sir."

"Ah, good evening, Professor! So sorry you could not come to dinner." They both said this almost simultaneously as the man of science walked in.

"My wife and I were just discussing the ethics of this storage scheme when you came in," he went on. "Have you anything fresh to tell us about the practical aspects of it? I'm afraid she doesn't altogether approve of it, but as she is very anxious to hear all about it, I thought you wouldn't mind her making one of the audience."

"On the contrary, I shall be delighted," replied the Professor; "the more so as it will give me a sympathiser."

"I'm very glad to hear it," said Mrs. Calvert approvingly. "I think it will be a very wicked scheme if it succeeds, and a very foolish and expensive one if it fails."

"After which there is of course nothing more to be said," laughed her husband, "except for the Professor to give his dispassionate opinion."

"Oh, it shall be dispassionate, I can assure you," he replied, noticing a little emphasis on the word. "The ethics of the matter are no business of mine, nor have I anything to do with its commercial bearings. You have asked me merely to look at technical possibilities and scientific probabilities, and of course I don't propose to go beyond these."

He took another sip at a cup of coffee that Mrs. Calvert had handed him, and went on:

"I've had a long talk with Markovitch this afternoon, and I must confess that I never met a more ingenious man or one who knew as much about magnetism and electricity as he does. His theory that they are the celestial and terrestrial manifestations of the same force, and that what is popularly called electric fluid is developed only at the stage where they become one, is itself quite a stroke of genius, or, at least, it will be if the theory stands the test of experience. His idea of locating the storage works over the Magnetic Pole of the earth is another, and I am bound to confess that, after a very careful examination of his plans and designs, I am distinctly of opinion that, subject to one or two reservations, he will be able to do what he contemplates."

"And the reservations what are they?" asked Calvert a trifle eagerly.

"The first is one that it is absolutely necessary to make with regard to all untried schemes, and especially to such a gigantic one as this. Nature, you know, has a way of playing most unexpected pranks with people who take liberties with her. Just at the last moment, when you are on the verge of success, something that you confidently expect to happen doesn't happen, and there you are left in the lurch. It is utterly impossible to foresee anything of this kind, but you must clearly understand that if such a thing did happen it would ruin the enterprise just when you have spent the greatest part of the money on it—that is to say, at the end and not at the beginning."

"All right," said Calvert, "we'll take that risk. Now, what's the other reservation?"

"I was going to say something about the immense cost, but that I presume you are prepared for."

Calvert nodded, and he went on:

"Well, that point being disposed of, it remains to be said that it may be very dangerous—I mean to those who live on the spot, and will be actually engaged in the work."

"Then, I hope you won't think of going near the place, Sid!" interrupted Mrs. Calvert, with a very pretty assumption of wifely authority.

"We'll see about that later, little woman. It's early days yet to get frightened about possibilities. Well, Professor, what was it you were going to say? Any more warnings?"

The Professor's manner stiffened a little as he replied:

"Yes, it is a warning, Mr. Calvert. The fact is I feel bound to tell you that you propose to interfere very seriously with the distribution of one of the subtlest and least-known forces of Nature, and that the consequences of such an interference might be most disastrous, not only for those engaged in the work, but even the whole hemisphere, and possibly the whole planet.

"On the other hand, I think it is only fair to say that nothing more than a temporary disturbance may take place. You may, for instance, give us a series of very violent thunderstorms, with very heavy rains; or you may abolish thunderstorms and rain altogether until you get to work. Both prospects are within the bounds of possibility, and, at the same time, neither may come to anything."

"Well, I think that quite good enough to gamble on, Professor," said Calvert, who was thoroughly fascinated by the grandeur and magnitude, to say nothing of the dazzling financial aspects of the scheme. "I am very much obliged to you for putting it so clearly and nicely. Unless something very unexpected happens, we shall get to work on it at once. Just fancy what a glorious thing it will be to play Jove to the nations of the earth, and dole out lightning to them at so much a flash!"

"Well, I don't want to be ill-natured," said Mrs. Calvert,

"but I must say that I hope the unexpected will happen. I think the whole thing is very wrong to begin with, and I shouldn't be at all surprised if you blew us all up, or struck us all dead with lightning, or even brought on the Day of Judgment before its time. I think I shall go to Australia while you're doing it."

II

A little more than a year had passed since this after-dinner conversation in the dining-room of Mr. Sidney Calvert's London house. During that time the preparations for the great experiment had been swiftly but secretly carried out. Ship after ship loaded with machinery, fuel, and provisions, and carrying labourers and artificers to the number of some hundreds, had sailed away into the Atlantic, and had come back in ballast and with bare working crews on board of them. Mr. Calvert himself had disappeared and reappeared two or three times, and on his return he had neither admitted nor denied any of the various rumours which gradually got into circulation in the City and in the Press.

Some said that it was an expedition to the Pole, and that the machinery consisted partly of improved ice-breakers and newly-invented steam sledges, which were to attack the ice-hummocks after the fashion of battering rams, and so gradually smooth a road to the Pole. To these little details others added flying machines and navigable balloons. Others again declared that the object was to plough out the North-West passage and keep a waterway clear from Hudson's Bay to the Pacific all the year round, and yet others, somewhat less imaginative, pinned their faith to the founding of a great astronomical and meteorological observatory at the nearest possible point to the Pole, one of the objects of which was to be the determination of the true nature of the Aurora Borealis and the Zodiacal Light.

It was this last hypothesis that Mr. Calvert favoured as far as he could be said to favour any. There was a vagueness, and, at the same time, a distinction about a great scientific expedition which made it possible for him to give a sort of qualified countenance to the rumours without committing himself to anything, but so well had all his precautions been taken that not even a suspicion of the true object of the expedition to Boothia Land had got outside the little circle of those who were in his confidence.

So far everything had gone as Orloff Markovitch, the Russian Pole to whose extraordinary genius the inception and working out of the gigantic project were due, had expected and predicted. He himself was in supreme control of the unique and costly works which had grown up under his constant supervision on that lonely and desolate spot in the far North where the magnetic needle points straight down to the centre of the planet.

Professor Kenyon had paid a couple of visits with Calvert, once at the beginning of the work and once when it was nearing completion. So far not the slightest hitch or accident had occurred, and nothing abnormal had been noticed in connection with the earth's electrical phenomena save unusually frequent appearances of the Aurora Borealis, and a singular decrease in the deviation of the mariner's compass. Nevertheless, the Professor had firmly but politely refused to remain until the gigantic apparatus was set to work, and Calvert, too, had, with extreme reluctance, yielded to his wife's intreaties, and had come back to England about a month before the initial experiment was to be begun.

The twentieth of March, which was the day fixed for the commencement of operations, came and went, to Mrs. Calvert's intense relief, without anything out of the common happening. Though she knew that over a hundred thousand pounds of her husband's money had been sunk, she found it impossible not to feel a thrill of satisfaction in the hope that Markovitch had made his experiment and failed.

She knew that the great Calvert Company, which was practically himself, could very well afford it, and she would not have regretted the loss of three times the sum in exchange for the knowledge that Nature was to be allowed to dispose of her electrical forces as seemed good to her. As for her husband, he went about his business as usual, only displaying slight signs of suppressed excitement and anticipation now and then, as the weeks went by and nothing happened.

She had not carried out her threat of going to Australia. She had, however, escaped from the rigours of the English spring to a villa near Nice, where she was awaiting the arrival of her second baby, an event which she had found very useful in persuading her husband to stop away from the Magnetic Pole. Calvert himself was so busy with what might be called the home details of the scheme that he had to spend the greater part of his time in London, and could only run over to Nice now and then.

It so happened that Miss Calvert put in an appearance a few days before she was expected, and therefore while her father was still in London. Her mother very naturally sent her maid with a telegram to inform him of the fact and ask him to come over at once. In about half-an-hour the maid came back with the form in her hand bringing a message from the telegraph office that, in consequence of some extraordinary accident, the wires had almost ceased to work properly and that no messages could be got through distinctly.

In the rapture of her new motherhood Kate Calvert had forgotten all about the great Storage Scheme, so she sent the maid back again with the request that the message should be sent off as soon as possible. Two hours later she sent again to ask if it had gone, and the reply came back that the wires had ceased working altogether and that no electrical communication by telegraph or telephone was for the present possible.

Then a terrible fear came to her. The experiment had been a success after all, and Markovitch's mysterious engines had been all this time imperceptibly draining the earth of its electric fluid and storing it up in the vast accumulators which would only yield it back again at the bidding of the Trust which was controlled by her husband! Still she was a sensible little woman, and after the first shock she managed, for her baby's sake, to put the fear out of her mind, at any rate until her husband came. He would be with her in a day or two, and, perhaps, after all, it was only some strange but perfectly natural occurrence which Nature herself would set right in a few hours.

When it got dusk that night, and the electric lights were turned on, it was noticed that they gave an unusually dim and wavering light. The engines were worked to their highest power, and the lines were carefully examined. Nothing could be found wrong with them, but the lights refused to behave as usual, and the most extraordinary feature of the phenomenon was that exactly the same thing was happening in all the electrically lighted cities and towns in the northern hemisphere. By midnight, too, telegraphic and telephonic communication north of the Equator had practically ceased, and the electricians of Europe and America were at their wits' ends to discover any reason for this unheard of disaster, for such in sober truth it would be unless the apparently suspended force quickly resumed action on its own account. The next morning it was found that, so far as all the marvels of electrical science were concerned, the world had gone back a hundred years.

Then people began to awake to the magnitude of the catastrophe that had befallen the world. Civilised mankind had been suddenly deprived of the services of an obedient slave which it had come to look upon as indispensable.

But there was something even more serious than this to

come. Observers in various parts of the hemisphere remembered that there hadn't been a thunder-storm anywhere for some weeks. Even the regions most frequently visited by them had had none. A most remarkable drought had also set in almost universally. A strange sickness, beginning with physical lassitude and depression of spirits which confounded the best medical science of the world was manifesting itself far and wide, and rapidly assuming the proportions of a gigantic epidemic.

In the physical world, too, metals were found to be afflicted with the same incomprehensible disease. Machinery of all sorts got "sick," to use a technical expression, and absolutely refused to act, and forges and foundries everywhere came to a standstill for the simple reason that metals seemed to have lost their best properties, and could no longer be utilised as they had been. Railway accidents and breakdowns on steamers, too, became matters of every day occurrence, for metals and driving wheels, piston rods and propeller shafts, had acquired an incomprehensible brittleness which only began to be understood when it was discovered that the electrical properties which iron and steel had formerly possessed had almost entirely disappeared.

So far Calvert had not wavered in his determination to make, as he thought, a colossal amount of money by his usurpation of one of the functions of Nature. To him the calamities which, it must be confessed, he had deliberately brought upon the world were only so many arguments for the ultimate success of the stupendous scheme. They were proof positive to the world, or at least they very soon would be, that the Calvert Storage Trust really did control the electricity of the Northern Hemisphere. From the Southern nothing had yet been heard beyond the news that the cables had ceased working.

Hence, as soon as he had demonstrated his power to restore matters to their normal condition, it was obvious that the world would have to pay his price under penalty of having the supply cut off again.

It was now getting towards the end of May. On the 1st of June, according to arrangement, Markovitch would stop his engines and permit the vast accumulation of electric fluid in his storage batteries to flow back into its accustomed channels. Then the Trust would issue its prospectus, setting forth the terms upon which it was prepared to permit the nations to enjoy that gift of Nature whose pricelessness the Trust had proved by demonstrating its own ability to corner it.

On the evening of May 25th Calvert was sitting in his sumptuous office in Victoria Street, writing by the light of a dozen wax candles in silver candelabra. He had just finished a letter to his wife, telling her to keep up her spirits and fear nothing; that in a few days the experiment would be over and everything restored to its former condition, shortly after which she would be the wife of a man who would soon be able to buy up all the other millionaires in the world.

As he put the letter into the envelope there was a knock at the door, and Professor Kenyon was announced. Calvert greeted him stiffly and coldly, for he more than half guessed the errand he had come on. There had been two or three heated discussions between them of late, and Calvert knew before the Professor opened his lips that he had come to tell him that he was about to fulfil a threat that he had made a few days before. And this the Professor did tell him in a few dry, quiet words.

"It's no use, Professor," he replied, "you know yourself that I am powerless, as powerless as you are. I have no means of communicating with Markovitch, and the work cannot be stopped until the appointed time."

"But you were warned, sir!" the Professor interrupted warmly. "You were warned, and when you saw the effects coming you might have stopped. I wish to goodness that I had had nothing to do with the infernal business, for infernal it really is. Who are you that you should usurp one of the functions of the Almighty, for it is nothing less than that? I have kept your criminal secret too long, and I will keep it no longer. You have made yourself the enemy of Society, and Society still has the power to deal with you—"

"My dear Professor, that's all nonsense, and you know it!" said Calvert, interrupting him with a contemptuous gesture: "If Society were to lock me up, it should do without electricity till I were free. If it hung one it would get none, except on Markovitch's terms, which would be higher than mine. So you can tell your story whenever you please. Meanwhile you'll excuse me if I remind you that I am rather busy."

Just as the Professor was about to take his leave the door opened and a boy brought in an envelope deeply edged with black. Calvert turned white to the lips and his hand trembled as he took it and opened it. It was in his wife's handwriting, and was dated five days before, as most of the journey had to be made on horseback. He read it through with fixed, staring eyes, then he crushed it into his pocket and strode towards the telephone. He rang the bell furiously, and then he started back with an oath on his lips, remembering that he had made it useless. The sound of the bell brought a clerk into the room immediately.

"Get me a hansom at once!" he almost shouted, and the clerk vanished.

"What is the matter? Where are you going?" asked the Professor.

"Matter? Read that!" he said, thrusting the crumpled letter into his hand. "My little girl is dead—dead of that accursed sickness which, as you justly say, I have brought on the world, and my wife is down with it, too, and may be dead by this time. That letter's five days old. My God, what have I done? What can I do? I'd give fifty thousand pounds to get a telegram to Markovitch. Curse him and his infernal scheme! If she dies I'll go to Boothia Land and kill him! Hullo! What's that? Lightning—by all that's holy—and thunder!"

As he spoke such a flash of lightning as had never split the skies of London before flared in a huge ragged stream of flame across the zenith, and a roar of thunder such as London's ears had never heard shook every house in the vast city to its foundation. Another and another followed in rapid succession, and all through the night and well into the next day there raged, as it was afterwards found, almost all over the whole Northern hemisphere, such a thunderstorm as had never been known in the world before and never would be again.

With it, too, came hurricanes and cyclones and deluges of rain; and when, after raging for nearly twenty-four hours, it at length ceased convulsing the atmosphere and growled itself away into silence, the first fact that came out of the chaos and desolation that it had left behind it was that the normal electrical conditions of the world had been restored—after which mankind set itself to repair the damage done by the cataclysm and went about its business in the usual way.

The epidemic vanished instantly and Mrs. Calvert did not die. Nearly six months later a white-haired wreck of a man crawled into her husband's office and said feebly:

"Don't you know me, Mr. Calvert? I'm Markovitch, or what there is left of him."

"Good heavens, so you are!" said Calvert. "What has happened to you? Sit down and tell me all about it."

The whole works suddenly burst into white flame. "It is not a long story," said Markovitch, sitting down and beginning to speak in a thin, trembling voice. "It is not long, but it is very bad. Everything went well at first. All succeeded as I said it would and then, I think it was just four days before we should have stopped, it happened."

"What happened?"

"I don't know. We must have gone too far, or by some means an accidental discharge must have taken place. The whole works suddenly burst into white flame. Everything made of metal melted like tallow. Every man in the works died instantly, burnt, you know, to a cinder. I was four or five miles away, with some others, seal shooting. We were all struck down insensible. When I came to myself I found I was the only one alive. Yes, Mr. Calvert, I am the only man that has returned from Boothia alive. The works are gone. There are only some heaps of melted metal lying about on the ice. After that I don't know what happened. I must have gone mad. It was enough to make a man mad, you know. But some Indians and Eskimos, who used to trade with us, found me wandering about, so they told me, starving and out of my mind, and they took me to the coast. There I got better and then was picked up by a whaler and so I got home. That is all. It was very awful, wasn't it?"

Then he reeled backward. Then his face fell forward into his trembling hands, and Calvert saw the tears trickling between his fingers. Then he reeled backward, and suddenly his body slipped gently out of the chair and on to the floor. When Calvert tried to pick him up he was dead. And so the secret of the Great Experiment, so far as the world at large was concerned, never got beyond the walls of Mr. Sidney Calvert's cosy dining-room after all.

A MAN WITH TWO LIVES

Ambrose Bierce

Here is the queer story of David William Duck, related by himself. Duck is an old man living in Aurora, Illinois, where he is universally respected. He is commonly known, however, as "Dead Duck."

"In the autumn of 1866 I was a private soldier of the Eighteenth Infantry. My company was one of those stationed at Fort Phil Kearney, commanded by Colonel Carrington. The country is more or less familiar with the history of that garrison, particularly with the slaughter by the Sioux of a detachment of eighty-one men and officers—not one escaping—through disobedience of orders by its commander, the brave but reckless Captain Fetterman. When that occurred, I was trying to make my way with important dispatches to Fort C. F. Smith, on the Big Horn. As the country swarmed with hostile Indians, I traveled by night and concealed myself as best I could before daybreak. The better to do so, I went afoot, armed with a Henry rifle and carrying three days' rations in my haversack.

"For my second place of concealment I chose what seemed in the darkness a narrow canon leading through a range of rocky hills. It contained many large bowlders, detached from the slopes of the hills. Behind one of these, in a clump of sage-brush, I made my bed for the day, and soon fell asleep. It seemed as if I had hardly closed my eyes, though in fact it was near midday, when I was awakened by the report of a rifle, the bullet striking the bowlder just above my body. A band of Indians had trailed me and had me nearly surrounded; the shot had been fired with an execrable aim by a fellow who had caught sight of me from the hillside above. The smoke of his rifle betrayed him, and I was no sooner on my feet than he was off his and rolling down the declivity. Then I ran in a stooping posture, dodging among the clumps of sage-brush in a storm of bullets from invisible enemies. The rascals did not rise and pursue, which I thought rather queer, for they must have known by my trail that they had to deal with only one man. The reason for their inaction was soon made clear. I had not gone a hundred yards before I reached the limit of my run—the head of the gulch which I had mistaken for a canon. It terminated in a concave breast of rock, nearly vertical and destitute of vegetation. In that cul-de-sac I was caught like a bear in a pen. Pursuit was needless; they had only to wait.

"They waited. For two days and nights, crouching behind a rock topped with a growth of mesquite, and with the cliff at my back, suffering agonies of thirst and absolutely hopeless of deliverance, I fought the fellows at long range, firing occasionally at the smoke of their rifles, as they did at that of mine. Of course, I did not dare to close my eyes at night, and lack of sleep was a keen torture.

"I remember the morning of the third day, which I knew was to be my last. I remember, rather indistinctly, that in my desperation and delirium I sprang out into the open and began firing my repeating rifle without seeing anybody to fire at. And I remember no more of that fight.

"The next thing that I recollect was my pulling myself out of a river just at nightfall. I had not a rag of clothing and knew nothing of my whereabouts, but all that night I traveled, cold and footsore, toward the north. At daybreak I found myself at Fort C. F. Smith, my destination, but without my dispatches. The first man that I met was a sergeant named William Briscoe, whom I knew very well. You can fancy his astonishment at seeing me in that condition, and my own at his asking who the devil I was.

"'Dave Duck,' I answered; 'who should I be?'

"He stared like an owl.

"'You do look it,' he said, and I observed that he drew a little away from me. 'What's up?' he added.

"I told him what had happened to me the day before. He heard me through, still staring; then he said:

"'My dear fellow, if you are Dave Duck I ought to inform you that I buried you two months ago. I was out with a small scouting party and found your body, full of bullet-holes and newly scalped— somewhat mutilated otherwise, too, I am sorry to say—right where you say you made your fight. Come to my tent and I'll show you your clothing and some letters that I took from your person; the commandant has your dispatches.'

"He performed that promise. He showed me the clothing, which I resolutely put on; the letters, which I put into my pocket. He made no objection, then took me to the commandant, who heard my story and coldly ordered Briscoe to take me to the guardhouse. On the way I said:

"'Bill Briscoe, did you really and truly bury the dead body that you found in these togs?'

"'Sure,' he answered—'just as I told you. It was Dave Duck, all right; most of us knew him. And now, you damned impostor, you'd better tell me who you are.'

"'I'd give something to know,' I said.

"A week later, I escaped from the guardhouse and got out of the country as fast as I could. Twice I have been back, seeking for that fateful spot in the hills, but unable to find it."

A THOUSAND DEATHS

Jack London

I had been in the water about an hour, and cold, exhausted, with a terrible cramp in my right calf, it seemed as though my hour had come. Fruitlessly struggling against the strong ebb tide, I had beheld the maddening procession of the water-front lights slip by, but now I gave up attempting to breast the stream and contended myself with the bitter thoughts of a wasted career, now drawing to a close.

It had been my luck to come of good, English stock, but of parents whose account with the bankers far exceeded their knowledge of child-nature and the rearing of children. While born with a silver spoon in my mouth, the blessed atmosphere of the home circle was to me unknown. My father, a very learned man and a celebrated antiquarian, gave no thought to his family, being constantly lost in the abstractions of his study; while my mother, noted far more for her good looks than her good sense, sated herself with the adulation of the society in which she was perpetually plunged. I went through the regular school and college routine of a boy of the English bourgeoisie, and as the years brought me increasing strength and passions, my parents suddenly became aware that I was possessed of an immortal soul, and endeavoured to draw the curb. But it was too late; I perpetrated the wildest and most audacious folly, and was disowned by my people, ostracised by the society I had so long outraged, and with the thousand pounds my father gave me, with the declaration that he would neither see me again nor give me more, I took a first-class passage to Australia.

Since then my life had been one long peregrination—from the Orient to the Occident, from the Arctic to the Antarctic—to find myself at last, an able seaman at thirty, in the full vigour of my manhood, drowning in San Francisco bay because of a disastrously successful attempt to desert my ship.

My right leg was drawn up by the cramp, and I was suffering the keenest agony. A slight breeze stirred up a choppy sea, which washed into my mouth and down my throat, nor could I prevent it. Though I still contrived to keep afloat, it was merely mechanical, for I was rapidly becoming unconscious. I have a dim recollection of drifting past the sea-wall, and of catching a glimpse of an upriver steamer's starboard light; then everything became a blank.

◆

I heard the low hum of insect life, and felt the balmy air of a spring morning fanning my cheek. Gradually it assumed a rhythmic flow, to whose soft pulsations my body seemed to respond. I floated on the gentle bosom of a summer's sea, rising and falling with dreamy pleasure on each crooning wave. But the pulsations grew stronger; the humming, louder; the waves, larger, fiercer—I was dashed about on a stormy sea. A great agony fastened upon me. Brilliant, intermittent sparks of light flashed athwart my inner consciousness; in my ears there was the sound of many waters; then a sudden snapping of an intangible something, and I awoke.

The scene, of which I was protagonist, was a curious one. A glance sufficed to inform me that I lay on the cabin floor of some gentleman's yacht, in a most uncomfortable posture. On either side, grasping my arms and working them up and down like pump handles, were two peculiarly clad, dark-skinned creatures. Though conversant with most aboriginal types, I could not conjecture their nationality. Some attachment had been fastened about my head, which connected my respiratory organs with the machine I shall next describe. My nostrils, however, had been closed, forcing me to breathe through my mouth. Foreshortened by the obliquity of my line of vision, I beheld two tubes, similar to small hosing but of different composition, which emerged from my mouth and went off at an acute angle from each other. The first came to an abrupt termination and lay on the floor beside me; the second traversed the floor in numerous coils, connecting with the apparatus I have promised to describe.

In the days before my life had become tangential, I had dabbled not a little in science, and, conversant with the appurtenances and general paraphernalia of the laboratory, I appreciated the machine I now beheld. It was composed chiefly of glass, the construction being of that crude sort which is employed for experimentative purposes. A vessel of water was surrounded by an air chamber, to which was fixed a vertical tube, surmounted by a globe. In the centre of this was a vacuum gauge. The water in the tube moved upwards and downwards, creating alternate inhalations and exhalations, which were in turn communicated to me through the hose. With this, and the aid of the men who pumped my arms, so vigorously, had the process of breathing been artificially carried on, my chest rising and falling and my lungs expanding and contracting, till nature could be persuaded to again take up her wonted labour.

As I opened my eyes the appliance about my head, nostrils and mouth was removed. Draining a stiff three fingers of brandy, I staggered to my feet to thank my preserver, and confronted—my father. But long years of fellowship with danger had taught me self-control, and I waited to see if he would recognise me. Not so; he saw in me no more than a runaway sailor and treated me accordingly.

Leaving me to the care of the blackies, he fell to revising the notes he had made on my resuscitation. As I ate of the handsome fare served up to me, confusion began on deck, and from the chanteys of the sailors and the rattling of blocks and tackles I surmised that we were getting under way. What a lark! Off on a cruise with my recluse father into the wide Pacific! Little did I realise, as I laughed to myself, which side the joke was to be on. Aye, had I known, I would have plunged overboard and welcomed the dirty fo'c'sle from which I had just escaped.

I was not allowed on deck till we had sunk the Farallones and the last pilot boat. I appreciated this forethought on the part of my father and made it a point to thank him heartily, in my bluff seaman's manner. I could not suspect that he had his own ends in view, in thus keeping my presence secret to all save the crew. He told me briefly of my rescue by his sailors, assuring me that the obligation was on his side, as my appearance had been most opportune. He had constructed the apparatus for the vindication of a theory concerning certain biological phenomena, and had been waiting for an opportunity to use it.

"You have proved it beyond all doubt," he said; then added with a sigh, "But only in the small matter of drowning."

But, to take a reef in my yarn—he offered me an advance of two pounds on my previous wages to sail with him, and this I considered handsome, for he really did not need me. Contrary to my expectations, I did not join the sailor' mess, for'ard, being assigned to a comfortable stateroom and eating at the captain's table. He had perceived that I was no common sailor, and I resolved to take this chance for reinstating myself in his good graces. I wove a fictitious past to account for my education and present position, and did my best to come in touch with him. I was not long in disclosing a predilection for scientific pursuits, nor he in appreciating my aptitude. I became his assistant, with a corresponding increase in wages, and before long, as he grew confidential and expounded his theories, I was as enthusiastic as himself.

The days flew quickly by, for I was deeply interested in my new studies, passing my waking hours in his well-stocked library, or listening to his plans and aiding him in his laboratory work. But we were forced to forego many enticing experiments, a rolling ship not being exactly the proper place for delicate or intricate work. He promised me, however, many delightful hours in the magnificent laboratory for which we were bound. He had taken possession of an uncharted South Sea island, as he said, and turned it into a scientific paradise.

We had not been on the island long, before I discovered the horrible mare's nest I had fallen into. But before I describe the strange things which came to pass, I must briefly outline the causes which culminated in as startling an experience as ever fell to the lot of man.

Late in life, my father had abandoned the musty charms of antiquity and succumbed to the more fascinating ones embraced under the general head of biology. Having been thoroughly grounded during his youth in the fundamentals, he rapidly explored all the higher branches as far as the scientific world had gone, and found himself on the no man's land of the unknowable. It was his intention to pre-empt some of this unclaimed territory, and it was at this stage of his investigations that we had been thrown together. Having a good brain, though I say it myself, I had mastered his speculations and methods of reasoning, becoming almost as mad as himself. But I should not say this. The marvellous results we afterwards obtained can only go to prove his sanity. I can but say that he was the most abnormal specimen of cold-blooded cruelty I have ever seen.

After having penetrated the dual mysteries of physiology

and psychology, his thought had led him to the verge of a great field, for which, the better to explore, he began studies in higher organic chemistry, pathology, toxicology and other sciences and sub-sciences rendered kindred as accessories to his speculative hypotheses. Starting from the proposition that the direct cause of the temporary and permanent arrest of vitality was due to the coagulation of certain elements and compounds in the protoplasm, he had isolated and subjected these various substances to innumerable experiments. Since the temporary arrest of vitality in an organism brought coma, and a permanent arrest death, he held that by artificial means this coagulation of the protoplasm could be retarded, prevented, and even overcome in the extreme states of solidification. Or, to do away with the technical nomenclature, he argued that death, when not violent and in which none of the organs had suffered injury, was merely suspended vitality; and that, in such instances, life could be induced to resume its functions by the use of proper methods. This, then, was his idea: To discover the method—and by practical experimentation prove the possibility—of renewing vitality in a structure from which life had seemingly fled. Of course, he recognised the futility of such endeavour after decomposition had set in; he must have organisms which but the moment, the hour, or the day before, had been quick with life. With me, in a crude way, he had proved this theory. I was really drowned, really dead, when picked from the water of San Francisco bay—but the vital spark had been renewed by means of his aerotherapeutical apparatus, as he called it.

Now to his dark purpose concerning me. He first showed me how completely I was in his power. He had sent the yacht away for a year, retaining only his two blackies, who were utterly devoted to him. He then made an exhaustive review of his theory and outlined the method of proof he had adopted, concluding with the startling announcement that I was to be his subject.

I had faced death and weighed my chances in many a desperate venture, but never in one of this nature. I can swear I am no coward, yet this proposition of journeying back and forth across the borderland of death put the yellow fear upon me. I asked for time, which he granted, at the same time assuring me that but the one course was open—I must submit. Escape from the Island was out of the question; escape by suicide was not to be entertained, though really preferable to what it seemed I must undergo; my only hope was to destroy my captors. But this latter was frustrated through the precautions taken by my father. I was subjected to a constant surveillance, even in my sleep being guarded by one or the other of the blacks.

Having pleaded in vain, I announced and proved that I was his son. It was my last card, and I had played all my hopes upon it. But he was inexorable; he was not a father but a scientific machine. I wonder yet how it ever came to pass that he married my mother or begat me, for there was not the slightest grain of emotion in his make-up. Reason was all in all to him, nor could he understand such things as love or sympathy in others, except as petty weaknesses which should be overcome. So he informed me that in the beginning he had given me life, and who had better right to take it away than he? Such, he said, was not his desire, however; he merely wished to borrow it occasionally, promising to return it punctually at the appointed time. Of course, there was a liability of mishaps, but I could do no more than take the chances, since the affairs of men were full of such.

The better to insure success, he wished me to be in the best possible condition, so I was dieted and trained like a great athlete before a decisive contest. What could I do? If I had to undergo the peril, it were best to be in good shape. In my intervals of relaxation he allowed me to assist in the arranging of the apparatus and in the various subsidiary experiments. The interest I took in all such operations can be imagined. I mastered the work as thoroughly as he, and often had the pleasure of seeing some of my suggestions or alterations put into effect. After such events I would smile grimly, conscious of officiating at my own funeral.

He began by inaugurating a series of experiments in toxicology. When all was ready, I was killed by a stiff dose of strychnine and allowed to lie dead for some twenty hours. During that period my body was dead, absolutely dead. All respiration and circulation ceased; but the frightful part of it was, that while the protoplasmic coagulation proceeded, I retained consciousness and was enabled to study it in all its ghastly details.

The apparatus to bring me back to life was an air-tight chamber, fitted to receive my body. The mechanism was simple—a few valves, a rotary shaft and crank, and an electric motor. When in operation, the interior atmosphere was alternately condenses and rarefied, thus communicating to my lungs an artificial respiration without the agency of the hosing previously used. Though my body was inert, and, for all I knew, in the first stages of decomposition, I was cognisant of everything that transpired. I knew when they placed me in the chamber, and though all my senses were quiescent, I was aware of hypodermic injections of a compound to react upon the coagulatory process. Then the chamber was closed and the machinery started. My anxiety was terrible; but the circulation became gradually restored, the different organs began to carry on their respective functions, and in an hour's time I was eating a hearty dinner.

It cannot be said that I participated in this series, nor in the subsequent ones, with much verve; but after two ineffectual attempts of escape, I began to take quite an interest. Besides, I was becoming accustomed. My father was beside himself at his success, and as the months rolled by his speculations took wilder and yet wilder flights. We ranged through the three great classes of poisons, the neurotics, the gaseous and the irritants, but carefully avoided some of the mineral irritants and passed the whole group of corrosives. During the poison regime I became quite accustomed to dying, and had but one mishap to shake my growing confidence. Scarifying a number of lesser blood vessels in my arm, he introduced a minute quantity of that most frightful of poisons, the arrow poison, or curare. I lost consciousness at the start, quickly followed by the cessation of respiration and circulation, and so far had the solidification of the protoplasm advanced, that he gave up all hope. But at the last moment he applied a discovery he had been working upon, receiving such encouragement as to redouble his efforts.

In a glass vacuum, similar but not exactly like a Crookes' tube, was placed a magnetic field. When penetrated by polarised light, it gave no phenomena of phosphorescence nor the rectilinear projection of atoms, but emitted non-luminous rays, similar to the X-ray. While the X-ray could reveal opaque objects hidden in dense mediums, this was possessed of far subtler penetration. By this he photographed my body, and found on the negative an infinite number of blurred shadows, due to the chemical and electric motions still going on. This was an infallible proof that the rigor mortis in which I lay was not genuine; that is, those mysterious forces, those delicate bonds which held my soul to my body, were still in action. The resultants of all other poisons were unapparent, save those of mercurial compounds, which usually left me languid for several days.

Another series of delightful experiments was with electricity. We verified Tesla's assertion that high currents were utterly harmless by passing 100,000 volts through my body. As this did not affect me, the current was reduced to 2,500, and I was quickly electrocuted. This time he ventured so far as to allow me to remain dead, or in a state of suspended vitality, for three days. It took four hours to bring me back.

Once, he superinduced lockjaw; but the agony of dying was so great that I positively refused to undergo similar experiments. The easiest deaths were by asphyxiation, such as drowning, strangling, and suffocation by gas; while those by morphine, opium, cocaine, and chloroform, were not at all hard.

Another time, after being suffocated, he kept me in cold storage for three months, not permitting me to freeze or decay. This was without my knowledge, and I was in a great fright on discovering the lapse of time. I became afraid of what he might do with me when I lay dead, my alarm being increased by the predilection he was beginning to betray towards vivisection. The last time I was resurrected, I discovered that he had been tampering with my breast. Though he had carefully dressed and sewed the incisions up, they were so severe that I had to take to my bed for some time. It was during this convalescence that I evolved the plan by which I ultimately escaped.

While feigning unbounded enthusiasm in the work, I asked and received a vacation from my moribund occupation. During this period I devoted myself to laboratory work, while he was too deep in the vivisection of the many animals captured by the blacks to take notice of my work.

It was on these two propositions that I constructed my theory: First, electrolysis, or the decomposition of water into its constituent gases by means of electricity; and, second, by the hypothetical existence of a force, the converse of gravitation, which Astor has named "apergy". Terrestrial attraction, for instance, merely draws objects together but does not combine them; hence, apergy is merely repulsion. Now, atomic or molecular attraction not only draws objects together but integrates them; and it was the converse of this, or a disintegrative force, which I wished to not only discover and produce, but to direct at will. Thus, the molecules of hydrogen and oxygen reacting on each other, separate and create new molecules, containing both elements and forming water. Electrolysis causes these molecules to split up and resume their original condition, producing the two gases separately. The force I wished to find must not only do this with two, but with all elements, no matter in what compounds they exist. If I could then entice my father within its radius, he would be instantly disintegrated and sent flying to the four quarters, a mass of isolated elements.

It must not be understood that this force, which I finally came to control, annihilated matter; it merely annihilated form. Nor, as I soon discovered, had it any effect on inorganic structure; but to all organic form it was absolutely fatal. This partiality puzzled me at first, though had I stopped to think deeper I would have seen through it. Since the number of atoms in organic molecules is far greater than in the most complex mineral molecules, organic compounds are characterised by their instability and the ease with which they are split up by physical forces and chemical reagents.

By two powerful batteries, connected with magnets constructed specially for this purpose, two tremendous forces were projected. Considered apart from each other, they were perfectly harmless; but they accomplished their purpose by focusing at an invisible point in mid-air. After practically demonstrating its success, besides narrowly escaping being blown into nothingness, I laid my trap. Concealing the magnets, so that their force made the whole space of my chamber doorway a field of death, and placing by my couch a button by which I could throw on the current from the storage batteries, I climbed into bed.

The blackies still guarded my sleeping quarters, one relieving the other at midnight. I turned on the current as soon as the first man arrived. Hardly had I begun to doze, when I was aroused by a sharp, metallic tinkle. There, on the mid-threshold, lay the collar of Dan, my father's St. Bernard. My keeper ran to pick it up. He disappeared like a gust of wind, his clothes falling to the floor in a heap. There was a slight wiff of ozone in the air, but since the principal gaseous components of his body were hydrogen, oxygen and nitrogen, which are equally colourless and odourless, there was no other manifestation of his departure. Yet when I shut off the current and removed the garments, I found a deposit of carbon in the form of animal charcoal; also other powders, the isolated, solid elements of his organism, such as sulphur, potassium and iron. Resetting the trap, I crawled back to bed. At midnight I got up and removed the remains of the second black, and then slept peacefully till morning.

I was awakened by the strident voice of my father, who was calling to me from across the laboratory. I laughed to myself. There had been no one to call him and he had overslept. I could hear him as he approached my room with the intention of rousing me, and so I sat up in bed, the better to observe his translation—perhaps apotheosis were a better term. He paused a moment at the threshold, then took the fatal step. Puff! It was like the wind sighing among the pines. He was gone. His clothes fell in a fantastic heap on the floor. Besides ozone, I noticed the faint, garlic-like odour of phosphorus. A little pile of elementary solids lay among his garments. That was all. The wide world lay before me. My captors were no more.

A WIFE MANUFACTURED TO ORDER

Alice W. Fuller

As I was going down G Street in the city of W— a strange sign attracted my attention. I stopped, looked, fairly rubbed my eyes to see if they were rightly focused; yes, there it was plainly lettered in gilt: "Wives made to order! Satisfaction guaranteed or money refunded."

Well! well! does some lunatic live here, I wonder? By Jove! I will investigate. I had inherited (I suppose from my mother) a bit of curiosity, and the truth of the matter was this: now nearing the age of forty, I thought it might be advisable to settle down in a home of my own; but alas! to settle down to a life of strife and turmoil, that would not be pleasant; and that I should have to do, I knew very well, if I should marry any of my numerous lady acquaintances—especially Florence Ward, the one I most admired. She unfortunately had strong-minded ways, and inclinations to be investigating woman's rights, politics, theosophy, and all that sort of thing. Bah! I could never endure it. I should be miserable, and the outcome would be a separation; I knew it. To be dictated to, perhaps found fault with—no, no, it would never do; better be a bachelor and at least live in peace. But—what does this sign mean? I'll find out for myself.

A ring of the bell brought a little white-haired, wiry sort of a man to the door. "Walk in, walk in, sir," he said.

I asked for an explanation of the strange sign over the door.

"Just step right in here and be seated, sir. My master is engaged at present, sir, with a great politician who had to separate from his wife; was so fractious, sir, got so many strange notions in her head; in fact, she wanted to hold the reins herself. You may have seen it—the papers have been full of it. Why, law bless you, sir, the poor man couldn't say his soul was his own, and he is here now making arrangements with master to make him a quieter sort of wife, some one to do the honors of the home without feelin' neglected if he happens to be a little courteous to some of his young lady friends. You see, master makes 'em to order, makes 'em to think just as you do, just as you want 'em to; then you've got a happy home, something to live for. Beautiful—golly! I've seen some of the beautifulest women turned out, 'most make your mouth water to look at." And so the old man rattled on until I was quite bewildered.

I interrupted him by asking if I could see his master.

"Oh, certainly, sir; you just make yourself comfortable and I will let you know when he is through."

I sat for some time like one in a dream, wondering if this could be so, and with many wonderful modern inventions in mind I began to think it possible. And then there was a vision of a happy home, a wife beautiful as a dream, gentle and loving, without a thought for anyone but me; one who would never reproach me if I didn't happen to get home just at what she thought was the proper time; one who would not ask me to go to church when she knew it was against my wishes; one who would never find fault with me if I wished to go to a base-ball game on Sunday, or bother me to take her to the theatre or opera. A man, you know, can't give much time to such things without interfering greatly with his comfort. Oh! could all this be realized? But just then my reverie was broken by the old man, who was saying: "Just step this way. Master, let me introduce you to Mr. Charles Fitzsimmons."

Short, thick-set, florid complexion, pale blue eyes with a sinister twinkle, was the description of Mr. Sharper, whom I confronted. Reaching out his hand, which was cold and clammy and reminded me very much of a piece of cold boiled pork, he said:

"Now, young man, what can I do for you? Want a life-companion, a pleasant one? Man of means, no doubt, and can enjoy yourself; a little fun now and then with the boys and no harm at all—none in the least. When a man comes home tired, doesn't like to be dictated to; want some one always to meet you with a smile, some one that doesn't expect you to be fondlin' and pettin' 'em all the time. I understand it—I know just how it is. Law bless my soul, I'e made more'n one man happy, and I've only been in the business a short time, too. Now, sir, I can get you up any style you want—*wax*, but can't be detected."

"Do you mean to say you manufacture a woman out of wax, who will talk?"

"That's just what I do; you give me the subjects you most enjoy talking upon, and tell me what kind of a looking wife you want, and leave the rest to me, and you will never regret it. I will furnish as many 'phones' as you wish; most men don't care for such a variety for a wife—too much talk, you know;" and he chuckled and laughed like a big baby.

"What are your prices, may I ask?"

"Well, it's owing a good deal to how they are got up—from five hundred to a thousand dollars."

"Well," I said, "I think that rather high."

"Dear man alive, a pleasant companion for life for a few hundred dollars! Most men don't grumble at all for the sake of having their own way and a pleasant home, and you see she ain't always asking for money." (Sure enough, I hadn't thought of that.)

"Very well, I will decide upon the matter and let you know."

"All right, young man; you'll come back. They all do, them as knows about it."

I went to my room at the hotel and thought it all out, thought of the pleasant evenings I could have with some one whose thoughts were like my own, some one who would not vex me by differing in opinion. I wondered what Florence would say. I really believed she cared for me, but she knew how I disliked so many of the topics she persisted in talking upon. What mattered it to me what Emerson said, or Edward Bellamy wrote, or Henry George, or Pentecost? what did I care about Hume or Huxley or Stuart Mill? any of those sciences, Christian Science or Divine Science or mind cure?—bah! it was all nonsense. The topics of the day were enough, and if I attended closely to my business I needed recreation, not such things as she would prescribe. Still Florence was interesting to talk to, and I rather liked her at times when she talked every-day talk; but I could not marry her, and it was her own fault. She knew my sentiments, and if she would persist in going on as she did I couldn't help it.

Yes, I decided I would have a home of my own, and a wife made to order at once. Before leaving the city I made all necessary arrangements, hurried home, rented a house, and went to see old Susan Tyler, whom I engaged as housekeeper; she was deaf and had an impediment in her speech, but she was a fine housekeeper. All my preparations made, the ideal home! Oh! how my heart beat as I looked around!—what happiness to do as I liked, a beautiful, uncomplaining wife ready to grant every wish and meet me with a smile! What would the boys say when, out a little late at night, I should be so perfectly at ease? I could just see jealousy on their faces, and I laughed outright for joy. To-morrow I was going for my bride. Side-looks and innuendos were thrust at me from all quarters, but I was too happy to demur or explain. When I reached the city I could scarcely wait for the appointed time.

Alighting from the carriage the door was opened, and I was

ushered into the presence of the most beautiful creature I had ever beheld. The hands extended towards mine, the lips opened, and a low, sweet voice said, "Dear Charles, how glad I am you have come!" I stood spellbound, and only a chuckle from Mr. Sharper brought me to my senses.

"Kiss your affianced, why don't you?" he said, and chuckled again.

I felt as though I wanted to knock him down for speaking so in that beautiful creature's presence. And then a little soft rippling laugh, and she moved towards me. Oh, could I get that beast to leave the room! Why did he stand there chuckling in that manner?

"Sir," I said, "you will oblige me by leaving the room for a few moments."

With that he chuckled still louder and muttered, "Bless me, I really believe he thinks her alive." Then to me: "To be sure, to be sure, but you only have a short time before going to the minister's, and I must show you how to adjust her. When you get home"—and he chuckled again—"you can be just as sentimental as you please, but just now we will attend to business. Here are a box of tubes made to talk as you wished them. They are adjusted so. Place the one you wish in your sleeve. You can carelessly touch her right here if there is any one around. Here is a spring in each hand and the tips of her fingers. I will give you a book of instructions, and you will soon learn to arrange her with very little effort, just to suit yourself, and I am sure you will be very happy. Now, sir, the time is up; you can go to the minister's."

As I put her wraps around her and drew her arm through mine she murmured so sweetly, "Thank you, dear." How glad I was to get out of the presence of that vile man who was constantly pulling or pushing her; I could scarcely keep my hands off from him, and my serene Margurette—for I decided to call her that—

would only smile and say, "Thank you!" "Oh, how lovely!" "Ah, indeed!" I was almost vexed with her to think she did not resent it. I wanted her all to myself where I could have the smiles, and thought I should be thankful when we were in our own home.

During our journey I could not help noticing the admiring glances from my fellow travellers, but my beautiful wife did not return any of their looks. In fact, I overheard a couple of young dudes say, "Just wait till that old codger's back is turned, and we shall see whether she will have no smiles for any but him." I had half a notion to adjust her to give them some cutting reply and then go into the smoker awhile, for I was sure they would try to get into conversation with her; but pshaw! I hadn't ordered any tubes of that kind. I believed I'd send and get one in case of an emergency. No, I wouldn't have such in the house; I wanted an amiable wife, and when we were once at home it would not be necessary. I wouldn't *have* to go with her anywhere unless I wanted to. Only think of that!—never feel that my wife would ask me to go with her and I have to refuse, then ten to one have her cry and make a fuss about it. I knew how it was, for I had seen too much of that sort of thing in the homes of my friends.

Business ran smoothly; everything was perfect harmony; my home was heaven on earth. I smoked when I wished to, I went to my base-ball games, I stayed out as long as I pleased, played cards when I wished, drank champagne or whatever I fancied, in fact had as good a time as I did before marriage. My male friends congratulated me upon my good fortune, and I was considered the luckiest man anywhere around. No one knew how I had made the good luck for myself.

There are some things in life I could never understand. One of them is that, when everything seems so prosperous, calamity is so often in the wake. And that was the case with me. After so many prosperous years a financial crash came. I tried to ward it off; I was up early and late. Margurette never complained, but was always sweet and smiling, with the same endearing words. Sometimes as the years went by I felt as though I would not object to her differing with me a little, for variety's sake; still it was best. When I would say, "Margurette, do you really think so?" and I would speak so cross to her often—I don't know but that I did so more than was necessary; still a man must have some place where he can be himself, and if he can't have that privilege at home, what's the use of having a home? —but she was never out of patience, and my wife would only say, "Yes, darling," so low and sweet. I remember once I said, when I was worried more than usual, "I am damned tired of this sort of thing," and she laughed so sweetly and called me her "own precious boy."

But the crash came, and there was no use trying to stay it any longer. I came home sick and tired. It was nine o'clock at night, with a cold, drizzling rain falling. Susan had gone to bed sick, and forgotten to light a fire in the grate. I went into the library, where Margurette always waited for me. No lights; I stumbled over a chair. I accidentally touched Margurette. She put up her lips to kiss me and laughingly said, "Precious darling, tired tonight?" Great God! I came very near striking her.

"Margurette, don't call me darling, talk to me; talk to me about something—anything sensible. Don't you know I am a ruined man? Everything I have got has been swept away from me."

"There, precious, I love you;" and she laughed again.

"Did you not hear what I said?" I screamed.

But she only laughed the more and said, "Oh, how lovely!"

I rushed from the house. I could not endure it longer; I was like one mad. My first thought was, Where can I go, to whom can I go for sympathy? I cannot stand this strain much longer, and to show weakness to men, I could never do that. I will go to Florence, I said. I will see what she says. Strange I should think of her just then!

I asked the servant who admitted me for Miss Florence.

"She is indisposed and cannot see anyone to-night."

"But," I said, writing on a card hastily, "take this to her."

Only a few moments elapsed and she came in, holding out her hand in an assuring and friendly way. "I am surprised to see you to-night, Mr. Fitzsimmons."

"O Florence!" I cried, "I am in trouble. I believe I shall lose my mind if I cannot have someone to go to; and you, dear Florence, you will know my needs; you can counsel, you can understand me."

"Sir!" Florence said, "are you mad, that you come here to insult me?"

"But I love you. I know it. I love the traits that I once thought I despised."

"Stop where you are! I did not receive you to hear such language. You forget yourself and me; you forget that you are a married man—shame upon you for humiliating me so!"

"Florence, Florence, I am not married; it is all a lie, a deception."

"Have you lost your reason, Mr. Fitzsimmons? Sit down, pray, and let me call my father. You are ill."

"Stop," I cried, "I do not need your father. I need you. Listen to me. I imagined I could never be happy with a wife who differed in opinion from me. In fact, I had almost decided to remain single all the rest of my days, until I came across a man who manufactured wives to order. Wait, Florence, until I have finished—do not look at me so. I am indeed sane. My wife was manufactured to my own ideas, a perfect human being as I supposed."

"Mr. Fitzsimmons, let me call my father." And Florence

started towards the door. She was so pale that she frightened me, but I clutched her frantically.

"Listen," I said; "will you go with me? I will prove that all I have told you is true."

My earnestness seemed to reassure her. She stopped as if carefully thinking, then asked me to repeat what I had already told her. Finally she said yes, she would go.

We were soon in the presence of my beautiful Margurette, whom I literally hated—I could not endure her face. "Now, Florence, see," I cried; and I had my wife talk the namby-pamby lingo I once thought so sweet. "Oh! how I hate her!" and I glared at her like a madman. "Florence, save me. I am a ruined man. Everything has been swept away—the last to-day. I am a pauper, an egotist, a bigot, a selfish."

"Stop!" cried Florence. "You wrong yourself; you are a man in your prime. What if your money has gone, you have your health and your faculties, I guess" (and there was a merry twinkle in her eyes); "the whole world is before you, and best of all, no one to interfere with you or argue on disagreeable topics."

"O Florence! I am punished enough for my selfishness. O God!" and I threw myself on the couch, "were I not a pauper, too, there might be some hope for happiness yet."

"You are not a pauper," said Florence; "you are the master of your fate, and if you are not happy it is your own fault."

"Florence, I can never be happy without you. I know now it is too late."

"Too late—never say that. But could you be happy with me, 'a woman wedded to an idea,' 'strongminded'? Why, Charles, I am liable to investigate all sorts of scientific subjects and reforms. And then supposing I should talk about it sometimes; if it was not for that I might think of the matter. As far as money is concerned, that would have little to do with my actions. Still,

Charles, upon the whole I should be afraid to marry the 'divorced' husband of so amiable a wife as your present one is. I, with my faults and imperfections! —the contrast would be too great."

"Florence, Florence," I said, "say no more. All I ask is, can you overlook my folly and take me for better, for worse? I have learned my lesson. I see now it is only a petty and narrow type of man who would wish to live only with his own personal echo. I want a woman, one who retains her individuality, a thinking woman. Will you be mine?"

"I will consider the matter favorably," said Florence; "but we shall have to wait a year, for opinion's sake, as I suppose there are not many who know how you had your late wife manufactured to order."

And we both laughed.

AN EXPRESS OF THE FUTURE

Michel Verne

"Take care!" cried my conductor, "there's a step!"

Safely descending the step thus indicated to me, I entered a vast room, illuminated by blinding electric reflectors, the sound of our feet alone breaking the solitude and silence of the place. Where was I? What had I come there to do? Who was my mysterious guide? Questions unanswered. A long walk in the night, iron doors opened and reclosed with a clang, stairs descending, it seemed to me, deep into the earth—that is all I could remember. I had, however, no time for thinking.

"No doubt you are asking yourself who I am?" said my guide: "Colonel Pierce, at your service. Where are you? In America, at Boston—in a station."

"A station?"

"Yes, the starting-point of the 'Boston to Liverpool Pneumatic Tubes Company'."

And, with an explanatory gesture, the Colonel pointed out to me two long iron cylinders, about a metre and a half in diameter, lying upon the ground a few paces off.

I looked at these two cylinders, ending on the right in a mass of masonry, and closed on the left with heavy metallic caps, from which a cluster of tubes were carried up to the roof; and suddenly I comprehended the purpose of all this.

Had I not, a short time before, read, in an American newspaper, an article describing this extraordinary project for linking Europe with the New World by means of two gigantic submarines tubes? An inventor had claimed to have accomplished the task; and that inventor, Colonel Pierce, I had before me.

In thought I realized the newspaper article.

Complaisantly the journalist entered into the details of the enterprise. He stated that more than 3,000 miles of iron tubes, weighing over 13,000,000 tons, were required, with the number of ships necessary, for the transport of this material—200 ships of 2,000 tons, each making thirty-three voyages. He described this Armada of science bearing the steel to two special vessels, on board of which the ends of the tubes were joined to each other, and incased in a triple netting of iron, the whole covered with a resinous preparation to preserve it from the action of the seawater.

Coming at once to the question of working, he filled the tubes—transformed into a sort of pea-shooter of interminable length—with a series of carriages, to be carried with their travellers by powerful currents of air, in the same way that despatches are conveyed pneumatically round Paris.

A parallel with the railways closed the article, and the author enumerated with enthusiasm the advantages of the new and audacious system. According to him, there would be, in passing through these tubes, a suppression of all nervous trepidation, thanks to the interior surface being of finely polished steel; equality of temperature secured by means of currents of air, by which the heat could be modified according to the seasons; incredibly low fares, owing to the cheapness of construction and working expenses—forgetting, or waving aside, all considerations of the question of gravitation and of wear and tear.

All that now came back to my mind.

So, then, this "Utopia" had become a reality, and these two cylinders of iron at my feet passed thence under the Atlantic and reached to the coast of England!

In spite of the evidence, I could not bring myself to believe in the thing having been done. That the tubes had been laid I could not doubt; but that men could travel by this route—never!

"Was it not impossible even to obtain a current of air of that length?"—I expressed that opinion aloud.

"Quite easy, on the contrary!" protested Colonel Pierce; "to obtain it, all that is required is a great number of steam fans similar to those used in blast furnaces. The air is driven by them with a force which is practically unlimited, propelling it at the speed of 1,800 kilometres an hour—almost that of a cannon-ball!—so that our carriages with their travellers, in the space of two hours and forty minutes, accomplish the journey between Boston and Liverpool."

"Eighteen hundred kilometres an hour!" I exclaimed.

"Not one less. And what extraordinary consequences arise from such a rate of speed! The time at Liverpool being four hours and forty minutes in advance of ours, a traveller starting from Boston at nine o'clock in the morning, arrives in England at 3.53 in the afternoon. Isn't that a journey quickly made? In another sense, on the contrary, our trains, in this latitude, gain over the sun more than 900 kilometres an hour, beating that planet hand over hand: quitting Liverpool at noon, for example, the traveller will reach the station where we now are at thirty-four minutes past nine in the morning—that is to say, earlier than he started! Ha! Ha! I don't think one can travel quicker than that!"

I did not know what to think. Was I talking with a madman?—or must I credit these fabulous theories, in spite of the objections which rose in my mind?

"Very well, so be it!" I said. "I will admit that travellers may take this madbrained route, and that you can obtain this incredible speed. But, when you have got this speed, how do you check it? When you come to a stop, everything must be shattered to pieces!"

"Not at all," replied the Colonel, shrugging his shoulders.

"Between our tubes—one for the out, the other for the home journey—consequently worked by currents going in opposite directions—a communication exists at every joint. When a train is approaching, an electric spark advertises us of the fact; left to itself, the train would continue its course by reason of the speed it had acquired; but, simply by the turning of a handle, we are able to let in the opposing current of compressed air from the parallel tube, and, little by little, reduce to nothing the final shock or stopping. But what is the use of all these explanations? Would not a trial be a hundred times better?"

And, without waiting for an answer to his questions, the Colonel pulled sharply a bright brass knob projecting from the side of one of the tubes: a panel slid smoothly in its grooves, and in the opening left by its removal I perceived a row of seats, on each of which two persons might sit comfortably side by side.

"The carriage!" exclaimed the Colonel. "Come in."

I followed him without offering any objection, and the panel immediately slid back into its place.

By the light of an electric lamp in the roof I carefully examined the carriage I was in.

Nothing could be more simple: a long cylinder, comfortably upholstered, along which some fifty arm-chairs, in pairs, were ranged in twenty-five parallel ranks. At either end a valve regulated the atmospheric pressure, that at the farther end allowing breathable air to enter the carriage, that in front allowing for the discharge of any excess beyond a normal pressure.

After spending a few moments on this examination, I became impatient.

"Well," I said, "are we not going to start?"

"Going to start?" cried the Colonel. "We have started!"

Started—like that—without the least jerk, was it possible? I listened attentively, trying to detect a sound of some kind that might have guided me.

If we had really started—if the Colonel had not deceived me in talking of a speed of eighteen hundred kilometres an hour—we must already be far from any land, under the sea; above our heads the huge, foam-crested waves; even at that moment, perhaps taking it for a monstrous sea-serpent of an unknown kind—whales were battering with their powerful tails our long, iron prison!

But I heard nothing but a dull rumble, produced, no doubt, by the passage of our carriage, and, plunged in boundless astonishment, unable to believe in the reality of all that had happened to me, I sat silently, allowing the time to pass.

At the end of about an hour, a sense of freshness upon my forehead suddenly aroused me from the torpor into which I had sunk by degrees.

I raised my hand to my brow: it was moist.

Moist! Why was that? Had the tube burst under pressure of the waters—a pressure which could not but be formidable, since it increases at the rate of "an atmosphere" every ten metres of depth? Had the ocean broken in upon us?

Fear seized upon me. Terrified, I tried to call out—and—and I found myself in my garden, generously sprinkled by a driving rain, the big drops of which had awakened me. I had simply fallen asleep while reading the article devoted by an American journalist to the fantastic projects of Colonel Pierce—who, also, I much fear, has only dreamed.

THE BRINK OF INFINITY

Stanley G. Weinbaum

One would hardly choose the life of an assistant professor of mathematics at an Eastern University as an adventurous one. Professors in general are reputed to drone out in a quiet, scholarly existence, and an instructor of mathematics might seem the driest and least lively of men, since his subject is perhaps the most desiccated. And yet—even the lifeless science of figures has had its dreamers—Clerk Maxwell, Lobachevsky, Einstein and the rest. The latter, the great Albert Einstein himself who is forging the only chain that ever tied a philosophers' dream to experimental science, is pounding his links of tenuous mathematical symbols, shadowy as thought, but unbreakable.

And don't forget that "Alice in Wonderland" was written by a dreamer who happened also to be a mathematician. Not that I class myself with them; I'm practical enough to leave fantasies alone. Teaching is my business.

At least, teaching is my main business. I do a little statistical work for industrial corporations when the occasion presents itself—in fact, you'll find my name in the classified section: Abner Aarons, Statistician and Consulting Mathematician. I eke out my professional salary, and I do at times strike something interesting. Of course, in the main such work consists of graphing trends of consumption for manufacturers, or population increase for public utilities.

And occasionally some up-and-coming advertising agency will consult me on how many sardine cans would be needed to fill the Panama Canal, or some such material to use as catchy advertising copy. Not exactly exciting work, but it helps financially.

Thus I was not particularly surprised that July morning to receive a call. The university had been closed for some weeks; the summer session was about to open, without however, the benefit of my presence. I was taking a vacation, leaving in two or three days for a Vermont village I knew, where the brook trout cared not a bit whether a prizefighter, president, or professor was on the hither end of the line. And I was going alone; three-quarters of the year before a classroom full of the tadpoles called college students had thoroughly wearied me of any further desire for human companionship; my social instincts were temporarily in abeyance.

Nevertheless, I'm not unthrifty enough to disregard an opportunity to turn an honest penny, and the call was far from unwelcome. Even the modest holiday I planned can bite deeply enough into the financial foundation of an assistant professor's pittance. And the work sounded like one of these fairly lucrative and rather simple propositions.

"This is Court Strawn," the telephone announced. "I'm an experimental chemist, and I've completed a rather long series of experiments. I want them tabulated and the results analyzed; do you do that sort of work?"

I did, and acknowledged as much.

"It will be necessary for you to call here for your data," the voice continued. Strangely unctuous, that voice. "It is impossible for me to leave." There followed an address on West Seventieth Street.

Well, I had called for data before. Generally the stuff was delivered or mailed to me, but his request wasn't extraordinary, I agreed, and added that I'd be over shortly. No use delaying my vacation if I could help it.

I took the subway. Taxis are a needless luxury to a professor, and a car of my own was an unrealized ambition. It wasn't long before I entered one of the nondescript brown houses that still survive west of the Avenue. Strawn let me in, and I perceived the reason for his request. The man was horribly crippled; his whole left side was warped like a gnarled oak, and he was hard put to hobble about the house. For the rest—stringy dark hair, and little tense eyes.

He greeted me pleasantly enough, and I entered a small library, while my host hobbled over to a littered desk, seating himself facing me. The deep-set eyes looked me over, and he chuckled.

"Are you a good mathematician, Dr. Aarons?" he asked. There was more than a hint of a sneer in his voice.

"My work has been satisfactory," I answered, somewhat nettled. "I've been doing statistical work for several years."

He waved a shriveled left hand.

"Of course—of course! I don't doubt your practical ability. Are you, however, well versed in the more abstract branches—the theory of numbers, for instance, or the hyper-spatial mathematics?"

I was feeling rather irritated. There was something about the man—

"I don't see that any of this is necessary in statistical analysis of experimental results," I said. "If you'll give me your data, I'll be going."

He chuckled again, seemingly hugely amused. "As a matter of fact, Dr. Aarons," he said smirking, "the experiment isn't completed yet. Indeed, to tell the truth, it is just beginning."

"What!" I was really angry. "If this is your idea of a joke—" I started to rise, thoroughly aroused.

"Just a moment," said Strawn coolly. He leveled a very effective-looking blue-barreled automatic at me. I sat down again open-mouthed; I confess to a feeling of panic at the sight of the cripple's beady little eyes peering along the ugly weapon.

"Common politeness dictates that you at least hear me out, Dr. Aarons." I didn't like the oily smoothness of his voice, but what was I to do? "As I was saying, the experiment is just beginning. As a matter of fact, you are the experiment!"

"Eh?" I said, wondering again if the whole thing might not be a joke of some sort.

"You're a mathematician, aren't you?" Strawn continued. "Well, that makes you fair game for me. A mathematician, my good friend, is no more to me than something to be hunted down. And I'm doing it!"

The man was crazy! The realization dawned on me as I strove to hold myself calm. Best to reason with him, I thought.

"But why?" I asked. "We're a harmless lot."

His eyes blazed up with a fierce light.

"Harmless, eh, harmless! Well, it was one of your colleagues that did —this!" He indicated his withered leg with his withered arm. "He did this with his lying calculations!" He leaned forward confidentially. "Listen to me, Dr. Aarons. I am a chemist, or was once. I used to work with explosives, and was pretty good, too. And then one of you damned calculators figured out a formula for me! A misplaced decimal point—bah! You're all fair game to me!" He paused, and the sneer came back to his lips. "That's simple justice, now, isn't it?"

Well, you can imagine how thoroughly horrified I was, sitting there facing a homicidal maniac with a loaded gun in his hand. Humor him! I'd heard that was the best treatment. Use persuasion, reason!

"Now, Mr. Strawn," I said, "you're certainly entitled to justice. Yes, you certainly are! But surely, Mr. Strawn, you are not serving the ends of justice by venting your anger on me! Surely that isn't justice."

He laughed wildly and continued. "A very specious argument, Dr. Aarons. You are simply unfortunate in that your name is the first in the classified section of the directory. Had your colleague given me a chance—any slightest chance to save my body from this that you see, I might be forgiving. But I trusted that fool's calculations!" He twisted his face again into that bitter leer. "As it is, I am giving you far more of a chance than I had. If, as you claim, you are a good mathematician, you shall have your opportunity to escape. I have no quarrel with the real students of figures, but only"—his leer became a very sinister scowl—"only with the dullards, the fakes and the blunderers. Yes, you'll have your chance!" The grin returned to his lips, but his eyes behind the blue automatic never wavered.

I saw no other alternative but to continue the ghastly farce. Certainly open opposition to any of his suggestions might only inflame the maniac to violence, so I merely questioned. "And what is the proposition, Mr. Strawn?"

The scowl became a sneer again.

"A very fair one, sir. A very fair proposition, indeed." He chuckled.

"I should like to hear it," I said, hoping for an interruption of some sort.

"You shall. It is just this: You are a mathematician, and you say, a good one. Very well. We shall put your claim to the test. I am thinking of a mathematical quantity, a numerical expression, if you prefer. You have ten questions to discover it. If you do so you are free as far as I am concerned. But if you fail"—his scowl reappeared—"well, if you fail I shall recognize you as one of the tribe of blunderers against whom I war, and the outcome will not be pleasant!"

Well! It was several moments before I found my voice, and began to babble protests. "But, Mr. Strawn! That's an utter impossibility! The range of numbers is infinite; how can I identify one with ten questions? Give me a fair test, man! This one offers not a chance in a million! In a billion!"

He silenced me with a wave of the blue barrel of his weapon.

"Remember, Dr. Aarons, I did not say it was a number. I said a numerical expression, which is a vastly wider field. I am giving you this hint without deducting a question; you must appreciate my magnanimity!" He laughed. "The rules of our little game are as follows: You may ask me any questions except the direct question, 'What is the expression?' I am bound to answer you in full and to the best of my knowledge any question except the direct inquiry. You may ask me as many questions at a time as you wish up to your limit of ten, but in any event I will answer not less than two per day. That should give you sufficient time for reflection"—again that horrible chuckle —"and my time too is limited."

"But, Mr. Strawn," I argued, "that may keep me here five days. Don't you know that by tomorrow my wife will have the police searching for me?"

A glint of anger flashed in the mad eyes. "You are not being fair, Dr. Aarons! I know you are not married! I checked up on you before you came here. I know you will not be missed. Do not attempt to lie to me; rather help me serve the ends of justice! You should be more than willing to prove your worth to survive as one of the true mathematicians." He rose suddenly. "And now, sir, you will please precede me through the door and up those stairs!"

Nothing to do but obey! The stubby gun in his hand was enough authority, at least to an unadventurous soul like myself. I rose and stalked out of the room at his direction, up the stairs and through a door he indicated. Beyond was a windowless little cell ventilated by a skylight, and the first glance revealed that this was barred. A piece of furniture of the type known as a day-bed, a straight chair, a deep overstuffed chair, and a desk made up the furnishings.

"Here," said the self-appointed host, "is your student's cell. On the desk is a carafe of water, and, as you see, an unabridged dictionary. That is the only reference allowed in our little game." He glanced at his watch. "It is ten minutes to four. By four tomorrow you must have asked me two questions, and have them well thought out! The ten minutes over are a gift from me, lest you doubt my generosity!" He moved toward the door. "I will see that your meals are on time," he added. "My best wishes, Dr. Aarons."

The door clicked shut and I at once commenced a survey of the room. The skylight was hopeless, and the door even more so; I was securely and ingloriously imprisoned. I spent perhaps half an hour in painstaking and fruitless inspection, but the room had been well designed or adapted to its purpose; the massive door was barred on the outside, the skylight was guarded by a heavy iron grating, and the walls offered no slightest hope. Abner Aarons was most certainly a prisoner!

My mind turned to Strawn's insane game. Perhaps I could solve his mad mystery; at least, I could keep him from violence for five days, and something might occur in the interim. I found cigars on the desk, and, forcing myself to a degree of calm, I lit one and sat down to think.

Certainly there was no use in getting at his lunatic concept from a quantitative angle, I could waste all ten questions too easily by asking, "Is it greater or less than a million? Is it greater or less than a thousand? Is it greater or less than a hundred?" Impossible to pin the thing by that sort of elimination when it might be a negative number, a fraction or a decimal, or even an imaginary number like the square root of minus one—or, for that matter, any possible combination of these. And that reflection gave me my impulse for the first question; by the time my cigar had been consumed to a tattered stub I had formulated my initial inquiry. Nor had I very long to wait; it was just past six when the door opened. "Stand away from the door, Dr. Aarons," came the voice of my host. I complied perforce; the madman entered, pushing before him a tea caddy bearing a really respectable meal, complete from bouillon to a bottle of wine. He propelled the cart with his withered left hand; the right brandished the evil automatic.

"I trust you have used your time well," he sneered.

"At least I have my first question," I responded.

"Good, Dr. Aarons! Very good! Let us hear it."

"Well," I continued, "among numbers, expressions of quantity, mathematicians recognize two broad distinctions—two fields in which every possible numerical expression may be classified. These two classifications are known as real numbers on the one hand, including every number both positive and negative, all fractions, decimals, and multiples of these numbers, and on the other hand the class of imaginary numbers, which include all products of operations on the quantity called 'e', otherwise expressed as the square root of minus one."

"Of course, Dr. Aarons. That is elementary!"

"Now then—is this quantity of yours real or imaginary?"

He beamed with a sinister satisfaction.

"A very fair question, sir! Very fair! And the answer—may it assist you—is that it is either!"

A light seemed to burst in my brain! Any student of numbers knows that only one figure is both real and imaginary, the one that marks the point of intersection between the real and imaginary numbergraphs. "I've got it!" The phrase kept running through my mind like a crazy drumbeat! With an effort I kept an appearance of calm.

"Mr. Strawn," I said, "is the quantity you have in mind zero?"

He laughed—a nasty, superior laugh that rasped in my ears.

"It is not, Dr. Aarons! I know as well as you that zero is both a real and imaginary number! Let me call your attention to my answer: I did not say that my concept was both real and imaginary; I said it was either!" He was backing toward the door. "Let me further remind you that you have eight guesses remaining, since I am forced to consider this premature shot in the dark as one chance! Good evening!"

He was gone; I heard the bar outside the door settle into its socket with a thump. I stood in the throes of despair, and cast scarcely a glance at the rather sumptuous repast he had served me, but slumped back into my chair.

It seemed hours before my thoughts were coherent again; actually I never knew the interval, since I did not glance at my watch. However, sooner or later I recovered enough to pour a tumbler of wine and eat a bit of the roast beef; the bouillon was hopelessly cold. And then I settled down to the consideration of my third question. From Strawn's several hints in the wording of his terms and the answers to my first and second queries, I tabulated what information I could glean. He had specifically designated a numerical expression; that eliminated the x's and y's of algebraic usage. The quantity was either real or imaginary and was not zero; well, the square of any imaginary is a real number. If the quantity contained more than one figure, or if an exponent was used, then I felt sure his expression was merely the square of an imaginary; one could consider such a quantity either real or imaginary. A means of determining this by a single question occurred to me. I scribbled a few symbols on a sheet of paper, and then, feeling a sudden and thorough exhaustion, I threw myself on the daybed and slept. I dreamed Strawn was pushing me into a nightmarish sea of grinning mathematical monsters.

The creaking of the door aroused me. Sunbeams illumined the skylight; I had slept out the night. Strawn entered balancing a tray on his left arm, holding the ever-present weapon in his free hand. He placed a half dozen covered dishes on the tea-cart, removing the remains of the evening meal to his tray.

"A poor appetite, Dr. Aarons," he commented. "You should not permit your anxiety to serve the ends of justice to upset you!" He chuckled with enjoyment of his sarcasm. "No questions yet? No matter; you have until four tomorrow for your next two."

"I have a question," I said, more thoroughly awakened. I rose and spread the sheet of paper on the desk.

"A numerical quantity, Mr. Strawn, can be expressed as an operation on numbers. Thus, instead of writing the numeral '4' one may prefer to express it as a product, such as '2×2,' or as a sum, as '3+1,' or as a quotient, as '8÷2' or 8/2 or as a remainder, as '5–1.' Or even in other ways—as a square, such as 2², or as a root, such as $\sqrt{16}$ or $3\sqrt{64}$. All different methods of expressing the single quantity '4.' Now here I have written out the various mathematical symbols of operations; my question is this: Which if any of these symbols is used in the expression you have in mind?"

"Very neatly put, Dr. Aarons! You have succeeded in combining several questions in one." He took the paper from me, spreading it on the desk before him. "This symbol, sir, is the one used." He indicated the first one in my list—the subtraction sign, a simple dash!

And my hopes, to use the triviality of a pun, were dashed as well! For that sign eliminated my carefully thought-out theory of a product or square of imaginaries to form a real number. You can't change imaginary to real by addition or subtraction; it takes multiplication, squaring or division to perform that mathematical magic! Once more I was thoroughly at sea, and for a long time I was unable to marshal my thoughts.

And so the hours dragged into days with the tantalizing slow swiftness that tortures the condemned in a prison death house. I seemed checkmated at every turn; curious paradoxical answers defeated my questions.

My fourth query, "Are there any imaginaries in your quantity?" elicited a cool, definite "No", My fifth, "How many digits are used in this expression?" brought forth an equally definite "Two."

Now there you are! What two digits connected by a minus sign can you name whose remainder is either real or imaginary? "An impossibility," I thought. "This maniac's merely torturing me!" And yet—somehow Strawn's madness seemed too ingenious, too clever, for such an answer. He was sincere in his perverted search for justice. I'd have sworn to that.

On my sixth question, I had an inspiration! By the terms of our game, Strawn was to answer any question save the direct one, "What is this expression?" I saw a way out! On his next appearance I met him with feverish excitement, barely waiting for his entrance to begin my query.

"Mr. Strawn! Here is a question you are bound by your own rules to answer. Suppose we place an equal sign after your quantity, what number or numbers will complete the equation: What is the quantity equal to?"

Why was the fiend laughing? Could he squirm out of that poser?

"Very clever, Dr. Aarons. A very clever question. And the answer is —anything!"

I suppose I shouted. "Anything! Anything! Then you're a fraud, and your game's a damnable trickery. There's no such expression!"

"But there is, Doctor! A good mathematician could find it!"

And he departed, still laughing.

I spent a sleepless night. Hour after hour I sat at that hateful desk, checking my scraps of information, thinking, trying to remember fragments of all-but-forgotten theories. And I found solutions! Not one, but several. Lord, how I sweated over them! With four questions—two days—left to me, the solution of the problem began to loom very close. The things dinned in my brain; my judgment counseled me to proceed slowly, to check my progress with another question, but my nature was rebelling against the incessant strain. "Stake it all on your last four questions! Ask them all at once, and end this agony one way or the other!"

I thought I saw the answer. Oh, the fiendish, insane cleverness of the man! He had pointed to the minus sign of my list, deliberately misled me, for all the time the symbol had meant the bar of a fraction. Do you see? The two symbols are identical—just a simple dash—but one use means subtraction and the other division! "1−1" means zero, but "1/1" means one! And by division his problem could be solved. For there is a quantity that means literally anything, real number or imaginary, and that quantity is "0/0"! Yes, zero divided by zero. You'd think offhand that the answer'd be zero, or perhaps one, but it isn't, not necessarily. Look at it like this: take the equation "2×3 = 6." See? That's another way of saying that two goes into six three times. Now take "0×6 = 0." Perfectly correct, isn't it? Well, in that equation zero goes into zero six times! Or "0/0 = 6"! And so on for any number, real or imaginary—zero divided by zero equals anything!

And that's what I figured the fiend had done. Pointed to the minus sign when he meant the bar of a fraction, or division!

He came in grinning at dawn.

"Are your questions ready, Dr. Aarons? I believe you have four remaining."

I looked at him. "Mr. Strawn, is your concept zero divided by zero?"

He grinned, "No, sir, it is not!"

I wasn't disheartened. There was just one other symbol I had been thinking of that would meet the requirement—one other possibility. My eighth question followed. "Then is it infinity divided by infinity?"

The grin widened. "It is not, Dr. Aarons."

I was a little panicky then! The end loomed awfully near! There was one way to find out if the thing was fraudulent or not; I used my ninth question:

"Mr. Strawn, when you designated the dash as the mathematical symbol used in your expression, did you mean it as the bar of a fraction or as the sign of subtraction?"

"As the subtraction sign, Dr. Aarons, You have one more question. Will you wait until tomorrow to ask it?"

The fiend was grinning in huge enjoyment. Thoroughly confident, he was, in the intricacies of his insane game. I hesitated in a torture of frenzied indecision. The appalling prospect of another agonized night of doubts decided me.

"I'll ask it now, Mr. Strawn!"

It had to be right! There weren't any other possibilities; I'd exhausted all of them in hour after hour of miserable conjecture!

"Is the expression—the one you're thinking of—infinity minus infinity?"

It was! I knew it by the madman's glare of amazed disappointment.

"The devil must have told you!" he shrieked. I think there were flecks of froth on his lips. He lowered the gun in his hand as I edged toward the door; he made no move to stop me, but stood in a sort of desolate silence, until I gained the top of the stairway. Then—

"Wait a minute!" he screamed. "You'll tell them! Wait just a minute, Dr. Aarons!"

I was down the stairs in two leaps, and tugging at the door. Strawn came after me, his gun leveled. I heard it crash as the door opened and I slipped out into a welcome daylight.

Yes, I reported him. The police got him as he was slipping away and dragged him before an alienist. Crazy, but his story was true; he had been mangled in an experimental laboratory explosion.

Oh, the problem? Don't you see? Infinity is the greatest expression of number possible—a number greater than any conceivable. Figure it out like this:

The mathematician's symbol for infinity is a tipsy eight—so:
∞

Well, take the question, $\infty+6=\infty$. That's true, because you can't add anything to infinity that will make it any greater than it is. See? It's the greatest possible number already. Well then, just by transposition, $\infty-\infty=6$. And so on; the same system applies to any conceivable number, real or imaginary.

There you are! Infinity minus itself may equal any quantity, absolutely any number, real or imaginary, from zero to infinity. No, there was nothing wrong with Court Strawn's mathematics.

CHRISTMAS 200,000 B.C.

Stanley Waterloo

It was Christmas in the year 200,000 B.C. It is true that it was not called Christmas then—our ancestors at that date were not much given to the celebration of religious festivals—but, taking the Gregorian calendar and counting backward just 200,000 plus 1887 years this particular day would be located. There was no formal celebration, but, nevertheless, a good deal was going on in the neighborhood of the home of Fangs. Names were not common at the time mentioned, but the more advanced of the cave-dwellers had them. Man had so far advanced that only traces of his ape origin remained, and he had begun to have a language. It was a queer "clucking" sort of language, something like that of the Bushmen, the low type of man yet to be found in Africa, and it was not very useful in the expression of ideas, but then primitive man didn't have many ideas to express. Names, so far as used, were at this time derived merely from some personal quality or peculiarity. Fangs was so called because of his huge teeth. His mate was called She Fox; his daughter, not Nellie, nor Jennie, nor Mamie—young ladies did not affect the "ie" then—but Red Lips. She was, for the age, remarkably pretty and refined. She could cast eyes which told a story at a suitor, and there were several kinds of snake she would not eat. She was a merry, energetic girl, and was the most useful member of the family in tree-climbing. She was an only child and rather petted. Her father or mother rarely knocked her down with a very heavy club when angry, and after her fourteenth year rarely assaulted her at all. So far as She Fox was concerned, this kindness largely resulted from discretion, the daughter having in the last encounter so belabored the mother that she was laid up for a week. The father abstained chiefly because the daughter had become useful. Red Lips was now eighteen.

Fangs was a cave-dweller. His home was sumptuously furnished. The floor of the cave was strewn with dry grass, something that in most other caves was lacking. Fangs was a prominent citizen. He was one of the strongest men in the valley. He had killed Red Beard, another prominent citizen, in a little dispute over priority of right to possession of a dead mastodon discovered in a swamp, and had for years been the terror of every cave man in the region who possessed anything worth taking.

On this particular morning, which would have been Christmas morning had it not come too early in the world's history, Fangs left the cave after eating the whole of a waterfowl he had killed with a stone the night before and some half dozen field mice which his wife had brought in. She Fox and Red Lips had for breakfast only the bones of the duck and some roots dug in the forest. Fangs carried with him a huge club, and in a rough pouch made of the skin of some small wild animal a collection of stones of convenient size for throwing. This was before man had invented the bow or even the crude stone ax. He came back in a surly mood because he had found nothing and killed nothing, but he brought a companion with him. This companion, whom he had met in the woods, was known as Wolf, because his countenance reminded one of a wolf. He could hardly be called a gentleman, even as times and terms went then. He was evidently not of an old family, for he possessed something more than a rudimentary tail, and, had his face looked less like that of a wolf, it would have been that of a baboon. He was hairy, and his speech of rough gutturals was imperfect. He could pronounce but few words. He was, however, very strong, and

Fangs rather liked him.

What Fangs did when he came in was to propose a matrimonial alliance. That is, he grasped his daughter by the arm and led her up to Wolf, and then pointing to an abandoned cave in the hillside not far distant, pushed them toward it. They did not have marriage ceremonies 200,000 B.C. Wolf, who had evidently been informed of Fangs's desire and who was himself in favor of the alliance, seized the girl and began dragging her off to the new home and the honeymoon. She resisted, and shrieked, and clawed like a wild-cat. Her mother, She Fox, came running out, club in hand, but was promptly knocked down by Fangs, who then dragged her into the cave again. Meanwhile the bridegroom was hauling the bride away through furze and bushes at a rapid rate. Red Lips had ceased to struggle, and was thinking. Her thoughts were not very well defined nor Clear, but one thing she knew well—she did not want to live in a cave with Wolf. She had a fancy that she would prefer to live instead with Yellow Hair, a young cave man who had not yet selected a mate, and who was remarkably fleet of foot. They were now very near the cave, and she knew that unless she exerted herself housekeeping would begin within a very few moments. Wolf was strong, but slow of movement. Red Lips was only less swift than Yellow Hair. An idea occurred to her. She bent her head and buried her strong teeth deep in the wrist of the man who was half-carrying, half-dragging her through the underwood.

With a howl which justified his name, Wolf for an instant released his hold. That instant allowed the girl's escape. She leaped away like a deer and darted into the forest. Yelling with pain and rage, Wolf pursued her. She gained on him steadily as she ran, but there was a light snow upon the ground, and she could be followed by the trail which her pursuer took up doggedly and determinedly. He knew that he could tire her out and catch her in time. He solaced himself for her temporary escape by thinking, as he ran, how fiercely he would beat his bride before starting for the cave again, and as he thought his teeth showed like those of a dog of to-day.

The chase lasted for hours, and Red Lips had gained perhaps a mile upon her pursuer when her strength began to flag. The pace was telling upon her. She had run many miles. She was almost hopeless of escape when she emerged into a little glade, where sat a man gnawing contentedly at a raw rabbit. He leaped to his feet as the girl appeared, but a moment later recognized her and smiled. The man was Yellow Hair. He reached out part of the rabbit he was devouring, and Red Lips, whose breakfast had, as already mentioned, been a light one, tore at it and consumed it in a moment. Then she told of what had happened.

"We will kill Wolf, and you shall live with me," said Yellow Hair.

Red Lips assented eagerly, and the two consulted together. Near them was a hill, one side of which was a precipice. At the base of the precipice ran a path. The result of the consultation was that Yellow Hair left the girl, and making a swift circuit, came upon the precipice from the farther side, and crouched low upon its summit. The girl ran along the path at the bottom of the declivity for some distance, then, entering a defile which crossed it at right angles, herself made a turn, climbed the hill and joined Yellow Hair. From where they were lying they could see the glade they had just left.

Wolf entered the glade, and noted where the footsteps of the girl and those of a man came together. For a moment or two he appeared troubled and suspicious; then his face cleared. He saw that the tracks had diverged again. He had recognized the man's tracks as those of Yellow Hair.

"Yellow Hair is afraid of my strong arm," he thought. "He

dare not stay with Red Lips. I shall catch her soon and beat her and take her with me."

The two crouching upon the precipice watched his every movement. They had rolled to the edge of the declivity a rock as huge as they could control, and now together held it poised over the pathway. Wolf came hurrying along, his head bent down like that of a hound on the scent of game. He reached a spot just beneath the two, and then with a sudden united effort they shoved over the rock. It thundered down upon the unfortunate Wolf with an accuracy which spoke well for the eyes and hands of the lovers. The man was crushed horribly. The two above scrambled down, laughing, and Yellow Hair took from the dead Wolf a necklace of claws and fastened it proudly upon his own person.

"Now we will go to my cave," said he.

"No," said Red Lips; "my father will look for Wolf to-morrow, and will find him. Then he will come and kill us. We must go and kill him tonight."

"Yes," said Yellow Hair.

Hand in hand the two started for the cave of Fangs. The side hill in which it was situated was very steep, and the lovers thought they could duplicate the affair with Wolf. "We must cripple him, anyway," said Yellow Hair, "for I am not strong enough to fight him alone. His club is heavy."

They reached the vicinity of the cave and crept above it. Having, with great difficulty, secured a rock in position to be rolled down, they waited for Fangs to appear. He came out about dusk, and stretched out his arms lazily, when the two above released the rock. It rolled down swiftly and with great force, but there was no such sheer drop afforded as when Wolf was killed, and Fangs heard the stone coming and almost eluded it. It caught one of his legs, as he tried to leap aside, and broke it.

Fangs fell to the ground.

With a yell of triumph Yellow Hair bounded to where the crippled man lay and began pounding him upon the head with his club. Fangs had a very thick head. He struggled vigorously, and succeeded in catching Yellow Hair by the wrist. Then he drew the younger man to him and began to throttle him. The case of Yellow Hair was desperate. Fangs's great strength was too much for him. His stifled yells told of his agony.

It was at this juncture that Red Lips demonstrated her quality as a girl of decision and of action. A sharp fragment of slate, several pounds in weight, lay at her feet. She seized it and bounded forward to where the struggle was going on. The back of Fangs's head was fairly exposed. The girl brought down the sharp stone upon it just where the head and spinal column joined, and the crashing thud told of the force of the blow. Delivered with such strength upon such a spot there could be but one result. The man could not have been killed more quickly. Yellow Hair released himself from the dead giant's embrace and rose to his feet. Then, after a short breathing time, to make assurance sure, he picked up his club and battered the head of Fangs until there could be no chance of his resuscitation. The performance was unnecessary, but neither Yellow Hair nor Red Lips was aware of the fact. Their knowledge of anatomy was limited. Neither knew the effect of such a blow delivered properly at the base of the brain.

Yellow Hair finally ceased his exercise and rested on his club.

"Shall we go to my cave now?" said he.

"Why should we?" said Red Lips. "Let us take this cave. There is dry grass on the floor."

They entered the cave. She Fox, who had witnessed what had occurred, sat in one corner, and looked up doubtfully as they entered. "I am tired," said Yellow Hair, and he laid himself down and went to sleep.

She Fox looked at her daughter. "I killed three hedgehogs to-day," she whispered.

The new mistress of the cave looked at her kindly. "Go out and dig some roots," she said, "and come back with them, and then with them and the hedgehogs we will have a feast."

She Fox went out and returned in an hour with roots and nuts. Red Lips awakened Yellow Hair, and all three fed ravenously and merrily. It was a great occasion in the cave of the late Fangs. There was no such Christmas feast, at the same time a wedding feast, in any other cave in all the region. And the sequel to the events of the day was as happy as the day itself. Yellow Hair and Red Lips somehow avoided being killed, and grew old together, and left a numerous progeny.

DR. HEIDEGGER'S EXPERIMENT

Nathaniel Hawthorne

That very singular man, old Dr. Heidegger, once invited four venerable friends to meet him in his study. There were three white-bearded gentlemen, Mr. Medbourne, Colonel Killigrew, and Mr. Gascoigne, and a withered gentlewoman, whose name was the Widow Wycherly. They were all melancholy old creatures, who had been unfortunate in life, and whose greatest misfortune it was that they were not long ago in their graves. Mr. Medbourne, in the vigor of his age, had been a prosperous merchant, but had lost his all by a frantic speculation, and was now little better than a mendicant. Colonel Killigrew had wasted his best years, and his health and substance, in the pursuit of sinful pleasures, which had given birth to a brood of pains, such as the gout, and divers other torments of soul and body. Mr. Gascoigne was a ruined politician, a man of evil fame, or at least had been so, till time had buried him from the knowledge of the present generation, and made him obscure instead of infamous. As for the Widow Wycherly, tradition tells us that she was a great beauty in her day; but, for a long while past, she had lived in deep seclusion, on account of certain scandalous stories, which had prejudiced the gentry of the town against her. It is a circumstance worth mentioning, that each of these three old gentlemen, Mr. Medbourne, Colonel Killigrew, and Mr. Gascoigne, were early lovers of the Widow Wycherly, and had once been on the point of cutting each other's throats for her sake. And, before proceeding further, I will merely hint, that Dr. Heidegger and all his four guests were sometimes thought to be a little beside themselves; as is not unfrequently the case with old people, when worried either by present troubles or woful recollections.

"My dear old friends," said Dr. Heidegger, motioning them to be seated, "I am desirous of your assistance in one of those little experiments with which I amuse myself here in my study."

If all stories were true, Dr. Heidegger's study must have been a very curious place. It was a dim, old-fashioned chamber, festooned with cobwebs and besprinkled with antique dust. Around the walls stood several oaken bookcases, the lower shelves of which were filled with rows of gigantic folios and black-letter quartos, and the upper with little parchment-covered duodecimos. Over the central bookcase was a bronze bust of Hippocrates, with which, according to some authorities, Dr. Heidegger was accustomed to hold consultations, in all difficult cases of his practice. In the obscurest corner of the room stood a tall and narrow oaken closet, with its door ajar, within which doubtfully appeared a skeleton. Between two of the bookcases hung a looking-glass, presenting its high and dusty plate within a tarnished gilt frame. Among many wonderful stories related of this mirror, it was fabled that the spirits of all the doctor's deceased patients dwelt within its verge, and would stare him in the face whenever he looked thitherward. The opposite side of the chamber was ornamented with the full-length portrait of a young lady, arrayed in the faded magnificence of silk, satin, and brocade, and with a visage as faded as her dress. Above half a century ago, Dr. Heidegger had been on the point of marriage with this young lady; but, being affected with some slight disorder, she had swallowed one of her lover's prescriptions, and died on the bridal evening. The greatest curiosity of the study remains to be mentioned; it was a ponderous folio volume, bound in black leather, with massive silver clasps. There were no letters on the back, and nobody could tell the title of the book. But it was well known to be a book of magic; and once, when a chambermaid had lifted it, merely to brush away the dust, the skeleton had rattled in its closet, the picture of the young lady had stepped one foot upon the floor, and several ghastly faces had peeped forth from the mirror; while the brazen head of Hippocrates frowned, and said, "Forbear!"

Such was Dr. Heidegger's study. On the summer afternoon of our tale, a small round table, as black as ebony, stood in the centre of the room, sustaining a cut-glass vase, of beautiful form and elaborate workmanship. The sunshine came through the window, between the heavy festoons of two faded damask curtains, and fell directly across this vase; so that a mild splendor was reflected from it on the ashen visages of the five old people who sat around. Four champagne-glasses were also on the table.

"My dear old friends," repeated Dr. Heidegger, "may I reckon on your aid in performing an exceedingly curious experiment?"

Now Dr. Heidegger was a very strange old gentleman, whose eccentricity had become the nucleus for a thousand fantastic stories. Some of these fables, to my shame be it spoken, might possibly be traced back to mine own veracious self; and if any passages of the present tale should startle the reader's faith, I must be content to bear the stigma of a fiction-monger.

When the doctor's four guests heard him talk of his proposed experiment, they anticipated nothing more wonderful than the murder of a mouse in an air-pump, or the examination of a cobweb by the microscope, or some similar nonsense, with which he was constantly in the habit of pestering his intimates. But without waiting for a reply, Dr. Heidegger hobbled across the chamber, and returned with the same ponderous folio, bound in black leather, which common report affirmed to be a book of magic. Undoing the silver clasps, he opened the volume, and took from among its black-letter pages a rose, or what was once a rose, though now the green leaves and crimson petals had assumed one brownish hue, and the ancient flower seemed ready to crumble to dust in the doctor's hands.

"This rose," said Dr. Heidegger, with a sigh, "this same withered and crumbling flower, blossomed five-and-fifty years ago. It was given me by Sylvia Ward, whose portrait hangs yonder; and I meant to wear it in my bosom at our wedding. Five-and-fifty years it has been treasured between the leaves of this old volume. Now, would you deem it possible that this rose of half a century could ever bloom again?"

"Nonsense!" said the Widow Wycherly, with a peevish toss of her head. "You might as well ask whether an old woman's wrinkled face could ever bloom again."

"See!" answered Dr. Heidegger.

He uncovered the vase, and threw the faded rose into the water which it contained. At first, it lay lightly on the surface of the fluid, appearing to imbibe none of its moisture. Soon, however, a singular change began to be visible. The crushed and dried petals stirred, and assumed a deepening tinge of crimson, as if the flower were reviving from a death-like slumber; the slender stalk and twigs of foliage became green; and there was the rose of half a century, looking as fresh as when Sylvia Ward had first given it to her lover. It was scarcely full blown; for some of its delicate red leaves curled modestly around its moist bosom, within which two or three dewdrops were sparkling.

"That is certainly a very pretty deception," said the doctor's friends; carelessly, however, for they had witnessed greater miracles at a conjurer's show; "pray how was it effected?"

"Did you never hear of the 'Fountain of Youth'," asked Dr. Heidegger, "which Ponce de Leon, the Spanish adventurer, went in search of, two or three centuries ago?"

"But did Ponce de Leon ever find it?" said the Widow

Wycherly.

"No," answered Dr. Heidegger, "for he never sought it in the right place. The famous Fountain of Youth, if I am rightly informed, is situated in the southern part of the Floridian peninsula, not far from Lake Macaco. Its source is overshadowed by several gigantic magnolias, which, though numberless centuries old, have been kept as fresh as violets, by the virtues of this wonderful water. An acquaintance of mine, knowing my curiosity in such matters, has sent me what you see in the vase.

"Ahem!" said Colonel Killigrew, who believed not a word of the doctor's story; "and what may be the effect of this fluid on the human frame?"

"You shall judge for yourself, my dear Colonel," replied Dr. Heidegger; "and all of you, my respected friends, are welcome to so much of this admirable fluid as may restore to you the bloom of youth. For my own part, having had much trouble in growing old, I am in no hurry to grow young again. With your permission, therefore, I will merely watch the progress of the experiment."

While he spoke, Dr. Heidegger had been filling the four champagne-glasses with the water of the Fountain of Youth. It was apparently impregnated with an effervescent gas, for little bubbles were continually ascending from the depths of the glasses, and bursting in silvery spray at the surface. As the liquor diffused a pleasant perfume, the old people doubted not that it possessed cordial and comfortable properties; and, though utter sceptics as to its rejuvenescent power, they were inclined to swallow it at once. But Dr. Heidegger besought them to stay a moment.

"Before you drink, my respectable old friends," said he, "it would be well that, with the experience of a lifetime to direct you, you should draw up a few general rules for your guidance, in passing a second time through the perils of youth. Think what a sin and shame it would be, if, with your peculiar advantages, you should not become patterns of virtue and wisdom to all the young people of the age."

The doctor's four venerable friends made him no answer, except by a feeble and tremulous laugh; so very ridiculous was the idea, that, knowing how closely repentance treads behind the steps of error, they should ever go astray again.

"Drink, then," said the doctor, bowing. "I rejoice that I have so well selected the subjects of my experiment."

With palsied hands, they raised the glasses to their lips. The liquor, if it really possessed such virtues as Dr. Heidegger imputed to it, could not have been bestowed on four human beings who needed it more wofully. They looked as if they had never known what youth or pleasure was, but had been the off-spring of Nature's dotage, and always the gray, decrepit, sapless, miserable creatures who now sat stooping round the doctor's table, without life enough in their souls or bodies to be animated even by the prospect of growing young again. They drank off the water, and replaced their glasses on the table.

Assuredly there was an almost immediate improvement in the aspect of the party, not unlike what might have been produced by a glass of generous wine, together with a sudden glow of cheerful sunshine, brightening over all their visages at once. There was a healthful suffusion on their cheeks, instead of the ashen hue that had made them look so corpse-like. They gazed at one another, and fancied that some magic power had really begun to smooth away the deep and sad inscriptions which Father Time had been so long engraving on their brows. The Widow Wycherly adjusted her cap, for she felt almost like a woman again.

"Give us more of this wondrous water!" cried they, eagerly. "We are younger,—but we are still too old! Quick,—give us more!"

"Patience, patience!" quoth Dr. Heidegger, who sat watching the experiment, with philosophic coolness. "You have been a long time growing old. Surely, you might be content to grow young in half an hour! But the water is at your service."

Again he filled their glasses with the liquor of youth, enough of which still remained in the vase to turn half the old people in the city to the age of their own grandchildren. While the bubbles were yet sparkling on the brim, the doctor's four guests snatched their glasses from the table, and swallowed the contents at a single gulp. Was it delusion? even while the draught was passing down their throats, it seemed to have wrought a change on their whole systems. Their eyes grew clear and bright; a dark shade deepened among their silvery locks; they sat around the table, three gentlemen of middle age, and a woman, hardly beyond her buxom prime.

"My dear widow, you are charming!" cried Colonel Killigrew, whose eyes had been fixed upon her face, while the shadows of age were flitting from it like darkness from the crimson daybreak.

The fair widow knew, of old, that Colonel Killigrew's compliments were not always measured by sober truth; so she started up and ran to the mirror, still dreading that the ugly visage of an old woman would meet her gaze. Meanwhile, the three gentlemen behaved in such a manner, as proved that the water of the Fountain of Youth possessed some intoxicating qualities; unless, indeed, their exhilaration of spirits were merely a lightsome dizziness, caused by the sudden removal of the weight of years. Mr. Gascoigne's mind seemed to run on political topics, but whether relating to the past, present, or future, could not easily be determined, since the same ideas and phrases have been in vogue these fifty years. Now he rattled forth full-throated sentences about patriotism, national glory, and the people's right; now he muttered some perilous stuff or other, in a sly and doubtful whisper, so cautiously that even his own conscience could scarcely catch the secret; and now, again, he spoke in measured accents, and a deeply deferential tone, as if a royal ear were listening to his well-turned periods. Colonel Killigrew all this time had been trolling forth a jolly bottle-song, and ringing his glass in symphony with the chorus, while his eyes wandered toward the buxom figure of the Widow Wycherly. On the other side of the table, Mr. Medbourne was involved in a calculation of dollars and cents, with which was strangely intermingled a project for supplying the East Indies with ice, by harnessing a team of whales to the polar icebergs.

As for the Widow Wycherly, she stood before the mirror courtesying and simpering to her own image, and greeting it as the friend whom she loved better than all the world beside. She thrust her face close to the glass, to see whether some long-remembered wrinkle or crow's-foot had indeed vanished. She examined whether the snow had so entirely melted from her hair, that the venerable cap could be safely thrown aside. At last, turning briskly away, she came with a sort of dancing step to the table.

"My dear old doctor," cried she, "pray favor me with another glass!"

"Certainly, my dear madam, certainly!" replied the complaisant doctor; "see! I have already filled the glasses."

There, in fact, stood the four glasses, brimful of this wonderful water, the delicate spray of which, as it effervesced from the surface, resembled the tremulous glitter of diamonds. It was now so nearly sunset, that the chamber had grown duskier than ever; but a mild and moonlike splendor gleamed from within the vase, and rested alike on the four guests, and on the doctor's venerable figure. He sat in a high-backed, elaborately carved oaken arm-chair, with a gray dignity of aspect that might have well befitted that very Father Time, whose power had never been disputed, save by this fortunate company. Even while quaffing the third draught of the Fountain of Youth, they were almost awed by the expression of his mysterious visage.

But, the next moment, the exhilarating gush of young life shot through their veins. They were now in the happy prime of youth. Age, with its miserable train of cares, and sorrows, and diseases, was remembered only as the trouble of a dream, from which they had joyously awoke. The fresh gloss of the soul, so early lost, and without which the world's successive scenes had been but a gallery of faded pictures, again threw its enchantment over all their prospects. They felt like new-created beings, in a new-created universe.

"We are young! We are young!" they cried exultingly.

Youth, like the extremity of age, had effaced the strongly marked characteristics of middle life, and mutually assimilated them all. They were a group of merry youngsters, almost maddened with the exuberant frolicsomeness of their years. The most singular effect of their gayety was an impulse to mock the infirmity and decrepitude of which they had so lately been the victims. They laughed loudly at their old-fashioned attire, the wide-skirted coats and flapped waistcoats of the young men, and the ancient cap and gown of the blooming girl. One limped across the floor, like a gouty grandfather; one set a pair of spectacles astride of his nose, and pretended to pore over the black-letter pages of the book of magic; a third seated himself in an arm-chair, and strove to imitate the venerable dignity of Dr. Heidegger. Then all shouted mirthfully, and leaped about the room. The Widow Wycherly—if so fresh a damsel could be called a widow—tripped up to the doctor's chair, with a mischievous merriment in her rosy face.

"Doctor, you dear old soul," cried she, "get up and dance

with me!" And then the four young people laughed louder than ever, to think what a queer figure the poor old doctor would cut.

"Pray excuse me," answered the doctor, quietly. "I am old and rheumatic, and my dancing days were over long ago. But either of these gay young gentlemen will be glad of so pretty a partner."

"Dance with me, Clara!" cried Colonel Killigrew.

"No, no, I will be her partner!" shouted Mr. Gascoigne.

"She promised me her hand, fifty years ago!" exclaimed Mr. Medbourne.

They all gathered round her. One caught both her hands in his passionate grasp—another threw his arm about her waist—the third buried his hand among the glossy curls that clustered beneath the widow's cap. Blushing, panting, struggling, chiding, laughing, her warm breath fanning each of their faces by turns, she strove to disengage herself, yet still remained in their triple embrace. Never was there a livelier picture of youthful rivalship, with bewitching beauty for the prize. Yet, by a strange deception, owing to the duskiness of the chamber, and the antique dresses which they still wore, the tall mirror is said to have reflected the figures of the three old, gray, withered grandsires, ridiculously contending for the skinny ugliness of a shrivelled grandam.

But they were young: their burning passions proved them so. Inflamed to madness by the coquetry of the girl-widow, who neither granted nor quite withheld her favors, the three rivals began to interchange threatening glances. Still keeping hold of the fair prize, they grappled fiercely at one another's throats. As they struggled to and fro, the table was overturned, and the vase dashed into a thousand fragments. The precious Water of Youth flowed in a bright stream across the floor, moistening the wings of a butterfly, which, grown old in the decline of summer, had alighted there to die. The insect fluttered lightly through the chamber, and settled on the snowy head of Dr. Heidegger.

"Come, come, gentlemen!—come, Madam Wycherly," exclaimed the doctor, "I really must protest against this riot."

They stood still and shivered; for it seemed as if gray Time were calling them back from their sunny youth, far down into the chill and darksome vale of years. They looked at old Dr. Heidegger, who sat in his carved arm-chair, holding the rose of half a century, which he had rescued from among the fragments of the shattered vase. At the motion of his hand, the four rioters resumed their seats; the more readily, because their violent exertions had wearied them, youthful though they were.

"My poor Sylvia's rose!" ejaculated Dr. Heidegger, holding it in the light of the sunset clouds; "it appears to be fading again."

And so it was. Even while the party were looking at it, the flower continued to shrivel up, till it became as dry and fragile as when the doctor had first thrown it into the vase. He shook off the few drops of moisture which clung to its petals.

"I love it as well thus, as in its dewy freshness," observed he, pressing the withered rose to his withered lips. While he spoke, the butterfly fluttered down from the doctor's snowy head, and fell upon the floor.

His guests shivered again. A strange chillness, whether of the body or spirit they could not tell, was creeping gradually over them all. They gazed at one another, and fancied that each fleeting moment snatched away a charm, and left a deepening furrow where none had been before. Was it an illusion? Had the changes of a lifetime been crowded into so brief a space, and were they now four aged people, sitting with their old friend, Dr. Heidegger?

"Are we grown old again, so soon?" cried they, dolefully.

In truth, they had. The Water of Youth possessed merely a virtue more transient than that of wine. The delirium which it created had effervesced away. Yes! they were old again. With a shuddering impulse, that showed her a woman still, the widow clasped her skinny hands before her face, and wished that the coffin-lid were over it, since it could be no longer beautiful.

"Yes, friends, ye are old again," said Dr. Heidegger; "and lo! the Water of Youth is all lavished on the ground. Well, I bemoan it not; for if the fountain gushed at my very doorstep, I would not stoop to bathe my lips in it; no, though its delirium were for years instead of moments. Such is the lesson ye have taught me!"

But the doctor's four friends had taught no such lesson to themselves. They resolved forthwith to make a pilgrimage to Florida, and quaff at morning, noon, and night from the Fountain of Youth.

Note: In an English Review, not long since, I have been accused of plagiarizing the idea of this story from a chapter in one of the novels of Alexandre Dumas. There has undoubtedly been a plagiarism on one side or the other; but as my story was written a good deal more than twenty years ago, and as the novel is of considerably more recent date, I take pleasure in thinking that M. Dumas has done me the honor to appropriate one of the fanciful conceptions of my earlier days. He is heartily welcome to it: nor is it the only instance, by many, in which the great French romancer has exercised the privilege of commanding genius by confiscating the intellectual property of less famous people to his own use and behoof.

September, 1860.

FINIS

Frank L. Pollock

"I'm getting tired," complained Davis, lounging in the window of the Physics Building, "and sleepy. It's after eleven o'clock. This makes the fourth night I've sat up to see your new star, and it'll be the last. Why, the thing was billed to appear three weeks ago."

"Are *you* tired, Miss Wardour?" asked Eastwood, and the girl glanced up with a quick flush and a negative murmur.

Eastwood made the reflection anew that she certainly was painfully shy. She was almost as plain as she was shy, though her hair had an unusual beauty of its own, fine as silk and coloured like palest flame.

Probably she had brains; Eastwood had seen her reading some extremely "deep" books, but she seemed to have no amusements, few interests. She worked daily at the Art Students' League, and boarded where he did, and he had thus come to ask her with the Davis's to watch for the new star from the laboratory windows on the Heights.

"Do you really think that it's worthwhile to wait any longer, professor?" enquired Mrs. Davis, concealing a yawn.

Eastwood was somewhat annoyed by the continued failure of the star to show itself and he hated to be called "professor", being only an assistant professor of physics.

"I don't know," he answered somewhat curtly. "This is the twelfth night that I have waited for it. Of course, it would have been a mathematical miracle if astronomers should have solved such a problem exactly, though they've been figuring on it for a quarter of a century."

The new Physics Building of Columbia University was about twelve storeys high. The physics laboratory occupied the ninth and tenth floors, with the astronomical rooms above it, an arrangement which would have been impossible before the invention of the oil vibration cushion, which practically isolated the instrument rooms from the earth.

Eastwood had arranged a small telescope at the window, and below them spread the illuminated map of Greater New York, sending up a faintly musical roar. All the streets were crowded, as they had been every night since the fifth of the month, when the great new star, or sun, was expected to come into view.

Some error had been made in the calculations, though, as Eastwood said, astronomers had been figuring on them for twenty-five years.

It was, in fact, nearly forty years since Professor Adolphe Bernier first announced his theory of a limited universe at the International Congress of Sciences in Paris, where it was counted as little more than a masterpiece of imagination.

Professor Bernier did not believe that the universe was infinite. Somewhere, he argued, the universe must have a centre, which is the pivot for its revolution.

The moon revolves around the earth, the planetary system revolves about the sun, the solar system revolves about one of the fixed stars, and this whole system in its turn undoubtedly revolve around some more distant point. But this sort of progression must definitely stop somewhere.

Somewhere there must be a central sun, a vast incandescent body which does not move at all. And as a sun is always larger and hotter than its satellites, therefore the body at the centre of the universe must be of an immensity and temperature beyond anything known or imagined.

It was objected that this hypothetical body should then be

large enough to be visible from the earth, and Professor Bernier replied that some day it undoubtedly would be visible. Its light had simply not yet had time to reach the earth.

The passage of light from the nearest of the fixed stars is a matter of three years, and there must be many stars so distant that their rays have not yet reached us. The great central sun must be so inconceivably remote that perhaps hundreds, perhaps thousands of years would elapse before its light should burst upon the solar system.

All this was contemptuously classed as "newspaper science" till the extraordinary mathematical revival a little after the middle of the twentieth century afforded the means of verifying it.

Following the new theorems discovered by Professor Burnside, of Princeton, and elaborated by Dr. Taneka, of Tokyo, astronomers succeeded in calculating the arc of the sun's movements through space, and its ratio to the orbit of its satellites. With this as a basis, it was possible to follow the widening circles, the consecutive systems of the heavenly bodies and their rotations.

The theory of Professor Bernier was justified. It was demonstrated that there really was a gigantic mass of incandescent matter, which, whether the central point of the universe or not, appeared to be without motion.

The weight and distance of this new sun were approximately calculated, and, the speed of light being known, it was an easy matter to reckon when its rays would reach the earth.

It was then estimated that the approaching rays would arrive at the earth in twenty-six years, and that was twenty-six years ago. Three weeks had passed since the date when the new heavenly body was expected to become visible, and it had not yet appeared.

Popular interest had risen to a high pitch, stimulated by innumerable newspaper and magazine articles, and the streets were nightly thronged with excited crowds armed with opera-glasses and star maps, while at every corner a telescope man had planted his tripod instrument at a nickel a look.

Similar scenes were taking place in every civilized city on the globe.

It was generally supposed that the new luminary would appear in size about midway between Venus and the moon. Better informed persons expected something like the sun, and a syndicate of capitalists quietly leased large areas on the coast of Greenland in anticipation of a great rise in temperature and a northward movement in population.

Even the business situation was appreciably affected by the public uncertainty and excitement. There was a decline in stocks, and a minor religious sect boldly prophesied the end of the world.

"I've had enough of this," said Davis, looking at his watch again. "Are you ready to go, Grace? By the way, isn't it getting warmer?"

It had been a sharp February day, but the temperature was certainly rising. Water was dripping from the roofs, and from the icicles that fringed the window ledges, as if a warm wave had suddenly arrived.

"What's that light?" suddenly asked Alice Wardour, who was lingering by the open window.

"It must be moonrise," said Eastwood, though the illumination of the horizon was almost like daybreak.

Davis abandoned his intention of leaving, and they watched the east grow pale and flushed till at last a brilliant white disc heaved itself above the horizon.

It resembled the full moon, but as if trebled in lustre, and the streets grew almost as light as by day.

"Good heavens, that must be the new star, after all!" said Davis in an awed voice.

"No, it's only the moon. This is the hour and minute for her rising," answered Eastwood, who had grasped the cause of the phenomenon. "But the new sun must have appeared on the other side of the earth. Its light is what makes the moon so brilliant. It will rise here just as the sun does, no telling how soon. It must be brighter than was expected—and maybe hotter," he added with a vague uneasiness.

"Isn't it getting very warm in here?" said Mrs. Davis, loosening her jacket. "Couldn't you turn off some of the steam heat?"

Eastwood turned it all off, for, in spite of the open window, the room was really growing uncomfortably close. But the warmth appeared to come from without; it was like a warm spring evening, and the icicles were breaking loose from the cornices.

For half an hour they leaned from the windows with but desultory conversation, and below them the streets were black with people and whitened with upturned faces. The brilliant moon rose higher, and the mildness of the night sensibly increased.

It was after midnight when Eastwood first noticed the reddish flush tinging the clouds low in the east, and he pointed it out to his companions.

"That must be it at last," he exclaimed, with a thrill of vibrating excitement at what he was going to see, a cosmic event unprecedented in intensity.

The brightness waxed rapidly.

"By Jove, see it redden!" Davis ejaculated. "It's getting lighter than day—and hot! Whew!"

The whole eastern sky glowed with a deepening pink that extended half round the horizon. Sparrows chirped from the roofs, and it looked as if the disc of the unknown star might at any moment be expected to lift above the Atlantic, but it delayed long.

The heavens continued to burn with myriad hues, gathering at last to a fiery furnace glow on the skyline.

Mrs. Davis suddenly screamed. An American flag blowing freely from its staff on the roof of the tall building had all at once burst into flame.

Low in the east lay a long streak of intense fire which broadened as they squinted with watering eyes. It was as if the edge of the world had been heated to whiteness.

The brilliant moon faded to a feathery white film in the glare. There was a confused outcry from the observatory overhead, and a crash of something being broken, and as the strange new sunlight fell through the window the onlookers leaped back as if a blast furnace had been opened before them.

The glass cracked and fell inward. Something like the sun, but magnified fifty times in size and hotness, was rising out of the sea. An iron instrument-table by the window began to smoke with an acrid smell of varnish.

"What the devil is this, Eastwood?" shouted Davis accusingly.

From the streets rose a sudden, enormous wail of fright and pain, the outcry of a million throats at once, and the roar of a stampede followed. The pavements were choked with struggling, panic-stricken people in the fierce glare, and above the din arose the clanging rush of fire engines and trucks.

Smoke began to rise from several points below Central Park, and two or three church chimes pealed crazily.

The observers from overhead came running down the stairs with a thunderous trampling, for the elevator man had deserted his post.

"Here, we've got to get out of this," shouted Davis, seizing his wife by the arm and hustling her toward the door. "This place'll be on fire directly."

"Hold on. You can't go down into that crush on the street," Eastwood cried, trying to prevent him.

But Davis broke away and raced down the stairs, half carrying his terrified wife. Eastwood got his back against the door in time to prevent Alice from following them.

"There's nothing in this building that will burn, Miss Wardour," he said as calmly as he could. "We had better stay here for the present. It would be sure death to get involved in that stampede below. Just listen to it."

The crowds on the street seemed to sway to and fro in contending waves, and the cries, curses, and screams came up in a savage chorus.

The heat was already almost blistering to the skin, though they carefully avoided the direct rays, and instruments of glass in the laboratory cracked loudly one by one.

A vast cloud of dark smoke began to rise from the harbour, where the shipping must have caught fire, and something exploded with a terrific report. A few minutes later half a dozen fires broke out in the lower part of the city, rolling up volumes of smoke that faded to a thin mist in the dazzling light.

The great new sun was now fully above the horizon, and the whole east seemed ablaze. The stampede in the streets had quieted all at once, for the survivors had taken refuge in the nearest houses, and the pavements were black with motionless forms of men and women.

"I'll do whatever you say," said Alice, who was deadly pale, but remarkably collected. Even at that moment Eastwood was struck by the splendour of her ethereally brilliant hair that burned like pale flame above her pallid face. "But we can't stay here, can we?"

"No," replied Eastwood, trying to collect his faculties in the face of this catastrophic revolution of nature. "We'd better go to the basement, I think."

In the basement were deep vaults used for the storage of delicate instruments, and these would afford shelter for a time at least. It occurred to him as he spoke that perhaps temporary safety was the best that any living thing on earth could hope for.

But he led the way down the well staircase. They had gone down six or seven flights when a gloom seemed to grow upon the air, with a welcome relief.

It seemed almost cool, and the sky had clouded heavily, with the appearance of polished and heated silver.

A deep but distant roaring arose and grew from the southeast, and they stopped on the second landing to look from the window.

A vast black mass seemed to fill the space between sea and sky, and it was sweeping towards the city, probably from the harbour, Eastwood thought, at a speed that made it visibly grow as they watched it.

"A cyclone—and a waterspout!" muttered Eastwood, appalled.

He might have foreseen it from the sudden, excessive evaporation and the heating of the air. The gigantic black pillar drove towards them swaying and reeling, and a gale came with it, and a wall of impenetrable mist behind.

As Eastwood watched its progress he saw its cloudy bulk illumined momentarily by a dozen lightning-like flashes, and a moment later, above its roar, came the tremendous detonations of heavy cannon. The forts and the warships were firing shells to break the waterspout, but the shots seemed to produce no effect. It was the city's last and useless attempt at resistance. A moment later forts and ships alike must have been engulfed.

"Hurry! This building will collapse!" Eastwood shouted.

They rushed down another flight, and heard the crash with which the monster broke over the city. A deluge of water, like the emptying of a reservoir, thundered upon the street, and the water was steaming hot as it fell.

There was a rending crash of falling walls, and in another

instant the Physics Building seemed to be twisted around by a powerful hand. The walls blew out, and the whole structure sank in a chaotic mass.

But the tough steel frame was practically unwreckable, and, in fact, the upper portion was simply bent down upon the lower storeys, peeling off most of the shell of masonry and stucco.

Eastwood was stunned as he was hurled to the floor, but when he came to himself he was still upon the landing, which was tilted at an alarming angle. A tangled mass of steel rods and beams hung a yard over his head, and a huge steel girder had plunged down perpendicularly from above, smashing everything in its way.

Wreckage choked the well of the staircase, a mass of plaster, bricks, and shattered furniture surrounded him, and he could look out in almost every direction through the rent iron skeleton.

A yard away Alice was sitting up, mechanically wiping the mud and water from her face, and apparently uninjured. Tepid water was pouring through the interstices of the wreck in torrents, though it did not appear to be raining.

A steady, powerful gale had followed the whirlwind, and it brought a little coolness with it. Eastwood enquired perfunctorily of Alice if she were hurt, without being able to feel any degree of interest in the matter. His faculty of sympathy seemed paralysed.

"I don't know. I thought—I thought that we were all dead!" the girl murmured in a sort of daze. "What was it? Is it all over?"

"I think it's only beginning," Eastwood answered dully.

The gale had brought up more clouds and the skies were thickly overcast, but shining white-hot. Presently the rain came down in almost scalding floods and as it fell upon the hissing streets it steamed again into the air.

In three minutes all the world was choked with hot vapour, and from the roar and splash the streets seemed to be running rivers.

The downpour seemed too violent to endure, and after an hour it did cease, while the city reeked with mist. Through the whirling fog Eastwood caught glimpses of ruined buildings, vast heaps of debris, all the wreckage of the greatest city of the twentieth century.

Then the torrents fell again, like a cataract, as if the waters of the earth were shuttlecocking between sea and heaven. With a jarring tremor of the ground a landslide went down into the Hudson.

The atmosphere was like a vapour bath, choking and sickening. The physical agony of respiration aroused Alice from a sort of stupor, and she cried out pitifully that she would die.

The strong wind drove the hot spray and steam through the shattered building till it seemed impossible that human lungs could extract life from the semi-liquid that had replaced the air, but the two lived.

After hours of this parboiling the rain slackened, and, as the clouds parted, Eastwood caught a glimpse of a familiar form halfway up the heavens. It was the sun, the old sun, looking small and watery.

But the intense heat and brightness told that the enormous body still blazed behind the clouds. The rain seemed to have ceased definitely, and the hard, shining whiteness of the sky grew rapidly hotter.

The heat of the air increased to an oven-like degree; the mists were dissipated, the clouds licked up, and the earth seemed to dry itself almost immediately. The heat from the two suns beat down simultaneously till it became a monstrous terror, unendurable.

An odour of smoke began to permeate the air; there was a dazzling shimmer over the streets, and great clouds of mist arose from the bay, but these appeared to evaporate before they could darken the sky.

The piled wreck of the building sheltered the two refugees from the direct rays of the new sun, now almost overhead, but not from the penetrating heat of the air. But the body will endure almost anything, short of tearing asunder, for a time at least; it is the finer mechanism of the nerves that suffers most.

Alice lay face down among the bricks, gasping and moaning. The blood hammered in Eastwood's brain, and the strangest mirages flickered before his eyes.

Alternately he lapsed into heavy stupors, and awoke to the agony of the day. In his lucid moments he reflected that this could not last long, and tried to remember what degree of heat would cause death.

Within an hour after the drenching rains he was feverishly thirsty, and the skin felt as if peeling from his whole body.

This fever and horror lasted until he forgot that he had ever known another state; but at last the west reddened, and the flaming sun went down. It left the familiar planet high in the heavens, and there was no darkness until the usual hour, though there was a slight lowering of the temperature.

But when night did come it brought life-giving coolness, and though the heat was still intense it seemed temperate by comparison. More than all, the kindly darkness seemed to set a limit to the cataclysmic disorders of the day.

"Ouf! This is heavenly!" said Eastwood, drawing long breaths and feeling mind and body revived in the gloom.

"It won't last long," replied Alice, and her voice sounded extraordinarily calm through the darkness. "The heat will come again when the new sun rises in a few hours."

"We might find some better place in the meanwhile—a deep cellar; or we might get into the subway," Eastwood suggested.

"It would be no use. Don't you understand? I have been thinking it all out. After this, the new sun will always shine, and we could not endure it even another day. The wave of heat is passing round the world as it revolves, and in a few hours the whole earth will be a burnt-up ball. Very likely we are the only people left alive in New York, or perhaps in America."

She seemed to have taken the intellectual initiative, and spoke with an assumption of authority that amazed him.

"But there must be others," said Eastwood, after thinking for a moment. "Other people have found sheltered places, or miners, or men underground."

"They would have been drowned by the rain. At any rate, there will be none left alive by tomorrow night.

"Think of it," she went dreamily, "for a thousand years this wave of fire has been rushing towards us, while life has been going on so happily in the world, so unconscious that the world was doomed all the time. And now this is the end of life."

"I don't know," Eastwood said slowly. "It may be the end of human life, but there must be some forms that will survive—some micro-organisms perhaps capable of resisting high temperatures, if nothing higher. The seed of life will be left at any rate, and that is everything. Evolution will begin over again, producing new types to suit the changed conditions. I only wish I could see what creatures will be here in a few thousand years.

"But I can't realize it at all—this thing!" he cried passionately, after a pause. "Is it real? Or have we all gone mad? It seems too much like a bad dream."

The rain crashed down again as he spoke, and the earth steamed, though not with the dense reek of the day. For hours the waters roared and splashed against the earth in hot billows till the streets were foaming yellow rivers, dammed by the wreck of fallen buildings.

There was a continual rumble as earth and rock slid into the East River, and at last the Brooklyn Bridge collapsed with a thunderous crash and splash that made all Manhattan vibrate. A gigantic billow like a tidal wave swept up the river from its fall.

The downpour slackened and ceased soon after the moon began to shed an obscured but brilliant light through the clouds.

Presently the east commenced to grow luminous, and this time there could be no doubt as to what was coming.

Alice crept closer to the man as the grey light rose upon the watery air.

"Kiss me!" she whispered suddenly, throwing her arms around his neck. He could feel her trembling. "Say you love me; hold me in your arms. There is only an hour."

"Don't be afraid. Try to face it bravely," stammered Eastwood.

"I don't fear it—not death. But I have never lived. I have always been timid and wretched and afraid—afraid to speak—and I've almost wished for suffering and misery or anything rather than to be stupid and dumb and dead, the way I've always been.

"I've never dared to tell anyone what I was, what I wanted. I've been afraid all my life, but I'm not afraid now. I have never lived; I have never been happy; and now we must die together!"

It seemed to Eastwood the cry of the perishing world. He held her in his arms and kissed her wet, tremulous face that was strained to his.

The twilight was gone before they knew it. The sky was blue already, with crimson flakes mounting to the zenith, and the heat was growing once more intense.

"This is the end, Alice," said Eastwood, and his voice trembled.

She looked at him, her eyes shining with an unearthly softness and brilliancy, and turned her face to the east.

There, in crimson and orange, flamed the last dawn that human eyes would ever see.

FROM THE "LONDON TIMES" OF 1904

Mark Twain

Correspondence of the "London Times" Chicago, April 1, 1904

I resume by cable-telephone where I left off yesterday. For many hours now, this vast city—along with the rest of the globe, of course—has talked of nothing but the extraordinary episode mentioned in my last report. In accordance with your instructions, I will now trace the romance from its beginnings down to the culmination of yesterday—or today; call it which you like. By an odd chance, I was a personal actor in a part of this drama myself. The opening scene plays in Vienna. Date, one o'clock in the morning, March 31, 1898. I had spent the evening at a social entertainment. About midnight I went away, in company with the military attaches of the British, Italian, and American embassies, to finish with a late smoke. This function had been appointed to take place in the house of Lieutenant Hillyer, the third attache mentioned in the above list. When we arrived there we found several visitors in the room; young Szczepanik; [1] Mr. K., his financial backer; Mr. W., the latter's secretary; and Lieutenant Clayton, of the United States Army. War was at that time threatening between Spain and our country, and Lieutenant Clayton had been sent to Europe on military business. I was well acquainted with young Szczepanik and his two friends, and I knew Mr. Clayton slightly. I had met him at West Point years before, when he was a cadet. It was when General Merritt was superintendent. He had the reputation of being an able officer, and also of being quick-tempered and plain-spoken.

This smoking-party had been gathered together partly for business. This business was to consider the availability of the telelectroscope for military service. It sounds oddly enough now, but it is nevertheless true that at that time the invention was not taken seriously by any one except its inventor. Even his financial supporter regarded it merely as a curious and interesting toy. Indeed, he was so convinced of this that he had actually postponed its use by the general world to the end of the dying century by granting a two years' exclusive lease of it to a syndicate, whose intent was to exploit it at the Paris World's Fair. When we entered the smoking-room we found Lieutenant Clayton and Szczepanik engaged in a warm talk over the telelectroscope in the German tongue. Clayton was saying:

"Well, you know my opinion of it, anyway!" and he brought his fist down with emphasis upon the table.

"And I do not value it," retorted the young inventor, with provoking calmness of tone and manner.

Clayton turned to Mr. K., and said:

"I cannot see why you are wasting money on this toy. In my opinion, the day will never come when it will do a farthing's worth of real service for any human being."

"That may be; yes, that may be; still, I have put the money in it, and am content. I think, myself, that it is only a toy; but Szczepanik claims more for it, and I know him well enough to believe that he can see father than I can—either with his telelectroscope or without it."

The soft answer did not cool Clayton down; it seemed only to irritate him the more; and he repeated and emphasised his conviction that the invention would never do any man a farthing's worth of real service. He even made it a "brass" farthing, this time. Then he laid an English farthing on the table, and added:

"Take that, Mr. K., and put it away; and if ever the

telelectroscope does any man an actual service—mind, a real service—please mail it to me as a reminder, and I will take back what I have been saying. Will you?"

"I will," and Mr. K. put the coin in his pocket.

Mr. Clayton now turned toward Szczepanik, and began with a taunt—a taunt which did not reach a finish; Szczepanik interrupted it with a hardy retort, and followed this with a blow. There was a brisk fight for a moment or two; then the attaches separated the men.

The scene now changes to Chicago. Time, the autumn of 1901. As soon as the Paris contract released the telelectroscope, it was delivered to public use, and was soon connected with the telephonic systems of the whole world. The improved "limitless-distance" telephone was presently introduced, and the daily doings of the globe made visible to everybody, and audibly discussible, too, by witnesses separated by any number of leagues.

By-and-by Szczepanik arrived in Chicago. Clayton (now captain) was serving in that military department at the time. The two men resumed the Viennese quarrel of 1898. On three different occasions they quarrelled, and were separated by witnesses. Then came an interval of two months, during which time Szczepanik was not seen by any of his friends, and it was at first supposed that he had gone off on a sight seeing tour and would soon be heard from. But no; no word came from him. Then it was supposed that he had returned to Europe. Still, time drifted on, and he was not heard from. Nobody was troubled, for he was like most inventors and other kinds of poets, and went and came in a capricious way, and often without notice.

Now comes the tragedy. On December 29, in a dark and unused compartment of the cellar under Captain Clayton's house, a corpse was discovered by one of Clayton's maid-servants. Friends of deceased identified it as Szczepanik's. The man had died by violence. Clayton was arrested, indicted, and brought to trial, charged with this murder. The evidence against him was perfect in every detail, and absolutely unassailable. Clayton admitted this himself. He said that a reasonable man could not examine this testimony with a dispassionate mind and not be convinced by it; yet the man would be in error, nevertheless. Clayton swore that he did not commit the murder, and that he had had nothing to do with it.

As your readers will remember, he was condemned to death. He had numerous and powerful friends, and they worked hard to save him, for none of them doubted the truth of his assertion. I did what little I could to help, for I had long since become a close friend of his, and thought I knew that it was not in his character to inveigle an enemy into a corner and assassinate him. During 1902 and 1903 he was several times reprieved by the governor; he was reprieved once more in the beginning of the present year, and the execution day postponed to March 31.

The governor's situation has been embarrassing, from the day of the condemnation, because of the fact that Clayton's wife is the governor's niece. The marriage took place in 1899, when Clayton was thirty-four and the girl twenty-three, and has been a happy one. There is one child, a little girl three years old. Pity for the poor mother and child kept the mouths of grumblers closed at first; but this could not last for ever—for in America politics has a hand in everything—and by-and-by the governor's political opponents began to call attention to his delay in allowing the law to take its course. These hints have grown more and more frequent of late, and more and more pronounced. As a natural result, his own party grew nervous. Its leaders began to visit Springfield and hold long private conferences with him. He was now between two fires. On the one hand, his niece was imploring him to pardon her husband; on the other were the leaders, insisting that he stand to his plain duty as chief magistrate of the State, and place no further bar to Clayton's execution. Duty won in the struggle, and the Governor gave his word that he would not again respite the condemned man. This was two weeks ago. Mrs. Clayton now said:

"Now that you have given your word, my last hope is gone, for I know you will never go back from it. But you have done the best you could for John, and I have no reproaches for you. You love him, and you love me, and we know that if you could honourable save him, you would do it. I will go to him now, and be what help I can to him, and get what comfort I may out of the few days that are left to us before the night comes which will have no end for me in life. You will be with me that day? You will not let me bear it alone?"

"I will take you to him myself, poor child, and I will be near you to the last."

By the governor's command, Clayton was now allowed every indulgence he might ask for which could interest his mind and soften the hardships of his imprisonment. His wife and child spent the days with him; I was his companion by night. He was removed from the narrow cell which he had occupied during such a dreary stretch of time, and given the chief warden's roomy and comfortable quarters. His mind was always busy with the catastrophe of his life, and with the slaughtered inventor, and he now took the fancy that he would like to have the telelectroscope and divert his mind with it. He had his wish. The connection was made with the international telephone-station, and day by day, and night by night, he called up one corner of the globe after another, and looked upon its life, and studied its strange sights, and spoke with its people, and realised that by grace of this marvellous instrument he was almost as free as the birds of the air, although a prisoner under locks and bars. He seldom spoke, and I never interrupted him when he was absorbed in this amusement. I sat in his parlour and read, and smoked, and the nights were very quiet and reposefully sociable, and I found them pleasant. Now and then I would her him say "Give me Yedo;" next, "Give me Hong-Kong;" next, "Give me Melbourne." And I smoked on, and read in comfort, while he wandered about the remote underworld, where the sun was shining in the sky, and the people were at their daily work. Sometimes the talk that came from those far regions through the microphone attachment interested me, and I listened.

Yesterday—I keep calling it yesterday, which is quite natural, for certain reasons—the instrument remained unused, and that also was natural, for it was the eve of the execution day. It was spent in tears and lamentations and farewells. The governor and the wife and child remained until a quarter-past eleven at night, and the scenes I witnessed were pitiful to see. The execution was to take place at four in the morning. A little after eleven a sound of hammering broke out upon the still night, and there was a glare of light, and the child cried out, "What is that, papa?" and ran to the window before she could be stopped and clapped her small hands and said, "Oh, come and see, mamma—such a pretty thing they are making!" The mother knew—and fainted. It was the gallows!

She was carried away to her lodging, poor woman, and Clayton and I were alone—alone, and thinking, brooding, dreaming. We might have been statues, we sat so motionless and still. It was a wild night, for winter was come again for a moment, after the habit of this region in the early spring. The sky was starless and black, and a strong wind was blowing from the lake. The silence in the room was so deep that all outside sounds seemed exaggerated by contrast with it. These sounds were fitting ones: they harmonised with the situation and the conditions: the boom and thunder of sudden storm-gusts among the roofs and chimneys, then the dying down into moanings and wailings about the eaves and angles; now and then a gnashing and lashing rush of sleet along the window-panes; and always the muffled and uncanny hammering of the gallows-builders in the court-yard. After an age of this, another sound—far off, and coming smothered and faint through the riot of the tempest—a bell tolling twelve! Another age, and it was tolled again. By-and-by, again. A dreary long interval after this, then the spectral sound floated to us once more—one, two three; and this time we caught our breath; sixty minutes of life left!

Clayton rose, and stood by the window, and looked up into the black sky, and listened to the thrashing sleet and the piping wind; then he said: "That a dying man's last of earth should be—this!" After a little he said: "I must see the sun again—the sun!" and the next moment he was feverishly calling: "China! Give me China—Peking!"

I was strangely stirred, and said to myself: "To think that it is a mere human being who does this unimaginable miracle—turns winter into summer, night into day, storm into calm, gives the freedom of the great globe to a prisoner in his cell, and the sun in his naked splendour to a man dying in Egyptian darkness."

I was listening.

"What light! what brilliancy! what radiance!... This is Peking?"

"Yes."

"The time?"

"Mid-afternoon."

"What is the great crowd for, and in such gorgeous costumes? What masses and masses of rich colour and barbaric magnificence! And how they flash and glow and burn in the flooding sunlight! What is the occasion of it all?"

"The coronation of our new emperor—the Czar."

"But I thought that that was to take place yesterday."

"This is yesterday—to you."

"Certainly it is. But my mind is confused, these days: there are reasons for it... Is this the beginning of the procession?"

"Oh, no; it began to move an hour ago."

"Is there much more of it still to come?"

"Two hours of it. Why do you sigh?"

"Because I should like to see it all."

"And why can't you?"

"I have to go—presently."

"You have an engagement?"

After a pause, softly: "Yes." After another pause: "Who are these in the splendid pavilion?"

"The imperial family, and visiting royalties from here and there and yonder in the earth."

"And who are those in the adjoining pavilions to the right and left?"

"Ambassadors and their families and suites to the right; unofficial foreigners to the left."

"If you will be so good, I—"

Boom! That distant bell again, tolling the half-hour faintly through the tempest of wind and sleet. The door opened, and the governor and the mother and child entered—the woman in widow's weeds! She fell upon her husband's breast in a passion of sobs, and I—I could not stay; I could not bear it. I went into the bedchamber, and closed the door. I sat there waiting—waiting—waiting, and listening to the rattling sashes and the blustering of the storm. After what seemed a long, long time, I heard a rustle and movement in the parlour, and knew that the clergyman and the sheriff and the guard were come. There was some low-voiced talking; then a hush; then a prayer, with a sound of sobbing; presently, footfalls—the departure for the gallows; then the child's happy voice: "Don't cry now, mamma, when we've got papa again, and taking him home."

The door closed; they were gone. I was ashamed: I was the only friend of the dying man that had no spirit, no courage. I stepped into the room, and said I would be a man and would follow. But we are made as we are made, and we cannot help it. I did not go.

I fidgeted about the room nervously, and presently went to the window and softly raised it—drawn by that dread fascination which the terrible and the awful exert—and looked down upon the court-yard. By the garish light of the electric lamps I saw the little group of privileged witnesses, the wife crying on her uncle's breast, the condemned man standing on the scaffold with the halter around his neck, his arms strapped to his body, the black cap on his head, the sheriff at his side with his hand on the drop, the clergyman in front of him with bare head and his book in his hand.

"I am the resurrection and the life—"

I turned away. I could not listen; I could not look. I did not know whither to go or what to do. Mechanically and without knowing it, I put my eye to that strange instrument, and there was Peking and the Czar's procession! The next moment I was leaning out of the window, gasping, suffocating, trying to speak, but dumb from the very imminence of the necessity of speaking. The preacher could speak, but I, who had such need of words—
"And may God have mercy upon your soul. Amen."

The sheriff drew down the black cap, and laid his hand upon the lever. I got my voice.

"Stop, for God's sake! The man is innocent. Come here and see Szczepanik face to face!"

Hardly three minutes later the governor had my place at the window, and was saying:

"Strike off his bonds and set him free!"

Three minutes later all were in the parlour again. The reader will imagine the scene; I have no need to describe it. It was a sort of mad orgy of joy.

A messenger carried word to Szczepanik in the pavilion, and one could see the distressed amazement in his face as he listened to the tale. Then he came to his end of the line, and talked with Clayton and the governor and the others; and the wife poured out her gratitude upon him for saving her husband's life, and in her deep thankfulness she kissed him at twelve thousand miles' range.

The telelectroscopes of the world were put to service now, and for many hours the kings and queens of many realms (with here and there a reporter) talked with Szczepanik, and praised him; and the few scientific societies which had not already made him an honorary member conferred that grace upon him.

How had he come to disappear from among us? It was easily explained. He had not grown used to being a world-famous person, and had been forced to break away from the lionising that was robbing him of all privacy and repose. So he grew a beard, put on coloured glasses, disguised himself a little in other ways, then took a fictitious name, and went off to wander about the earth in peace.

Such is the tale of the drama which began with an inconsequential quarrel in Vienna in the spring of 1898, and came near ending as a tragedy in the spring of 1904.

Mark Twain.

II

Correspondence of the "London Times" Chicago, April 5, 1904

To-day, by a clipper of the Electric Line, and the latter's Electric Railway connections, arrived an envelope from Vienna, for

Captain Clayton, containing an English farthing. The receiver of it was a good deal moved. He called up Vienna, and stood face to face with Mr. K., and said:

"I do not need to say anything: you can see it all in my face. My wife has the farthing. Do not be afraid—she will not throw it away."

M.T.

III

Correspondence of the "London Times" Chicago, April 23, 1904

Now that the after developments of the Clayton case have run their course and reached a finish, I will sum them up. Clayton's romantic escape from a shameful death steeped all this region in an enchantment of wonder and joy—during the proverbial nine days. Then the sobering process followed, and men began to take thought, and to say: "But a man was killed, and Clayton killed him." Others replied: "That is true: we have been overlooking that important detail; we have been led away by excitement."

The telling soon became general that Clayton ought to be tried again. Measures were taken accordingly, and the proper representations conveyed to Washington; for in America under the new paragraph added to the Constitution in 1889, second trials are not State affairs, but national, and must be tried by the most august body in the land—the Supreme Court of the United States. The justices were therefore summoned to sit in Chicago. The session was held day before yesterday, and was opened with the usual impressive formalities, the nine judges appearing in their black robes, and the new chief justice (Lemaitre) presiding. In opening the case the chief justice said:

"It is my opinion that this matter is quite simple. The prisoner at the bar was charged with murdering the man Szczepanik; he was tried for murdering the man Szczepanik; he was fairly tried and justly condemned and sentenced to death for murdering the man Szczepanik. It turns out that the man Szczepanik was not murdered at all. By the decision of the French courts in the Dreyfus matter, it is established beyond cavil or question that the decisions of courts are permanent and cannot be revised. We are obliged to respect and adopt this precedent. It is upon precedents that the enduring edifice of jurisprudence is reared. The prisoner at the bar has been fairly and righteously condemned to death for the murder of the man Szczepanik, and, in my opinion, there is but one course to pursue in the matter: he must be hanged."

Mr. Justice Crawford said:

"But, your Excellency, he was pardoned on the scaffold for that."

"The pardon is not valid, and cannot stand, because he was pardoned for killing Szczepanik, a man whom he had not killed. A man cannot be pardoned for a crime which he has not committed; it would be an absurdity."

"But, your Excellency, he did kill a man."

"That is an extraneous detail; we have nothing to do with it. The court cannot take up this crime until the prisoner has expiated the other one."

Mr. Justice Halleck said:

"If we order his execution, your Excellency, we shall bring about a miscarriage of justice, for the governor will pardon him again."

"He will not have the power. He cannot pardon a man for a crime which he has not committed. As I observed before, it would be an absurdity."

After a consultation, Mr. Justice Wadsworth said:

"Several of us have arrived at the conclusion, your Excellency, that it would be an error to hang the prisoner for killing Szczepanik, instead of for killing the other man, since it is proven that he did not kill Szczepanik."

"On the contrary, it is proven that he did kill Szczepanik. By the French precedent, it is plain that we must abide by the finding of the court."

"But Szczepanik is still alive."

"So is Dreyfus."

In the end it was found impossible to ignore or get around the French precedent. There could be but one result: Clayton was delivered over for the execution. It made an immense excitement; the State rose as one man and clamored for Clayton's pardon and retrial. The governor issued the pardon, but the Supreme Court was in duty bound to annul it, and did so, and poor Clayton was hanged yesterday. The city is draped in black, and, indeed, the like may be said of the State. All America is vocal with scorn of "French justice", and of the malignant little soldiers who invented it and inflicted it upon the other Christian lands.

[1] Pronounced (approximately) Shepannik.

GRAPH

Stanley G. Weinbaum

"You're on the mend again," said Dr. Felix Kurtius, tossing his black case carelessly on the desk. "Let's see how permanent it is this time!"

Isaac Levinson—mail-order Levinson—rolled down his sleeve and stared sardonically at the doctor.

"Thanks," he growled. "I've heard that before."

"You're feeling better, aren't you?"

The merchandise king nodded reluctantly, staring about his elaborate office. "Sure," he said. "But for how long? And anyway, why don't you do something? Is this the new medical practice—to let a patient get well by himself? For that I don't need a doctor!"

"I gave you my suggestions," retorted Kurtius. "Three and a half years ago—when you first called me—I told you what to do. Don't blame me because you refuse to follow my advice."

"Vacations!" sneered Levinson. "Rest—change—travel—retire! Could I leave my business with conditions like they were?"

"You certainly could! What's a little more money to you—or a little less?"

"Money—bah! It's my business that needs me."

"Same thing."

"No," said Levinson abruptly. "Not the same thing! My stockholders, my employees, I have obligations to them. The business must be run right, or the one loses money and the other jobs. Could I let some schlemiehl make a botch of things while I was telling how the biggest tarpon got away from me. Oser!"

"Just excuses," observed Kurtius. "What you mean is that you didn't want to leave."

"Couldn't is what I said."

"Wouldn't is what you mean."

The doctor gestured at the fittings of his patient's office. "You don't mean to tell me you're so busy that you haven't time to walk two blocks to my office, do you?—Instead of having me call here to examine you?"

Levinson silently indicated the welter of papers on his desk. "And that's what you've wedded to!" scoffed Kurtius. "Charts, summaries, statistics. Any clerk could tabulate them for you."

"Charts and statistics," growled Levinson, "are the life-blood of my business."

"And your business is the life-blood of you!"

"Yet you want I should get away from it."

"That's my advice. No man can live year after year on his own blood. You can't; that's the whole trouble with you. That's why medicine or operations are perfectly useless in your case."

"Bah!" Levinson was frowning again. "I have a notion that you doctors recommend the rest cure when you don't know what's wrong. I don't want to rest; I want something that will put me in shape to keep on working. I don't believe it's my business that's doing this to me; for twenty-five years I've lived, eaten, slept, and dreamt this business, and never, until that first time I called you, have I felt an hour's sickness. And now these damned spells—better, worse, better worse—How could it be my business?"

"Well," observed Kurtius, "there's no way of proving it to you. I've told you my diagnosis; that's all I can do. You'll find out sooner or later that I am right."

"I don't believe it," said Levinson stubbornly.

"Well, as I said, there's no way of proving it to you."

"You doctors," continued Levinson, "spend your efforts

treating symptoms instead of causes. Because I am tired, I must go somewhere and rest; because I can't sleep, I must get out somewhere and exercise; because I have no appetite, I must go away from my business! Why don't you find why I am tired, and can't sleep or eat? I should run my business like that and in a year I'd be broke—machullah!"

"Didn't you ever hear of functional disorders?" queried Kurtius mildly.

"Am I the doctor or you?"

"Functional disorders are those where there's nothing the matter with the patient—that is organically. Nothing wrong except in the mind or nervous system."

"Hah! Imaginary sickness I've got."

"It's not imaginary. Functional troubles are just as real as organic ones, and sometimes a damn sight harder to treat— Especially," he added, "if the patient won't cooperate."

"And you think my business is doing that?"

"Just as I told you."

"Bah! For more than twenty years I have had no trouble. And why do I get better and then worse again? You should make a study of your cases."

"Do you think I don't?" snapped Kurtius. "I can give you this case history by heart. Why, look here! Here's something you ought to be able to understand!"

He reached toward his black bag, noting that the catch had opened, spilling a stethoscope and a parer or two on the littered desk. He seized a paper and spread it out before his patient. "What's that?" grunted Levinson.

"Graph of your metabolism," replied the doctor. "Make a study of my cases, eh! Here's your chart month by month for three and a half years."

Levinson scanned the irregular black lines. Suddenly he

narrowed his eyes, leaned closer. A moment more and he burst into a snickering laugh.

"What's the matter?" queried Kurtius impatiently.

"The chart!" chuckled Levinson. "Hee-hee! It's a graph of our sales I was looking at before you came! Case-record, huh?" Kurtius glanced at the paper, frowned perplexedly, and suddenly gave vent to a shout of laughter. "Ho!" He roared, slapping the desk. "Funny! Oh, Lord!"

"What's that funny?" asked his patient.

"The graph! The sales-chart!" bellowed the doctor. "Your business doesn't affect you, eh? Look!"

He pulled another bit of paper from his bag, spread it beside the first.

"Here's your metabolism! Look it over!"

Peak for peak, valley for valley, the two graphs were identical!

HERE LIES

Howard Wandrei

Chauncey knocked the dottle out of his corncob and briefly startled Old Shep by inquiring unemotionally, "Will you never finish that blasted stick?"

Which in Old Chauncey was tantamount to fury. Words being precious things, both old boys hoarded every syllable; Shep tightened his leathery lips and with the scalpel-point of the knife flicked away a mote of pine. Each link of the chain he was whittling from that interminable stick of soft pine resembled ivory in its satin finish. He might produce one link in a day or let it require a full week. No hurry. The current chain numbered four hundred and seventy-two links. A masterpiece.

Under Shep's surreptitious scrutiny, Old Chauncey stood erect purposefully and stalked to the woodpile. There a fat log stood on end. With one swift, seemingly effortless stroke of the ax he cleft the log in two, spat explosively and hiked into the house wagging his jaw.

The log-built house, a jewel of conscientious carpentry, stood on the wooded elevation called St. Paul's Hill, near town. On the side hill one hundred and twenty feet below stood another log-built affair, formerly the ice-house. Since Old Shep had become Chauncey's permanent guest, this structure had been equipped with furnishings as complete and comfortable as the house, including plumbing. So there was no reason for Shep to hang around Old Chauncey's kitchen.

The housekeeper, Celia Lilleoden, performed the chores incidental to both houses with such easy efficiency that old

Chauncey was repeatedly reminded of his bachelorhood. From continually sunning themselves behind the kitchen like two old snakes the men had acquired a wrinkled black-walnut finish, but Celia still retained the firm, buxom ripeness of an apple.

As a practical communist Old Chauncey kept his latch-key out by inclination. His generosity was limitless.

Thus, Old Shep did not have to ask for anything he wanted. It was share and share alike.

For example, he charged tobacco to Old Chauncey's account at the store in town. He always had. If he preferred a grade of tobacco superior to what Old Chauncey himself used, such was his privilege. A plug is a plug.

Shep and Chauncey once had occupied the same double desk of raw cherrywood in the schoolhouse which was now a weedy hill of rubble and rotten wood a half-mile out on the backroad.

Besides words, Old Shep hoarded tobacco plugs in case the cause of communism ever collapsed.

In accordance with this scheme of living, Old Chauncey gradually became accustomed to being spared the nuisance of opening the occasional letter he received from another old soldier in Sackett's Harbor, New York. At first Shep had gone to the trouble of sneaking the mail down to the ice-house and steaming it open. But currently the mail arrived slit open without any subterfuge. The knife, incidentally, was the better of Old Chauncey's two. Shep had borrowed it, knowing that in communism there can be no Indian giving.

On one occasion Chauncey accosted Old Shep behind the kitchen with a crumpled letter in his fingers.

"Shep," he suggested casually, "I wish you'd slit my letters open at the top instead of an end. It wouldn't bunch the writing up so much when you shove it back inside."

"Chauncey," Old Shep replied tremblingly, "you're not serious with me, are you? If you want to keep secrets from your old crony, why, you just tell me seriously not to open those letters any more and I won't."

It used to give Chauncey a funny feeling when Old Shep talked like that.

Of a somnolent summer morning while Chauncey was scrubbing his long yellow teeth he glimpsed blurred movement through the starched white bathroom curtain. Tweaking the curtain somewhat aside he witnessed Old Shep scampering down the side hill to the ice-house with a load of kindling in his arms.

"I'll be dog-goned," swore Old Chauncey with toothpaste foam dribbling down his chin. "He complains he can't do his chopping on account of his rheumatism, and look at the old turkey go! I see where I chop kindling for both of us from now on."

When Old Shep showed up to get in a few licks of whittling before breakfast, Chauncey inquired, "How's that rheumatism?"

"Fierce, Chauncey. I'm getting mighty creaky."

"Well, help yourself to my kindling, Shep. Long as I *know* where it's disappearing to, I don't give a durn."

"Thanks, Chauncey; thanks! I knew you'd feel that way."

The bacon, eggs, and delicately crusty fried potatoes hit the palate so ambrosially that, after breakfast, Chauncey was seduced into the disastrous error of mentioning to Shep the chances of marrying Miss Lilleoden: error, for it was only human nature to covet the goods which another man prized most.

Thenceforward Old Shep neglected his whittling or idled awkwardly with it in the kitchen, where a housekeeper spends most of her time. Chauncey observed blackly that Old Shep had a cunning way with him, too.

"Durn it," Chauncey ruminated dismally, "everything I want, he gets. If I tell him to stay away from her he won't take me seriously. The old hoodoo always has his way. Anyhow, his durned whittling is out of my sight."

Befell a morning when Old Shep didn't appear, and Chauncey found him stretched out stiff half-way down the side hill. In Shep's vulturine right fist was clenched a small crumple of bills. This pilfering had occurred with such regularity that the companion of Chauncey's childhood had accumulated just about enough to get started with Celia Lilleoden.

Chauncey asked the coroner, a glistening little round man like a wet dumpling, "Is he dead?"

"Of course he's dead," said the coroner. "Obviously."

"He has no kin," Celia reminded Old Chauncey in her slow, soft contralto.

"I'll do him one more favor," Chauncey offered unblinkingly. "He can have my lot in the cemet'ry."

The lot in Dream Hill Cemetery measured eight feet long, five feet wide and ten feet deep, meaning that it had been excavated and ready for occupancy these past five years. The walls were common brick. On the floor was a stone bed to lie on. Whimsically Chauncey had also installed a small table furnished with a tobacco bag and pipe, matches, an alarm clock with an illuminated dial, and an ashtray. And a thick, plumber's candle. The old pagan!

Anchored in the foot-wall of this cell, ladder-like, were iron rungs which had enabled him on past occasions to descend and inspect his subterranean property; as, on this occasion, he made the trip to deposit Shep's unfinished wooden chain.

The stone slab sealing the cell had long been cut with the dangerous advertisement:

Here Lies Chauncey
D'autreville Whose Worldly

*Goods Were any Man's For
The Asking.*

Naturally, a new inscription had to be chiseled.

"But there ain't any more room in that piece, Chauncey," the stone-cutter objected. "You want 'nother stone."

"Turn it upside down and cut it in the bottom," Old Chauncey directed. "With that topside staring him in the face, he'll have something to read in the hereafter."

The underside, becoming the face, carried the inscription:

*Here Lies Shepard
Frankenfield Who Feels
No Anxiety for the Future
Nor Regret for the Past.*

On the day preceding Old Shep's interment, Old Chauncey paid a visit to the nearest justice of the peace with Celia Lilleoden and no one thought it was in the least peculiar. As Chauncey balanced accounts with himself, the state would otherwise inherit his property eventually, as was right, but he wished to insure Celia's staying on as his housekeeper, in which capacity she beggared superlatives.

While four huskies furnished by the undertaker replaced the granite sheet over the brick chamber, Old Chauncey recollected the particulars of a certain fit of Shep's, dating about five years before, shortly before Celia. That catalepsy, or whatever it was, had gripped Shep as though in death for nearly three days until Old Chauncey had thought of making a brassy rumpus next to his ear with the big dinner bell. The alarm clock in the subterranean mausoleum was set for eleven o'clock, terminating a like period of time, when Old Shep might be expected to wake up and yawn in the hereafter. Just a whim of Chauncey's, since the coroner had pronounced Old Shep indisputably defunct.

Late that night Celia surmised worriedly that her absent husband might be visiting the tomb of his lifelong crony, and there he was in the sickly forest of tombstones, hunkering down on Shep's horizontal tombstone like a boy watching a game of marbles.

But he was listening, not watching. He knocked again on the slab with his bony knuckles, cocked his head. Listening for the response while the lazy breeze lifted his silken gray hair in the starry cave of night, he asked, "Cele, do you hear him down there?"

Celia's gentle mind recoiled from the idea that the dead might rise in answer to a human summons. The stoically restrained grief for his departed friend must have touched her husband somewhat in the head.

On the fifth night Chauncey observed, "That Old Shep's ghost must be getting tuckered out."

Celia decided that there was a limit to indulgence.

"Chauncey," she ordered firmly, "you mustn't come down here any more. You'll be taking pneumonia."

He accepted the order without protest.

"Maybe *that*," he commented to the frankly puzzled Mrs. Old Chauncey, "will teach the old grasshopper when to take a man seriously."

IN THE AVU OBSERVATORY

H.G. Wells

The observatory at Avu, in Borneo, stands on the spur of the mountain. To the north rises the old crater, black against the unfathomable blue of the sky. From the little circular building, with its mushroom dome, the slopes plunge steeply downward into the black mysteries of the tropical forest beneath. The little house in which the observer and his assistant live is about fifty yards from the observatory, and beyond this are the huts of their native attendants.

Thaddy, the chief observer, was down with a slight fever. His assistant, Woodhouse, paused for a moment in silent contemplation of the tropical night before commencing his solitary vigil. The night was very silent. Now and then voices and laughter came from the native huts, or the cry of some strange animal was heard from the midst of the mystery of the forest. Nocturnal insects appeared in ghostly fashion out of the darkness, and fluttered round his light. He thought, perhaps, of all the possibilities of discovery that still lay in the black tangle beneath him; for to the naturalist the virgin forests of Borneo are still a wonderland, full of strange questions and half-suspected discoveries. Woodhouse carried a small lantern in his hand, and its yellow glow contrasted vividly with the infinite series of tints between lavender-blue and black in which the landscape was painted. His hands and face were smeared with ointment against the attacks of the mosquitoes.

Even in these days of celestial photography, work done in a purely temporary erection, and with only the most primitive appliances in addition to the telescope, still involves a very large amount of cramped and motionless watching. He sighed as he thought of the physical fatigues before him, stretched himself, and entered the observatory.

The reader is probably familiar with the structure of an ordinary astronomical observatory. The building is usually cylindrical in shape, with a very light hemispherical roof capable of being turned round from the interior. The telescope is supported upon a stone pillar in the centre, and a clockwork arrangement compensates for the earth's rotation, and allows a star once found to be continuously observed. Besides this, there is a compact tracery of wheels and screws about its point of support, by which the astronomer adjusts it. There is, of course, a slit in the movable roof which follows the eye of the telescope in its survey of the heavens. The observer sits or lies on a sloping wooden arrangement, which he can wheel to any part of the observatory as the position of the telescope may require. Within it is advisable to have things as dark as possible, in order to enhance the brilliance of the stars observed.

The lantern flared as Woodhouse entered his circular den, and the general darkness fled into black shadows behind the big machine, from which it presently seemed to creep back over the whole place again as the light waned. The slit was a profound transparent blue, in which six stars shone with tropical brilliance, and their light lay, a pallid gleam, along the black tube of the instrument. Woodhouse shifted the roof, and then proceeding to the telescope, turned first one wheel and then another, the great cylinder slowly swinging into a new position. Then he glanced through the finder, the little companion telescope, moved the roof a little more, made some further adjustments, and set the clockwork in motion. He took off his jacket, for the night was very hot, and pushed into position the uncomfortable seat to which he was condemned for the next four hours. Then with a sigh he resigned himself to his watch upon the mysteries of space.

There was no sound now in the observatory, and the lantern waned steadily. Outside there was the occasional cry of some animal in alarm or pain, or calling to its mate, and the intermittent sounds of the Malay and Dyak servants. Presently one of the men began a queer chanting song, in which the others joined at intervals. After this it would seem that they turned in for the night, for no further sound came from their direction, and the whispering stillness became more and more profound.

The clockwork ticked steadily. The shrill hum of a mosquito explored the place and grew shriller in indignation at Woodhouse's ointment. Then the lantern went out and all the observatory was black.

Woodhouse shifted his position presently, when the slow movement of the telescope had carried it beyond the limits of his comfort.

He was watching a little group of stars in the Milky Way, in one of which his chief had seen or fancied a remarkable colour variability. It was not a part of the regular work for which the establishment existed, and for that reason perhaps Woodhouse was deeply interested. He must have forgotten things terrestrial. All his attention was concentrated upon the great blue circle of the telescope field—a circle powdered, so it seemed, with an innumerable multitude of stars, and all luminous against the blackness of its setting. As he watched he seemed to himself to become incorporeal, as if he too were floating in the ether of space. Infinitely remote was the faint red spot he was observing.

Suddenly the stars were blotted out. A flash of blackness passed, and they were visible again.

"Queer," said Woodhouse. "Must have been a bird."

The thing happened again, and immediately after the great

tube shivered as though it had been struck. Then the dome of the observatory resounded with a series of thundering blows. The stars seemed to sweep aside as the telescope swung round and away from the slit in the roof.

"Great Scott!" cried Woodhouse. "What's this?"

Some huge, vague, black shape, with a flapping something like a wing, seemed to be struggling in the aperture of the roof. In another moment the slit was clear again, and the luminous haze of the Milky Way shone warm and bright.

The interior of the roof was perfectly black, and only a scraping sound marked the whereabouts of the unknown creature.

Woodhouse had scrambled from the seat to his feet. He was trembling violently and in a perspiration with the suddenness of the occurrence. Was the thing, whatever it was, inside or out? It was big, whatever else it might be. Something shot across the skylight, and the telescope swayed. He started violently and put his arm up. It was in the observatory, then, with him. It was clinging to the roof, apparently. What the devil was it? Could it see him?

He stood for perhaps a minute in a state of stupefaction. The beast, whatever it was, clawed at the interior of the dome, and then something flapped almost into his face, and he saw the momentary gleam of starlight on a skin like oiled leather. His water-bottle was knocked off his little table with a smash.

The sense of some strange bird-creature hovering a few yards from his face in the darkness was indescribably unpleasant to Woodhouse. As his thought returned he concluded that it must be some night-bird or large bat. At any risk he would see what it was, and pulling a match from his pocket, he tried to strike it on the telescope seat. There was a smoking streak of phosphorescent light, the match flared for a moment, and he saw a vast wing sweeping towards him, a gleam of grey-brown fur, and then he was struck in the face and the match knocked out of his hand. The blow was aimed at his temple, and a claw tore sideways down to his cheek. He reeled and fell, and he heard the extinguished lantern smash. Another blow followed as he fell. He was partly stunned, he felt his own warm blood stream out upon his face. Instinctively he felt his eyes had been struck at, and, turning over on his face to protect them, tried to crawl under the protection of the telescope.

He was struck again upon the back, and he heard his jacket rip, and then the thing hit the roof of the observatory. He edged as far as he could between the wooden seat and the eyepiece of the instrument, and turned his body round so that it was chiefly his feet that were exposed. With these he could at least kick. He was still in a mystified state. The strange beast banged about in the darkness, and presently clung to the telescope, making it sway and the gear rattle. Once it flapped near him, and he kicked out madly and felt a soft body with his feet. He was horribly scared now. It must be a big thing to swing the telescope like that. He saw for a moment the outline of a head black against the starlight, with sharply-pointed upstanding ears and a crest between them. It seemed to him to be as big as a mastiff's. Then he began to bawl out as loudly as he could for help.

At that the thing came down upon him again. As it did so his hand touched something beside him on the floor. He kicked out, and the next moment his ankle was gripped and held by a row of keen teeth. He yelled again, and tried to free his leg by kicking with the other. Then he realised he had the broken water-bottle at his hand, and, snatching it, he struggled into a sitting posture, and feeling in the darkness towards his foot, gripped a velvety ear, like the ear of a big cat. He had seized the water-bottle by its neck and brought it down with a shivering crash upon the head of the strange beast. He repeated the blow, and then stabbed and jobbed with the jagged end of it, in the darkness, where he judged the face might be.

The small teeth relaxed their hold, and at once Woodhouse pulled his leg free and kicked hard. He felt the sickening feel of fur and bone giving under his boot. There was a tearing bite at his arm, and he struck over it at the face, as he judged, and hit damp fur.

There was a pause; then he heard the sound of claws and the dragging of a heavy body away from him over the observatory floor. Then there was silence, broken only by his own sobbing breathing, and a sound like licking. Everything was black except the parallelogram of the blue skylight with the luminous dust of stars, against which the end of the telescope now appeared in silhouette. He waited, as it seemed, an interminable time.

Was the thing coming on again? He felt in his trouser-pocket for some matches, and found one remaining. He tried to strike this, but the floor was wet, and it spat and went out. He cursed. He could not see where the door was situated. In his struggle he had quite lost his bearings. The strange beast, disturbed by the splutter of the match, began to move again. "Time!" called Woodhouse, with a sudden gleam of mirth, but the thing was not coming at him again. He must have hurt it, he thought, with the broken bottle. He felt a dull pain in his ankle. Probably he was bleeding there. He wondered if it would support him if he tried to stand up. The night outside was very still. There was no sound of any one moving. The sleepy fools had not heard those wings battering upon the dome, nor his shouts. It was no good wasting strength in shouting. The monster flapped its wings and startled him into a defensive attitude. He hit his elbow against the seat, and it fell over with a crash. He cursed this, and then he cursed the darkness.

Suddenly the oblong patch of starlight seemed to sway to

and fro. Was he going to faint? It would never do to faint. He clenched his fists and set his teeth to hold himself together. Where had the door got to? It occurred to him he could get his bearings by the stars visible through the skylight. The patch of stars he saw was in Sagittarius and south-eastward; the door was north—or was it north by west? He tried to think. If he could get the door open he might retreat. It might be the thing was wounded. The suspense was beastly. "Look here!" he said, "if you don't come on, I shall come at you."

Then the thing began clambering up the side of the observatory, and he saw its black outline gradually blot out the skylight. Was it in retreat? He forgot about the door, and watched as the dome shifted and creaked. Somehow he did not feel very frightened or excited now. He felt a curious sinking sensation inside him. The sharply-defined patch of light, with the black form moving across it, seemed to be growing smaller and smaller. That was curious. He began to feel very thirsty, and yet he did not feel inclined to get anything to drink. He seemed to be sliding down a long funnel.

He felt a burning sensation in his throat, and then he perceived it was broad daylight, and that one of the Dyak servants was looking at him with a curious expression. Then there was the top of Thaddy's face upside down. Funny fellow Thaddy, to go about like that! Then he grasped the situation better, and perceived that his head was on Thaddy's knee, and Thaddy was giving him brandy. And then he saw the eyepiece of the telescope with a lot of red smears on it. He began to remember.

"You've made this observatory in a pretty mess," said Thaddy.

The Dyak boy was beating up an egg in brandy. Woodhouse took this and sat up. He felt a sharp twinge of pain. His ankle was tied up, so were his arm and the side of his face. The smashed glass, red-stained, lay about the floor, the telescope seat was overturned, and by the opposite wall was a dark pool. The door was open, and he saw the grey summit of the mountain against a brilliant background of blue sky.

"Pah!" said Woodhouse. "Who's been killing calves here? Take me out of it."

Then he remembered the Thing, and the fight he had had with it.

"What was it?" he said to Thaddy—"the Thing I fought with?"

"You know that best," said Thaddy. "But, anyhow, don't worry yourself now about it. Have some more to drink."

Thaddy, however, was curious enough, and it was a hard struggle between duty and inclination to keep Woodhouse quiet until he was decently put away in bed, and had slept upon the copious dose of meat-extract Thaddy considered advisable. They then talked it over together.

"It was," said Woodhouse, "more like a big bat than anything else in the world. It had sharp, short ears, and soft fur, and its wings were leathery. Its teeth were little, but devilish sharp, and its jaw could not have been very strong or else it would have bitten through my ankle."

"It has pretty nearly," said Thaddy.

"It seemed to me to hit out with its claws pretty freely. That is about as much as I know about the beast. Our conversation was intimate, so to speak, and yet not confidential."

"The Dyak chaps talk about a Big Colugo, a Klang-utang—whatever that may be. It does not often attack man, but I suppose you made it nervous. They say there is a Big Colugo and a Little Colugo, and a something else that sounds like gobble. They all fly about at night. For my own part I know there are flying foxes and flying lemurs about here; but they are none of them very big beasts."

"There are more things in heaven and earth," said Woodhouse,—and Thaddy groaned at the quotation,—"and more particularly in the forests of Borneo, than are dreamt of in our philosophies. On the whole, if the Borneo fauna is going to disgorge any more of its novelties upon me, I should prefer that it did so when I was not occupied in the observatory at night and alone."

IN THE COURT OF THE DRAGON

Robert W. Chambers

> *"Oh, thou who burn'st in heart for those who burn*
> *In Hell, whose fires thyself shall feed in turn;*
> *How long be crying—'Mercy on them.' God!*
> *Why, who art thou to teach and He to learn?"*

In the Church of St. Barnabé vespers were over; the clergy left the altar; the little choir-boys flocked across the chancel and settled in the stalls. A Suisse in rich uniform marched down the south aisle, sounding his staff at every fourth step on the stone pavement; behind him came that eloquent preacher and good man, Monseigneur C—.

My chair was near the chancel rail, I now turned toward the west end of the church. The other people between the altar and the pulpit turned too. There was a little scraping and rustling while the congregation seated itself again; the preacher mounted the pulpit stairs, and the organ voluntary ceased.

I had always found the organ-playing at St. Barnabé highly interesting. Learned and scientific it was, too much so for my small knowledge, but expressing a vivid if cold intelligence. Moreover, it possessed the French quality of taste: taste reigned supreme, self-controlled, dignified and reticent.

To-day, however, from the first chord I had felt a change for the worse, a sinister change. During vespers it had been chiefly the chancel organ which supported the beautiful choir, but now and again, quite wantonly as it seemed, from the west gallery where the great organ stands, a heavy hand had struck across the church at the serene peace of those clear voices. It was something more than harsh and dissonant, and it betrayed no lack of skill. As it recurred again and again, it set me thinking of what my architect's books say about the custom in early times to consecrate the choir as soon as it was built, and that the nave, being finished sometimes half a century later, often did not get any blessing at all: I wondered idly if that had been the case at St. Barnabé, and whether something not usually supposed to be at home in a Christian church might have entered undetected and taken possession of the west gallery. I had read of such things happening, too, but not in works on architecture.

Then I remembered that St. Barnabé was not much more than a hundred years old, and smiled at the incongruous association of mediaeval superstitions with that cheerful little piece of eighteenth-century rococo.

But now vespers were over, and there should have followed a few quiet chords, fit to accompany meditation, while we waited for the sermon. Instead of that, the discord at the lower end of the church broke out with the departure of the clergy, as if now nothing could control it.

I belong to those children of an older and simpler generation who do not love to seek for psychological subtleties in art; and I have ever refused to find in music anything more than melody and harmony, but I felt that in the labyrinth of sounds now issuing from that instrument there was something being hunted. Up and down the pedals chased him, while the manuals blared approval. Poor devil! whoever he was, there seemed small hope of escape!

My nervous annoyance changed to anger. Who was doing this? How dare he play like that in the midst of divine service? I glanced at the people near me: not one appeared to be in the least disturbed. The placid brows of the kneeling nuns, still turned towards the altar, lost none of their devout abstraction under the pale shadow of their white head-dress. The fashionable lady beside me was looking expectantly at Monseigneur C—. For all her face betrayed, the organ might have been singing an Ave Maria.

But now, at last, the preacher had made the sign of the cross, and commanded silence. I turned to him gladly. Thus far I had not found the rest I had counted on when I entered St. Barnabé that afternoon.

I was worn out by three nights of physical suffering and mental trouble: the last had been the worst, and it was an exhausted body, and a mind benumbed and yet acutely sensitive, which I had brought to my favourite church for healing. For I had been reading *The King in Yellow*.

"The sun ariseth; they gather themselves together and lay them down in their dens." Monseigneur C—delivered his text in a calm voice, glancing quietly over the congregation. My eyes turned, I knew not why, toward the lower end of the church. The organist was coming from behind his pipes, and passing along the gallery on his way out, I saw him disappear by a small door that leads to some stairs which descend directly to the street. He was a slender man, and his face was as white as his coat was black. "Good riddance!" I thought, "with your wicked music! I hope your assistant will play the closing voluntary."

With a feeling of relief—with a deep, calm feeling of relief, I turned back to the mild face in the pulpit and settled myself to listen. Here, at last, was the ease of mind I longed for.

"My children," said the preacher, "one truth the human soul finds hardest of all to learn: that it has nothing to fear. It can never be made to see that nothing can really harm it."

"Curious doctrine!" I thought, "for a Catholic priest. Let us see how he will reconcile that with the Fathers."

"Nothing can really harm the soul," he went on, in, his coolest, clearest tones, "because—"

But I never heard the rest; my eye left his face, I knew not for what reason, and sought the lower end of the church. The same man was coming out from behind the organ, and was passing along the gallery *the same way*. But there had not been time for him to return, and if he had returned, I must have seen him. I felt a faint chill, and my heart sank; and yet, his going and coming were no affair of mine. I looked at him: I could not look away from his black figure and his white face. When he was exactly opposite to me, he turned and sent across the church straight into my eyes, a look of hate, intense and deadly: I have never seen any other like it; would to God I might never see it again! Then he disappeared by the same door through which I had watched him depart less than sixty seconds before.

I sat and tried to collect my thoughts. My first sensation was like that of a very young child badly hurt, when it catches its breath before crying out.

To suddenly find myself the object of such hatred was exquisitely painful: and this man was an utter stranger. Why should he hate me so?—me, whom he had never seen before? For the moment all other sensation was merged in this one pang: even fear was subordinate to grief, and for that moment I never doubted; but in the next I began to reason, and a sense of the incongruous came to my aid.

As I have said, St. Barnabé is a modern church. It is small and well lighted; one sees all over it almost at a glance. The organ gallery gets a strong white light from a row of long windows in the clerestory, which have not even coloured glass.

The pulpit being in the middle of the church, it followed that, when I was turned toward it, whatever moved at the west end could not fail to attract my eye. When the organist passed it was no wonder that I saw him: I had simply miscalculated the interval between his first and his second passing. He had come in that last time by the other side-door. As for the look which had so upset me, there had been no such thing, and I was a nervous fool.

I looked about. This was a likely place to harbour supernatural horrors! That clear-cut, reasonable face of Monseigneur C—, his collected manner and easy, graceful gestures, were they not just a little discouraging to the notion of a gruesome mystery? I glanced above his head, and almost laughed. That flyaway lady supporting one corner of the pulpit canopy, which looked like a fringed damask table-cloth in a high wind, at the first attempt of a basilisk to pose up there in the organ loft, she would point her gold trumpet at him, and puff him out of existence! I laughed to myself over this conceit, which, at the time, I thought very amusing, and sat and chaffed myself and everything else, from the old harpy outside the railing, who had made me pay ten centimes for my chair, before she would let me in (she was more like a basilisk, I told myself, than was my organist with the anaemic complexion): from that grim old dame, to, yes, alas! Monseigneur C—himself. For all devoutness had fled. I had never yet done such a thing in my life, but now I felt a desire to mock.

As for the sermon, I could not hear a word of it for the jingle in my ears of

"The skirts of St. Paul has reached.
Having preached us those six Lent lectures,
More unctuous than ever he preached,"

keeping time to the most fantastic and irreverent thoughts.

It was no use to sit there any longer: I must get out of doors and shake myself free from this hateful mood. I knew the rudeness I was committing, but still I rose and left the church.

A spring sun was shining on the Rue St. Honoré, as I ran down the church steps. On one corner stood a barrow full of yellow jonquils, pale violets from the Riviera, dark Russian violets, and white Roman hyacinths in a golden cloud of mimosa. The street was full of Sunday pleasure-seekers. I swung my cane and laughed with the rest. Some one overtook and passed me. He never turned, but there was the same deadly malignity in his white profile that there had been in his eyes. I watched him as long as I could see him. His lithe back expressed the same menace; every step that carried him away from me seemed to bear him on some errand connected with my destruction.

I was creeping along, my feet almost refusing to move. There began to dawn in me a sense of responsibility for something long forgotten. It began to seem as if I deserved that which he threatened: it reached a long way back—a long, long way back. It had lain dormant all these years: it was there, though, and presently it would rise and confront me. But I would try to escape; and I stumbled as best I could into the Rue de Rivoli, across the Place de la Concorde and on to the Quai. I looked with sick eyes upon the sun, shining through the white foam of the fountain, pouring over the backs of the dusky bronze river-gods, on the far-away Arc, a structure of amethyst mist, on the countless vistas of grey stems and bare branches faintly green. Then I saw him again coming down one of the chestnut alleys of the Cours la Reine.

I left the river-side, plunged blindly across to the Champs Elysées and turned toward the Arc. The setting sun was sending its rays along the green sward of the Rond-point: in the full glow he sat on a bench, children and young mothers all about him. He was nothing but a Sunday lounger, like the others, like myself. I said the words almost aloud, and all the while I gazed on the malignant hatred of his face. But he was not looking at me. I crept past and dragged my leaden feet up the Avenue. I knew that every time I met him brought him nearer to the accomplishment of his purpose and my fate. And still I tried to save myself.

The last rays of sunset were pouring through the great Arc. I passed under it, and met him face to face. I had left him far down the Champs Elysées, and yet he came in with a stream of people who were returning from the Bois de Boulogne. He came so close that he brushed me. His slender frame felt like iron inside its loose black covering. He showed no signs of haste, nor of fatigue, nor of any human feeling. His whole being expressed one thing: the will, and the power to work me evil.

In anguish I watched him where he went down the broad crowded Avenue, that was all flashing with wheels and the trappings of horses and the helmets of the Garde Republicaine.

He was soon lost to sight; then I turned and fled. Into the Bois, and far out beyond it—I know not where I went, but after a long while as it seemed to me, night had fallen, and I found myself sitting at a table before a small café. I had wandered back into the Bois. It was hours now since I had seen him. Physical fatigue and mental suffering had left me no power to think or feel. I was tired, so tired! I longed to hide away in my own den. I resolved to go home. But that was a long way off.

I live in the Court of the Dragon, a narrow passage that leads from the Rue de Rennes to the Rue du Dragon.

It is an "impasse"; traversable only for foot passengers. Over the entrance on the Rue de Rennes is a balcony, supported by an iron dragon. Within the court tall old houses rise on either side, and close the ends that give on the two streets. Huge gates, swung back during the day into the walls of the deep archways, close this court, after midnight, and one must enter then by ringing at certain small doors on the side. The sunken pavement collects unsavoury pools. Steep stairways pitch down to doors that open on the court. The ground floors are occupied by shops of second-hand dealers, and by iron workers. All day long the place rings with the clink of hammers and the clang of metal bars.

Unsavoury as it is below, there is cheerfulness, and comfort, and hard, honest work above.

Five flights up are the ateliers of architects and painters, and the hiding-places of middle-aged students like myself who want to live alone. When I first came here to live I was young, and not alone.

I had to walk a while before any conveyance appeared, but at last, when I had almost reached the Arc de Triomphe again, an empty cab came along and I took it.

From the Arc to the Rue de Rennes is a drive of more than half an hour, especially when one is conveyed by a tired cab horse that has been at the mercy of Sunday fête-makers.

There had been time before I passed under the Dragon's wings to meet my enemy over and over again, but I never saw him once, and now refuge was close at hand.

Before the wide gateway a small mob of children were playing. Our concierge and his wife walked among them, with their black poodle, keeping order; some couples were waltzing on the sidewalk. I returned their greetings and hurried in.

All the inhabitants of the court had trooped out into the street. The place was quite deserted, lighted by a few lanterns hung high up, in which the gas burned dimly.

My apartment was at the top of a house, halfway down the court, reached by a staircase that descended almost into the street, with only a bit of passage-way intervening, I set my foot on the threshold of the open door, the friendly old ruinous stairs rose before me, leading up to rest and shelter. Looking back over my right shoulder, I saw *him*, ten paces off. He must have entered the court with me.

He was coming straight on, neither slowly, nor swiftly, but straight on to me. And now he was looking at me. For the first time since our eyes encountered across the church they met now again, and I knew that the time had come.

Retreating backward, down the court, I faced him. I meant to escape by the entrance on the Rue du Dragon. His eyes told me that I never should escape.

It seemed ages while we were going, I retreating, he advancing, down the court in perfect silence; but at last I felt the shadow of the archway, and the next step brought me within it. I had meant to turn here and spring through into the street. But the shadow was not that of an archway; it was that of a vault. The great doors on the Rue du Dragon were closed. I felt this by the blackness which surrounded me, and at the same instant I read it in his face. How his face gleamed in the darkness, drawing swiftly nearer! The deep vaults, the huge closed doors, their cold iron clamps were all on his side. The thing which he had threatened had arrived: it gathered and bore down on me from the fathomless shadows; the point from which it would strike was his infernal eyes. Hopeless, I set my back against the barred doors and defied him.

There was a scraping of chairs on the stone floor, and a rustling as the congregation rose. I could hear the Suisse's staff in the south aisle, preceding Monseigneur C—to the sacristy.

The kneeling nuns, roused from their devout abstraction, made their reverence and went away. The fashionable lady, my neighbour, rose also, with graceful reserve. As she departed her glance just flitted over my face in disapproval.

Half dead, or so it seemed to me, yet intensely alive to every trifle, I sat among the leisurely moving crowd, then rose too and went toward the door.

I had slept through the sermon. Had I slept through the sermon? I looked up and saw him passing along the gallery to his place. Only his side I saw; the thin bent arm in its black covering looked like one of those devilish, nameless instruments which lie in the disused torture-chambers of mediaeval castles.

But I had escaped him, though his eyes had said I should not. *Had* I escaped him? That which gave him the power over me came back out of oblivion, where I had hoped to keep it. For I knew him now. Death and the awful abode of lost souls, whither my weakness long ago had sent him—they had changed him for every other eye, but not for mine. I had recognized him almost from the first; I had never doubted what he was come to do; and now I knew while my body sat safe in the cheerful little church, he had been hunting my soul in the Court of the Dragon.

I crept to the door: the organ broke out overhead with a blare. A dazzling light filled the church, blotting the altar from my eyes. The people faded away, the arches, the vaulted roof vanished. I raised my seared eyes to the fathomless glare, and I saw the black stars hanging in the heavens: and the wet winds from the lake of Hali chilled my face.

And now, far away, over leagues of tossing cloud-waves, I saw the moon dripping with spray; and beyond, the towers of Carcosa rose behind the moon.

Death and the awful abode of lost souls, whither my weakness long ago had sent him, had changed him for every other eye but mine. And now I heard *his voice*, rising, swelling, thundering through the flaring light, and as I fell, the radiance increasing, increasing, poured over me in waves of flame. Then I sank into the depths, and I heard the King in Yellow whispering to my soul: "It is a fearful thing to fall into the hands of the living God!"

IN THE YEAR TEN THOUSAND

William Harben

A. D. 10,000. An old man, more than six hundred years of age, was walking with a boy through a great museum. The people who were moving around them had beautiful forms, and faces which were indescribably refined and spiritual.

"Father," said the boy, "you promised to tell me to-day about the Dark Ages. I like to hear how men lived and thought long ago."

"It is no easy task to make you understand the past," was the reply. "It is hard to realize that man could have been so ignorant as he was eight thousand years ago, but come with me; I will show you something."

He led the boy to a cabinet containing a few time-worn books bound in solid gold.

"You have never seen a book," he said, taking out a large volume and carefully placing it on a silk cushion on a table. "There are only a few in the leading museums of the world. Time was when there were as many books on earth as inhabitants."

"I cannot understand," said the boy with a look of perplexity on his intellectual face. "I cannot see what people could have wanted with them; they are not attractive; they seem to be useless."

The old man smiled. "When I was your age, the subject was too deep for me; but as I grew older and made a close study of the history of the past, the use of books gradually became plain to me. We know that in the year 2000 they were read by the best minds. To make you understand this, I shall first have to explain that eight thousand years ago human beings communicated their thoughts to one another by making sounds with their tongues, and not by mind-reading, as you and I do. To understand me, you have simply to read my thoughts as well as your education will permit; but primitive man knew nothing about thought-intercourse, so he invented speech. Humanity then was divided up in various races, and each race had a separate language. As certain sounds conveyed definite ideas, so did signs and letters; and later, to facilitate the exchange of thought, writing and printing were invented. This book was printed."

The boy leaned forward and examined the pages closely; his young brow clouded. "I cannot understand," he said, "it seems so useless."

The old man put his delicate fingers on the page. "A line of these words may have conveyed a valuable thought to a reader long ago," he said, reflectively. "In fact, this book purports to be a history of the world up to the year 2000. Here are some pictures," he continued, turning the worn leaves carefully. "This is George Washington; this a pope of a church called the Roman Catholic; this is a man named Gladstone, who was a great political leader in England. Pictures then, as you see, were very crude. We have preserved some of the oil paintings made in those days. Art was in its cradle. In producing a painting of an object, the early artists mixed colored paints and spread them according to taste on stretched canvas or on the walls or windows of buildings. You know that our artists simply throw light and darkness into space in the necessary variations, and the effect is all that could be desired in the way of imitating nature. See that landscape in the alcove before you. The foliage of the trees, the grass, the flowers, the stretch of water, have every appearance of life because the light which produces them is alive."

The boy looked at the scene admiringly for a few minutes, then bent again over the book. Presently he recoiled from the pictures, a strange look of disgust struggling in his tender features.

"These men have awful faces," he said. "They are so unlike people living now. The man you call a pope looks like an animal. They all have huge mouths and frightfully heavy jaws. Surely men could not have looked like that."

"Yes," the old man replied, gently. "There is no doubt that human beings then bore a nearer resemblance to the lower animals than we now do. In the sculpture and portraits of all ages we can trace a gradual refinement in the appearances of men. The features of the human race to-day are more ideal. Thought has always given form and expression to faces. In those dark days the thoughts of men were not refined. Human beings died of starvation and lack of attention in cities where there were people so wealthy that they could not use their fortunes. And they were so nearly related to the lower animals that they believed in war. George Washington was for several centuries reverenced by millions of people as a great and good man; and yet under his leadership thousands of human beings lost their lives in battle."

The boy's susceptible face turned white.

"Do you mean that he encouraged men to kill one another?" he asked, bending more closely over the book.

"Yes, but we cannot blame him; he thought he was right. Millions of his countrymen applauded him. A greater warrior than he was a man named Napoleon Bonaparte. Washington fought under the belief that he was doing his country a service in defending it against enemies, but everything in history goes to prove that Bonaparte waged war to gratify a personal ambition to distinguish himself as a hero. Wild animals of the lowest orders were courageous, and would fight one another till they died; and yet the most refined of the human race, eight or nine thousand years ago, prided themselves on the same ferocity of nature. Women, the gentlest half of humanity, honored men more for bold achievements in shedding blood than for any other quality. But murder was not only committed in wars; men in private life killed one another; fathers and mothers were now and then so depraved as to put their own children to death; and the highest tribunals of the world executed murderers without dreaming that it was wrong, erroneously believing that to kill was the only way to prevent killing."

"Did no one in those days realize that it was horrible?" asked the youth.

"Yes," answered the father, "as far back as ten thousand years ago there was an humble man, it is said, who was called Jesus Christ. He went from place to place, telling every one he met that the world would be better if men would love one another as themselves."

"What kind of man was he?" asked the boy, with kindling eyes.

"He was a spiritual genius," was the earnest reply, "and the greatest that has ever lived."

"Did he prevent them from killing one another?" asked the youth, with a tender upward glance.

"No, for he himself was killed by men who were too barbarous to understand him. But long after his death his words were remembered. People were not civilized enough to put his teachings into practice, but they were able to see that he was right."

"After he was killed, did the people not do as he had told them?" asked the youth, after a pause of several minutes.

"It seems not," was the reply. "They said no human being could live as he had directed. And when he had been dead for several centuries, people began to say that he was the Son of God who had come to earth to show men how to live. Some even believed that he was God himself."

"Did they believe that he was a person like ourselves?"

The old man reflected for a few minutes, then, looking into the boy's eager face, he answered: "That subject will be hard for you to understand. I will try to make it plain. To the unformed minds of early humanity there could be nothing without a personal creator. As man could build a house with his own hands, and was superior to his work, so he argued that some unknown being, greater than all visible things, had made the universe. They called that being by different names according to the language they spoke. In English the word used was 'God.'"

"They believed that somebody had made the universe!" said the boy, "how very strange!"

"No, not somebody as you comprehend it," replied the father gently, "but some vague, infinite being who punished the evil and rewarded the good. Men could form no idea of a creator that did not in some way resemble themselves; and as they could subdue their enemies through fear and by the infliction of pain, so did they believe that God would punish those who did not please him. Some people long ago believed that God's punishment was inflicted after death for eternity. The numerous beliefs about the personality and laws of the creator caused more bloodshed in the gloomy days of the past than anything else. Religion was the foundation of many of the most horrible wars. People committed thousands of crimes in the name of the God of the universe. Men and women were burned alive because they would not believe certain creeds, and yet they adhered to convictions equally as preposterous; but you will learn all these things later in life. That picture before you was the last queen of England, called Victoria."

"I hoped that the women would not have such repulsive features as the men," said the boy, looking critically at the picture, "but this face makes me shudder. Why do they all look so coarse and brutal?"

"People living when this queen reigned had the most degrading habit that ever blackened the history of mankind."

"What was that?" asked the youth.

"The consumption of flesh. They believed that animals, fowls, and fish were created to be eaten."

"Is it possible?" The boy shuddered convulsively, and turned away from the book. "I understand now why their faces repel me so. I do not like to think that we have descended from such people."

"They knew no better," said the father. "As they gradually became more refined they learned to burn the meat over flames and to cook it in heated vessels to change its appearance. The places where animals were killed and sold were withdrawn to retired places. Mankind was slowly turning from the habit, but they did not know it. As early as 2050 learned men, calling themselves vegetarians, proved conclusively that the consumption of such food was cruel and barbarous, and that it retarded refinement and mental growth. However, it was not till about 2300 that the vegetarian movement became of marked importance. The most highly educated classes in all lands adopted vegetarianism, and only the uneducated continued to kill and eat animals. The vegetarians tried for years to enact laws prohibiting the consumption of flesh, but opposition was very strong. In America in 2320 a colony was formed consisting of about three hundred thousand vegetarians. They purchased large tracts of land in what was known as the Indian Territory, and there made their homes, determined to prove by example the efficacy of their tenets. Within the first year the colony had doubled its number: people joined it from all parts of the globe. In the year 4000 it was a country of its own, and was the wonder of the world. The brightest minds were born there. The greatest discoveries and inventions were made by its inhabitants. In 4030 Gillette discovered the process of manufacturing crystal. Up to that time people had built their houses of natural stone, inflammable wood, and metals; but the new material, being fireproof and beautiful in its various colors, was used for all building purposes. In 4050 Holloway found the submerged succession of mountain chains across the Atlantic Ocean, and intended to construct a bridge on their summits; but the vast improvement in air ships rendered his plans impracticable.

"In 4051 John Saunders discovered and put into practice thought-telegraphy. This discovery was the signal for the introduction in schools and colleges of the science of mind-reading, and by the year 5000 so great had been the progress in that branch of knowledge that words were spoken only among the lowest of the uneducated. In no age of the world's history has there been such an important discovery. It civilized the world. Its early promoters did not dream of the vast good mind-reading would accomplish. Slowly it killed evil. Societies for the prevention of evil thought were organized in all lands. Children were born pure of mind and grew up in purity. Crime was choked out of existence. If a man had an evil thought, it was read in his heart, and he was not allowed to keep it. Men at first shunned evil for fear of detection, and then grew to love purity.

"In the year 6021 all countries of the world, having then a common language, and being drawn together in brotherly love by constant exchange of thought, agreed to call themselves a union without ruler or rulers. It was the greatest event in the history of the world. Certain sensitive mind students in Germany, who had for years been trying to communicate with other planets through the channel of thought, declared that, owing to the terrestrial unanimity of purpose in that direction, they had received mental impressions from other worlds, and that thorough interplanetary intercourse was a future possibility.

"Important inventions were made as the mind of humanity grew more elevated. Thornton discovered the plan to heat the earth's surface from its internal fire, and this discovery made journeys to the wonderful ice-bound countries situated at the North and the South Poles easy of accomplishment. At the North Pole, in the extensive concave lands, was found a peculiar race of men. Their sun was the great perpetually boiling lake of lava which bubbled from the centre of the earth in the bottom of their bowl-shaped world. And a strange religion was theirs! They believed that the earth was a monster on whose hide they had to live for a mortal lifetime, and that to the good was given the power after death to walk over the icy waste to their god, whose starry eyes they could see twinkling in space, and that the evil were condemned to feed the fire in the stomach of the monster as long as it lived. They told beautiful stories about the creation of their world, and held that if they lived too near the hot, dazzling mouth of evil, they would become blinded to the soft, forgiving eyes of the god of space. Hence they suffered the extreme cold of the lands near the frozen seas, believing that the physical ordeal prepared them for the icy journey to immortal rest after death. But there were those who hungered after the balmy atmosphere and the wonderful fruits and flowers that grew in the lowlands, and they lived there in indolence and so-called sin."

The old man and his son left the museum and walked into a wonderful park. Flowers of the most beautiful kinds and of sweetest fragrance grew on all sides. They came to a tall tower, four thousand feet in height, built of manufactured crystal. Something, like a great white bird, a thousand feet long, flew across the sky and settled down on the tower's summit.

"This was one of the most wonderful inventions of the Seventieth century," said the old man. "The early inhabitants of the earth could not have dreamed that it would be possible to go around it in twenty-four hours. In fact, there was a time when they were not able to go around it at all. Scientists were astonished when a man called Malburn, a great inventor, announced that, at a height of four thousand feet, he could disconnect an air ship from the laws of gravitation, and cause it to stand still in space till the earth had turned over. Fancy what must have been that immortal genius' feelings when he stood in space and saw the earth for the first time whirling beneath him!"

They walked on for some distance across the park till they came to a great instrument made to magnify the music in light. Here they paused and seated themselves.

"It will soon be night," said the old man. "The tones are those of bleeding sunset. I came here last evening to listen to the musical struggle between the light of dying day and that of the coming stars. The sunlight had been playing a powerful solo; but the gentle chorus of the stars, led by the moon, was inexplicably touching. Light is the voice of immortality; it speaks in all things."

An hour passed. It was growing dark.

"Tell me what immortality is," said the boy. "What does life lead to?"

"We do not know," replied the old man. "If we knew we would be infinite. Immortality is increasing happiness for all time; it is—"

A meteor shot across the sky. There was a burst of musical laughter among the singing stars. The old man bent over the boy's face and kissed it. "Immortality," said he—"immortality must be love immortal."

THE INCREDIBLE ALIENS

William Bender Jr.

It was only a tiny dot on the view screen when the military lookout on the armed cruiser identified it as an alien spaceship and sounded the general alert. Technicist Ninth Class Narant, chief psychanalyst aboard, studied its approach with a rebellious, almost passionate hope that the impossible was at last going to happen.

Or was it impossible? They were the first men to visit this planetary system. Why couldn't they expect to encounter a truly superior race for a change?

Intently, Narant examined the course of the alien craft. Rather mischievously he hoped the stranger would suddenly adopt evasion tactics showing it had detected their presence in the black void between the 6th and 7th planets of the Star Restus. That would certainly be a sign of superiority! And what a blow to Central Scientific Headquarters back home. The anti-detection shield was one of their proudest accomplishments.

And yet, though still wishful, Narant realized deep in his heart that such hopes were blighted. Illogical and improbable. No people in the Universe could even compare with them. Explorers and merchants and military ships and privateers had prowled all the great planetary systems of the galaxy. They and their technology reigned supreme everywhere. Indeed, the accumulated evidence of their supremacy even formed the irrefutable foundation of Central Scientific's dogma on selective breeding.

"I must ask you to leave the bridge now, doctor." The voice, crisp and authoritative, crackled over Narant's shoulder.

Commander Karsine had entered the control room during Narant's brief reverie in front of the viewing screen. An able and successful combat officer still in his early thirties, Karsine wore the light weight space armor the regulations prescribed for moments of impending action. Even if the enemy blasted a hole in the control room itself, that armor could protect Karsine long enough to save or disintegrate the cruiser, as the case might be.

"Commander," Narant suddenly blurted. "One request. I should like to remain this one time and observe your tactics right here."

"Denied." Karsine explained brusquely that only combat personnel were allowed in the central control room during contact with a strange vessel. "But," he ended, patronizingly, "you can watch from the observation room. When we have made the capture, I'll be happy to review my operations with you."

When we have made the capture. The Commander's abundant self confidence only served to further depress Narant. Out there in the void rode a space vessel of an altogether unknown race. And there was no question in Karsine's mind but that their cruiser would take the alien. Not "*if*" we make the capture. Simply, "*when*." It was small solace for Narant to recall that he himself had firmly established Self Confidence as one of the highest-rated mental traits for military command. It had been one of his major projects as a Psychanalyst 4th Class.

As he left the bridge, the airlock rumbled shut behind him, sealing off the control room from the rest of the ship. Narant climbed the spiral staircase into the observation room. One entire wall was a thick quartzite pane over-looking the control center. You could see as much from up here as down below. But somehow it wasn't the same.

Other technicists with non-combatant specialties were already strapped to seats in the room, prepared to watch the show on which their very lives might depend. The "VM" lamp winked slowly on and off, its orange glow warning against "possible violent maneuvers." Narant found a seat and obediently fastened the safety harness. He studied the view screen on the bridge below. The alien ship, seemingly unaware of the danger that now threatened it, still followed its initial course.

Narant tried to concentrate on the scrambling activity in the control center, but his rebellious mind would have none of it. Unwanted memories rose up to haunt him. He had been assigned to this trip mainly to purge those thoughts from his mind with work and action, but the cure appeared no cure at all.

Three months ago his final request for the marriage permit had returned disapproved. The accompanying explanation had been a masterpiece of scientific doggerel. It analyzed the genetic composition of Narant and Technicist 3rd Class Melda. It presented carefully worked-out Tables of Probability regarding the nature and potential achievement of the offspring of such a union. It called attention to the low probability rate of Melda and Narant begetting a genius. "Therefore," it had concluded, "it is not in the best interests of the intended participants, nor will it serve to build the race, if the aforementioned are joined in matrimony."

There followed a rare bit of sterilized philosophy: "It is to be hoped that each party mentioned in the above will readily find another individual in whom to repose his and her natural emotional interest." Narant felt, with a startling sense of the primeval, that if he should find the person who phrased that report he would delightfully club him to death.

But of course emotionalism was absurd. The whole thing had been handled dispassionately. Certain basic factors had been fed into banks of electronic calculators and, a few micro-seconds later, the resultant statistical data came out. It simply failed to measure up. There was no arguing or quibbling about the results for the calculators were mechanically infallible.

However, Narant had taken one more step: an application for "random mating." But the retention drums of the master calculators had accumulated a far too overwhelming amount of information about the advantages of scientific breeding. So that application, too, had been refused.

And shortly after, Narant found himself assigned to this cruiser bound for Restus. A report that the inhabitants had begun space flight. A distant, but conceivable threat to the security of the home planet. He knew the assignment resulted from some scientific effort to mollify his disappointment. So he left home. But he took with him the forlorn hope that on this voyage, or the next, or the one after that, he would find somewhere in the vast reaches of space an advanced people who still practiced random mating; that he might find them, analyze them and feed that information back to the master calculators. For only by placing hard new facts into the "brain" could there be any chance of changing the decision.

In the sealed combat control center, Commander Karsine finished strapping himself into the anthropometric chair in front of the view screen. A subordinate lowered the master control panel into position. Narant perked up with new interest. A specialist of Karsine's class, he realized, could manipulate that control panel with the consummate skill of a master musician at a great organ. The battery of keys, buttons and switches built into the panel gave Karsine complete domination over the thousands of small engines and servo-mechanisms, tens-of-thousands of electric tubes, and the millions of electrical synapses that comprised the fighting apparatus of the space cruiser.

Abruptly the "VM" sign began flashing more rapidly, its color changing from orange to red. A siren whooped throughout the ship. Karsine's voice, somewhat metallic over the speakers, gave the "Imminent Combat" alert. The ship was going into action.

Narant felt the seat straps pull at his chest. In the view screen below, the alien vessel began to swell rapidly. A low hum permeated the observation room. Narant glanced out the nearest port. Glistening metallic spines were expanding outward from the body of the cruiser. At the tip of each bulged the glowing cone of the force and detection heads, the cruiser's most potent tools of attack and defense.

"Engine room!" Karsine's peremptory voice snapped through the speakers.

"Engine room standing by."

"For ten seconds only, do not...repeat, do *not* act on manual signal control. This is a test only. Read them off. "

"Yes, sir. Reading test signals: Fire eight...fire six...fire nine...fire one...fire main." The voice paused. "Is that all, sir?"

"The ten seconds are up," reproached Karsine. Henceforth, his every command would have to be acted upon instantly. "Divert seventy per cent of main power supply into armament system."

"Yes, sir."

"Check spinal extension."

"Extended and locked. All force heads burning, Commander." Another voice had answered this time.

"Good." Karsine's brief acknowledgment for an efficient crew. "Activate the combat calculator."

"In action, sir."

There, Narant realized, was another de-humanizing achievement of Central Scientific. Years ago in the war with the repulsive exoskeletal inhabitants of Sirius 13, earth's military commanders had gone into battle with terrible ardor. To destroy the Sirians they had taken frequent, unnecessary risks, and in so doing had sacrificed dozens of brand new combat ships. So a special calculator had been designed for all craft except humble merchantmen. It kept a running check on the enemy's tactics, his power output, his course, speed and relative aggressiveness; it measured the power consumption of its own ship in counteracting enemy weapons, and a score of other factors. Once activated, the "brain" computed the mathematical probabilities of ultimate success at each instant of the battle. If the scale ever tipped in favor of the enemy craft, the calculator instantly selected the best evasion course, fired auxiliary rockets and broke off the engagement.

Narant unconsciously shook his head in disapproval. He wondered if he was getting old? Such efficiency disturbed him more than he cared to admit. Only in the histories, it seemed, could you find those thrilling battles where human ingenuity played the decisive role. Where a handful of courageous men could face outrageous odds and win through to victory by wit and resourcefulness. Yes, only in the histories.

Nowadays warfare, like love, revolved about mathematics and probability curves and trillions of electrons chasing themselves through a maze of wires and throwing switches and making decisions that once had been the prerogative of man alone.

Narant yearned for man's lost freedom to make an honest error.

Suddenly Karsine's harsh voice came blasting over the loudspeaker. "Prepare to grapple!"

Narant glanced quickly out through the port into the black sky. The alien ship, its bright metal reflecting the light of the distant sun, floated a mile away. Motionless. Or so it seemed against the unchanging stellar background.

It possessed hard sleek lines, pointed nose, flaring tail vanes. Its designers, he guessed, must still be thinking in terms of atmospheric flight. It hardly seemed the type of craft that could cross the broad interstellar reaches; probably had been built simply to plod about its neighboring planets. It must be an early development, for spaceships had never before been detected in the Restus system. More than likely the ship had not even become aware of their presence. Small wonder Karsine had decided to grapple.

The force heads on Narant's side of the cruiser began to shimmer under the surge of power being fed to them. They grew red hot, almost translucent. They would hold fire until the beam became powerful enough to withstand tremendous forces. Sometimes in grappling, an enemy craft had been known to discharge its main rocket batteries in an effort to wrench loose. But any second now...

"Execute grapple!" Karsine ordered.

The cruiser shuddered. Lights dimmed as the force heads sucked at every available bit of power. With a blinding flash, a blue-white ribbon of energy streaked across the mile-wide void to the alien ship. It flicked the nose of the Restus craft, gripped, and swept over the entire hull like a glittering cocoon.

"Tension indicator: Nine-eight-point-eight," reported a too-casual voice over the speaker. "Enemy ship secured."

"Opposing force?"

"Negative."

Karsine cautiously studied his dials, alert for the first sign of a counter-blow. Nothing happened. A minute dragged by. The tension indicators remained constant; detection heads, zero. And then: "Bring it alongside."

The grappling beam slowly began to contract, bringing the alien ship closer. As it passed through the invisibility screen, multi-colored de-action rays focussed upon it, nullifying virtually every weapon known to man.

Narant's hopes dissolved. The emptiness left only an aching

futility. As usual, the capture had been simple...and complete.

"Advance parties prepare to go aboard," commanded the loudspeaker.

A man behind Narant unbuckled his straps, got up and stretched. "Here we go again," he said. And then, to nobody in particular: "I used to get a kick out of investigating strange creatures. Now it's work. Just work."

Narant looked over his shoulder at the cruiser's anthropometrist. He would have to board the ship right behind the combat team, analyze the tools, controls, living conditions of the crew. Perhaps he, too, experienced this ennui of persistent success?

Narant had ended his preparations in the psych-examination chamber by the time they brought the first of the alien people to him. Narant stared in sudden amazement. The creature was humanoid. It had a well-formed head with a squat, shrunken nose and steep brows; there were prehensile arms, and hands with five fingers. But the man was hairy and, Narant winced, immodestly naked.

The humanoid was still in the grip of the paralytic when they took him into the examination chamber and strapped him to the table. Narant judged the alien a little taller, give or take a few inches, than a normal human being. His interest began to perk up. It always did when he could study another creature that had learned to conquer space. For perhaps the first time in three months, thoughts of Melda were over-shadowed by the immediate prospect of exploring the mysteries of an alien mind.

As the attendant came back out of the chamber, Narant secured the door. "How many of them?" he asked.

The attendant shook his head in evident amazement. "Four. I don't know how they do it, but that ship had only a four man crew."

"Impossible," Narant exclaimed.

"That's all there are," the man insisted. "We've covered the whole ship."

"But how could they...?"

"The engineers are working on that now. I heard one of them remark about the great number of automatic controls, but even so...isn't that one for the book?"

That, Narant agreed, was one for the book. Four men. The space vessels he knew usually held scores of crewmen and specialists to handle the manifold emergencies that arose in flight. His imagination soaring, Narant turned rapidly to begin his experiments.

He started the automatic recorder that would code his findings on a thin strip of tape and then, more excited than usual, began the examination. Inside the chamber, a giant multi-faceted crystal began to rotate slowly in the gimbals which held it suspended from the ceiling. Sharp individual beams of light swept over the face of the alien being on the table. One by one, the lights flickered over him and passed on, each one probing, measuring, comparing with universal norms, and then recording its findings on both dial and tape.

Long before the five-hour examination was over, the hopes of Technicist 9th Class Narant far transcended any he had experienced in the past three months. The aliens had almost human potential. They were fun-loving, kindly, clannish. Their resourcefulness *and their ingenuity* were literally unsurpassed.

But then the most amazing fact of all revealed itself: The time-lapse since this race had been entirely primitive was fantastically short. In one brief—almost abrupt—transition, they had gone from jungle to the conquest of space. The mind, the racial background and the obvious achievements of these creatures presented such a picture of rapid advancement as to stagger the imagination.

Once he had transmitted the coded tapes to Central Scientific, Narant sought out the anthropometrist. His lingering doubts vanished when the two compared findings. Everything inside the spaceship had been designed expressly for these strange creatures with the five fingers and the prehensile hands and arms.

As the cruiser finally pointed toward home, Narant was a new man. Of course their information would set the scientific world spinning on its collective ear. But more important, it would have vast personal significance. According to the crystal, the mating pattern of these surprisingly progressive beings was entirely one of random selection!

Already that data would be digesting inside the master calculators. The knowledge would become a part of all future decisions. Probability rates would change strikingly...especially those that governed the issuance of "random-mating" licenses. For Narant, the voyage had been a tremendous success.

However, in the space experimental laboratories near the Nevada desert on the third planet of the sun Restus, no such optimism existed.

Twenty-four hours had passed since the S-X-2 had vanished. They had had a precise fix on it as it blistered through the void on an elliptic course that would return it automatically to Earth. Everything had seemed to be going perfectly. All the bugs of the first Spacerocket Experimental had evidently been straightened out in making the "2". And then, some 250-thousand miles beyond Saturn, it had disappeared. Just like that.

Dr. Gordon Basset glanced distastefully at the telephone on his desk. Then he began thumbing through the metropolitan directory for a number. The hands that held the directory were strong, supple. They would have been a revelation to Technicist Ninth Class Narant, if he had seen them.

But then Technicist Ninth Class Narant himself would have

been something of a revelation to Dr. Gordon Basset, what with his twenty claw-like extensors.

Basset found the number, dialed, and waited for the connection.

"Hello, Dr. Farrell? Basset here. I've got bad news on the S-X-2... No details yet, but the ship has broken contact... Yes, I must presume it's lost... I'll file a complete report as soon as possible... What's that?... I suppose you're right—we'll have the S.P.C.A. on our necks for sacrificing four more test animals. What the hell, they can't expect us to send men on these experimental flights!"

Basset talked for a moment longer and then replaced the phone. He sighed. Another report. Another failure. Another requiem to be written for a lost ship—and four chimpanzees.

MESMERIC REVELATION

Edgar Allan Poe

Whatever doubt may still envelop the *rationale* of mesmerism, its startling *facts* are now almost universally admitted. Of these latter, those who doubt, are your mere doubters by profession—an unprofitable and disreputable tribe. There can be no more absolute waste of time than the attempt to *prove*, at the present day, that man, by mere exercise of will, can so impress his fellow, as to cast him into an abnormal condition, of which the phenomena resemble very closely those of *death*, or at least resemble them more nearly than they do the phenomena of any other normal condition within our cognizance; that, while in this state, the person so impressed employs only with effort, and then feebly, the external organs of sense, yet perceives, with keenly refined perception, and through channels supposed unknown, matters beyond the scope of the physical organs; that, moreover, his intellectual faculties are wonderfully exalted and invigorated; that his sympathies with the person so impressing him are profound; and, finally, that his susceptibility to the impression increases with its frequency, while, in the same proportion, the peculiar phenomena elicited are more extended and more *pronounced*.

I say that these—which are the laws of mesmerism in its general features—it would be supererogation to demonstrate; nor shall I inflict upon my readers so needless a demonstration; to-day. My purpose at present is a very different one indeed. I am impelled, even in the teeth of a world of prejudice, to detail without comment the very remarkable substance of a colloquy, occurring between a sleep-waker and myself.

I had been long in the habit of mesmerizing the person in question (Mr. Vankirk), and the usual acute susceptibility and exaltation of the mesmeric perception had supervened. For many months he had been laboring under confirmed phthisis, the more distressing effects of which had been relieved by my manipulations; and on the night of Wednesday, the fifteenth instant, I was summoned to his bedside.

The invalid was suffering with acute pain in the region of the heart, and breathed with great difficulty, having all the ordinary symptoms of asthma. In spasms such as these he had usually found relief from the application of mustard to the nervous centres, but to-night this had been attempted in vain.

As I entered his room he greeted me with a cheerful smile, and although evidently in much bodily pain, appeared to be, mentally, quite at ease.

"I sent for you to-night," he said, "not so much to administer to my bodily ailment, as to satisfy me concerning certain psychal impressions which, of late, have occasioned me much anxiety and surprise. I need not tell you how sceptical I have hitherto been on the topic of the soul's immortality. I cannot deny that there has always existed, as if in that very soul which I have been denying, a vague half-sentiment of its own existence. But this half-sentiment at no time amounted to conviction. With it my reason had nothing to do. All attempts at logical inquiry resulted, indeed, in leaving me more sceptical than before. I had been advised to study Cousin. I studied him in his own works as well as in those of his European and American echoes. The 'Charles Elwood' of Mr. Brownson, for example, was placed in my hands. I read it with profound attention. Throughout I found it logical, but the portions which were not *merely* logical were unhappily the initial arguments of the disbelieving hero of the book. In his summing up it seemed evident to me that the reasoner had not even succeeded in convincing himself. His end had plainly forgotten his beginning, like the government of Trinculo. In short, I was not long in perceiving that if man is to be intellectually convinced of his own immortality, he will never be so convinced by the mere abstractions which have been so long the fashion of the moralists of England, of France, and of Germany. Abstractions may amuse and exercise, but take no hold on the mind. Here upon earth, at least, philosophy, I am persuaded, will always in vain call upon us to look upon qualities as things. The will may assent—the soul—the intellect, never.

"I repeat, then, that I only half felt, and never intellectually believed. But latterly there has been a certain deepening of the feeling, until it has come so nearly to resemble the acquiescence of reason, that I find it difficult to distinguish between the two. I am enabled, too, plainly to trace this effect to the mesmeric influence. I cannot better explain my meaning than by the hypothesis that the mesmeric exaltation enables me to perceive a train of ratiocination which, in my abnormal existence, convinces, but which, in full accordance with the mesmeric phenomena, does not extend, except through its *effect*, into my normal condition. In sleep-waking, the reasoning and its conclusion—the cause and its effect—are present together. In my natural state, the cause vanishing, the effect only, and perhaps only partially, remains.

"These considerations have led me to think that some good results might ensue from a series of well-directed questions propounded to me while mesmerized. You have often observed the profound self-cognizance evinced by the sleep-waker—the extensive knowledge he displays upon all points relating to the mesmeric condition itself; and from this self-cognizance may be deduced hints for the proper conduct of a catechism."

I consented of course to make this experiment. A few passes

threw Mr. Vankirk into the mesmeric sleep. His breathing became immediately more easy, and he seemed to suffer no physical uneasiness. The following conversation then ensued:—V. in the dialogue representing the patient, and P. myself.

P. Are you asleep?

V. Yes—no; I would rather sleep more soundly.

P. [*After a few more passes.*] Do you sleep now?

V. Yes.

P. How do you think your present illness will result?

V. [*After a long hesitation and speaking as if with effort.*] I must die.

P. Does the idea of death afflict you?

V. [*Very quickly.*] No—no!

P. Are you pleased with the prospect?

V. If I were awake I should like to die, but now it is no matter. The mesmeric condition is so near death as to content me.

P. I wish you would explain yourself, Mr. Vankirk.

V. I am willing to do so, but it requires more effort than I feel able to make. You do not question me properly.

P. What then shall I ask?

V. You must begin at the beginning.

P. The beginning! But where is the beginning?

V. You know that the beginning is GOD. [*This was said in a low, fluctuating tone, and with every sign of the most profound veneration.*]

P. What then, is God?

V. [*Hesitating for many minutes.*] I cannot tell.

P. Is not God spirit?

V. While I was awake I knew what you meant by "spirit," but now it seems only a word—such, for instance, as truth, beauty—a quality, I mean.

P. Is not God immaterial?

V. There is no immateriality—it is a mere word. That which is not matter, is not at all—unless qualities are things.

P. Is God, then, material?

V. No. [*This reply startled me very much.*]

P. What, then, is he?

V. [*After a long pause, and mutteringly.*] I see—but it is a thing difficult to tell. [*Another long pause.*] He is not spirit, for he exists. Nor is he matter, as *you understand it*. But there are *gradations* of matter of which man knows nothing; the grosser impelling the finer, the finer pervading the grosser. The atmosphere, for example, impels the electric principle, while the electric principle permeates the atmosphere. These gradations of matter increase in rarity or fineness, until we arrive at a matter *unparticled*—without particles—indivisible—*one;* and here the law of impulsion and permeation is modified. The ultimate, or unparticled matter, not only permeates all things but impels all things; and thus *is* all things within itself. This matter is God. What men attempt to embody in the word "thought," is this matter in motion.

P. The metaphysicians maintain that all action is reducible to motion and thinking, and that the latter is the origin of the former.

V. Yes; and I now see the confusion of idea. Motion is the action of *mind*, not of *thinking*. The unparticled matter, or God, in quiescence, is (as nearly as we can conceive it) what men call mind. And the power of self-movement (equivalent in effect to human volition) is, in the unparticled matter, the result of its unity and omniprevalence; *how* I know not, and now clearly see that I shall never know. But the unparticled matter, set in motion by a law, or quality, existing within itself, is thinking.

P. Can you give me no more precise idea of what you term the unparticled matter?

V. The matters of which man is cognizant escape the senses in gradation. We have, for example, a metal, a piece of wood, a drop of water, the atmosphere, a gas, caloric, electricity, the luminiferous ether. Now we call all these things matter, and embrace all matter in one general definition; but in spite of this, there can be no two ideas more essentially distinct than that which we attach to a metal, and that which we attach to the luminiferous ether. When we reach the latter, we feel an almost irresistible inclination to class it with spirit, or with nihility. The only consideration which restrains us is our conception of its atomic constitution; and here, even, we have to seek aid from our notion of an atom, as something possessing in infinite minuteness, solidity, palpability, weight. Destroy the idea of the atomic constitution and we should no longer be able to regard the ether as an entity, or at least as matter. For want of a better word we might term it spirit. Take, now, a step beyond the luminiferous ether—conceive a matter as much more rare than the ether, as this ether is more rare than the metal, and we arrive at once (in spite of all the school dogmas) at a unique mass—an unparticled matter. For although we may admit infinite littleness in the atoms themselves, the infinitude of littleness in the spaces between them is an absurdity. There will be a point—there will be a degree of rarity, at which, if the atoms are sufficiently numerous, the interspaces must vanish, and the mass absolutely coalesce. But the consideration of the atomic constitution being now taken away, the nature of the mass inevitably glides into what we conceive of spirit. It is clear, however, that it is as fully matter as before. The truth is, it is impossible to conceive spirit, since it is impossible to imagine what is not. When we flatter ourselves that we have formed its conception, we have merely deceived our understanding by the consideration of infinitely rarified matter.

P. There seems to me an insurmountable objection to the idea of absolute coalescence—and is the very slight resistance experienced by the heavenly bodies in their revolutions through space—a resistance now ascertained, it is true, to exist in *some* degree, but which is, nevertheless, so slight as to have been quite overlooked by the sagacity even of Newton. We know that the resistance of bodies is, chiefly, in proportion to their density. Absolute coalescence is absolute density. Where there are no interspaces, there can be no yielding. An ether, absolutely dense, would put an infinitely more effectual stop to the progress of a star than would an ether of adamant or of iron.

V. Your objection is answered with an ease which is nearly in the ratio of its apparent unanswerability—as regards the progress of the star, it can make no difference whether the star passes through the ether *or the ether through it*. There is no astronomical error more unaccountable than that which reconciles the known retardation of the comets with the idea of their passage through an ether: for, however rare this ether be supposed, it would put a stop to all sidereal revolution in a very far briefer period than has been admitted by those astronomers who have endeavored to slur over a point which they found it impossible to comprehend. The retardation actually experienced is, on the other hand, about that which might be expected from the *friction* of the ether in the instantaneous passage through the orb. In the one case, the retarding force is momentary and complete within itself—in the other it is endlessly accumulative.

P. But in all this—in this identification of mere matter with

God—is there nothing of irreverence? [*I was forced to repeat this question before the sleep-waker fully comprehended my meaning.*]

V. Can you say *why* matter should be less reverenced than mind? But you forget that the matter of which I speak is, in all respects, the very "mind" or "spirit" of the schools, so far as regards its high capacities, and is, moreover, the "matter" of these schools at the same time. God, with all the powers attributed to spirit, is but the perfection of matter.

P. You assert, then, that the unparticled matter, in motion, is thought?

V. In general, this motion is the universal thought of the universal mind. This thought creates. All created things are but the thoughts of God.

P. You say "in general."

V. Yes. The universal mind is God. For new individualities, *matter* is necessary.

P. But you now speak of "mind" and "matter" as do the metaphysicians.

V. Yes—to avoid confusion. When I say "mind", I mean the unparticled or ultimate matter; by "matter", I intend all else.

P. You were saying that "for new individualities matter is necessary".

V. Yes; for mind, existing unincorporate, is merely God. To create individual, thinking beings, it was necessary to incarnate portions of the divine mind. Thus man is individualized. Divested of corporate investiture, he were God. Now, the particular motion of the incarnated portions of the unparticled matter is the thought of man; as the motion of the whole is that of God.

P. You say that divested of the body man will be God?

V. [*After much hesitation.*] I could not have said this; it is an absurdity.

P. [*Referring to my notes.*] You *did* say that "divested of corporate investiture man were God."

V. And this is true. Man thus divested *would be* God—would be unindividualized. But he can never be thus divested—at least never *will be*—else we must imagine an action of God returning upon itself—a purposeless and futile action. Man is a creature. Creatures are thoughts of God. It is the nature of thought to be irrevocable.

P. I do not comprehend. You say that man will never put off the body?

V. I say that he will never be bodiless.

P. Explain.

V. There are two bodies—the rudimental and the complete; corresponding with the two conditions of the worm and the butterfly. What we call "death," is but the painful metamorphosis. Our present incarnation is progressive, preparatory, temporary. Our future is perfected, ultimate, immortal. The ultimate life is the full design.

P. But of the worm's metamorphosis we are palpably cognizant.

V. *We*, certainly—but not the worm. The matter of which our rudimental body is composed, is within the ken of the organs of that body; or, more distinctly, our rudimental organs are adapted to the matter of which is formed the rudimental body; but not to that of which the ultimate is composed. The ultimate body thus escapes our rudimental senses, and we perceive only the shell which falls, in decaying, from the inner form; not that inner form itself; but this inner form, as well as the shell, is appreciable by those who have already acquired the ultimate life.

P. You have often said that the mesmeric state very nearly resembles death. How is this?

V. When I say that it resembles death, I mean that it resembles the ultimate life; for when I am entranced the senses of my rudimental life are in abeyance, and I perceive external things directly, without organs, through a medium which I shall employ in the ultimate, unorganized life.

P. Unorganized?

V. Yes; organs are contrivances by which the individual is brought into sensible relation with particular classes and forms of matter, to the exclusion of other classes and forms. The organs of man are adapted to his rudimental condition, and to that only; his ultimate condition, being unorganized, is of unlimited comprehension in all points but one—the nature of the volition of God—that is to say, the motion of the unparticled matter. You will have a distinct idea of the ultimate body by conceiving it to be entire brain. This it is *not*; but a conception of this nature will bring you near a comprehension of what it *is*. A luminous body imparts vibration to the luminiferous ether. The vibrations generate similar ones within the retina; these again communicate similar ones to the optic nerve. The nerve conveys similar ones to the brain; the brain, also, similar ones to the unparticled matter which permeates it. The motion of this latter is thought, of which perception is the first undulation. This is the mode by which the mind of the rudimental life communicates with the external world; and this external world is, to the rudimental life, limited, through the idiosyncrasy of its organs. But in the ultimate, unorganized life, the external world reaches the whole body, (which is of a substance having affinity to brain, as I have said) with no other intervention than that of an infinitely rarer ether than even the luminiferous; and to this ether—in unison with it—the whole body vibrates, setting in motion the unparticled matter which permeates it. It is to the absence of idiosyncratic organs, therefore, that we must attribute the nearly unlimited perception of the ultimate life. To rudimental beings, organs are the cages necessary to confine them until fledged.

P. You speak of rudimental "beings". Are there other rudimental thinking beings than man?

V. The multitudinous conglomeration of rare matter into nebulæ, planets, suns, and other bodies which are neither nebulæ, suns, nor planets, is for the sole purpose of supplying *pabulum* for the idiosyncrasy of the organs of an infinity of rudimental beings. But for the necessity of the rudimental, prior to the ultimate life, there would have been no bodies such as these. Each of these is tenanted by a distinct variety of organic, rudimental, thinking creatures. In all, the organs vary with the features of the place tenanted. At death, or metamorphosis, these creatures, enjoying the ultimate life—immortality—and cognizant of all secrets but *the one*, act all things and pass everywhere by mere volition—indwelling, not the stars, which to us seem the sole palpabilities, and for the accommodation of which we blindly deem space created—but that SPACE itself—that infinity of which the truly substantive vastness swallows up the star-shadows—blotting them out as non-entities from the perception of the angels.

P. You say that "but for the *necessity* of the rudimental life" there would have been no stars. But why this necessity?

V. In the inorganic life, as well as in the inorganic matter generally, there is nothing to impede the action of one simple *unique* law—the Divine Volition. With the view of producing impediment, the organic life and matter, (complex, substantial, and law-encumbered,) were contrived.

P. But again—why need this impediment have been produced?

V. The result of law inviolate is perfection—right—negative happiness. The result of law violate is imperfection, wrong, positive pain. Through the impediments afforded by the number, complexity, and substantiality of the laws of organic life and matter, the violation of law is rendered, to a certain extent, practicable. Thus pain, which in the inorganic life is impossible, is possible in the organic.

P. But to what good end is pain thus rendered possible?

V. All things are either good or bad by comparison. A sufficient analysis will show that pleasure, in all cases, is but the contrast of pain. *Positive* pleasure is a mere idea. To be happy at any one point we must have suffered at the same. Never to suffer would have been never to have been blessed. But it has been shown that, in the inorganic life, pain cannot be thus the necessity for the organic. The pain of the primitive life of Earth, is the sole basis of the bliss of the ultimate life in Heaven.

P. Still, there is one of your expressions which I find it impossible to comprehend—"the truly *substantive* vastness of infinity."

V. This, probably, is because you have no sufficiently generic conception of the term "*substance*" itself. We must not regard it as a quality, but as a sentiment:—it is the perception, in thinking beings, of the adaptation of matter to their organization. There are many things on the Earth, which would be nihility to the inhabitants of Venus—many things visible and tangible in Venus, which we could not be brought to appreciate as existing at all. But to the inorganic beings—to the angels—the whole of the unparticled matter is substance—that is to say, the whole of what we term "space" is to them the truest substantiality;—the stars, meantime, through what we consider their materiality, escaping the angelic sense, just in proportion as the unparticled matter, through what we consider its immateriality, eludes the organic.

As the sleep-waker pronounced these latter words, in a feeble tone, I observed on his countenance a singular expression, which somewhat alarmed me, and induced me to awake him at once. No sooner had I done this, than, with a bright smile irradiating all his features, he fell back upon his pillow and expired. I noticed that in less than a minute afterward his corpse had all the stern rigidity of stone. His brow was of the coldness of ice. Thus, ordinarily, should it have appeared, only after long pressure from Azrael's hand. Had the sleep-waker, indeed, during the latter portion of his discourse, been addressing me from out the region of the shadows?

MOXON'S MASTER

Ambrose Bierce

Are you serious?—do you really believe that a machine thinks?"

I got no immediate reply; Moxon was apparently intent upon the coals in the grate, touching them deftly here and there with the fire-poker till they signified a sense of his attention by a brighter glow. For several weeks I had been observing in him a growing habit of delay in answering even the most trivial of commonplace questions. His air, however, was that of preoccupation rather than deliberation: one might have said that he had "something on his mind."

Presently he said:

"What is a 'machine'? The word has been variously defined. Here is one definition from a popular dictionary: 'Any instrument or organization by which power is applied and made effective, or a desired effect produced.' Well, then, is not a man a machine? And you will admit that he thinks—or thinks he thinks."

"If you do not wish to answer my question," I said, rather testily, "why not say so?—all that you say is mere evasion. You know well enough that when I say 'machine' I do not mean a man, but something that man has made and controls."

"When it does not control him," he said, rising abruptly and looking out of a window, whence nothing was visible in the blackness of a stormy night. A moment later he turned about and with a smile said: "I beg your pardon; I had no thought of evasion. I considered the dictionary man's unconscious testimony suggestive and worth something in the discussion. I can give your question a direct answer easily enough: I do believe that a machine thinks about the work that it is doing."

That was direct enough, certainly. It was not altogether pleasing, for it tended to confirm a sad suspicion that Moxon's devotion to study and work in his machine-shop had not been good for him. I knew, for one thing, that he suffered from insomnia, and that is no light affliction. Had it affected his mind? His reply to my question seemed to me then evidence that it had; perhaps I should think differently about it now. I was younger then, and among the blessings that are not denied to youth is ignorance. Incited by that great stimulant to controversy, I said:

"And what, pray, does it think with—in the absence of a brain?"

The reply, coming with less than his customary delay, took his favorite form of counter-interrogation:

"With what does a plant think—in the absence of a brain?"

"Ah, plants also belong to the philosopher class! I should be pleased to know some of their conclusions; you may omit the premises."

"Perhaps," he replied, apparently unaffected by my foolish irony, "you may be able to infer their convictions from their acts. I will spare you the familiar examples of the sensitive mimosa, the several insectivorous flowers and those whose stamens bend down and shake their pollen upon the entering bee in order that he may fertilize their distant mates. But observe this. In an open spot in my garden I planted a climbing vine. When it was barely above the surface I set a stake into the soil a yard away. The vine at once made for it, but as it was about to reach it after several days I removed it a few feet. The vine at once altered its course, making an acute angle, and again made for the stake. This manœuvre was repeated several times, but finally, as if discouraged, the vine abandoned the pursuit and ignoring further attempts to divert it traveled to a small tree, further away, which it climbed.

"Roots of the eucalyptus will prolong themselves incredibly in search of moisture. A well-known horticulturist relates that one entered an old drain pipe and followed it until it came to a break, where a section of the pipe had been removed to make way for a stone wall that had been built across its course. The root left the drain and followed the wall until it found an opening where a stone had fallen out. It crept through and following the other side of the wall back to the drain, entered the unexplored part and resumed its journey."

"And all this?"

"Can you miss the significance of it? It shows the consciousness of plants. It proves that they think."

"Even if it did—what then? We were speaking, not of plants, but of machines. They may be composed partly of wood—wood that has no longer vitality—or wholly of metal. Is thought an attribute also of the mineral kingdom?"

"How else do you explain the phenomena, for example, of crystallization?"

"I do not explain them."

"Because you cannot without affirming what you wish to deny, namely, intelligent cooperation among the constituent elements of the crystals. When soldiers form lines, or hollow squares, you call it reason. When wild geese in flight take the form of a letter V you say instinct. When the homogeneous atoms of a mineral, moving freely in solution, arrange themselves into shapes mathematically perfect, or particles of frozen moisture into the symmetrical and beautiful forms of snowflakes, you have nothing to say. You have not even invented a name to conceal your heroic unreason."

Moxon was speaking with unusual animation and earnestness. As he paused I heard in an adjoining room known to me as his "machine-shop," which no one but himself was permitted to enter, a singular thumping sound, as of some one pounding upon a table with an open hand. Moxon heard it at the same moment and, visibly agitated, rose and hurriedly passed into the room whence it came. I thought it odd that any one else should be in there, and my interest in my friend—with doubtless a touch of unwarrantable curiosity—led me to listen intently, though, I am happy to say, not at the keyhole. There were confused sounds, as of a struggle or scuffle; the floor shook. I distinctly heard hard breathing and a hoarse whisper which said "Damn you!" Then all was silent, and presently Moxon reappeared and said, with a rather sorry smile:

"Pardon me for leaving you so abruptly. I have a machine in there that lost its temper and cut up rough."

Fixing my eyes steadily upon his left cheek, which was traversed by four parallel excoriations showing blood, I said:

"How would it do to trim its nails?"

I could have spared myself the jest; he gave it no attention, but seated himself in the chair that he had left and resumed the interrupted monologue as if nothing had occurred:

"Doubtless you do not hold with those (I need not name them to a man of your reading) who have taught that all matter is sentient, that every atom is a living, feeling, conscious being. I do. There is no such thing as dead, inert matter: it is all alive; all instinct with force, actual and potential; all sensitive to the same forces in its environment and susceptible to the contagion of higher and subtler ones residing in such superior organisms as it may be brought into relation with, as those of man when he is fashioning it into an instrument of his will. It absorbs something of his intelligence and purpose—more of them in proportion to the complexity of the resulting machine and that of its work.

"Do you happen to recall Herbert Spencer's definition of

'Life'? I read it thirty years ago. He may have altered it afterward, for anything I know, but in all that time I have been unable to think of a single word that could profitably be changed or added or removed. It seems to me not only the best definition, but the only possible one.

"'Life,' he says, 'is a definite combination of heterogeneous changes, both simultaneous and successive, in correspondence with external coexistences and sequences.'"

"That defines the phenomenon," I said, "but gives no hint of its cause."

"That," he replied, "is all that any definition can do. As Mill points out, we know nothing of cause except as an antecedent—nothing of effect except as a consequent. Of certain phenomena, one never occurs without another, which is dissimilar: the first in point of time we call cause, the second, effect. One who had many times seen a rabbit pursued by a dog, and had never seen rabbits and dogs otherwise, would think the rabbit the cause of the dog.

"But I fear," he added, laughing naturally enough, "that my rabbit is leading me a long way from the track of my legitimate quarry: I'm indulging in the pleasure of the chase for its own sake. What I want you to observe is that in Herbert Spencer's definition of 'life' the activity of a machine is included—there is nothing in the definition that is not applicable to it. According to this sharpest of observers and deepest of thinkers, if a man during his period of activity is alive, so is a machine when in operation. As an inventor and constructor of machines I know that to be true."

Moxon was silent for a long time, gazing absently into the fire. It was growing late and I thought it time to be going, but somehow I did not like the notion of leaving him in that isolated house, all alone except for the presence of some person of whose nature my conjectures could go no further than that it was unfriendly, perhaps malign. Leaning toward him and looking earnestly into his eyes while making a motion with my hand through the door of his workshop, I said:

"Moxon, whom have you in there?"

Somewhat to my surprise he laughed lightly and answered without hesitation:

"Nobody; the incident that you have in mind was caused by my folly in leaving a machine in action with nothing to act upon, while I undertook the interminable task of enlightening your understanding. Do you happen to know that Consciousness is the creature of Rhythm?"

"O bother them both!" I replied, rising and laying hold of my overcoat. "I'm going to wish you good night; and I'll add the hope that the machine which you inadvertently left in action will have her gloves on the next time you think it needful to stop her."

Without waiting to observe the effect of my shot I left the house.

Rain was falling, and the darkness was intense. In the sky beyond the crest of a hill toward which I groped my way along precarious plank sidewalks and across miry, unpaved streets I could see the faint glow of the city's lights, but behind me nothing was visible but a single window of Moxon's house. It glowed with what seemed to me a mysterious and fateful meaning. I knew it was an uncurtained aperture in my friend's "machine-shop," and I had little doubt that he had resumed the studies interrupted by his duties as my instructor in mechanical consciousness and the fatherhood of Rhythm. Odd, and in some degree humorous, as his convictions seemed to me at that time, I could not wholly divest myself of the feeling that they had some tragic relation to his life and character—perhaps to his destiny—although I no longer entertained the notion that they were the vagaries of a disordered mind. Whatever might be thought of his views, his exposition of them was too logical for that. Over and over, his last words came back to me: "Consciousness is the creature of Rhythm." Bald and terse as the statement was, I now found it infinitely alluring. At each recurrence it broadened in meaning and deepened in suggestion. Why, here, (I thought) is something upon which to found a philosophy. If consciousness is the product of rhythm all things are conscious, for all have motion, and all motion is rhythmic. I wondered if Moxon knew the significance and breadth of his thought—the scope of this momentous generalization; or had he arrived at his philosophic faith by the tortuous and uncertain road of observation?

That faith was then new to me, and all Moxon's expounding had failed to make me a convert; but now it seemed as if a great light shone about me, like that which fell upon Saul of Tarsus; and out there in the storm and darkness and solitude I experienced what Lewes calls "The endless variety and excitement of philosophic thought." I exulted in a new sense of knowledge, a new pride of reason. My feet seemed hardly to touch the earth; it was as if I were uplifted and borne through the air by invisible wings.

Yielding to an impulse to seek further light from him whom I now recognized as my master and guide, I had unconsciously turned about, and almost before I was aware of having done so found myself again at Moxon's door. I was drenched with rain, but felt no discomfort. Unable in my excitement to find the doorbell I instinctively tried the knob. It turned and, entering, I mounted the stairs to the room that I had so recently left. All was dark and silent; Moxon, as I had supposed, was in the adjoining room—the "machine-shop." Groping along the wall until I found the communicating door I knocked loudly several times, but got no response, which I attributed to the uproar outside, for the wind was blowing a gale and dashing the rain against the thin walls in sheets. The drumming upon the shingle roof spanning the unceiled room was loud and incessant.

I had never been invited into the machine-shop—had, indeed, been denied admittance, as had all others, with one exception, a skilled metal worker, of whom no one knew anything except that his name was Haley and his habit silence. But in my spiritual exaltation, discretion and civility were alike forgotten and I opened the door. What I saw took all philosophical speculation out of me in short order.

Moxon sat facing me at the farther side of a small table upon which a single candle made all the light that was in the room. Opposite him, his back toward me, sat another person. On the table between the two was a chessboard; the men were playing. I knew little of chess, but as only a few pieces were on the board it was obvious that the game was near its close. Moxon was intensely interested—not so much, it seemed to me, in the game as in his antagonist, upon whom he had fixed so intent a look that, standing though I did directly in the line of his vision, I was altogether unobserved. His face was ghastly white, and his eyes glittered like diamonds. Of his antagonist I had only a back view, but that was sufficient; I should not have cared to see his face.

He was apparently not more than five feet in height, with proportions suggesting those of a gorilla—a tremendous breadth of shoulders, thick, short neck and broad, squat head, which had a tangled growth of black hair and was topped with a crimson fez. A tunic of the same color, belted tightly to the waist, reached the seat—apparently a box—upon which he sat; his legs and feet were not seen. His left forearm appeared to rest in his lap; he moved his pieces with his right hand, which seemed disproportionately long.

I had shrunk back and now stood a little to one side of the doorway and in shadow. If Moxon had looked farther than the face of his opponent he could have observed nothing now, except that the door was open. Something forbade me either to enter or to retire, a feeling—I know not how it came—that I was in the presence of an imminent tragedy and might serve my friend by remaining. With a scarcely conscious rebellion against the indelicacy of the act I remained.

The play was rapid. Moxon hardly glanced at the board before making his moves, and to my unskilled eye seemed to move the piece most convenient to his hand, his motions in doing so being quick, nervous and lacking in precision. The response of his antagonist, while equally prompt in the inception, was made with a slow, uniform, mechanical and, I thought, somewhat theatrical movement of the arm, that was a sore trial to my patience. There was something unearthly about it all, and I caught myself shuddering. But I was wet and cold.

Two or three times after moving a piece the stranger slightly inclined his head, and each time I observed that Moxon shifted his king. All at once the thought came to me that the man was dumb. And then that he was a machine—an automaton chess-player! Then I remembered that Moxon had once spoken to me of having invented such a piece of mechanism, though I did not understand that it had actually been constructed. Was all his talk about the consciousness and intelligence of machines merely a prelude to eventual exhibition of this device—only a trick to intensify the effect of its mechanical action upon me in my ignorance of its secret?

A fine end, this, of all my intellectual transports—my "endless variety and excitement of philosophic thought!" I was about to retire in disgust when something occurred to hold my curiosity. I observed a shrug of the thing's great shoulders, as if it were irritated: and so natural was this—so entirely human—that in my new view of the matter it startled me. Nor was that all, for a moment later it struck the table sharply with its clenched hand. At that gesture Moxon seemed even more startled than I: he pushed his chair a little backward, as in alarm.

Presently Moxon, whose play it was, raised his hand high above the board, pounced upon one of his pieces like a sparrow-hawk and with the exclamation "checkmate!" rose quickly to his feet and stepped behind his chair. The automaton sat motionless.

The wind had now gone down, but I heard, at lessening intervals and progressively louder, the rumble and roll of thunder. In the pauses between I now became conscious of a low humming or buzzing which, like the thunder, grew momentarily louder and more distinct. It seemed to come from the body of the automaton, and was unmistakably a whirring of wheels. It gave me the impression of a disordered mechanism which had escaped the repressive and regulating action of some controlling part—an effect such as might be expected if a pawl should be jostled from the teeth of a ratchet-wheel. But before I had time for much conjecture as to its nature my attention was taken by the strange motions of the automaton itself. A slight but continuous convulsion appeared to have possession of it. In body and head it shook like a man with palsy or an ague chill, and the motion augmented every moment until the entire figure was in violent agitation. Suddenly it sprang to its feet and with a movement almost too quick for the eye to follow shot forward across table and chair, with both arms thrust forth to their full length—the posture and lunge of a diver. Moxon tried to throw himself backward out of reach, but he was too late: I saw the horrible thing's hands close upon his throat, his own clutch its wrists. Then the table was overturned, the candle thrown to the floor and extinguished, and all was black dark. But the noise of the struggle was dreadfully distinct, and most terrible of all were the raucous, squawking sounds made by the strangled man's efforts to breathe. Guided by the infernal hubbub, I sprang to the rescue of my friend, but had hardly taken a stride in the darkness when the whole room blazed with a blinding white light that burned into my brain and heart and memory a vivid picture of the combatants on the floor, Moxon underneath, his throat still in the clutch of those iron hands, his head forced backward, his eyes protruding, his mouth wide open and his tongue thrust out; and—horrible contrast!—upon the painted face of his assassin an expression of tranquil and profound thought, as in the solution of a problem in chess! This I observed, then all was blackness and silence.

Three days later I recovered consciousness in a hospital. As the memory of that tragic night slowly evolved in my ailing brain I recognized in my attendant Moxon's confidential workman, Haley. Responding to a look he approached, smiling.

"Tell me about it," I managed to say, faintly—"all about it."

"Certainly," he said; "you were carried unconscious from a burning house—Moxon's. Nobody knows how you came to be there. You may have to do a little explaining. The origin of the fire is a bit mysterious, too. My own notion is that the house was struck by lightning."

"And Moxon?"

"Buried yesterday—what was left of him."

Apparently this reticent person could unfold himself on occasion. When imparting shocking intelligence to the sick he was affable enough. After some moments of the keenest mental suffering I ventured to ask another question:

"Who rescued me?"

"Well, if that interests you—I did."

"Thank you, Mr. Haley, and may God bless you for it. Did you rescue, also, that charming product of your skill, the automaton chess-player that murdered its inventor?"

The man was silent a long time, looking away from me. Presently he turned and gravely said:

"Do you know that?"

"I do," I replied; "I saw it done."

That was many years ago. If asked to-day I should answer less confidently.

MR. BRISHER'S TREASURE

H.G. Wells

"You can't be TOO careful WHO you marry," said Mr. Brisher, and pulled thoughtfully with a fat-wristed hand at the lank moustache that hides his want of chin.

"That's why—" I ventured.

"Yes," said Mr. Brisher, with a solemn light in his bleary, blue-grey eyes, moving his head expressively and breathing alcohol INTIMATELY at me. "There's lots as 'ave 'ad a try at me—many as I could name in this town—but none 'ave done it—none."

I surveyed the flushed countenance, the equatorial expansion, the masterly carelessness of his attire, and heaved a sigh to think that by reason of the unworthiness of women he must needs be the last of his race.

"I was a smart young chap when I was younger," said Mr. Brisher. "I 'ad my work cut out. But I was very careful—very. And I got through..."

He leant over the taproom table and thought visibly on the subject of my trustworthiness. I was relieved at last by his confidence.

"I was engaged once," he said at last, with a reminiscent eye on the shuv-a'penny board.

"So near as that?"

He looked at me. "So near as that. Fact is—" He looked about him, brought his face close to mine, lowered his voice, and fenced off an unsympathetic world with a grimy hand. "If she ain't dead or married to some one else or anything—I'm engaged still. Now." He confirmed this statement with nods and facial contortions. "STILL," he said, ending the pantomime, and broke into a reckless smile at my surprise. "ME!"

"Run away," he explained further, with coruscating eyebrows. "Come 'ome.

"That ain't all.

"You'd 'ardly believe it," he said, "but I found a treasure. Found a regular treasure."

I fancied this was irony, and did not, perhaps, greet it with proper surprise. "Yes," he said, "I found a treasure. And come 'ome. I tell you I could surprise you with things that has happened to me." And for some time he was content to repeat that he had found a treasure—and left it.

I made no vulgar clamour for a story, but I became attentive to Mr. Brisher's bodily needs, and presently I led him back to the deserted lady.

"She was a nice girl," he said—a little sadly, I thought. "AND respectable."

He raised his eyebrows and tightened his mouth to express extreme respectability—beyond the likes of us elderly men.

"It was a long way from 'ere. Essex, in fact. Near Colchester. It was when I was up in London—in the buildin' trade. I was a smart young chap then, I can tell you. Slim. 'Ad best clo'es 's good as anybody. 'At—SILK 'at, mind you." Mr. Brisher's hand shot above his head towards the infinite to indicate it silk hat of the highest. "Umbrella—nice umbrella with a 'orn 'andle. Savin's. Very careful I was..."

He was pensive for a little while, thinking, as we must all come to think sooner or later, of the vanished brightness of youth. But he refrained, as one may do in taprooms, from the obvious moral.

"I got to know 'er through a chap what was engaged to 'er sister. She was stopping in London for a bit with an aunt that 'ad a 'am an' beef shop. This aunt was very particular—they was all very particular people, all 'er people was—and wouldn't let 'er sister go out with this feller except 'er other sister, MY girl that is, went with them. So 'e brought me into it, sort of to ease the crowding. We used to go walks in Battersea Park of a Sunday afternoon. Me in my topper, and 'im in 'is; and the girl's—well—stylish. There wasn't many in Battersea Park 'ad the larf of us. She wasn't what you'd call pretty, but a nicer girl I never met. *I* liked 'er from the start, and, well—though I say it who shouldn't—she liked me. You know 'ow it is, I dessay?"

I pretended I did.

"And when this chap married 'er sister—'im and me was great friends—what must 'e do but arst me down to Colchester, close by where She lived. Naturally I was introjuced to 'er people, and well, very soon, her and me was engaged."

He repeated, "engaged."

"She lived at 'ome with 'er father and mother, quite the lady, in a very nice little 'ouse with a garden—and remarkable respectable people they was. Rich you might call 'em a'most. They owned their own 'ouse—got it out of the Building Society, and cheap because the chap who had it before was a burglar and in prison—and they 'ad a bit of free'old land, and some cottages and money 'nvested—all nice and tight: they was what you'd call snug and warm. I tell you, I was On. Furniture too. Why! They 'ad a pianner. Jane—'er name was Jane—used to play it Sundays, and very nice she played too. There wasn't 'ardly a 'im toon in the book she COULDN'T play...

"Many's the evenin' we've met and sung 'ims there, me and 'er and the family.

"'Er father was quite a leadin' man in chapel. You should ha' seen him Sundays, interruptin' the minister and givin' out 'ims. He had gold spectacles, I remember, and used to look over 'em at you while he sang hearty—he was always great on singing 'earty to the Lord—and when HE got out o' toon 'arf the people went after 'im—always. 'E was that sort of man. And to walk be'ind 'im in 'is nice black clo'es—'is 'at was a brimmer—made one regular proud to be engaged to such a father-in-law. And when the summer came I went down there and stopped a fortnight.

"Now, you know there was a sort of Itch," said Mr. Brisher. "We wanted to marry, me and Jane did, and get things settled. But 'E said I 'ad to get a proper position first. Consequently there was a Itch. Consequently, when I went down there, I was anxious to show that I was a good useful sort of chap like. Show I could do pretty nearly everything like. See?"

I made a sympathetic noise.

"And down at the bottom of their garden was a bit of wild part like. So I says to 'im, 'Why don't you 'ave a rockery 'ere?' I says. 'It 'ud look nice.'

"'Too much expense,' he says.

"'Not a penny,' says I. 'I'm a dab at rockeries. Lemme make you one.' You see, I'd 'elped my brother make a rockery in the beer garden be'ind 'is tap, so I knew 'ow to do it to rights. 'Lemme make you one,' I says. 'It's 'olidays, but I'm that sort of chap, I 'ate doing nothing,' I says. 'I'll make you one to rights.' And the long and the short of it was, he said I might.

"And that's 'ow I come on the treasure."

"What treasure?" I asked.

"Why!" said Mr. Brisher, "the treasure I'm telling you about, what's the reason why I never married."

"What!—a treasure—dug up?"

"Yes—buried wealth—treasure trove. Come out of the ground. What I kept on saying—regular treasure..." He looked at me with unusual disrespect.

"It wasn't more than a foot deep, not the top of it," he said.

"I'd 'ardly got thirsty like, before I come on the corner."

"Go on," I said. "I didn't understand."

"Why! Directly I 'it the box I knew it was treasure. A sort of instinct told me. Something seemed to shout inside of me—'Now's your chance—lie low.' It's lucky I knew the laws of treasure trove or I'd 'ave been shoutin' there and then. I daresay you know—"

"Crown bags it," I said, "all but one per cent. Go on. It's a shame. What did you do?"

"Uncovered the top of the box. There wasn't anybody in the garden or about like. Jane was 'elping 'er mother do the 'ouse. I WAS excited—I tell you. I tried the lock and then gave a whack at the hinges. Open it came. Silver coins—full! Shining. It made me tremble to see 'em. And jest then—I'm blessed if the dustman didn't come round the back of the 'ouse. It pretty nearly gave me 'eart disease to think what a fool I was to 'ave that money showing. And directly after I 'eard the chap next door—'e was 'olidaying, too—I 'eard him watering 'is beans. If only 'e'd looked over the fence!"

"What did you do?"

"Kicked the lid on again and covered it up like a shot, and went on digging about a yard away from it—like mad. And my face, so to speak, was laughing on its own account till I had it hid. I tell you I was regular scared like at my luck. I jest thought that it 'ad to be kep' close and that was all. 'Treasure,' I kep' whisperin' to myself, 'Treasure' and ''undreds of pounds, 'undreds, 'undreds of pounds.' Whispering to myself like, and digging like blazes. It seemed to me the box was regular sticking out and showing, like your legs do under the sheets in bed, and I went and put all the earth I'd got out of my ''ole for the rockery slap on top of it. I WAS in a sweat. And in the midst of it all out toddles 'er father. He didn't say anything to me, jest stood behind me and stared, but Jane tole me afterwards when he went indoors, 'e says, 'That there jackanapes of yours, Jane'—he always called me a jackanapes some'ow—'knows 'ow to put 'is back into it after all.' Seemed quite impressed by it, 'e did."

"How long was the box?" I asked, suddenly.

"'Ow long?" said Mr. Brisher.

"Yes—in length?"

"Oh! 'bout so-by-so." Mr. Brisher indicated a moderate-sized trunk.

"FULL?" said I.

"Full up of silver coins—'arf-crowns, I believe."

"Why!" I cried, "that would mean—hundreds of pounds."

"Thousands," said Mr. Brisher, in a sort of sad calm. "I calc'lated it out."

"But how did they get there?"

"All I know is what I found. What I thought at the time was this. The chap who'd owned the 'ouse before 'er father 'd been a regular slap-up burglar. What you'd call a 'igh-class criminal. Used to drive 'is trap—like Peace did." Mr. Brisher meditated on the difficulties of narration and embarked on a complicated parenthesis. "I don't know if I told you it'd been a burglar's 'ouse before it was my girl's father's, and I knew 'e'd robbed a mail train once, I did know that. It seemed to me—"

"That's very likely," I said. "But what did you do?"

"Sweated," said Mr. Brisher. "Regular run orf me. All that morning," said Mr. Brisher, "I was at it, pretending to make that rockery and wondering what I should do. I'd 'ave told 'er father p'r'aps, only I was doubtful of 'is honesty—I was afraid he might rob me of it like, and give it up to the authorities—and besides, considering I was marrying into the family, I thought it would be nicer like if it came through me. Put me on a better footing, so to speak. Well, I 'ad three days before me left of my 'olidays, so there wasn't no hurry, so I covered it up and went on digging, and tried to puzzle out 'ow I was to make sure of it. Only I couldn't.

"I thought," said Mr. Brisher, "AND I thought. Once I got regular doubtful whether I'd seen it or not, and went down to it and 'ad it uncovered again, just as her ma came out to 'ang up a bit of washin' she'd done. Jumps again! Afterwards I was just thinking I'd 'ave another go at it, when Jane comes to tell me dinner was ready. 'You'll want it,' she said, 'seeing all the 'ole you've dug.'

"I was in a regular daze all dinner, wondering whether that chap next door wasn't over the fence and filling 'is pockets. But in the afternoon I got easier in my mind—it seemed to me it must 'ave been there so long it was pretty sure to stop a bit longer—and I tried to get up a bit of a discussion to dror out the old man and see what 'E thought of treasure trove."

Mr. Brisher paused, and affected amusement at the memory.

"The old man was a scorcher," he said; "a regular scorcher."

"What!" said I; "did he—?"

"It was like this," explained Mr. Brisher, laying a friendly hand on my arm and breathing into my face to calm me. "Just to dror 'im out, I told a story of a chap I said I knew—pretendin', you know—who'd found a sovring in a novercoat 'e'd borrowed. I said 'e stuck to it, but I said I wasn't sure whether that was right or not. And then the old man began. Lor'! 'e DID let me 'ave it!" Mr. Brisher affected an insincere amusement. "'E was, well—what you might call a rare 'and at Snacks. Said that was the sort of friend 'e'd naturally expect me to 'ave. Said 'e'd naturally expect that from the friend of a out-of-work loafer who took up with daughters who didn't belong to 'im. There! I couldn't tell you 'ARF 'e said. 'E went on most outrageous. I stood up to 'im about it, just to dror 'im out. 'Wouldn't you stick to a 'arf-sov', not if you found it in the street?' I says. 'Certainly not,"e says; 'certainly I wouldn't.' 'What! not if you found it as a sort of treasure?' 'Young man,' 'e says, 'there's 'i'er 'thority than mine—Render unto Caesar'—what is it? Yes. Well, he fetched up that. A rare 'and at 'itting you over the 'ed with the Bible, was the old man. And so he went on. 'E got to such Snacks about me at last I couldn't stand it. I'd promised Jane not to answer 'im back, but it got a bit TOO thick. I—I give it 'im..."

Mr. Brisher, by means of enigmatical facework, tried to make me think he had had the best of that argument, but I knew better.

"I went out in a 'uff at last. But not before I was pretty sure I 'ad to lift that treasure by myself. The only thing that kep' me up was thinking 'ow I'd take it out of 'im when I 'ad the cash."

There was a lengthy pause.

"Now, you'd 'ardly believe it, but all them three days I never 'ad a chance at the blessed treasure, never got out not even a 'arf-crown. There was always a Somethink—always.

"'Stonishing thing it isn't thought of more," said Mr. Brisher. "Finding treasure's no great shakes. It's gettin' it. I don't suppose I slep' a wink any of those nights, thinking where I was to take it, what I was to do with it, 'ow I was to explain it. It made me regular ill. And days I was that dull, it made Jane regular 'uffy. 'You ain't the same chap you was in London,' she says, several times. I tried to lay it on 'er father and 'is Snacks, but bless you, she knew better. What must she 'ave but that I'd got another girl on my mind! Said I wasn't True. Well, we had a bit of a row. But I was that set on the Treasure, I didn't seem to mind a bit Anything she said.

"Well, at last I got a sort of plan. I was always a bit good at planning, though carrying out isn't so much in my line. I thought it all out and settled on a plan. First, I was going to take all my pockets full of these 'ere 'arf-crowns—see?—and afterwards as I shall tell.

"Well, I got to that state I couldn't think of getting at the Treasure again in the daytime, so I waited until the night before I had to go, and then, when everything was still, up I gets and slips down to the back door, meaning to get my pockets full. What must I do in the scullery but fall over a pail! Up gets 'er father with a gun—'e was a light sleeper was 'er father, and very suspicious and there was me: 'ad to explain I'd come down to the pump for a drink because my water-bottle was bad. 'E didn't let me off a Snack or two over that bit, you lay a bob."

"And you mean to say—" I began.

"Wait a bit," said Mr. Brisher. "I say, I'd made my plan. That put the kybosh on one bit, but it didn't 'urt the general scheme not a bit. I went and I finished that rockery next day, as though there wasn't a Snack in the world; cemented over the stones, I did, dabbed it green and everythink. I put a dab of green just to show where the box was. They all came and looked at it, and sai' 'ow nice it was—even 'e was a bit softer like to see it, and all he said was, 'It's a pity you can't always work like that, then you might get something definite to do,' he says.

"'Yes,' I says—I couldn't 'elp it—'I put a lot in that rockery,' I says, like that. See? 'I put a lot in that rockery'—meaning—"

"I see," said I—for Mr. Brisher is apt to overelaborate his jokes.

"''E didn't," said Mr. Brisher. "Not then, anyhow.

"Ar'ever—after all that was over, off I set for London... Orf I set for London."

Pause.

"On'y I wasn't going to no London," said Mr. Brisher, with sudden animation, and thrusting his face into mine. "No fear! What do YOU think?

"I didn't go no further than Colchester—not a yard.

"I'd left the spade just where I could find it. I'd got everything planned and right. I 'ired a little trap in Colchester, and pretended I wanted to go to Ipswich and stop the night, and come back next day, and the chap I 'ired it from made me leave two sovrings on it right away, and off I set.

"I didn't go to no Ipswich neither.

"Midnight the 'orse and trap was 'itched by the little road that ran by the cottage where 'e lived—not sixty yards off, it wasn't—and I was at it like a good 'un. It was jest the night for such games—overcast—but a trifle too 'ot, and all round the sky there was summer lightning and presently a thunderstorm. Down it came. First big drops in a sort of fizzle, then 'ail. I kep'on. I whacked at it—I didn't dream the old man would 'ear. I didn't even trouble to go quiet with the spade, and the thunder and lightning and 'ail seemed to excite me like. I shouldn't wonder if I was singing. I got so 'ard at it I clean forgot the thunder and the 'orse and trap. I precious soon got the box showing, and started to lift it..."

"Heavy?" I said.

"I couldn't no more lift it than fly. I WAS sick. I'd never thought of that I got regular wild—I tell you, I cursed. I got sort of outrageous. I didn't think of dividing it like for the minute, and even then I couldn't 'ave took money about loose in a trap. I hoisted one end sort of wild like, and over the whole show went with a tremenjous noise. Perfeck smash of silver. And then right on the heels of that, Flash! Lightning like the day! and there was the back door open and the old man coming down the garden with 'is blooming old gun. He wasn't not a 'undred yards away!

"I tell you I was that upset—I didn't think what I was doing. I never stopped-not even to fill my pockets. I went over the fence like a shot, and ran like one o'clock for the trap, cussing and swearing as I went. I WAS in a state...

"And will you believe me, when I got to the place where I'd left the 'orse and trap, they'd gone. Orf! When I saw that I 'adn't a cuss left for it. I jest danced on the grass, and when I'd danced enough I started off to London... I was done."

Mr. Brisher was pensive for an interval. "I was done," he repeated, very bitterly.

"Well?" I said.

"That's all," said Mr. Brisher.

"You didn't go back?"

"No fear. I'd 'ad enough of THAT blooming treasure, any'ow for a bit. Besides, I didn't know what was done to chaps who tried to collar a treasure trove. I started off for London there and then..."

"And you never went back?"

"Never."

"But about Jane? Did you write?"

"Three times, fishing like. And no answer. We'd parted in a bit of a 'uff on account of 'er being jealous. So that I couldn't make out for certain what it meant.

"I didn't know what to do. I didn't even know whether the old man knew it was me. I sort of kep' an eye open on papers to see when he'd give up that treasure to the Crown, as I hadn't a doubt 'e would, considering 'ow respectable he'd always been."

"And did he?"

Mr. Brisher pursed his mouth and moved his head slowly from side to side. "Not 'IM," he said.

"Jane was a nice girl," he said, "a thorough nice girl mind you, if jealous, and there's no knowing I mightn't 'ave gone back to 'er after a bit. I thought if he didn't give up the treasure I might 'ave a sort of 'old on 'im... Well, one day I looks as usual under Colchester—and there I saw 'is name. What for, d'yer think?"

I could not guess.

Mr. Brisher's voice sank to a whisper, and once more he spoke behind his hand. His manner was suddenly suffused with a positive joy. "Issuing counterfeit coins," he said. "Counterfeit coins!"

"You don't mean to say—?"

"Yes-It. Bad. Quite a long case they made of it. But they got 'im, though he dodged tremenjous. Traced 'is 'aving passed, oh!—nearly a dozen bad 'arf-crowns."

"And you didn't—?"

"No fear. And it didn't do 'IM much good to say it was treasure trove."

ROGER DODSWORTH: THE REANIMATED ENGLISHMAN

Mary Wollstonecraft Shelley

It may be remembered, that on the fourth of July last, a paragraph appeared in the papers importing that Dr. Hotham, of Northumberland, returning from Italy, over Mount St. Gothard, a score or two of years ago, had dug out from under an avalanche, in the neighbourhood of the mountain, a human being whose animation had been suspended by the action of the frost. Upon the application of the usual remedies, the patient was resuscitated, and discovered himself to be Mr. Dodsworth, the son of the antiquary Dodsworth, who perished in the reign of Charles I. He was thirty-seven years of age at the time of his inhumation, which had taken place as he was returning from Italy, in 1654. It was added that as soon as he was sufficiently recovered he would return to England, under the protection of his preserver. We have since heard no more of him, and various plans for public benefit, which have started in philanthropic minds on reading the statement, have already returned to their pristine nothingness. The antiquarian society had eaten their way to several votes for medals, and had already begun, in idea, to consider what prices it could afford to offer for Mr. Dodsworth's old clothes, and to conjecture what treasures in the way of pamphlet, old song, or autographic letter his pockets might contain. Poems from all quarters, of all kinds, elegiac, congratulatory, burlesque and allegoric, were half written. Mr. Godwin had suspended for the sake of such authentic information the history of the Commonwealth he had just begun. It is hard not only that the world should be baulked of these destined gifts from the talents of the country, but also that it should be promised and then deprived of a new subject of romantic wonder and scientific interest. A novel idea is worth much in the commonplace routine of life, but a new fact, an astonishment, a miracle, a palpable wandering from the course of things into apparent impossibilities, is a circumstance to which the imagination must cling with delight, and we say again that it is hard, very hard, that Mr. Dodsworth refuses to appear, and that the believers in his resuscitation are forced to undergo the sarcasms and triumphant arguments of those sceptics who always keep on the safe side of the hedge.

Now we do not believe that any contradiction or impossibility is attached to the adventures of this youthful antique. Animation (I believe physiologists agree) can as easily be suspended for an hundred or two years, as for as many seconds. A body hermetically sealed up by the frost, is of necessity preserved in its pristine entireness. That which is totally secluded from the action of external agency, can neither have any thing added to nor taken away from it: no decay can take place, for something can never become nothing; under the influence of that state of being which we call death, change but not annihilation removes from our sight the corporeal atoma; the earth receives sustenance from them, the air is fed by them, each element takes its own, thus seizing forcible repayment of what it had lent. But the elements that hovered round Mr. Dodsworth's icy shroud had no power to overcome the obstacle it presented. No zephyr could gather a hair from his head, nor could the influence of dewy night or genial morn penetrate his more than adamantine panoply. The story of the Seven Sleepers rests on a miraculous interposition—they slept. Mr. Dodsworth did not sleep; his breast never heaved, his pulses were stopped; death had his finger pressed on his lips which no breath might pass. He has removed it now, the grim shadow is vanquished, and stands wondering. His victim has cast from him the frosty spell, and arises as perfect a man as he had lain down an hundred and fifty years before. We have eagerly desired to be furnished with some particulars of his first conversations, and the mode in which he has learnt to adapt himself to his new scene of life. But since facts are denied to us, let us be permitted to indulge in conjecture. What his first words were may be guessed from the expressions used by people exposed to shorter accidents of the like nature. But as his powers return, the plot thickens. His dress had already excited Doctor Hotham's astonishment—the peaked beard—the love locks—the frill, which, until it was thawed, stood stiff under the mingled influence of starch and frost; his dress fashioned like that of one of Vandyke's portraits, or (a more familiar similitude) Mr. Sapio's costume in Winter's Opera of the Oracle, his pointed shoes—all spoke of other times. The curiosity of his preserver was keenly awake, that of Mr. Dodsworth was about to be roused. But to be enabled to conjecture with any degree of likelihood the tenor of his first inquiries, we must endeavour to make out what part he played in his former life. He lived at the most interesting period of English History—he was lost to the world when Oliver Cromwell had arrived at the summit of his ambition, and in the eyes of all Europe the commonwealth of England appeared so established as to endure for ever. Charles I. was dead; Charles II. was an outcast, a beggar, bankrupt even in hope. Mr. Dodsworth's father, the antiquary, received a salary from the republican general, Lord Fairfax, who was himself a great lover of antiquities, and died the very year that his son went to his long, but not unending sleep, a curious coincidence this, for it would seem that our frost-preserved friend was returning to England on his father's death, to claim probably his inheritance—how short lived are human views! Where now is Mr. Dodsworth's patrimony? Where his co-heirs, executors, and fellow legatees? His protracted absence has, we should suppose, given the present possessors to his estate—the world's chronology is an hundred and seventy years older since he seceded from the busy scene, hands after hands have tilled his acres, and then become clods beneath them; we may be permitted to doubt whether one single particle of their surface is individually the same as those which were to have been his—the youthful soil would of itself reject the antique clay of its claimant.

Mr. Dodsworth, if we may judge from the circumstance of his being abroad, was no zealous commonwealth's man, yet his having chosen Italy as the country in which to make his tour and his projected return to England on his father's death, renders it probable that he was no violent loyalist. One of those men he seems to be (or to have been) who did not follow Cato's advice as recorded in the Pharsalia; a party, if to be of no party admits of such a term, which Dante recommends us utterly to despise, and which not unseldom falls between the two stools, a seat on either of which is so carefully avoided. Still Mr. Dodsworth could hardly fail to feel anxious for the latest news from his native country at so critical a period; his absence might have put his own property in jeopardy; we may imagine therefore that after his limbs had felt the cheerful return of circulation, and after he had refreshed himself with such of earth's products as from all analogy he never could have hoped to live to eat, after he had been told from what peril he had been rescued, and said a prayer thereon which even appeared enormously long to Dr. Hotham—we may imagine, we say, that his first question would be: "if any news had arrived lately from England?"

"I had letters yesterday," Dr. Hotham may well be supposed to reply.

"Indeed," cries Mr. Dodsworth, "and pray, sir, has any change for better or worse occurred in that poor distracted country?"

Dr. Hotham suspects a Radical, and coldly replies: "Why, sir, it would be difficult to say in what its distraction consists. People talk of starving manufacturers, bankruptcies, and the fall of the Joint Stock Companies—excrescences these, excrescences which will attach themselves to a state of full health. England, in fact, was never in a more prosperous condition."

Mr. Dodsworth now more than suspects the Republican, and, with what we have supposed to be his accustomed caution, sinks for awhile his loyalty, and in a moderate tone asks: "Do our governors look with careless eyes upon the symptoms of over-health?"

"Our governors," answers his preserver, "if you mean our ministry, are only too alive to temporary embarrassment." (We beg Doctor Hotham's pardon if we wrong him in making him a high Tory; such a quality appertains to our pure anticipated cognition of a Doctor, and such is the only cognizance that we have of this gentleman.) "It were to be wished that they showed themselves more firm—the king, God bless him!"

"Sir!" exclaims Mr. Dodsworth.

Doctor Hotham continues, not aware of the excessive astonishment exhibited by his patient: "The king, God bless him, spares immense sums from his privy purse for the relief of his subjects, and his example has been imitated by all the aristocracy and wealth of England."

"The King!" ejaculates Mr. Dodsworth.

"Yes, sir," emphatically rejoins his preserver; "the king, and I am happy to say that the prejudices that so unhappily and unwarrantably possessed the English people with regard to his Majesty are now, with a few" (with added severity) "and I may say contemptible exceptions, exchanged for dutiful love and such reverence as his talents, virtues, and paternal care deserve."

"Dear sir, you delight me," replies Mr. Dodsworth, while his loyalty late a tiny bud suddenly expands into full flower; "yet I hardly understand; the change is so sudden; and the man—Charles Stuart, King Charles, I may now call him, his murder is I trust execrated as it deserves?"

Dr. Hotham put his hand on the pulse of his patient—he feared an access of delirium from such a wandering from the subject. The pulse was calm, and Mr. Dodsworth continued: "That unfortunate martyr looking down from heaven is, I trust, appeased by the reverence paid to his name and the prayers dedicated to his memory. No sentiment, I think I may venture to assert, is so general in England as the compassion and love in which the memory of that hapless monarch is held?"

"And his son, who now reigns? —"

"Surely, sir, you forget; no son; that of course is impossible. No descendant of his fills the English throne, now worthily occupied by the house of Hanover. The despicable race of the Stuarts, long outcast and wandering, is now extinct, and the last days of the last Pretender to the crown of that family justified in the eyes of the world the sentence which ejected it from the kingdom for ever."

Such must have been Mr. Dodsworth's first lesson in politics. Soon, to the wonder of the preserver and preserved, the real state of the case must have been revealed; for a time, the strange and tremendous circumstance of his long trance may have threatened the wits of Mr. Dodsworth with a total overthrow. He had, as he crossed Mount Saint Gothard, mourned a father—now every human being he had ever seen is "lapped in lead," is dust, each voice he had ever heard is mute. The very sound of the English tongue is changed, as his experience in conversation with Dr. Hotham assures him. Empires, religions, races of men, have probably sprung up or faded; his own patrimony (the thought is idle, yet, without it, how can he live?) is sunk into the thirsty gulph that gapes ever greedy to swallow the past; his learning, his acquirements, are probably obsolete; with a bitter smile he thinks to himself, I must take to my father's profession, and turn antiquary. The familiar objects, thoughts, and habits of my boyhood, are now antiquities. He wonders where the hundred and sixty folio volumes of MS. that his father had compiled, and which, as a lad, he had regarded with religious reverence, now are—where—ah, where? His favourite play-mate, the friend of his later years, his destined and lovely bride, tears long frozen are uncongealed, and flow down his young old cheeks.

But we do not wish to be pathetic; surely since the days of the patriarchs, no fair lady had her death mourned by her lover so many years after it had taken place. Necessity, tyrant of the world, in some degree reconciles Mr. Dodsworth to his fate. At first he is persuaded that the later generation of man is much deteriorated from his contemporaries; they are neither so tall, so handsome, nor so intelligent. Then by degrees he begins to doubt his first impression. The ideas that had taken possession of his brain before his accident, and which had been frozen up for so many years, begin to thaw and dissolve away, making room for others. He dresses himself in the modern style, and does not object much to anything except the neck-cloth and hard-boarded hat. He admires the texture of his shoes and stockings, and looks with admiration on a small Genevese watch, which he often consults, as if he were not yet assured that time had made progress in its accustomed manner, and as if he should find on its dial plate ocular demonstration that he had exchanged his thirty-seventh year for his two hundredth and upwards, and had left A.D. 1654 far behind to find himself suddenly a beholder of the ways of men in this enlightened nineteenth century. His curiosity is insatiable; when he reads, his eyes cannot purvey fast enough to his mind, and every now and then he lights upon some inexplicable passage, some discovery and knowledge familiar to us, but undreamed of in his days, that throws him into wonder and interminable reverie. Indeed, he may be supposed to pass much of his time in that state, now and then interrupting himself with a royalist song against old Noll and the Roundheads, breaking off suddenly, and looking round fearfully to see who were his auditors, and on beholding the modern appearance of his friend the Doctor, sighing to think that it is no longer of import to any, whether he sing a cavalier catch or a puritanic psalm.

It were an endless task to develope all the philosophic ideas to which Mr. Dodsworth's resuscitation naturally gives birth. We should like much to converse with this gentleman, and still more to observe the progress of his mind, and the change of his ideas in his very novel situation. If he be a sprightly youth, fond of the shows of the world, careless of the higher human pursuits, he may proceed summarily to cast into the shade all trace of his former life, and endeavour to merge himself at once into the stream of humanity now flowing. It would be curious enough to observe the mistakes he would make, and the medley of manners which would thus be produced. He may think to enter into active life, become whig or tory as his inclinations lead, and get a seat in the, even to him, once called chapel of St. Stephens. He may content himself with turning contemplative philosopher, and find sufficient food for his mind in tracing the march of the human intellect, the changes which have been wrought in the dispositions, desires, and powers of mankind. Will he be an advocate for perfectibility or deterioration? He must admire our manufactures, the progress of science, the diffusion of knowledge, and the fresh spirit of enterprise characteristic of our countrymen. Will he find any individuals to be compared to the glorious spirits of his day? Moderate in his views as we have supposed him to be, he will probably fall at once into the temporising tone of mind now so much in vogue. He will be pleased to find a calm in politics; he will greatly admire the ministry who have succeeded in conciliating almost all parties—to find peace where he left feud. The same character which he bore a couple of hundred years ago, will influence him now; he will still be the moderate, peaceful, unenthusiastic Mr. Dodsworth that he was in 1647.

For notwithstanding education and circumstances may suffice to direct and form the rough material of the mind, it cannot create, nor give intellect, noble aspiration, and energetic constancy where dulness, wavering of purpose, and grovelling desires, are stamped by nature. Entertaining this belief we have (to forget Mr. Dodsworth for awhile) often made conjectures how such and such heroes of antiquity would act, if they were reborn in these times: and then awakened fancy has gone on to imagine that some of them are reborn; that according to the theory explained by Virgil in his sixth Æneid, every thousand years the dead return to life, and their souls endued with the same sensibilities and capacities as before, are turned naked of knowledge into this world, again to dress their skeleton powers in such habiliments as situation, education, and experience will furnish. Pythagoras, we are told, remembered many transmigrations of this sort, as having occurred to himself, though for a philosopher he made very little use of his anterior memories. It would prove an instructive school for kings and statesmen, and in fact for all human beings, called on as they are, to play their part on the stage of the world, could they remember what they had been. Thus we might obtain a glimpse of heaven and of hell, as, the secret of our former identity confined to our own bosoms, we winced or exulted in the blame or praise bestowed on our former selves. While the love of glory and posthumous reputation is as natural to man as his attachment to life itself, he must be, under such a state of things, tremblingly alive to the historic records of his honour or shame. The mild spirit of Fox would have been soothed by the recollection that he had played a worthy part as Marcus Antoninus—the former experiences of Alcibiades or even of the emasculated Steeny of James I. might have caused Sheridan to have refused to tread over again the same path of dazzling but fleeting brilliancy. The soul of our modern Corinna would have been purified and exalted by a consciousness that once it had given life to the form of Sappho. If at the present moment the witch, memory, were in a freak, to cause all the present generation to recollect that some ten centuries back they had been somebody else, would not several of our free thinking martyrs wonder to find that they had suffered as Christians under Domitian, while the judge as he passed sentence would suddenly become aware, that formerly he had condemned the saints of the early church to the torture, for not renouncing the religion he now upheld— nothing but benevolent actions and real goodness would come pure out of the ordeal. While it would be whimsical to perceive how some great men in parish affairs would strut under the consciousness that their hands had once held a sceptre, an honest artizan or pilfering domestic would find that he was little altered by being transformed into an idle noble or director of a joint stock company; in every way we may suppose that the humble would be exalted, and the noble and the proud would feel their stars and honours dwindle into baubles and child's play when they called to mind the lowly stations they had once occupied. If philosophical novels were in fashion, we conceive an excellent one might be written on the development of the same mind in various stations, in different periods of the world's history.

But to return to Mr. Dodsworth, and indeed with a few more words to bid him farewell. We entreat him no longer to bury himself in obscurity; or, if he modestly decline publicity, we beg him to make himself known personally to us. We have a thousand inquiries to make, doubts to clear up, facts to ascertain. If any fear that old habits and strangeness of appearance will make him ridiculous to those accustomed to associate with modern exquisites, we beg to assure him that we are not given to ridicule mere outward shows, and that worth and intrinsic excellence will always claim our respect.

This we say, if Mr. Dodsworth is alive. Perhaps he is again no more. Perhaps he opened his eyes only to shut them again more obstinately; perhaps his ancient clay could not thrive on the harvests of these latter days. After a little wonder; a little shuddering to find himself the dead alive—finding no affinity between himself and the present state of things—he has bidden once more an eternal farewell to the sun. Followed to his grave by his preserver and the wondering villagers, he may sleep the true death-sleep in the same valley where he so long reposed. Doctor Hotham may have erected a simple tablet over his twice-buried remains, inscribed—

> To the Memory of R. Dodsworth,
> An Englishman,
> Born April 1, 1617;
> Died July 16, 18; — Aged 187.

An inscription which, if it were preserved during any terrible convulsion that caused the world to begin its life again, would occasion many learned disquisitions and ingenious theories concerning a race which authentic records showed to have secured the privilege of attaining so vast an age.

SELLING POINT

Norman Arkawy

"Good morning, madam," Ira said. "I represent..."

"We don't want any," said the women, easing the door shut.

With the time tested finesse of door-to-door salesmen, Ira slipped his size twelve shoe between the swinging door and the jamb. "But madam, if you'll give me a few minutes of your time..."

The woman shook her head. "It won't do you any good," she said, trying to squeeze the door shut over his foot. "Whatever it is, we don't want any."

"I represent U.S. Robot Company," Ira persisted. He smiled pleasantly. His unyielding foot maintained a six inch wide avenue of communication between himself and the woman in the house. "Long the leader in commercial and industrial mechanicals, U.S. Robot is now introducing a new line of home servants, designed to assist the housewife in every possible task about the house."

"You're wasting your time," the woman said wearily.

Ira used his professional smile to indicate that he enjoyed wasting his time. "When you've seen the demonstration," he said, "I'm sure you'll agree that no home should be without a Model I household robot."

The woman looked out at him silently, patiently, resigned. She was pretty and petite and very young; and, from her appearance, had never done a day's work in her life. A typical newlywed, Ira thought. A perfect prospect, he decided.

"As you undoubtedly know, the outstanding characteristics of U.S. Robot mechanicals have always been ability, durability and reliability. Their performance in industry has earned for the United States Robot Company the enviable reputation it is proud to possess: 'Leader in the art, artist of the trade—if it's U.S. Robot, it's perfect!'"

The woman smiled and allowed the door to swing open slightly. "What about Amalgamated Androids?" she asked. "I understand they've got some pretty good models, too."

"Well," Ira admitted, "some of their models are pretty good; adequate, perhaps. But why take anything but the best? And, of course, our robots..."

"I've seen some AA models that *are* perfect," the woman said. A suggestion of a smile tugged at the corner of her mouth. "How can yours be any better than perfect?"

Ira's voice took on a confidential complexion. "Some of their models are beautiful," he conceded. "And they may seem to work well when they're new. But they're not built to last, like ours. Why..."

"I think," the woman tried to interrupt, "that some of..."

"How can you compare them to U.S. Robot?" Ira ran on. "We have had forty-seven years of experience in producing mechanicals for the most difficult jobs imaginable. Amalgamated Androids while producing an adequate household model, does not have the valuable know-how to build into their mechanicals the strength and quality that is taken for granted in every machine bearing the U.S. Robot label."

The woman was skeptical. "Maybe your company does make the best factory hands," she argued, "but household robots must be esthetic as well as rugged. And Amalgamated Androids are specialists in building humanoid robots, while your company..."

"But, madam," Ira said, grinning. "Our household models are perfectly human in appearance—I should say, *im*perfectly human because we even give them tiny blemishes to make them seem more natural."

The woman was obviously unconvinced. Ira applied the clincher. "What greater proof could you want than this?" He held up his left hand, baring his wrist so that she could read his identification stamp.

Model I (Masc.)
Serial No. 27146 12V
U.S. ROBOT CO., INC.

The woman's eyes widened. Her face took on an expression of delighted surprise.

"What better proof could you want?" Ira repeated. "Do I look like a robot? Am I not a perfect humanoid? Here," he said, extending his hand, "feel my skin and see if it isn't just like a man's."

The woman gingerly touched his hand. Her eyes mirrored her satisfaction.

Ira pressed his advantage. "Model I robots come in both masculine and feminine designs, built to your individual specifications as to size, coloring, strength, personality traits, apparent age, and so forth. For example, lonely people can have companionship built in, if they like. You can have an Ira or Inez possessing an almost human intelligence and free choice, or you can get one that is blindly servile and which will never volunteer advice or information. You can get an elderly, refined butler or a handsome young man-around-the-house. You can get a pretty, petite parlor maid or a buxom cook."

Ira paused to observe his customer. She was looking at him in a peculiar way. Knowing that he was a robot, she seemed to be appraising him as she would a man. Ira noted her odd reaction and puzzled over it. It usually went the other way—women lost interest in him when they learned that he was not a man.

"Why don't you come inside," the woman suggested suddenly, opening the door for him.

Ira smiled at her graciously and went into the house. Her reaction was not so puzzling, after all, he decided. A young and virtuous wife would feel the conventional fears that were "built into her" by society. She had to be careful. It was conceivably dangerous to be alone in the house with a handsome man. But, if he's a robot, she has nothing to fear—from him or herself.

"Sit down," the woman said, "and rest a while."

"Thank you, madam." He sat. "But, of course, I don't need the rest. Model I's can do strenuous work for twenty-three out of every twenty-four hours. In fact, in laboratory tests, they've been run for one hundred and eighty-six hours continuously, without a breakdown."

He was back in his sales pitch. "Work is the basic function of all U.S. Robot Company robots. With all their esthetic perfection, the household models are no exception to this rule. They are unequaled in efficient performance. Power is the keynote of the Model I."

He opened his demonstration case and removed a steel bar, three inches in diameter. Placing one hand on each end, he bent the metal into a V.

"The heart of the mechanism," he went on, "is a powerful twelve volt A-battery, perfectly shielded and guaranteed to give trouble-free service for at least forty years. Sixteen motor centers are fed by the central power plant, all coordinated and synchronized by the best flui-electronic brain ever devised. Sturdy TS steel alloy construction over all gives the Model I its phenomenal strength and durability. And the surface tissue, made of a new patented miracle material, combines the best features of esthetic and functional performance."

The woman was obviously impressed. Lips slightly parted, she watched Ira attentively and listened breathlessly to everything he said. Instinctively, he felt that he had made a sale. But the woman said nothing; only gazed at him in a way that might have been covetous, might have been adoring or might have been merely symptomatic of hypnosis.

"May I demonstrate the I's power and versatility in practical performance?" Ira asked. Taking her silence to be consent, he swung into his demonstration.

Swiftly, surely, he went about the room, cleaning. Effortlessly, he lifted large pieces of furniture and, holding them aloft with his right hand, he cleaned under them with his left. He talked as he worked. "Notice the quiet efficiency of the self-cleansing electro-static duster we have built in. We also have attachments for waxing, washing, spraying, painting, ironing, soldering..."

"You're wonderful," the woman sighed.

"And let me point out," Ira pursued, eager to clinch the sale, "that the Model I is so life-like that, in normal operation, it is almost completely silent. Only a faint throbbing—like that of a human heart—is noticeable."

The woman cocked her head to a side. "I don't hear *anything*," she said.

Ira smiled triumphantly. "Of course, you don't! Come here," he said. "Put your ear to my chest and you'll just be able to make it out."

She rested her head on his chest and listened. The delicate fragrance of her perfume mingled with that sweet human scent that not even the Model I robots could imitate. Ira bent his head and brushed his sensitized cheek against her hair. He felt emotions that no robot should feel.

He silently cursed his makers and the wonderfully human brain they had given him. Their theory was that a salesman, to be effective, should think exactly like a human being. To better satisfy the customers, he should appreciate every human drive and desire. But it was wrong to feel like a man, to desire like a man, to hurt like a man and be unable to ease the pain because he was not a man! For once, U.S. Robot had gone too far!

The woman looked up at him with the eyes that broadcast adoration. "You're wonderful!" she repeated. "Do you think...?" She hesitated, looked away. "Could I be in love with you?" she asked with child-like innocence. "Is it possible?"

Ira felt flustered, giddy, light-headed, exultant, confused, miserable and weak. Damn U.S. Robot and their perfected flui-electronics! "But madam," he protested, "I'm not a man! I'm only a..."

"Please call me Emma," the woman said. "You see, I'm not Mrs. Bartlett. I've tried to tell you—Madam is not at home. I only work here."

Gone was his exultant feeling, gone the light-headedness. Only the misery and weakness remained in the realization that his yearning was impossible of fulfillment and that, to top it off, he had wasted his time trying to sell himself to a servant.

"Do you think I could?" the maid repeated.

"Could what?"

"Be in love with you."

"But, miss don't you understand? I'm not..."

"My name is Emma," she said softly. She smiled and he fought down an overwhelming urge to touch her, to kiss her pink, inviting lips. He stood rigid. He wanted to cry out in his torment.

Her hand reached out to him and he felt her fingers touch his. Electricity tingled up his arm and through his chest. Automatically, he repeated his cursed disavowal of humanness. Vaguely, he heard his own words, sounding like an echo in his ears. "I'm a robot."

"I know," Emma said quietly. Then, she held up her right

hand, revealing the identification stamp on her wrist.

Model M (fem.)
Serial No. 6139 12V
AMALGAMATED ANDROIDS, INC.

A moment later the android was in his arms. He held her close, dizzy with the sensation of this new emotion with one of his own kind.

Several moments later he pushed her gently away from him. "Pack your bag, Emma," he said.

She looked at him starry-eyed but quizzically. "But my work—madam will be furious—"

"Your bag, Emma," he repeated. "When our companies built us they made us as near human as possible—perhaps too much so. If we can work for humans we can also live like them. U.S. Robots and Amalgamated Androids have just lost two employees. Your bag."

Being an android she could work faster than any human counter-part; her bag was packed in nothing flat.

THE CAGE

J.D. Beresford

I was not asleep. I have watched passengers who kept their eyes shut between the stations, but as yet I have not seen an indisputable case of anyone sound asleep on the Hampstead and Charing Cross Tube. Of the other passages that make up London's greater intestine I have less experience, and it may be that some tubes are more conducive to slumber than the one most familiar to me. I have no ambition to make a dogmatic generalisation concerning either the stimulative or soporific action of the Underground. I merely wish it to be understood that I was not asleep, and that it was hardly possible that I could have been, with a small portmanteau permanently on one foot, and the owner of it—a little man who must have wished that the straps were rather longer—intermittently on the other. Against this, however, I have to put the fact that I could not say at which station the little man removed from me the burden of himself and his portmanteau. Nor could I give particulars of the appearance of such of my innumerable fellow-passengers as were most nearly presented to me, although I do know that most of them were reading—even the strap-hangers. It was, indeed, this observation that started my vision or train of thought or preoccupation—call it anything you like except a dream.

The eyes in his otherwise repulsive face held a wistfulness, a hint of vague speculation that attracted me. He sat, hunched on the summit of the steeply rising ground overlooking the sea, the place where the forest comes so abruptly to an end that from a little distance it looks as if it had been gigantically planed to a hard edge.

He was alone and ruminatively quiescent after food. He had fed well and carelessly. Some of the bones that lay near him had been very indifferently picked. He leaned forward clasping his hairy legs with his equally hairy arms, and stared out with that hint of speculation and wistfulness in his eyes over the placid magnificence of the Western Sea—just disturbed enough to reflect a gorgeous road of fire that laid a vanishing track across the waters up to the open goal of the low sun. A faint breeze blew up the hill, and it seemed as if he leant his face forward to drink the first refreshment of that sweet, cool air.

I approached him more nearly, trying to read his thought, rejoicing in the knowledge that he could neither see nor apprehend me. For though a man may know something of the past, the future is hidden from him, and I represented to him a future that could only be reckoned in a vast procession of centuries. Yet as I came nearer, so near that I could rest my hands on his knees and gaze up closely into his eyes, he shrank a little and leaned slightly away from me, as if he were uncertainly aware of an unfamiliar, distasteful presence. I fancied that the mat of hair on his chest just perceptibly bristled.

I could read his thought, now, and I was thrilled to discover that the expression of his eyes had not misled me. He had attained to a form of consciousness. He, alone, of all the beasts had received the gift of constructive imagination. He could look forward, make plans to meet a possible emergency. He knew already something of tomorrow. Even then he was deep in speculation. That day he had hunted a slow but cunning little beast which found a refuge among the great boulders that lay piled in gigantic profusion along the foreshore. And he had failed. Another quarry had been his, but that particular little beast had outwitted him. And now, longing for it, he ruminated clumsy lethargic plans for its capture.

It may have been that the unusual effort tired him, for

presently he slept, still hunched into the same compact heap, crouching with an effect of swift alertness as if he were ready at the least alarm to leap up and vanish into the cover of the forest.

Then, a plan came to me, also. I would bring a vision to this primitive ancestor of mankind. I would merge myself with his being and he should dream a dream of the immensely distant future. Blessed and privileged above all the human race, he should know for an instant to what inconceivable developments, to what towering heights of intellectual and manipulative glory his descendants should one day be heir. I had no definite idea of the precise illustration I should choose to set forth the magnificence of man's latest attainment. Nor did I pause to consider what I myself might suffer in the process of this infamous liaison between the ages. I acted on an impulse that I found irresistible. I have myself longed so often to read the distant future of mankind, that I felt as a god bestowing an inestimable gift. But I should have known that in the mystical union it is the god and not the man who suffers.

I was wrapped in an awful darkness as we fell stupendously through time, but presently I knew that we were rising again, weighted with the burden of primitive flesh. Then in an instant came a strange yellow unnatural light, the roaring of a terrible sound—and the fearful vision. The horror of it was unendurable; the shock of it so great that spirit and flesh were rent asunder. I remained. He fell back to the sweetness of the cool air blowing up from the tranquil sea.

Did he rush frantically into the forest or sit with dripping mouth and wide alarmed eyes, rigidly staring at the scarlet rim of the setting sun? Yet what could he have understood of the future in that moment of detestable revelation? Could he have recognised men and women in their strange disguise of modern dress, as being even of the same species as himself? And if he had, what could he have known of them, seeing them packed so closely together, immoveably wedged into the terror of that rocking roaring cage of unknown material; seeing them occupied in staring so intently and incomprehensibly at those amazing little black-dotted white sheets? Impossible for him to guess that those speckled sheets held a magic that transported his descendants from the misery of their cage into imaginations so extensive and so various that some of them might, however dimly and allusively, include himself, hunched and ruminant, regarding the vast tranquillity of the sea.

The tunnel suddenly broke, the roaring gave place to a rattle that by contrast was gentle and soothing. I opened my eyes. We were under the sky again, slipping, with intermittent flashes of light, into the harbour of Golder's Green Station.

For a moment, I seemed to see the clumsy and violent shape of a beast that strove in panic to escape; and then I came back to my own world of the patient readers, with their white, controlled faces, forming now in solemn procession down the aisle of the carriage.

But it was his dream, not mine. And I have been wondering whether, if I dreamed also, the distant future might not seem equally unendurable to me?

THE CASE OF MR. HELMER

Robert W. Chambers

He had really been too ill to go; the penetrating dampness of the studio, the nervous strain, the tireless application, all had told on him heavily. But the feverish discomfort in his head and lungs gave him no rest; it was impossible to lie there in bed and do nothing; besides, he did not care to disappoint his hostess. So he managed to crawl into his clothes, summon a cab, and depart. The raw night air cooled his head and throat; he opened the cab window and let the snow blow in on him.

When he arrived he did not feel much better, although Catharine was glad to see him.

Somebody's wife was allotted to him to take in to dinner, and he executed the commission with that distinction of manner peculiar to men of his temperament.

When the women had withdrawn and the men had lighted cigars and cigarettes, and the conversation wavered between municipal reform and contes drolatiques, and the Boznovian attaché had begun an interminable story, and Count Fantozzi was emphasizing his opinion of women by joining the tips of his overmanicured thumb and forefinger and wafting spectral kisses at an annoyed Englishman opposite, Helmer laid down his unlighted cigar and, leaning over, touched his host on the sleeve.

"Hello! What's up, Philip?" said his host cordially; and Helmer, dropping his voice a tone below the sustained pitch of conversation, asked him the question that had been burning his feverish lips since dinner began.

To which his host replied, "What girl do you mean?" and

bent nearer to listen.

"I mean the girl in the fluffy black gown, with shoulders and arms of ivory, and the eyes of Aphrodite."

His host smiled. "Where did she sit, this human wonder?"

"Beside Colonel Farrar."

"Farrar? Let's see"—he knit his brows thoughtfully, then shook his head. "I can't recollect; we're going in now and you can find her and I'll—"

His words were lost in the laughter and hum around them; he nodded an abstracted assurance at Helmer; others claimed his attention, and by the time he rose to signal departure he had forgotten the girl in black.

As the men drifted toward the drawing-rooms, Helmer moved with the throng. There were a number of people there whom he knew and spoke to, although through the increasing feverishness he could scarce hear himself speak. He was too ill to stay; he would find his hostess and ask the name of that girl in black, and go.

The white drawing-rooms were hot and over-thronged. Attempting to find his hostess, he encountered Colonel Farrar, and together they threaded their way aimlessly forward.

"Who is the girl in black, Colonel?" he asked; "I mean the one that you took in to dinner."

"A girl in black? I don't think I saw her."

"She sat beside you!"

"Beside me?" The Colonel halted, and his inquiring gaze rested for a moment on the younger man, then swept the crowded rooms.

"Do you see her now?" he asked.

"No," said Helmer, after a moment.

They stood silent for a little while, then parted to allow the Chinese minister thoroughfare—a suave gentleman, all antique silks, and a smile "thousands of years old." The minister passed, leaning on the arm of the general commanding at Governor's Island, who signaled Colonel Farrar to join them; and Helmer drifted again, until a voice repeated his name insistently, and his hostess leaned forward from the brilliant group surrounding her, saying: "What in the world is the matter, Philip? You look wretchedly ill."

"It's a trifle close here—nothing's the matter."

He stepped nearer, dropping his voice: "Catharine, who was that girl in black?"

"What girl?"

"She sat beside Colonel Farrar at dinner—or I thought she did—"

"Do you mean Mrs. Van Siclen? She is in white, silly!"

"No—the girl in black."

His hostess bent her pretty head in perplexed silence, frowning a trifle with the effort to remember.

"There were so many," she murmured; "let me see—it is certainly strange that I cannot recollect. Wait a moment! Are you sure she wore black? Are you sure she sat next to Colonel Farrar?"

"A moment ago I was certain—" he said, hesitating. "Never mind, Catherine; I'll prowl about until I find her."

His hostess, already partly occupied with the animated stir around her, nodded brightly; Helmer turned his fevered eyes and then his steps toward the cool darkness of the conservatories.

But he found there a dozen people who greeted him by name, demanding not only his company but his immediate and undivided attention.

"Mr. Helmer might be able to explain to us what his own work means," said a young girl, laughing.

They had evidently been discussing his sculptured group, just completed for the new façade of the National Museum. Press and public had commented very freely on the work since the unveiling a week since; critics quarrelled concerning the significance of the strange composition in marble. The group was at the same time repellent and singularly beautiful; but nobody denied its technical perfection. This was the sculptured group: A vaquero, evidently dying, lay in a loose heap among some desert rocks. Beside him, chin on palm, sat an exquisite winged figure, calm eyes fixed on the dying man. It was plain that death was near; it was stamped on the ravaged visage, on the collapsed frame. And yet, in the dying boy's eyes there was nothing of agony, no fear, only an intense curiosity as the lovely winged figure gazed straight into the glazing eyes.

"It may be," observed an attractive girl, "that Mr. Helmer will say with Mr. Gilbert, 'It is really very clever, But I don't know what it means.'" Helmer laughed and started to move away. "I think I'd better admit that at once," he said, passing his hand over his aching eyes; but the tumult of protest blocked his retreat, and he was forced to find a chair under the palms and tree ferns. "It was merely an idea of mine," he protested, goodhumoredly, "an idea that has haunted me so persistently that, to save myself further annoyance, I locked it up in marble."

"Demoniac obsession?" suggested a very young man, with a taste for morbid literature.

"Not at all," protested Helmer, smiling; "the idea annoyed me until I gave it expression. It doesn't bother me any more." "You said," observed the attractive girl, "that you were going to tell us all about it."

"About the idea? Oh no, I didn't promise that—"

"Please, Mr. Helmer!"

A number of people had joined the circle; he could see others standing here and there among the palms, evidently pausing to listen.

"There is no logic in the idea," he said, uneasily—"nothing to attract your attention. I have only laid a ghost—"

He stopped short. The girl in black stood there among the others, intently watching him. When she caught his eye, she nodded with the friendliest little smile; and as he started to rise she shook her head and stepped back with a gesture for him to continue.

They looked steadily at one another for a moment.

"The idea that has always attracted me," he began slowly, "is purely instinctive and emotional, not logical. It is this: As long as I can remember I have taken it for granted that a person who is doomed to die, never dies utterly alone. We who die in our beds—or expect to—die surrounded by the living. So fall soldiers on the firing line; so end the great majority—never absolutely alone. Even in a murder, the murderer at least must be present. If not, something else is there.

"But how is it with those solitary souls isolated in the world—the lone herder who is found lifeless in some vast, waterless desert, the pioneer whose bones are stumbled over by the tardy pickets of civilization—and even those nearer us—here in our city—who are found in silent houses, in deserted streets, in the solitude of salt meadows, in the miserable desolation of vacant lands beyond the suburbs?"

The girl in black stood motionless, watching him intently.

"I like to believe," he went on, "that no living creature dies absolutely and utterly alone. I have thought that, perhaps in the desert, for instance, when a man is doomed, and there is no chance that he could live to relate the miracle, some winged sentinel from the uttermost outpost of Eternity, putting off the armor of invisibility, drops through space to watch beside him so that he may not die alone."

There was absolute quiet in the circle around him. Looking

always at the girl in black, he said:

"Perhaps those doomed on dark mountains or in solitary deserts, or the last survivor at sea, drifting to certain destruction after the wreck has foundered, finds death no terror, being guided to it by those invisible to all save the surely doomed. That is really all that suggested the marble—quite illogical, you see."

In the stillness, somebody drew a long, deep breath; the easy reaction followed; people moved, spoke together in low voices; a laugh rippled up out of the darkness. But Helmer had gone, making his way through the half light toward a figure that moved beyond through the deeper shadows of the foliage—moved slowly and more slowly. Once she looked back, and he followed, pushing forward and parting the heavy fronds of fern and palm and masses of moist blossoms. Suddenly he came upon her, standing there as though waiting for him.

"There is not a soul in this house charitable enough to present me," he began.

"Then," she answered laughingly, "charity should begin at home. Take pity on yourself—and on me. I have waited for you."

"Did you really care to know me?" he stammered.

"Why am I here alone with you?" she asked, bending above a scented mass of flowers.

"Indiscretion may be a part of valor, but it is the best part of—something else."

That blue radiance which a starless sky sheds lighted her white shoulders; transparent shadow veiled the contour of neck and cheeks.

"At dinner," he said, "I did not mean to stare so—but I simply could not keep my eyes from yours—"

"A hint that mine were on yours, too?"

She laughed a little laugh so sweet that the sound seemed part of the twilight and the floating fragrance. She turned gracefully, holding out her hand.

"Let us be friends," she said, "after all these years."

Her hand lay in his for an instant; then she withdrew it and dropped it caressingly upon a cluster of massed flowers.

"Forced bloom," she said, looking down at them, where her fingers, white as the blossoms, lay half buried. Then, raising her head, "You do not know me, do you?"

"Know you?" he faltered; "how could I know you? Do you think for a moment that I could have forgotten you?"

"Ah, you have not forgotten me!" she said, still with her wide smiling eyes on his; "you have not forgotten. There is a trace of me in the winged figure you cut in marble—not the features, not the massed hair, nor the rounded neck and limbs—but in the eyes. Who living, save yourself, can read those eyes?"

"Are you laughing at me?"

"Answer me; who alone in all the world can read the message in those sculptured eyes?"

"Can you?" he asked, curiously troubled. "Yes; I, and the dying man in marble."

"What do you read there?"

"Pardon for guilt. You have foreshadowed it unconsciously—the resurrection of the soul. That is what you have left in marble for the mercilessly just to ponder on; that alone is the meaning of your work."

Through the throbbing silence he stood thinking, searching his clouded mind.

"The eyes of the dying man are your own," she said. "Is it not true?"

And still he stood there, groping, probing through dim and forgotten corridors of thought toward a faint memory scarcely perceptible in the wavering mirage of the past.

"Let us talk of your career," she said, leaning back against the thick foliage—"your success, and all that it means to you," she added gayly.

He stood staring at the darkness. "You have set the phantoms of forgotten things stirring and whispering together somewhere within me. Now tell me more; tell me the truth."

"You are slowly reading it in my eyes," she said, laughing sweetly. "Read and remember."

The fever in him seared his sight as he stood there, his confused gaze on hers.

"Is it a threat of hell you read in the marble?" he asked.

"No, no thing of destruction, only resurrection and hope of Paradise. Look at me closely."

"Who are you?" he whispered, closing his eyes to steady his swimming senses. "When have we met?"

"You were very young," she said under her breath— "and I was younger—and the rains had swollen the Canadian river so that it boiled amber at the fords; and I could not cross—alas!"

A moment of stunning silence, then her voice again: "I said nothing, not a word even of thanks when you offered aid... I—was not too heavy in your arms, and the ford was soon passed—-soon passed. That was very long ago." Watching him from shadowy sweet eyes, she said:

"For a day you knew the language of my mouth and my arms around you, there in the white sun glare of the river. For every kiss taken and retaken, given and forgiven, we must account—-for every one, even to the last.

"But you have set a monument for us both, preaching the resurrection of the soul. Love is such a little thing—and ours endured a whole day long! Do you remember? Yet He who created love, designed that it should last a lifetime. Only the lost outlive it."

She leaned nearer:

"Tell me, you who have proclaimed the resurrection of dead souls, are you afraid to die?"

Her low voice ceased; lights broke out like stars through the foliage around them; the great glass doors of the ballroom were opening; the illuminated fountain flashed, a falling shower of silver. Through the outrush of music and laughter swelling around them, a clear far voice called "Françoise!"

Again, close by, the voice rang faintly, "Françoise! Françoise!"

She slowly turned, staring into the brilliant glare beyond.

"Who called?" he asked hoarsely.

"My mother," she said, listening intently. "Will you wait for me?"

His ashen face glowed again like a dull ember. She bent nearer, and caught his fingers in hers.

"By the memory of our last kiss, wait for me!" she pleaded, her little hand tightening on his.

"Where?" he said, with dry lips. "We cannot talk here!—we cannot say here the things that must be said."

"In your studio," she whispered. "Wait for me."

"Do you know the way?"

"I tell you I will come; truly I will! Only a moment with my mother—-then I will be there!"

Their hands clung together an instant, then she slipped away into the crowded rooms; and after a moment Helmer followed, head bent, blinded by the glare.

"You are ill, Philip," said his host, as he took his leave. "Your face is as ghastly as that dying vaquero's—by Heaven, man, you look like him!"

"Did you find your girl in black?" asked his hostess curiously.

"Yes," he said; "good night."

The air was bitter as he stepped out—bitter as death. Scores of carriage lamps twinkled as he descended the snowy steps, and a faint gust of music swept out of the darkness, silenced as the heavy doors closed behind him.

He turned west, shivering. A long smear of light bounded his horizon as he pressed toward it and entered the sordid avenue beneath the iron arcade which was even now trembling under the shock of an oncoming train. It passed overhead with a roar; he raised his hot eyes and saw, through the tangled girders above, the illuminated disk of the clock tower all distorted—for the fever in him was disturbing everything—even the cramped and twisted street into which he turned, fighting for breath like a man stabbed through and through.

"What folly!" he said aloud, stopping short in the darkness. "This is fever—all this. She could not know where to come—"

Where two blind alleys cut the shabby block, worming their way inward from the avenue and from Tenth Street, he stopped again, his hands working at his coat.

"It is fever, fever!" he muttered. "She was not there."

There was no light in the street save for the red fire lamp burning on the corner, and a glimmer from the Old Grapevine Tavern across the way. Yet all around him the darkness was illuminated with pale unsteady flames, lighting him as he groped through the shadows of the street to the blind alley. Dark old silent houses peered across the paved lane at their aged counterparts, waiting for him.

And at last he found a door that yielded, and he stumbled into the black passageway, always lighted on by the unsteady pallid flames which seemed to burn in infinite depths of night.

"She was not there—she was never there," he gasped, bolting the door and sinking down upon the floor. And, as his mind wandered, he raised his eyes and saw the great bare room growing whiter and whiter under the uneasy flames.

"It will burn as I burn," he said aloud—for the phantom

flames had crept into his body.

Suddenly he laughed, and the vast studio rang again.

"Hark!" he whispered, listening intently. "Who knocked?"

There was some one at the door; he managed to raise himself and drag back the bolt.

"You!" he breathed, as she entered hastily, her hair disordered and her black skirts powdered with snow.

"Who but I?" she whispered, breathless. "Listen! do you hear my mother calling me? It is too late; but she was with me to the end."

Through the silence, from an infinite distance, came a desolate cry of grief—"Françoise!"

He had fallen back into his chair again, and the little busy flames enveloped him so that the room began to whiten again into a restless glare. Through it he watched her.

The hour struck, passed, struck and passed again. Other hours grew, lengthening into night.

She sat beside him with never a word or sigh or whisper of breathing; and dream after dream swept him, like burning winds. Then sleep immersed him so that he lay senseless, sightless eyes still fixed on her. Hour after hour—and the white glare died out, fading to a glimmer. In densest darkness, he stirred, awoke, his mind quite clear, and spoke her name in a low voice.

"Yes, I am here," she answered gently.

"Is it death?" he asked, closing his eyes.

"Yes. Look at me, Philip."

His eyes unclosed; into his altered face there crept an intense curiosity. For he beheld a glimmering shape, wide-winged and deep-eyed, kneeling beside him, and looking him through and through.

THE CLOCK THAT WENT BACKWARD

Edward Page Mitchell

A row of Lombardy poplars stood in front of my great-aunt Gertrude's house, on the bank of the Sheepscot River. In personal appearance my aunt was surprisingly like one of those trees. She had the look of hopeless anemia that distinguishes them from fuller blooded sorts. She was tall, severe in outline, and extremely thin. Her habiliments clung to her. I am sure that had the gods found occasion to impose upon her the fate of Daphne she would have taken her place easily and naturally in the dismal row, as melancholy a poplar as the rest.

Some of my earliest recollections are of this venerable relative. Alive and dead she bore an important part in the events I am about to recount: events which I believe to be without parallel in the experience of mankind.

During our periodical visits of duty to Aunt Gertrude in Maine, my cousin Harry and myself were accustomed to speculate much on her age. Was she sixty, or was she six score? We had no precise information; she might have been either. The old lady was surrounded by old-fashioned things. She seemed to live altogether in the past. In her short half-hours of communicativeness, over her second cup of tea, or on the piazza where the poplars sent slim shadows directly toward the east, she used to tell us stories of her alleged ancestors. I say alleged, because we never fully believed that she had ancestors.

A genealogy is a stupid thing. Here is Aunt Gertrude's, reduced to its simplest forms:

Her great-great-grandmother (1599-1642) was a woman of

Holland who married a Puritan refugee, and sailed from Leyden to Plymouth in the ship Ann in the year of our Lord 1632. This Pilgrim mother had a daughter, Aunt Gertrude's great-grandmother (1640-1718). She came to the Eastern District of Massachusetts in the early part of the last century, and was carried off by the Indians in the Penobscot wars. Her daughter (1680-1776) lived to see these colonies free and independent, and contributed to the population of the coming republic not less than nineteen stalwart sons and comely daughters. One of the latter (1735-1802) married a Wiscasset skipper engaged in the West India trade, with whom she sailed. She was twice wrecked at sea—once on what is now Seguin Island and once on San Salvador. It was on San Salvador that Aunt Gertrude was born.

We got to be very tired of hearing this family history. Perhaps it was the constant repetition and the merciless persistency with which the above dates were driven into our young ears that made us skeptics. As I have said, we took little stock in Aunt Gertrude's ancestors. They seemed highly improbable. In our private opinion the great- grandmothers and grandmothers and so forth were pure myths, and Aunt Gertrude herself was the principal in all the adventures attributed to them, having lasted from century to century while generations of contemporaries went the way of all flesh.

On the first landing of the square stairway of the mansion loomed a tall Dutch clock. The case was more than eight feet high, of a dark red wood, not mahogany, and it was curiously inlaid with silver. No common piece of furniture was this. About a hundred years ago there flourished in the town of Brunswick a horologist named Cary, an industrious and accomplished workman. Few well-to-do houses on that part of the coast lacked a Cary timepiece. But Aunt Gertrude's clock had marked the hours and minutes of two full centuries before the Brunswick artisan was born. It was running when William the Taciturn pierced the dikes to relieve Leyden. The name of the maker, Jan Lipperdam, and the date, 1572, were still legible in broad black letters and figures reaching quite across the dial. Cary's masterpieces were plebeian and recent beside this ancient aristocrat. The jolly Dutch moon, made to exhibit the phases over a landscape of windmills and polders, was cunningly painted. A skilled hand had carved the grim ornament at the top, a death's head transfixed by a two-edged sword. Like all timepieces of the sixteenth century, it had no pendulum. A simple Van Wyck escapement governed the descent of the weights to the bottom of the tall case.

But these weights never moved. Year after year, when Harry and I returned to Maine, we found the hands of the old clock pointing to the quarter past three, as they had pointed when we first saw them. The fat moon hung perpetually in the third quarter, as motionless as the death's head above. There was a mystery about the silenced movement and the paralyzed hands. Aunt Gertrude told us that the works had never performed their functions since a bolt of lightning entered the clock; and she showed us a black hole in the side of the case near the top, with a yawning rift that extended downward for several feet. This explanation failed to satisfy us. It did not account for the sharpness of her refusal when we proposed to bring over the watchmaker from the village, or for her singular agitation once when she found Harry on a stepladder, with a borrowed key in his hand, about to test for himself the clock's suspended vitality.

One August night, after we had grown out of boyhood, I was awakened by a noise in the hallway. I shook my cousin. "Somebody's in the house," I whispered.

We crept out of our room and on to the stairs. A dim light came from below. We held breath and noiselessly descended to the second landing. Harry clutched my arm. He pointed down over the banisters, at the same time drawing me back into the shadow.

We saw a strange thing.

Aunt Gertrude stood on a chair in front of the old clock, as spectral in her white nightgown and white nightcap as one of the poplars when covered with snow. It chanced that the floor creaked slightly under our feet. She turned with a sudden movement, peering intently into the darkness, and holding a candle high toward us, so that the light was full upon her pale face. She looked many years older than when I bade her good night. For a few minutes she was motionless, except in the trembling arm that held aloft the candle. Then, evidently reassured, she placed the light upon a shelf and turned again to the clock.

We now saw the old lady take a key from behind the face and proceed to wind up the weights. We could hear her breath, quick and short. She rested a hand on either side of the case and held her face close to the dial, as if subjecting it to anxious scrutiny. In this attitude she remained for a long time. We heard her utter a sigh of relief, and she half turned toward us for a moment. I shall never forget the expression of wild joy that transfigured her features then.

The hands of the clock were moving; they were moving backward.

Aunt Gertrude put both arms around the clock and pressed her withered cheek against it. She kissed it repeatedly. She caressed it in a hundred ways, as if it had been a living and beloved thing. She fondled it and talked to it, using words which we could hear but could not understand. The hands continued to move backward.

Then she started back with a sudden cry. The clock had stopped. We saw her tall body swaying for an instant on the chair. She stretched out her arms in a convulsive gesture of terror and despair, wrenched the minute hand to its old place at a quarter past three, and fell heavily to the floor.

II

Aunt Gertrude's will left me her bank and gas stocks, real estate, railroad bonds, and city sevens, and gave Harry the clock. We thought at the time that this was a very unequal division, the more surprising because my cousin had always seemed to be the favorite. Half in seriousness we made a thorough examination of the ancient timepiece, sounding its wooden case for secret drawers, and even probing the not complicated works with a knitting needle to ascertain if our whimsical relative had bestowed there some codicil or other document changing the aspect of affairs. We discovered nothing.

There was testamentary provision for our education at the University of Leyden. We left the military school in which we had learned a little of the theory of war, and a good deal of the art of standing with our noses over our heels, and took ship without delay. The clock went with us. Before many months it was established in a corner of a room in the Breede Straat.

The fabric of Jan Lipperdam's ingenuity, thus restored to its native air, continued to tell the hour of quarter past three with its old fidelity. The author of the clock had been under the sod for nearly three hundred years. The combined skill of his successors in the craft at Leyden could make it go neither forward nor backward.

We readily picked up enough Dutch to make ourselves understood by the townspeople, the professors, and such of our eight hundred and odd fellow students as came into intercourse. This language, which looks so hard at first, is only a sort of polarized English. Puzzle over it a little while and it jumps into your comprehension like one of those simple cryptograms made by running together all the words of a sentence and then dividing in the wrong places.

The language acquired and the newness of our surroundings worn off, we settled into tolerably regular pursuits. Harry devoted himself with some assiduity to the study of sociology, with especial reference to the round-faced and not unkind maidens of Leyden. I went in for the higher metaphysics.

Outside of our respective studies, we had a common ground of unfailing interest. To our astonishment, we found that not one in twenty of the faculty or students knew or cared a sliver about the glorious history of the town, or even about the circumstances under which the university itself was founded by the Prince of Orange. In marked contrast with the general indifference was the enthusiasm of Professor Van Stopp, my chosen guide through the cloudiness of speculative philosophy.

This distinguished Hegelian was a tobacco-dried little old man, with a skullcap over features that reminded me strangely of Aunt Gertrude's. Had he been her own brother the facial resemblance could not have been closer. I told him so once, when we were together in the Stadthuis looking at the portrait of the hero of the siege, the Burgomaster Van der Werf. The professor laughed. "I will show you what is even a more extraordinary coincidence," said he; and, leading the way across the hall to the great picture of the siege, by Warmers, he pointed out the figure of a burgher participating in the defense. It was true. Van Stopp might have been the burgher's son; the burgher might have been Aunt Gertrude's father.

The professor seemed to be fond of us. We often went to his rooms in an old house in the Rapenburg Straat, one of the few houses remaining that antedate 1574. He would walk with us through the beautiful suburbs of the city, over straight roads lined with poplars that carried us back to the bank of the Sheepscot in our minds. He took us to the top of the ruined Roman tower in the center of the town, and from the same battlements from which anxious eyes three centuries ago had watched the slow approach of Admiral Boisot's fleet over the submerged polders, he pointed out the great dike of the Landscheiding, which was cut that the oceans might bring Boisot's Zealanders to raise the leaguer and feed the starving. He showed us the headquarters of the Spaniard Valdez at Leyderdorp, and told us how heaven sent a violent northwest wind on the night of the first of October, piling up the water deep where it had been shallow and sweeping the fleet on between Zoeterwoude and Zwieten up to the very walls of the fort at Lammen, the last stronghold of the besiegers and the last obstacle in the way of succor to the famishing inhabitants. Then he showed us where, on the very night before the retreat of the besieging army, a huge breach was made in the wall of Leyden, near the Cow Gate, by the Walloons from Lammen.

"Why!" cried Harry, catching fire from the eloquence of the professor's narrative, "that was the decisive moment of the siege."

The professor said nothing. He stood with his arms folded, looking intently into my cousin's eyes.

"For," continued Harry, "had that point not been watched, or had defense failed and the breach been carried by the night assault from Lammen, the town would have been burned and the people massacred under the eyes of Admiral Boisot and the fleet of relief. Who defended the breach?"

Van Stopp replied very slowly, as if weighing every word:

"History records the explosion of the mine under the city wall on the last night of the siege; it does not tell the story of the defense or give the defender's name. Yet no man that ever lived had a more tremendous charge than fate entrusted to this unknown hero. Was it chance that sent him to meet that unexpected danger? Consider some of the consequences had he failed. The fall of Leyden would have destroyed the last hope of the Prince of Orange and of the free states. The tyranny of Philip would have been reestablished. The birth of religious liberty and of self-government by the people would have been postponed, who knows for how many centuries? Who knows that there would or could have been a republic of the United States of America had there been no United Netherlands? Our University, which has given to the world Grotius, Scaliger, Arminius, and Descartes, was founded upon this hero's successful defense of the breach. We owe to him our presence here today. Nay, you owe to him your very existence. Your ancestors were of Leyden; between their lives and the butchers outside the walls he stood that night."

The little professor towered before us, a giant of enthusiasm and patriotism. Harry's eyes glistened and his cheeks reddened.

"Go home, boys," said Van Stopp, "and thank God that while the burghers of Leyden were straining their gaze toward Zoeterwoude and the fleet, there was one pair of vigilant eyes and one stout heart at the town wall just beyond the Cow Gate!"

III

The rain was splashing against the windows one evening in the autumn of our third year at Leyden, when Professor Van Stopp honored us with a visit in the Breede Straat. Never had I seen the old gentleman in such spirits. He talked incessantly. The gossip of the town, the news of Europe, science, poetry, philosophy, were in turn touched upon and treated with the same high and good humor. I sought to draw him out on Hegel, with whose chapter on the complexity and interdependency of things I was just then struggling.

"You do not grasp the return of the Itself into Itself through its Otherself?" he said smiling. "Well, you will, sometime."

Harry was silent and preoccupied. His taciturnity gradually

affected even the professor. The conversation flagged, and we sat a long while without a word. Now and then there was a flash of lightning succeeded by distant thunder.

"Your clock does not go," suddenly remarked the professor. "Does it ever go?"

"Never since we can remember," I replied. "That is, only once, and then it went backward. It was when Aunt Gertrude—"

Here I caught a warning glance from Harry. I laughed and stammered, "The clock is old and useless. It cannot be made to go."

"Only backward?" said the professor, calmly, and not appearing to notice my embarrassment. "Well, and why should not a clock go backward? Why should not Time itself turn and retrace its course?"

He seemed to be waiting for an answer. I had none to give.

"I thought you Hegelian enough," he continued, "to admit that every condition includes its own contradiction. Time is a condition, not an essential. Viewed from the Absolute, the sequence by which future follows present and present follows past is purely arbitrary. Yesterday, today, tomorrow; there is no reason in the nature of things why the order should not be tomorrow, today, yesterday."

A sharper peal of thunder interrupted the professor's speculations.

"The day is made by the planet's revolution on its axis from west to east. I fancy you can conceive conditions under which it might turn from east to west, unwinding, as it were, the revolutions of past ages. Is it so much more difficult to imagine Time unwinding itself; Time on the ebb, instead of on the flow; the past unfolding as the future recedes; the centuries countermarching; the course of events proceeding toward the Beginning and not, as now, toward the End?"

"But," I interposed, "we know that as far as we are concerned the—"

"We know!" exclaimed Van Stopp, with growing scorn. "Your intelligence has no wings. You follow in the trail of Compte and his slimy brood of creepers and crawlers. You speak with amazing assurance of your position in the universe. You seem to think that your wretched little individuality has a firm foothold in the Absolute. Yet you go to bed tonight and dream into existence men, women, children, beasts of the past or of the future. How do you know that at this moment you yourself, with all your conceit of nineteenth-century thought, are anything more than a creature of a dream of the future, dreamed, let us say, by some philosopher of the sixteenth century? How do you know that you are anything more than a creature of a dream of the past, dreamed by some Hegelian of the twenty-sixth century? How do you know, boy, that you will not vanish into the sixteenth century or 2060 the moment the dreamer awakes?"

There was no replying to this, for it was sound metaphysics. Harry yawned. I got up and went to the window. Professor Van Stopp approached the clock.

"Ah, my children," said he, "there is no fixed progress of human events. Past, present, and future are woven together in one inextricable mesh. Who shall say that this old clock is not right to go backward?"

A crash of thunder shook the house. The storm was over our heads.

When the blinding glare had passed away, Professor Van Stopp was standing upon a chair before the tall timepiece. His face looked more than ever like Aunt Gertrude's. He stood as she had stood in that last quarter of an hour when we saw her wind the clock.

The same thought struck Harry and myself.

"Hold!" we cried, as he began to wind the works. "It may be death if you—"

The professor's sallow features shone with the strange enthusiasm that had transformed Aunt Gertrude's.

"True," he said, "it may be death; but it may be the awakening. Past, present, future; all woven together! The shuttle goes to and fro, forward and back—"

He had wound the clock. The hands were whirling around the dial from right to left with inconceivable rapidity. In this whirl we ourselves seemed to be borne along. Eternities seemed to contract into minutes while lifetimes were thrown off at every tick. Van Stopp, both arms outstretched, was reeling in his chair. The house shook again under a tremendous peal of thunder. At the same instant a ball of fire, leaving a wake of sulphurous vapor and filling the room with dazzling light, passed over our heads and smote the clock. Van Stopp was prostrated. The hands ceased to revolve.

IV

The roar of the thunder sounded like heavy cannonading. The lightning's blaze appeared as the steady light of a conflagration. With our hands over our eyes, Harry and I rushed out into the night.

Under a red sky people were hurrying toward the Stadthuis. Flames in the direction of the Roman tower told us that the heart of the town was afire. The faces of those we saw were haggard and emaciated. From every side we caught disjointed phrases of complaint or despair. "Horseflesh at ten schillings the pound," said one, "and bread at sixteen schillings." "Bread indeed!" an old woman retorted: "It's eight weeks gone since I have seen a crumb." "My little grandchild, the lame one, went last night." "Do you know what Gekke Betje, the washerwoman, did? She was starving. Her babe died, and she and her man—"

A louder cannon burst cut short this revelation. We made our way on toward the citadel of the town, passing a few soldiers here and there and many burghers with grim faces under their broad-brimmed felt hats.

"There is bread plenty yonder where the gunpowder is, and full pardon, too. Valdez shot another amnesty over the walls this morning."

An excited crowd immediately surrounded the speaker. "But the fleet!" they cried.

"The fleet is grounded fast on the Greenway polder. Boisot may turn his one eye seaward for a wind till famine and pestilence have carried off every mother's son of ye, and his ark will not be a rope's length nearer. Death by plague, death by starvation, death by fire and musketry—that is what the burgomaster offers us in return for glory for himself and kingdom for Orange."

"He asks us," said a sturdy citizen, "to hold out only twenty-four hours longer, and to pray meanwhile for an ocean wind."

"Ah, yes!" sneered the first speaker. "Pray on. There is bread enough locked in Pieter Adriaanszoon van der Werf's cellar. I warrant you that is what gives him so wonderful a stomach for resisting the Most Catholic King."

A young girl, with braided yellow hair, pressed through the crowd and confronted the malcontent. "Good people," said the maiden, "do not listen to him. He is a traitor with a Spanish heart. I am Pieter's daughter. We have no bread. We ate malt cakes and rapeseed like the rest of you till that was gone. Then we stripped the green leaves from the lime trees and willows in our garden and ate them. We have eaten even the thistles and weeds that grew between the stones by the canal. The coward lies."

Nevertheless, the insinuation had its effect. The throng, now become a mob, surged off in the direction of the burgomaster's house. One ruffian raised his hand to strike the girl out of the way. In a wink the cur was under the feet of his fellows, and Harry, panting and glowing, stood at the maiden's side, shouting defiance in good English at the backs of the rapidly retreating crowd.

With the utmost frankness she put both her arms around Harry's neck and kissed him.

"Thank you," she said. "You are a hearty lad. My name is Gertruyd van der Wert."

Harry was fumbling in his vocabulary for the proper Dutch phrases, but the girl would not stay for compliments. "They mean mischief to my father"; and she hurried us through several exceedingly narrow streets into a three-cornered market place dominated by a church with two spires. "There he is," she exclaimed, "on the steps of St. Pancras."

There was a tumult in the market place. The conflagration raging beyond the church and the voices of the Spanish and Walloon cannon outside of the walls were less angry than the roar of this multitude of desperate men clamoring for the bread that a single word from their leader's lips would bring them. "Surrender to the King!" they cried, "or we will send your dead body to Lammen as Leyden's token of submission."

One tall man, taller by half a head than any of the burghers confronting him, and so dark of complexion that we wondered how he could be the father of Gertruyd, heard the threat in silence. When the burgomaster spoke, the mob listened in spite of themselves.

"What is it you ask, my friends? That we break our vow and surrender Leyden to the Spaniards? That is to devote ourselves to a fate far more horrible than starvation. I have to keep the oath! Kill me, if you will have it so. I can die only once, whether by your hands, by the enemy's, or by the hand of God. Let us starve, if we must, welcoming starvation because it comes before dishonor. Your menaces do not move me; my life is at your disposal. Here, take my sword, thrust it into my breast, and divide my flesh among you to appease your hunger. So long as I remain alive expect no surrender."

There was silence again while the mob wavered. Then there were mutterings around us. Above these rang out the clear voice of the girl whose hand Harry still held-unnecessarily, it seemed to me.

"Do you not feel the sea wind? It has come at last. To the tower! And the first man there will see by moonlight the full white sails of the prince's ships."

For several hours I scoured the streets of the town, seeking in vain my cousin and his companion; the sudden movement of the crowd toward the Roman tower had separated us. On every side I saw evidences of the terrible chastisement that had brought this stout-hearted people to the verge of despair. A man with hungry eyes chased a lean rat along the bank of the canal. A young mother, with two dead babes in her arms, sat in a doorway to which they bore the bodies of her husband and father, just killed at the walls. In the middle of a deserted street I passed unburied corpses in a pile twice as high as my head. The pestilence had been there-kinder than the Spaniard, because it held out no treacherous promises while it dealt its blows.

Toward morning the wind increased to a gale. There was no sleep in Leyden, no more talk of surrender, no longer any thought or care about defense. These words were on the lips of everybody I met: "Daylight will bring the fleet!"

Did daylight bring the fleet? History says so, but I was not a witness. I know only that before dawn the gale culminated in a violent thunderstorm, and that at the same time a muffled explosion, heavier than the thunder, shook the town. I was in the crowd that watched from the Roman Mound for the first signs of the approaching relief. The concussion shook hope out of every face. "Their mine has reached the wall!" But where? I pressed forward until I found the burgomaster, who was standing among the rest. "Quick!" I whispered. "It is beyond the Cow Gate, and this side of the Tower of Burgundy." He gave me a searching glance, and then strode away, without making any attempt to quiet the general panic. I followed close at his heels.

It was a tight run of nearly half a mile to the rampart in question. When we reached the Cow Gate this is what we saw:

A great gap, where the wall had been, opening to the swampy fields beyond: in the moat, outside and below, a confusion of upturned faces, belonging to men who struggled like demons to achieve the breach, and who now gained a few feet and now were forced back; on the shattered rampart a handful of soldiers and burghers forming a living wall where masonry had failed; perhaps a double handful of women and girls, serving stones to the defenders and boiling water in buckets, besides pitch and oil and unslaked lime, and some of them quoiting tarred and burning hoops over the necks of the Spaniards in the moat; my cousin Harry leading and directing the men; the burgomaster's daughter Gertruyd encouraging and inspiring the women.

But what attracted my attention more than anything else was the frantic activity of a little figure in black, who, with a huge ladle, was showering molten lead on the heads of the assailing party. As he turned to the bonfire and kettle which supplied him with ammunition, his features came into the full light. I gave a cry of surprise: the ladler of molten lead was Professor Van Stopp.

The burgomaster Van der Werf turned at my sudden exclamation. "Who is that?" I said. "The man at the kettle?"

"That," replied Van der Werf, "is the brother of my wife, the clockmaker Jan Lipperdam."

The affair at the breach was over almost before we had had time to grasp the situation. The Spaniards, who had overthrown the wall of brick and stone, found the living wall impregnable. They could not even maintain their position in the moat; they were driven off into the darkness. Now I felt a sharp pain in my left arm. Some stray missile must have hit me while we watched the fight.

"Who has done this thing?" demanded the burgomaster. "Who is it that has kept watch on today while the rest of us were straining fools' eyes toward tomorrow?"

Gertruyd van der Werf came forward proudly, leading my cousin. "My father," said the girl, "he has saved my life."

"That is much to me," said the burgomaster, "but it is not all. He has saved Leyden and he has saved Holland."

I was becoming dizzy. The faces around me seemed unreal. Why were we here with these people? Why did the thunder and lightning forever continue? Why did the clockmaker, Jan Lipperdam, turn always toward me the face of Professor Van Stopp? "Harry!" I said, "come back to our rooms."

But though he grasped my hand warmly his other hand still held that of the girl, and he did not move. Then nausea overcame me. My head swam, and the breach and its defenders faded from sight.

V

Three days later I sat with one arm bandaged in my accustomed seat in Van Stopp's lecture room. The place beside me was vacant.

"We hear much," said the Hegelian professor, reading from a notebook in his usual dry, hurried tone, "of the influence of the sixteenth century upon the nineteenth. No philosopher, as far as I am aware, has studied the influence of the nineteenth century upon the sixteenth. If cause produces effect, does effect never induce cause? Does the law of heredity, unlike all other laws of this universe of mind and matter, operate in one direction only? Does the descendant owe everything to the ancestor, and the ancestor nothing to the descendant? Does destiny, which may seize upon our existence, and for its own purposes bear us far into the future, never carry us back into the past?"

I went back to my rooms in the Breede Straat, where my only companion was the silent clock.

THE CONQUEST OF THE EARTH
BY THE MOON

Washington Irving

What right had the first discoverers of America to land and take possession of a country, without first gaining the consent of its inhabitants, or yielding them an adequate compensation for their territory? —a question which has withstood many fierce assaults, and has given much distress of mind to mulitudes of kind-hearted folk. And indeed, until it be totally vanquished, and put to rest, the worthy people of America can by no means enjoy the soil they inhabit, with clear right and title, and unsullied consciences.

The first source of right, by which property is acquired in a country, is DISCOVERY. For as all mankind have an equal right to any thing, which has never before been appropriated, so any nation, that discovers an uninhabited country, and takes possession thereof, is considered as enjoying full property, and absolute, unquestionable empire therein. This proposition being admitted, it follows clearly, that the Europeans who first visited America, were the real discoverers of the same; nothing being necessary to the establishment of this fact, but simply to prove that it was totally uninhabited by man. This would at first appear to be a point of some difficulty, for it is well known, that this quarter of the world abounded with certain animals, that walked erect on two feet, had something of the human countenance, uttered certain unintelligible sounds, very much like language, in short, had a marvellous resemblance to human beings.

But the zealous and enlightened fathers, who accompanied the discoverers, plainly proved (and as there were no Indian writers arose on the other side, the fact was considered as fully admitted and established) that the two-legged race of animals before mentioned were mere cannibals, detestable monsters, and many of them giants—which last description of vagrants have, since the times of Gog, Magog, and Goliath, been considered as outlaws, and have received no quarter in either history, chivalry, or song. This right of discovery being fully established, we now come to the next, which is the right acquired by CULTIVATION. Now it is notorious, that the savages knew nothing of agriculture, when first discovered by the Europeans, but lived a most vagabond, disorderly, unrighteous life—rambling from place to place, and prodigally rioting upon the spontaneous luxuries of nature, without tasking her generosity to yield them anything more; whereas it has been most unquestionably shown, that Heaven intended the earth should be ploughed and sown, and manured, and laid out into cities, and towns, and farms, and country seats, and pleasure grounds, and public gardens, all which the Indians knew nothing about—therefore, they did not improve the talents Providence had bestowed on them—therefore, they were careless stewards—therefore, they had no right to the soil—therefore, they deserved to be exterminated.

It is true, the savages might plead that they drew all the benefits from the land which their simple wants required - they found plenty of game to hunt, which, together with the roots and uncultivated fruits of the earth, furnished a sufficient variety for their frugal repasts; and that as Heaven merely designed the earth to form the abode, and satisfy the wants of man, so long as these purposes were answered, the will of Heaven was accomplished. But this only proves how undeserving they were of the blessings around them—they were so much the more savages, for not having more wants; for knowledge is in some degree an increase of desires, and it is this superiority both in the number and magnitude of his desires, that distinguishes the man from the beast

But a more irresistible right than either that I have mentioned, and one which will be the most readily admitted by my reader, provided he be blessed with bowels of charity and philanthropy, is the right acquired by CIVILIZATION. All the world knows the lamentable state in which these poor savages were found. Not only deficient in the comforts of life, but what is still worse, most piteously and unfortunately blind to the miseries of their situation. But no sooner did the benevolent inhabitants of Europe behold their sad condition than they immediately went to work to ameliorate and improve it They introduced among them rum, gin, brandy, and the other comforts of life—and it is astonishing to read how soon the poor savages learned to estimate those blessings; they likewise made known to them a thousand remedies, by which the most inveterate diseases are alleviated and healed; and that they might comprehend the benefits and enjoy the comforts of these medicines, they previously introduced among them the diseases which they were calculated to cure.

But the most important branch of civilization, and which has most strenuously been extolled by the zealous and pious fathers of the Romish Church, is the introduction of the Christian faith. It was truly a sight that might well inspire horror, to behold these savages tumbling among the dark mountains of paganism, and guilty of the most horrible ignorance of religion. It is true, they neither stole nor defrauded; they were sober, frugal, continent, and faithful to their word; but though they acted right habitually, it was all in vain, unless they acted so from precept. The newcomers, therefore, used every method to induce them to embrace and practise the true religion—except indeed that of setting them the example.

Here then are three complete and undeniable sources of right established, any one of which was more than ample to establish a property in the newly-discovered regions of America. Now, so it has happened in certain parts of this delightful quarter of the globe, that the right of discovery has been so strenuously asserted—the influence of cultivation so industriously extended, and the progress of salvation and civilization so zealously prosecuted, that, what with their attendant wars, persecutions, oppressions, diseases and other partial evils that often hang on the skirts of great benefits—the savage aborigines have, somehow or another, been utterly annihilated—and this all at once brings me to a fourth right, which is worth all the others put together: the RIGHT BY EXTERMINATION, or in other words, the RIGHT BY GUN-POWDER.

But as argument is never so well understood by us selfish mortals as when it comes home to ourselves, and as I am particularly anxious that this question should be put to rest forever, I will suppose a parallel case, by way of arousing the candid attention of my readers.

Let us suppose, then, that the inhabitants of the moon, by astonishing advancement in science, and by profound insight into that lunar philosophy, the mere flickerings of which have of late years dazzled the feeble optics, and addled the shallow brains of the good people of our globe - let us suppose, I say, that the inhabitants of the moon, by these means, had arrived at such a command of their energies, such an enviable state of perfectibility, as to control the elements, and navigate the boundless regions of space. Let us suppose a roving crew of these soaring philosophers, in the course of an aerial voyage of discovery among the stars, should chance to alight upon this outlandish planet.

And here I beg my readers will not have the uncharitableness to smile, as is too frequently the fault of volatile readers, when perusing the grave speculations of philosophers. I am far from indulging in any sportive vein at present; nor is the supposition I have been making so wild as many may deem it. It has long been a very serious and anxious question with me, and many a time and oft, in the course of my overwhelming cares and contrivances for the welfare and protection of this my native planet, have I lain awake whole nights debating in my mind, whether it were most probable we should first discover and civilize the moon, or the moon discover and civilize our globe. Neither would the prodigy of sailing in the air and cruising among the stars be a whit more astonishing and incomprehensible to us, than was the European mystery of navigating floating castles, through the world of waters, to the simple natives. We have already discovered the art of coasting along the aerial shores of our planet, by means of balloons, as the savages had of venturing along their sea coasts in canoes; and the disparity between the former, and the aerial vehicles of the philosophers from the moon, might not be greater than that between the bark canoes of the savages, and the mighty ships of their discoverers.

To return then to my supposition—let us suppose that the aerial visitants I have mentioned, possessed of vastly superior knowledge to ourselves; that is to say, possessed of superior knowledge in the art of extermination—riding on hyppogriffs—defended with impenetrable armour—armed with concentrated sunbeams, and provided with vast engines, to hurl enormous moon-stones: in short, let us suppose them, if our vanity will permit the supposition, as superior to us in knowledge, and consequently in power, as the Europeans were to the Indians, when they first discovered them. All this is very possible; it is only our self-sufficiency that makes us think otherwise; and I warrant the poor savages, before they had any knowledge of the white men, armed in all the terrors of glittering steel and tremendous gunpowder, were as perfectly convinced that they themselves were the wisest, the most virtuous, powerful, and perfect of created beings, as are, at this present moment, the lordly inhabitants of old England, the volatile populace of France, or even the self-satisfied citizens of this most enlightened republic.

Let us suppose, moreover, that the aerial voyagers, finding this planet to be nothing but a howling wilderness, inhabited by us, poor savages and wild beasts, shall take formal possession of it, in the name of his most gracious and philosophic excellency, the man in the moon. Finding, however, that their numbers are incompetent to hold it in complete subjection, on account of the ferocious barbarity of its inhabitants, they shall take our worthy President, the King of England, the Emperor of Hayti, the mighty Bonaparte, and the great King of Bantam, and returning to their native planet, shall carry them to court, as were the Indian chiefs led about as spectacles in the courts of Europe.

Then making such obeisance as the etiquette of the court requires, they shall address the puissant man in the moon, in, as near as I can conjecture, the following terms:

"Most serene and mighty Potentate, whose dominions extend as far as the eye can reach, who rideth on the Great Bear, useth the sun as a looking-glass, and maintaineth unrivalled control over tides, madmen, and sea-crabs. We thy liege subjects have just returned from a voyage of discovery, in the course of which we have landed and taken possession of that obscure little dirty planet, which thou beholdest rolling at a distance. The five uncouth monsters, which we have brought into this august presence, were once very important chiefs among their fellow savages, who are a race of beings totally destitute of the common attributes of humanity; and differing in every thing from the inhabitants of the moon, inasmuch as they carry their heads upon their shoulders, instead of under their arms—have two eyes instead of one - are utterly destitute of tails, and of a variety of unseemly complexions, particularly of horrible whiteness—instead of pea-green.

"We have moreover found these miserable savages sunk into a state of the utmost ignorance and depravity, every man shamelessly living with his own wife, and rearing his own children, instead of indulging in that community of wives enjoined by the law of nature, as expounded by the philosophers of the moon. In a word, they have scarcely a gleam of true philosophy among them, but are, in fact, utter heretics, ignoramuses, and barbarians. Taking compassion, therefore, on the sad condition of these sublunary wretches, we have endeavoured, while we remained on their planet, to introduce among them the light of reason—and the comforts of the moon. We have treated them to mouthfuls of moonshine, and draughts of nitrous oxide, which they swallowed with incredible voracity, particularly the females; and we have likewise endeavoured to instil into them the precepts of lunar philosophy. We have insisted upon their renouncing the contemptible shackles of religion and common sense, and adoring the profound, omnipotent, and all perfect energy, and the ecstatic, immutable, immovable perfection. But such was the unparalleled obstinacy of these wretched savages, that they persisted in cleaving to their wives, and adhering to their religion, and absolutely set at naught the sublime doctrines of the moon—nay, among other abominable heresies, they even went so far as blasphemously to declare, that this ineffable planet was made of nothing more nor less than green cheese!"

At these words, the great man in the moon (being a very profound philosopher) shall fall into a terrible passion, and possessing equal authority over things that do not belong to him, as did whilom his holiness the Pope, shall forthwith issue a formidable bull, specifying, "That, whereas a certain crew of Lunatics have lately discovered, and taken possession of a newly discovered planet called the earth—and that whereas it is inhabited by none but a race of two-legged animals that carry their heads on their shoulders instead of under their arms; cannot talk the lunatic language; have two eyes instead of one; are destitute of tails, and of a horrible whiteness, instead of pea-green—therefore, and for a variety of other excellent reasons, they are considered incapable of possessing any property in the planet they infest, and the right and title to it are confirmed to its original discoverers. And furthermore, the colonists who are now about to depart to the aforesaid planet are authorized and commanded to use every means to convert these infidel savages from the darkness of Christianity, and make them thorough and absolute lunatics."

In consequence of this benevolent bull, our philosophic benefactors go to work with hearty zeal. They seize upon our fertile territories, scourge us from our rightful possessions, relieve us from our wives, and when we are unreasonable enough to complain, they will turn upon us and say, "Miserable barbarians! Ungrateful wretches! Have we not come thousands of miles to improve your worthless planet; have we not fed you with moonshine; have we not intoxicated you with nitrous oxide; does not our moon give you light every night, and have you the baseness to murmur, when we claim a pitiful return for all these benefits?"

But finding that we not only persist in absolute contempt of their reasoning and disbelief in their philosophy, but even go so far as daringly to defend our property, their patience shall be exhausted, and they shall resort to their superior powers of argument; hunt us with hyppogriffs, transfix us with concentrated sunbeams, demolish our cities with moon-stones; until having, by main force, converted us to the true faith, they shall graciously permit us to exist in the torrid deserts of Arabia, or the frozen regions of Lapland, there to enjoy the charms of lunar philosophy, in much the same manner as the reformed and enlightened savages of this country are kindly suffered to inhabit the inhospitable forests of the north, or the impenetrable wildernesses of South America.

Thus, I hope, I have clearly proved, and strikingly illustrated, the right of the early colonists to the possession of this country; and thus is this gigantic question completely vanquished.

THE CONVERSATION OF EIROS AND CHARMION

Edgar Allan Poe

Πυρ σοι προσοισω.
I will bring fire to thee.

—EURIPIDES—Androm.

EIROS.
Why do you call me Eiros?

CHARMION.
So henceforward will you always be called. You must forget too, my earthly name, and speak to me as Charmion.

EIROS.
This is indeed no dream!

CHARMION.
Dreams are with us no more; but of these mysteries anon. I rejoice to see you looking life-like and rational. The film of the shadow has already passed from off your eyes. Be of heart and fear nothing. Your allotted days of stupor have expired and, to-morrow, I will myself induct you into the full joys and wonders of your novel existence.

EIROS.
True—I feel no stupor—none at all. The wild sickness and the terrible darkness have left me, and I hear no longer that mad, rushing, horrible sound, like the "voice of many waters." Yet

my senses are bewildered, Charmion, with the keenness of their perception of the new.

CHARMION.
A few days will remove all this;—but I fully understand you, and feel for you. It is now ten earthly years since I underwent what you undergo—yet the remembrance of it hangs by me still. You have now suffered all of pain, however, which you will suffer in Aidenn.

EIROS.
In Aidenn?

CHARMION.
In Aidenn.

EIROS.
Oh God!—pity me, Charmion!—I am overburthened with the majesty of all things—of the unknown now known—of the speculative Future merged in the august and certain Present.

CHARMION.
Grapple not now with such thoughts. To-morrow we will speak of this. Your mind wavers, and its agitation will find relief in the exercise of simple memories. Look not around, nor forward—but back. I am burning with anxiety to hear the details of that stupendous event which threw you among us. Tell me of it. Let us converse of familiar things, in the old familiar language of the world which has so fearfully perished.

EIROS.
Most fearfully, fearfully!—this is indeed no dream.

CHARMION.
Dreams are no more. Was I much mourned, my Eiros?

EIROS.

Mourned, Charmion?—oh deeply. To that last hour of all, there hung a cloud of intense gloom and devout sorrow over your household.

CHARMION.

And that last hour—speak of it. Remember that, beyond the naked fact of the catastrophe itself, I know nothing. When, coming out from among mankind, I passed into Night through the Grave—at that period, if I remember aright, the calamity which overwhelmed you was utterly unanticipated. But, indeed, I knew little of the speculative philosophy of the day.

EIROS.

The individual calamity was as you say entirely unanticipated; but analogous misfortunes had been long a subject of discussion with astronomers. I need scarce tell you, my friend, that, even when you left us, men had agreed to understand those passages in the most holy writings which speak of the final destruction of all things by fire, as having reference to the orb of the earth alone. But in regard to the immediate agency of the ruin, speculation had been at fault from that epoch in astronomical knowledge in which the comets were divested of the terrors of flame. The very moderate density of these bodies had been well established. They had been observed to pass among the satellites of Jupiter, without bringing about any sensible alteration either in the masses or in the orbits of these secondary planets. We had long regarded the wanderers as vapory creations of inconceivable tenuity, and as altogether incapable of doing injury to our substantial globe, even in the event of contact. But contact was not in any degree dreaded; for the elements of all the comets were accurately known. That among them we should look for the agency of the threatened fiery destruction had been for many years considered an inadmissible idea. But wonders and wild fancies had been, of late days, strangely rife among mankind; and, although it was only with a few of the ignorant that actual apprehension prevailed, upon the announcement by astronomers of a new comet, yet this announcement was generally received with I know not what of agitation and mistrust.

The elements of the strange orb were immediately calculated, and it was at once conceded by all observers, that its path, at perihelion, would bring it into very close proximity with the earth. There were two or three astronomers, of secondary note, who resolutely maintained that a contact was inevitable. I cannot very well express to you the effect of this intelligence upon the people. For a few short days they would not believe an assertion which their intellect so long employed among worldly considerations could not in any manner grasp. But the truth of a vitally important fact soon makes its way into the understanding of even the most stolid. Finally, all men saw that astronomical knowledge lied not, and they awaited the comet. Its approach was not, at first, seemingly rapid; nor was its appearance of very unusual character. It was of a dull red, and had little perceptible train. For seven or eight days we saw no material increase in its apparent diameter, and but a partial alteration in its color. Meantime, the ordinary affairs of men were discarded and all interests absorbed in a growing discussion, instituted by the philosophic, in respect to the cometary nature. Even the grossly ignorant aroused their sluggish capacities to such considerations. The learned now gave their intellect—their soul—to no such points as the allaying of fear, or to the sustenance of loved theory. They sought—they panted for right views. They groaned for perfected knowledge. Truth arose in the purity of her strength and exceeding majesty, and the wise bowed down and adored.

That material injury to our globe or to its inhabitants would result from the apprehended contact, was an opinion which hourly lost ground among the wise; and the wise were now freely permitted to rule the reason and the fancy of the crowd. It was demonstrated, that the density of the comet's nucleus was far less than that of our rarest gas; and the harmless passage of a similar visitor among the satellites of Jupiter was a point strongly insisted upon, and which served greatly to allay terror. Theologians with an earnestness fear-enkindled, dwelt upon the biblical prophecies, and expounded them to the people with a directness and simplicity of which no previous instance had been known. That the final destruction of the earth must be brought about by the agency of fire, was urged with a spirit that enforced every where conviction; and that the comets were of no fiery nature (as all men now knew) was a truth which relieved all, in a great measure, from the apprehension of the great calamity foretold. It is noticeable that the popular prejudices and vulgar errors in regard to pestilences and wars—errors which were wont to prevail upon every appearance of a comet—were now altogether unknown. As if by some sudden convulsive exertion, reason had at once hurled superstition from her throne. The feeblest intellect had derived vigor from excessive interest.

What minor evils might arise from the contact were points of elaborate question. The learned spoke of slight geological disturbances, of probable alterations in climate, and consequently in vegetation, of possible magnetic and electric influences. Many held that no visible or perceptible effect would in any manner be produced. While such discussions were going on, their subject gradually approached, growing larger in apparent diameter, and of a more brilliant lustre. Mankind grew paler as it came. All human operations were suspended.

There was an epoch in the course of the general sentiment when the comet had attained, at length, a size surpassing that of any previously recorded visitation. The people now, dismissing any lingering hope that the astronomers were wrong, experienced all the certainty of evil. The chimerical aspect of their terror was gone. The hearts of the stoutest of our race beat violently within their bosoms. A very few days sufficed, however, to merge even such feelings in sentiments more unendurable We could no longer apply to the strange orb any accustomed thoughts. Its historical attributes had disappeared. It oppressed us with a hideous novelty of emotion. We saw it not as an astronomical phenomenon in the heavens, but as an incubus upon our hearts, and a shadow upon our brains. It had taken, with inconceivable rapidity, the character of a gigantic mantle of rare flame, extending from horizon to horizon.

Yet a day, and men breathed with greater freedom. It was clear that we were already within the influence of the comet; yet we lived. We even felt an unusual elasticity of frame and vivacity of mind. The exceeding tenuity of the object of our dread was apparent; for all heavenly objects were plainly visible through it. Meantime, our vegetation had perceptibly altered; and we gained faith, from this predicted circumstance, in the foresight of the wise. A wild luxuriance of foliage, utterly unknown before, burst out upon every vegetable thing.

Yet another day—and the evil was not altogether upon us. It was now evident that its nucleus would first reach us. A wild change had come over all men; and the first sense of pain was the wild signal for general lamentation and horror. This first sense of pain lay in a rigorous constriction of the breast and lungs, and an insufferable dryness of the skin. It could not be denied that our atmosphere was radically affected; the conformation of this atmosphere and the possible modifications to which it might be subjected, were now the topics of discussion. The result of investigation sent an electric thrill of the intensest terror through the universal heart of man.

It had been long known that the air which encircled us was a compound of oxygen and nitrogen gases, in the proportion of twenty-one measures of oxygen, and seventy-nine of nitrogen in every one hundred of the atmosphere. Oxygen, which was the principle of combustion, and the vehicle of heat, was absolutely necessary to the support of animal life, and was the most powerful and energetic agent in nature. Nitrogen, on the contrary, was incapable of supporting either animal life or flame. An unnatural excess of oxygen would result, it had been ascertained in just such an elevation of the animal spirits as we had latterly experienced. It was the pursuit, the extension of the idea, which had engendered awe. What would be the result of a total extraction of the nitrogen? A combustion irresistible, all-devouring, omni-prevalent, immediate;—the entire fulfilment, in all their minute and terrible details, of the fiery and horror-inspiring denunciations of the prophecies of the Holy Book.

Why need I paint, Charmion, the now disenchained frenzy of mankind? That tenuity in the comet which had previously inspired us with hope, was now the source of the bitterness of despair. In its impalpable gaseous character we clearly perceived the consummation of Fate. Meantime a day again passed—bearing away with it the last shadow of Hope. We gasped in the rapid modification of the air. The red blood bounded tumultuously through its strict channels. A furious delirium possessed all men; and, with arms rigidly outstretched towards the threatening heavens, they trembled and shrieked aloud. But the nucleus of the destroyer was now upon us; even here in Aidenn, I shudder while I speak. Let me be brief—brief as the ruin that overwhelmed. For a moment there was a wild lurid light alone, visiting and penetrating all things. Then—let us bow down, Charmion, before the excessive majesty of the great God!—then, there came a shouting and pervading sound, as if from the mouth itself of HIM; while the whole incumbent mass of ether in which we existed, burst at once into a species of intense flame, for whose surpassing brilliancy and all-fervid heat even the angels in the high Heaven of pure knowledge have no name. Thus ended all.

IN THE YEAR 2889

Jules Verne and Michel Verne

Little though they seem to think of it, the people of this twenty-ninth century live continually in fairyland. Surfeited as they are with marvels, they are indifferent in presence of each new marvel. To them all seems natural. Could they but duly appreciate the refinements of civilization in our day; could they but compare the present with the past, and so better comprehend the advance we have made! How much fairer they would find our modern towns, with populations amounting sometimes to 10,000,000 souls; their streets 300 feet wide, their houses 1000 feet in height; with a temperature the same in all seasons; with their lines of aërial locomotion crossing the sky in every direction! If they would but picture to themselves the state of things that once existed, when through muddy streets rumbling boxes on wheels, drawn by horses—yes, by horses!—were the only means of conveyance. Think of the railroads of the olden time, and you will be able to appreciate the pneumatic tubes through which to-day one travels at the rate of 1000 miles an hour. Would not our contemporaries prize the telephone and the telephote more highly if they had not forgotten the telegraph?

Singularly enough, all these transformations rest upon principles which were perfectly familiar to our remote ancestors, but which they disregarded. Heat, for instance, is as ancient as man himself; electricity was known 3000 years ago, and steam 1100 years ago. Nay, so early as ten centuries ago it was known that the differences between the several chemical and physical forces depend on the mode of vibration of the etheric particles, which is for each specifically different. When at last the kinship of all these forces was discovered, it is simply astounding that 500 years should still have to elapse before men could analyze and describe the several modes of vibration that constitute these differences. Above all, it is singular that the mode of reproducing these forces directly from one another, and of reproducing one without the others, should have remained undiscovered till less than a hundred years ago. Nevertheless, such was the course of events, for it was not till the year 2792 that the famous Oswald Nier made this great discovery.

Truly was he a great benefactor of the human race. His admirable discovery led to many another. Hence is sprung a pleiad of inventors, its brightest star being our great Joseph Jackson. To Jackson we are indebted for those wonderful instruments the new accumulators. Some of these absorb and condense the living force contained in the sun's rays; others, the electricity stored in our globe; others again, the energy coming from whatever source, as a waterfall, a stream, the winds, etc. He, too, it was that invented the transformer, a more wonderful contrivance still, which takes the living force from the accumulator, and, on the simple pressure of a button, gives it back to space in whatever form may be desired, whether as heat, light, electricity, or mechanical force, after having first obtained from it the work required. From the day when these two instruments were contrived is to be dated the era of true progress. They have put into the hands of man a power that is almost infinite. As for their applications, they are numberless. Mitigating the rigors of winter, by giving back to the atmosphere the surplus heat stored up during the summer, they have revolutionized agriculture. By supplying motive power for aërial navigation, they have given to commerce a mighty impetus. To them we are indebted for the continuous production of electricity without batteries or dynamos, of light without combustion or incandescence, and for an unfailing supply of mechanical energy for all the needs of industry.

Yes, all these wonders have been wrought by the accumulator and the transformer. And can we not to them also trace, indirectly, this latest wonder of all, the great "Earth Chronicle" building in 253d Avenue, which was dedicated the other day? If George Washington Smith, the founder of the Manhattan "Chronicle," should come back to life to-day, what would he think were he to be told that this palace of marble and gold belongs to his remote descendant, Fritz Napoleon Smith, who, after thirty generations have come and gone, is owner of the same newspaper which his ancestor established!

For George Washington Smith's newspaper has lived generation after generation, now passing out of the family, anon coming back to it. When, 200 years ago, the political center of the United States was transferred from Washington to Centropolis, the newspaper followed the government and assumed the name of Earth Chronicle. Unfortunately, it was unable to maintain itself at the high level of its name. Pressed on all sides by rival journals of a more modern type, it was continually in danger of collapse. Twenty years ago its subscription list contained but a few hundred thousand names, and then Mr. Fritz Napoleon Smith bought it for a mere trifle, and originated telephonic journalism.

Every one is familiar with Fritz Napoleon Smith's system—a system made possible by the enormous development of telephony during the last hundred years. Instead of being printed, the Earth Chronicle is every morning spoken to subscribers, who, in interesting conversations with reporters, statesmen, and scientists, learn the news of the day. Furthermore, each subscriber owns a phonograph, and to this instrument he leaves the task of gathering the news whenever he happens not to be in a mood to listen directly himself. As for purchasers of single copies, they can at a very trifling cost learn all that is in the paper of the day at any of the innumerable phonographs set up nearly everywhere.

Fritz Napoleon Smith's innovation galvanized the old newspaper. In the course of a few years the number of subscribers grew to be 85,000,000, and Smith's wealth went on growing, till now it reaches the almost unimaginable figure of $10,000,000,000. This lucky hit has enabled him to erect his new building, a vast edifice with four *façades*, each 3,250 feet in length, over which proudly floats the hundred-starred flag of the Union. Thanks to the same lucky hit, he is to-day king of newspaperdom; indeed, he would be king of all the Americans, too, if Americans could ever accept a king. You do not believe it? Well, then, look at the plenipotentiaries of all nations and our own ministers themselves crowding about his door, entreating his counsels, begging for his approbation, imploring the aid of his all-powerful organ. Reckon up the number of scientists and artists that he supports, of inventors that he has under his pay.

Yes, a king is he. And in truth his is a royalty full of burdens. His labors are incessant, and there is no doubt at all that in earlier times any man would have succumbed under the overpowering stress of the toil which Mr. Smith has to perform. Very fortunately for him, thanks to the progress of hygiene, which, abating all the old sources of unhealthfulness, has lifted the mean of human life from 37 up to 52 years, men have stronger constitutions now than heretofore. The discovery of nutritive air is still in the future, but in the meantime men today consume food that is compounded and prepared according to scientific principles, and they breathe an atmosphere freed from the micro-organisms that formerly used to swarm in it; hence they live longer than their forefathers and know nothing of the innumerable diseases of olden times.

Nevertheless, and notwithstanding these considerations, Fritz

Napoleon Smith's mode of life may well astonish one. His iron constitution is taxed to the utmost by the heavy strain that is put upon it. Vain the attempt to estimate the amount of labor he undergoes; an example alone can give an idea of it. Let us then go about with him for one day as he attends to his multifarious concernments. What day? That matters little; it is the same every day. Let us then take at random September 25th of this present year 2889.

This morning Mr. Fritz Napoleon Smith awoke in very bad humor. His wife having left for France eight days ago, he was feeling disconsolate. Incredible though it seems, in all the ten years since their marriage, this is the first time that Mrs. Edith Smith, the professional beauty, has been so long absent from home; two or three days usually suffice for her frequent trips to Europe. The first thing that Mr. Smith does is to connect his phonotelephote, the wires of which communicate with his Paris mansion. The telephote! Here is another of the great triumphs of science in our time. The transmission of speech is an old story; the transmission of images by means of sensitive mirrors connected by wires is a thing but of yesterday. A valuable invention indeed, and Mr. Smith this morning was not niggard of blessings for the inventor, when by its aid he was able distinctly to see his wife notwithstanding the distance that separated him from her. Mrs. Smith, weary after the ball or the visit to the theater the preceding night, is still abed, though it is near noontide at Paris. She is asleep, her head sunk in the lace-covered pillows. What? She stirs? Her lips move. She is dreaming perhaps? Yes, dreaming. She is talking, pronouncing a name—his name—Fritz! The delightful vision gave a happier turn to Mr. Smith's thoughts. And now, at the call of imperative duty, light-hearted he springs from his bed and enters his mechanical dresser.

Two minutes later the machine deposited him all dressed at

the threshold of his office. The round of journalistic work was now begun. First he enters the hall of the novel-writers, a vast apartment crowned with an enormous transparent cupola. In one corner is a telephone, through which a hundred Earth Chronicle *littérateurs* in turn recount to the public in daily installments a hundred novels. Addressing one of these authors who was waiting his turn, "Capital! Capital! my dear fellow," said he, "your last story. The scene where the village maid discusses interesting philosophical problems with her lover shows your very acute power of observation. Never have the ways of country folk been better portrayed. Keep on, my dear Archibald, keep on! Since yesterday, thanks to you, there is a gain of 5000 subscribers."

"Mr. John Last," he began again, turning to a new arrival, "I am not so well pleased with your work. Your story is not a picture of life; it lacks the elements of truth. And why? Simply because you run straight on to the end; because you do not analyze. Your heroes do this thing or that from this or that motive, which you assign without ever a thought of dissecting their mental and moral natures. Our feelings, you must remember, are far more complex than all that. In real life every act is the resultant of a hundred thoughts that come and go, and these you must study, each by itself, if you would create a living character. 'But,' you will say, 'in order to note these fleeting thoughts one must know them, must be able to follow them in their capricious meanderings.' Why, any child can do that, as you know. You have simply to make use of hypnotism, electrical or human, which gives one a two-fold being, setting free the witness-personality so that it may see, understand, and remember the reasons which determine the personality that acts. Just study yourself as you live from day to day, my dear Last. Imitate your associate whom I was complimenting a moment ago. Let yourself be hypnotized. What's that? You have tried it already? Not sufficiently, then, not sufficiently!"

Mr. Smith continues his round and enters the reporters' hall. Here 1500 reporters, in their respective places, facing an equal number of telephones, are communicating to the subscribers the news of the world as gathered during the night. The organization of this matchless service has often been described. Besides his telephone, each reporter, as the reader is aware, has in front of him a set of commutators, which enable him to communicate with any desired telephotic line. Thus the subscribers not only hear the news but see the occurrences. When an incident is described that is already past, photographs of its main features are transmitted with the narrative. And there is no confusion withal. The reporters' items, just like the different stories and all the other component parts of the journal, are classified automatically according to an ingenious system, and reach the hearer in due succession. Furthermore, the hearers are free to listen only to what specially concerns them. They may at pleasure give attention to one editor and refuse it to another.

Mr. Smith next addresses one of the ten reporters in the astronomical department—a department still in the embryonic stage, but which will yet play an important part in journalism.

"Well, Cash, what's the news?"

"We have phototelegrams from Mercury, Venus, and Mars."

"Are those from Mars of any interest?"

"Yes, indeed. There is a revolution in the Central Empire."

"And what of Jupiter?" asked Mr. Smith.

"Nothing as yet. We cannot quite understand their signals. Perhaps ours do not reach them."

"That's bad," exclaimed Mr. Smith, as he hurried away, not in the best of humor, toward the hall of the scientific editors. With their heads bent down over their electric computers, thirty scientific men were absorbed in transcendental calculations. The coming of Mr. Smith was like the falling of a bomb among them.

"Well, gentlemen, what is this I hear? No answer from Jupiter? Is it always to be thus? Come, Cooley, you have been at work now twenty years on this problem, and yet—"

"True enough," replied the man addressed. "Our science of optics is still very defective, and through our mile-and-three-quarter telescopes—"

"Listen to that, Peer," broke in Mr. Smith, turning to a second scientist. "Optical science defective! Optical science is your specialty. But," he continued, again addressing William Cooley, "failing with Jupiter, are we getting any results from the moon?"

"The case is no better there."

"This time you do not lay the blame on the science of optics. The moon is immeasurably less distant than Mars, yet with Mars our communication is fully established. I presume you will not say that you lack telescopes?"

"Telescopes? O no, the trouble here is about—inhabitants!"

"That's it," added Peer.

"So, then, the moon is positively uninhabited?" asked Mr. Smith.

"At least," answered Cooley, "on the face which she presents to us. As for the opposite side, who knows?"

"Ah, the opposite side! You think, then," remarked Mr. Smith, musingly, "that if one could but—"

"Could what?"

"Why, turn the moon about-face."

"Ah, there's something in that," cried the two men at once. And indeed, so confident was their air, they seemed to have no doubt as to the possibility of success in such an undertaking.

"Meanwhile," asked Mr. Smith, after a moment's silence, "have you no news of interest to-day?"

"Indeed we have," answered Cooley. "The elements of Olympus are definitively settled. That great planet gravitates beyond Neptune at the mean distance of 11,400,799,642 miles from the sun, and to traverse its vast orbit takes 1311 years, 294 days, 12 hours, 43 minutes, 9 seconds."

"Why didn't you tell me that sooner?" cried Mr. Smith. "Now inform the reporters of this straightway. You know how eager is the curiosity of the public with regard to these astronomical questions. That news must go into to-day's issue."

Then, the two men bowing to him, Mr. Smith passed into the next hall, an enormous gallery upward of 3200 feet in length, devoted to atmospheric advertising. Every one has noticed those enormous advertisements reflected from the clouds, so large that they may be seen by the populations of whole cities or even of entire countries. This, too, is one of Mr. Fritz Napoleon Smith's ideas, and in the Earth Chronicle building a thousand projectors are constantly engaged in displaying upon the clouds these mammoth advertisements.

When Mr. Smith to-day entered the sky-advertising department, he found the operators sitting with folded arms at their motionless projectors, and inquired as to the cause of their inaction. In response, the man addressed simply pointed to the sky, which was of a pure blue. "Yes," muttered Mr. Smith, "a cloudless sky! That's too bad, but what's to be done? Shall we produce rain? That we might do, but is it of any use? What we need is clouds, not rain. Go," said he, addressing the head engineer, "go see Mr. Samuel Mark, of the meteorological division of the scientific department, and tell him for me to go to work in earnest on the question of artificial clouds. It will never do for us to be always thus at the mercy of cloudless skies!"

Mr. Smith's daily tour through the several departments of his newspaper is now finished. Next, from the advertisement hall he passes to the reception chamber, where the ambassadors accredited to the American government are awaiting him, desirous of having a word of counsel or advice from the all-powerful editor. A discussion was going on when he entered. "Your Excellency will pardon me," the French Ambassador was saying to the Russian, "but I see nothing in the map of Europe that requires change. 'The North for the Slavs?' Why, yes, of course; but the South for the Latins. Our common frontier, the Rhine, it seems to me, serves very well. Besides, my government, as you must know, will firmly oppose every movement, not only against Paris, our capital, or our two great prefectures, Rome and Madrid, but also against the kingdom of Jerusalem, the dominion of Saint Peter, of which France means to be the trusty defender."

"Well said!" exclaimed Mr. Smith. "How is it," he asked, turning to the Russian ambassador, "that you Russians are not content with your vast empire, the most extensive in the world, stretching from the banks of the Rhine to the Celestial Mountains and the Kara-Korum, whose shores are washed by the Frozen Ocean, the Atlantic, the Mediterranean, and the Indian Ocean? Then, what is the use of threats? Is war possible in view of modern inventions—asphyxiating shells capable of being projected a distance of 60 miles, an electric spark of 90 miles, that can at one stroke annihilate a battalion; to say nothing of the plague, the cholera, the yellow fever, that the belligerents might spread among their antagonists mutually, and which would in a few days destroy the greatest armies?"

"True," answered the Russian; "but can we do all that we wish? As for us Russians, pressed on our eastern frontier by the Chinese, we must at any cost put forth our strength for an effort toward the west."

"O, is that all? In that case," said Mr. Smith, "the thing can be arranged. I will speak to the Secretary of State about it. The attention of the Chinese government shall be called to the matter. This is not the first time that the Chinese have bothered us."

"Under these conditions, of course—" And the Russian ambassador declared himself satisfied.

"Ah, Sir John, what can I do for you?" asked Mr. Smith as he turned to the representative of the people of Great Britain, who till now had remained silent.

"A great deal," was the reply. "If the Earth Chronicle would but open a campaign on our behalf—"

"And for what object?"

"Simply for the annulment of the Act of Congress annexing to the United States the British islands."

Though, by a just turn-about of things here below, Great Britain has become a colony of the United States, the English are not yet reconciled to the situation. At regular intervals they are ever addressing to the American government vain complaints.

"A campaign against the annexation that has been an accomplished fact for 150 years!" exclaimed Mr. Smith. "How can your people suppose that I would do anything so unpatriotic?"

"We at home think that your people must now be sated. The Monroe doctrine is fully applied; the whole of America belongs to the Americans. What more do you want? Besides, we will pay for what we ask."

"Indeed!" answered Mr. Smith, without manifesting the slightest irritation. "Well, you English will ever be the same. No, no, Sir John, do not count on me for help. Give up our fairest province, Britain? Why not ask France generously to renounce possession of Africa, that magnificent colony the complete conquest of which cost her the labor of 800 years? You will be well received!"

"You decline! All is over then!" murmured the British agent sadly. "The United Kingdom falls to the share of the Americans; the Indies to that of—"

"The Russians," said Mr. Smith, completing the sentence.

"Australia—"

"Has an independent government."

"Then nothing at all remains for us!" sighed Sir John, downcast.

"Nothing?" asked Mr. Smith, laughing. "Well, now, there's Gibraltar!"

With this sally the audience ended. The clock was striking twelve, the hour of breakfast. Mr. Smith returns to his chamber. Where the bed stood in the morning a table all spread comes up through the floor. For Mr. Smith, being above all a practical man, has reduced the problem of existence to its simplest terms. For him, instead of the endless suites of apartments of the olden time, one room fitted with ingenious mechanical contrivances is enough. Here he sleeps, takes his meals, in short, lives.

He seats himself. In the mirror of the phonotelephote is seen the same chamber at Paris which appeared in it this morning. A table furnished forth is likewise in readiness here, for notwithstanding the difference of hours, Mr. Smith and his wife have arranged to take their meals simultaneously. It is delightful thus to take breakfast *tête-à-tête* with one who is 3000 miles or so away. Just now, Mrs. Smith's chamber has no occupant.

"She is late! Woman's punctuality! Progress everywhere except there!" muttered Mr. Smith as he turned the tap for the first dish. For like all wealthy folk in our day, Mr. Smith has done away with the domestic kitchen and is a subscriber to the Grand Alimentation Company, which sends through a great network of tubes to subscribers' residences all sorts of dishes, as a varied assortment is always in readiness. A subscription costs money, to be sure, but the *cuisine* is of the best, and the system has this advantage, that it does away with the pestering race of the *cordons-bleus*. Mr. Smith received and ate, all alone, the *hors-d'oeuvre*, *entrées*, *rôti*, and *legumes* that constituted the repast. He was just finishing the dessert when Mrs. Smith appeared in the mirror of the telephote.

"Why, where have you been?" asked Mr. Smith through the telephone.

"What! You are already at the dessert? Then I am late," she exclaimed, with a winsome *naïveté*. "Where have I been, you ask? Why, at my dress-maker's. The hats are just lovely this season! I suppose I forgot to note the time, and so am a little late."

"Yes, a little," growled Mr. Smith; "so little that I have already quite finished breakfast. Excuse me if I leave you now, but I must be going."

"O certainly, my dear; good-by till evening."

Smith stepped into his air-coach, which was in waiting for him at a window. "Where do you wish to go, sir?" inquired the coachman.

"Let me see; I have three hours," Mr. Smith mused. "Jack, take me to my accumulator works at Niagara."

For Mr. Smith has obtained a lease of the great falls of Niagara. For ages the energy developed by the falls went unutilized. Smith, applying Jackson's invention, now collects this energy, and lets or sells it. His visit to the works took more time than he had anticipated. It was four o'clock when he returned home, just in time for the daily audience which he grants to callers.

One readily understands how a man situated as Smith is must be beset with requests of all kinds. Now it is an inventor needing capital; again it is some visionary who comes to advocate a brilliant scheme which must surely yield millions of profit. A choice has to be made between these projects, rejecting the worthless, examining the questionable ones, accepting the meritorious. To this work Mr. Smith devotes every day two full hours.

The callers were fewer to-day than usual—only twelve of them. Of these, eight had only impracticable schemes to propose.

In fact, one of them wanted to revive painting, an art fallen into desuetude owing to the progress made in color-photography. Another, a physician, boasted that he had discovered a cure for nasal catarrh! These impracticables were dismissed in short order. Of the four projects favorably received, the first was that of a young man whose broad forehead betokened his intellectual power.

"Sir, I am a chemist," he began, "and as such I come to you."

"Well!"

"Once the elementary bodies," said the young chemist, "were held to be sixty-two in number; a hundred years ago they were reduced to ten; now only three remain irresolvable, as you are aware."

"Yes, yes."

"Well, sir, these also I will show to be composite. In a few months, a few weeks, I shall have succeeded in solving the problem. Indeed, it may take only a few days."

"And then?"

"Then, sir, I shall simply have determined the absolute. All I want is money enough to carry my research to a successful issue."

"Very well," said Mr. Smith. "And what will be the practical outcome of your discovery?"

"The practical outcome? Why, that we shall be able to produce easily all bodies whatever—stone, wood, metal, fibers—"

"And flesh and blood?" queried Mr. Smith, interrupting him. "Do you pretend that you expect to manufacture a human being out and out?"

"Why not?"

Mr. Smith advanced $100,000 to the young chemist, and engaged his services for the Earth Chronicle laboratory.

The second of the four successful applicants, starting from experiments made so long ago as the nineteenth century and again and again repeated, had conceived the idea of removing an entire city all at once from one place to another. His special project had to do with the city of Granton, situated, as everybody knows, some fifteen miles inland. He proposes to transport the city on rails and to change it into a watering-place. The profit, of course, would be enormous. Mr. Smith, captivated by the scheme, bought a half-interest in it.

"As you are aware, sir," began applicant No. 3, "by the aid of our solar and terrestrial accumulators and transformers, we are able to make all the seasons the same. I propose to do something better still. Transform into heat a portion of the surplus energy at our disposal; send this heat to the poles; then the polar regions, relieved of their snow-cap, will become a vast territory available for man's use. What think you of the scheme?"

"Leave your plans with me, and come back in a week. I will have them examined in the meantime."

Finally, the fourth announced the early solution of a weighty scientific problem. Every one will remember the bold experiment made a hundred years ago by Dr. Nathaniel Faithburn. The doctor, being a firm believer in human hibernation—in other words, in the possibility of our suspending our vital functions and of calling them into action again after a time—resolved to subject the theory to a practical test. To this end, having first made his last will and pointed out the proper method of awakening him; having also directed that his sleep was to continue a hundred years to a day from the date of his apparent death, he unhesitatingly put the theory to the proof in his own person. Reduced to the condition of a mummy, Dr. Faithburn was coffined and laid in a tomb. Time went on. September 25th, 2889, being the day set for his resurrection, it was proposed to Mr. Smith that he should permit the second part of the experiment to be performed at his residence this evening.

"Agreed. Be here at ten o'clock," answered Mr. Smith; and with that the day's audience was closed.

Left to himself, feeling tired, he lay down on an extension chair. Then, touching a knob, he established communication with the Central Concert Hall, whence our greatest *maestros* send out to subscribers their delightful successions of accords determined by recondite algebraic formulas. Night was approaching. Entranced by the harmony, forgetful of the hour, Smith did not notice that it was growing dark. It was quite dark when he was aroused by the sound of a door opening. "Who is there?" he asked, touching a commutator.

Suddenly, in consequence of the vibrations produced, the air became luminous.

"Ah! you, Doctor?"

"Yes," was the reply. "How are you?"

"I am feeling well."

"Good! Let me see your tongue. All right! Your pulse. Regular! And your appetite?"

"Only passably good."

"Yes, the stomach. There's the rub. You are over-worked. If your stomach is out of repair, it must be mended. That requires study. We must think about it."

"In the meantime," said Mr. Smith, "you will dine with me."

As in the morning, the table rose out of the floor. Again, as in the morning, the *potage*, *rôti*, *ragoûts*, and *legumes* were supplied through the food-pipes. Toward the close of the meal, phonotelephotic communication was made with Paris. Smith saw his wife, seated alone at the dinner-table, looking anything but pleased at her loneliness.

"Pardon me, my dear, for having left you alone," he said through the telephone. "I was with Dr. Wilkins."

"Ah, the good doctor!" remarked Mrs. Smith, her countenance

lighting up.

"Yes. But, pray, when are you coming home?"

"This evening."

"Very well. Do you come by tube or by air-train?"

"Oh, by tube."

"Yes; and at what hour will you arrive?"

"About eleven, I suppose."

"Eleven by Centropolis time, you mean?"

"Yes."

"Good-by, then, for a little while," said Mr. Smith as he severed communication with Paris.

Dinner over, Dr. Wilkins wished to depart. "I shall expect you at ten," said Mr Smith. "To-day, it seems, is the day for the return to life of the famous Dr. Faithburn. You did not think of it, I suppose. The awakening is to take place here in my house. You must come and see. I shall depend on your being here."

"I will come back," answered Dr. Wilkins.

Left alone, Mr. Smith busied himself with examining his accounts—a task of vast magnitude, having to do with transactions which involve a daily expenditure of upward of $800,000. Fortunately, indeed, the stupendous progress of mechanic art in modern times makes it comparatively easy. Thanks to the Piano Electro-Reckoner, the most complex calculations can be made in a few seconds. In two hours Mr. Smith completed his task. Just in time. Scarcely had he turned over the last page when Dr. Wilkins arrived. After him came the body of Dr. Faithburn, escorted by a numerous company of men of science. They commenced work at once. The casket being laid down in the middle of the room, the telephote was got in readiness. The outer world, already notified, was anxiously expectant, for the whole world could be eye-witnesses of the performance, a reporter meanwhile, like the chorus in the ancient drama, explaining it all *viva voce* through the telephone.

"They are opening the casket," he explained. "Now they are taking Faithburn out of it—a veritable mummy, yellow, hard, and dry. Strike the body and it resounds like a block of wood. They are now applying heat; now electricity. No result. These experiments are suspended for a moment while Dr. Wilkins makes an examination of the body. Dr. Wilkins, rising, declares the man to be dead. 'Dead!' exclaims every one present. 'Yes,' answers Dr. Wilkins, 'dead!' 'And how long has he been dead?' Dr. Wilkins makes another examination. 'A hundred years,' he replies."

The case stood just as the reporter said. Faithburn was dead, quite certainly dead! "Here is a method that needs improvement," remarked Mr. Smith to Dr. Wilkins, as the scientific committee on hibernation bore the casket out. "So much for that experiment. But if poor Faithburn is dead, at least he is sleeping," he continued. "I wish I could get some sleep. I am tired out, Doctor, quite tired out! Do you not think that a bath would refresh me?"

"Certainly. But you must wrap yourself up well before you go out into the hall-way. You must not expose yourself to cold."

"Hall-way? Why, Doctor, as you well know, everything is done by machinery here. It is not for me to go to the bath; the bath will come to me. Just look!" and he pressed a button. After a few seconds a faint rumbling was heard, which grew louder and louder. Suddenly the door opened, and the tub appeared.

Such, for this year of grace 2889, is the history of one day in the life of the editor of the Earth Chronicle. And the history of that one day is the history of 365 days every year, except leap-years, and then of 366 days—for as yet no means has been found of increasing the length of the terrestrial year.

THE END OF THE WORLD

Eugène Mouton

And the world will end by fire.

Of all the questions that interest humankind, none is more worthy of research than that of the destiny of the planet we inhabit. Geology and history have taught us many things about the Earth's past; we know the age of our world, within a few hundred million years or so; we know the order of development in which life progressively manifest itself and propagated over its surface; we know in which epoch humans finally arrived to sit down at the banquet that life had prepared for them, and for which it had taken several thousand years to set the table.

We know all that, or at least think we know it, which comes down to exactly the same thing—but if we are sure of our past, we are not of our future.

Humankind scarcely knows and more about the probable duration of its existence than each one of us knows about the number of years that he has yet to live:

The table is laid,
The exquisite parade,
That gives us cheer!
A toast, my dear!

All well and good—but are we on the soup, or the dessert? Who can tell us, alas, that the coffee will not be served very soon?

We go on and on, heedless of the future of the world, without ever asking ourselves whether, by chance, this frail boat that is carrying us across the ocean of infinity is not at risk of capsizing suddenly, or whether its old hull, worn away by time and impaired by the agitations of the voyage, does not have some leak though which death is filtering into its carcass—which is, of course, the very carcass of humankind—one drop at a time.

The world—which is to say, our terrestrial globe—has not always existed. It had begun, so it will end. The question is, when?

First of all, let us ask ourselves whether the world might end by virtue of an accident, a perturbation of present laws.

We cannot admit that. Such a hypothesis would, in fact, be in absolute contradiction with the opinion that we intend to sustain in this work. It is obvious, therefore, that we cannot adopt it. Any discussion is impossible if one admits the opinion that one is setting out to combat.

Thus, one point is definitely established: the Earth will not be destroyed by accident; it will end as a consequence of the continued action of the laws of its present existence. It will die, as they say, its appropriate death.

But will it die of old age? Will it die of a disease?

I have no hesitation in replying: no, it will not die of old age; yes, it will die of a disease—in consequence of excess.

I have said that the world will end as a consequence of the continued action of the laws of its present existence. It is now a matter of figuring out which, of all the agents functioning for the maintenance of the life of the terraqueous globe, is the one that will have the responsibility of destroying it someday.

I say this without hesitation: that agent is the same one to which the Earth owed is existence in the first place: heat. Heat will drink the sea; heat will eat the Earth—and this is how it will happen.

One day, with regard to the functioning of locomotives, the illustrious Stephenson asked a great English chemist what the force was that moved such machines. The chemist replied: "It's the Sun."

And, indeed, all the heat that we liberate when we burn combustible vegetable matter-wood or coal—has been stored there by the Sun; a piece of wood or coal is therefore, fundamentally, nothing but a preserve of solar radiation. The more vegetable life develops, the greater the accumulation of these preserves becomes. If a great deal is burned and a great deal created—that is to say, if cultivation and industry evolve, the storage the solar radiation absorbed by the Earth on one the hand and its liberation on the other will increase incessantly, and the Earth will become warmer in a continuous manner.

What would happen if the animal population, and the human population in its turn, followed the same progress? What would happen if considerable transformations, born of the very development of animal life on the surface of the globe, were to modify the structure of terrains, displace the basins of the seas, and reassemble humankind on continents that are both more fertile and more permeable to solar heat?

Now, that is exactly what will happen.

When one compares the world with what it once was, one is immediately struck by one fact that leaps to the eyes: the worldwide evolution of organic life. From the most elevated summits of mountains to the most profound gulfs of the sea, millions of billions of animalcules, animals, cryptogams and superior plants, have been working day and night for centuries, as have the foraminifera on which half our continents are built.

That work was going rapidly enough before the epoch when humans appeared on the Earth, but since the appearance of man it has developed with a rapidity that is accelerating every day. As long as humankind remained restricted to two or three parts of Asia, Europe and Africa, it was not noticeable, because, save for a few focal points of concentration, life in general still found it easy to pour into empty space the surplus accumulated at certain points of the civilized world; it was thus that colonization increasingly populated previously uninhabited countries innocent of all cultivation. Then commenced the first phase of the progress of life by human action: the agricultural phase.

Things moved in this direction for about six centuries, but large deposits of oil were developed, and, almost at the same time, chemistry and steam-power. The Earth then entered its industrial phase—which is only just beginning, since that was not much more than 60 years ago. But where this movement will lead us, and with what velocity we shall arrive, it is easy to presume, given that which has already happened before our eyes.

It is evident, for anyone with eyes to see, that for half a century, animals and people alike have tended to multiply, to proliferate, to pullulate in a truly disquieting proportion. More is eaten, more is drunk, silkworms are cultivated, poultry fed and cattle fattened. At the same time, planning is going on everywhere; ground has been cleared; fecund crop rotations and intensive cultures have been invented, which double the soil's yields; not content with what the earth produces, salmon at five francs a side have been sown in our rivers, and oysters at 24 sous a dozen in our gulfs.

In the meantime, enormous quantities of wine, beer and cider have been fermented; veritable rivers of eau-de-vie have been distilled, and millions of tons of oil burned—not to mention that heating equipment is improving incessantly, that more and more houses are being rendered draught-proof, and that the linen and cotton fabrics that humans employ to keep themselves warm are being fabricated more cheaply with every passing day.

To this already-sufficiently-somber picture it is necessary to add the insane developments of public education, which one can consider as a source of light and heat, for, if it does not emit them itself, it multiplies their production by giving humans the means of improving and extending their impact on nature.

This is where we are now; this is where a mere half-century of industrialism has brought us; obviously, there are, in all of this, manifest symptoms of an imminent exuberance, and one can conclude that within 100 years from now, the Earth will have developed a paunch.

Then will commence the redoubtable period in which the excess of production will lead to an excess of consumption, the excess of consumption to an excess of heat, and the excess of heat to the spontaneous combustion of the Earth and all its inhabitants.

It is not difficult to anticipate the series of phenomena that will lead the globe, by degrees, to that final catastrophe. Distressing as the depiction of these phenomena might be, I shall not hesitate to map them out, because the prevision of these facts, by enlightening future generations as to the dangers of the excesses of civilization, might perhaps serve to moderate the abuse of life and postpone the fatal final accounting by a few thousand years, or at least a few months.

This, therefore, is what will happen.

For ten centuries, everything will go progressively faster. Industry, above all, will make giant strides. To begin with, all the oil deposits will be exhausted, then all the sources of kerosene; then all the forests will be cut down; then the oxygen in the air and the hydrogen in the water will be burned directly. By that time, there will be something like a million steam-engines on the surface of the globe, averaging 1000 horse-power—the equivalent of a billion horse-power—functioning night and day.

All physical work is done by machines or animals; humans no longer do any, except for skilful gymnastics practiced solely for hygienic reasons. But while their machines incessantly vomit out torrents of manufactured products, an ever-denser host of sheep, chickens, turkeys, pigs, ducks, cows and geese emerges from their agricultural factories, all oozing fat, bleating, lowing, gobbling, quacking, bellowing, whistling and demanding consumers with loud cries!

Now, under the influence of ever more abundant and ever more succulent nutrition, the fecundity of the human and animal species is increasing from day to day. Houses rise up one floor at a time; first gardens are done away with, then courtyards. Cities, then villages, gradually begin to project lines of suburbs in every direction; soon, transversal lines connect these radii.

Movement progresses; neighboring cities begin to connect with one another. Paris annexes Saint-Germain, Versailles and then Bauvais, then Châlons, then Orléans, then Tours; Marseilles annexes Toulon, Draguignan, Nice, Carpentras, Nîmes and Montpellier; Bordeaux, Lyon and Lille share out the rest, and Paris ends up annexing Marseilles, Lyon, Lille and Bordeaux. And the same thing is happening throughout Europe, and the other four continents of the world.

But at the same time, the animal population is increasing. All useless species have disappeared; all that now remain are cattle sheep, horses and poultry. Now, to nourish all that, empty space is required for cultivation, and room is getting short.

A few terrains are then reserved for cultivation, fertilizer is piled herein, and there, lying amid grass six feet high, unprecedented species of sheep and cattle, devoid of hair, tails, feet and bones are seen rolling around, reduced by the art of husbandry to be nothing more than monstrous steaks alimented by four insatiable stomachs.

In the meantime, in the southern hemisphere, a formidable revolution is about to take place. What am I saying? Scarcely 50,000 years have gone by, and here it is, complete!

The polypers have joined all the continents together, and all the islands of the Pacific Ocean and the southern seas. America, Europe and Africa have disappeared beneath the waters of the ocean; nothing remains of them but a few islands formed by the last summits of the Alps, the Pyrenees, the buttes Montmartre, the Carpathians, the Atlas Mountains and the Cordilleras.

The human race, retreating gradually from the sea, has expanded over the incommensurable plains that the sea has abandoned, bringing its overwhelming civilization with it; already space is beginning to run out on the former continents. Here it is the final entrenchments: it is here that it will battle against the invasion of animal life. Here is where it will perish!

It is on a calcareous terrain; an enormous mass of animalized materials is incessantly converted into a chalky state; this mass, exposed to the rays of a torrid Sun, incessantly stores up new concentrations of heat, while the functioning of machines, the combustion of hearths and the development of animal heat cause the ambient temperature to rise incessantly.

And in the meantime, animal production continues to increase; there comes a time when the equilibrium breaks down; it becomes manifest that production will outstrip consumption. Then, in the Earth's crust, a sort kind of rind begins to form at first, and subsequently, an appreciable layer of irreducible detritus; the Earth is saturated with life.

Fermentation begins.

The thermometer rises, the barometer falls, the hygrometer marches toward zero. Flowers wither, leaves turn yellow, parchments curl up; everything dries out and becomes brittle. Animals shrink by virtue of the effects of heat and evaporation. Humans, in their turn, grow thin and desiccated; all temperaments melt into one—the bilious—and the last of the lymphatics offers his daughter and 100 millions in dowry to the last of the scrofulous, who has not a *sou* to his name, and who refuses out of pride.

The heat increases and the wells dry up. Water-carriers are elevated to the rank of capitalists, then millionaires, to the extent that the prince's Great Water-Carrier becomes one of the principal dignitaries of state. All the crimes and infamies that one sees committed today for a gold piece are committed for a glass of water, and Cupid himself, abandoning his quiver and arrows, replaces them with a carafe of ice-water.

In this torrid atmosphere, a lump of ice is worth 20 times its weight in diamonds. The Emperor of Australia, in a fit of mental aberration, orders a *tutti frutti* that cost an entire year's civil list. A scientist makes a colossal fortune by obtaining a hectoliter of fresh water at 45 degrees.

Streams dry up; crayfish, jostling one another tumultuously to run after the trickles of warm water that are abandoning them, change color as they go along, turning scarlet. Fish, their hearts weakening and their swim-bladders distended, let themselves drift on the currents, bellies up and fins inert.

And the human species begins to go visibly mad. Strange passions, unexpected angers, overwhelming infatuations and insane pleasures make life into a series of furious detonations—or, rather, one continuous explosion, which begins at birth and concludes with death. In a world cooked by an implacable combustion, everything is scorched, crackled, grilled and roasted, and after the water, which has evaporated, one senses the air diminishing as it becomes more rarefied.

A terrible calamity! The rivers, great and small, have disappeared; the seas are beginning to warm up, then to heat up; now they are already simmering as if over a gentle fire. First the little fish, asphyxiated, show their bellies at the surface; then come the algae, detached from the sea-bed by the heat; finally, cooked in red wine and rendering up their fat in large stains, the sharks, whales and giant squid rise up, along with the fabulous kraken and the much-contested sea serpent; and with all this fat, vegetation and fish cooked together, the steaming ocean becomes an incommensurable bouillabaisse.

A nauseating odor of cooking expands over the entire inhabited earth; it reigns there for barely a century; the ocean evaporates and leaves no other trace of its existence than fish bones scattered over desert plains...

It is the beginning of the end.

Under the triple influence of heat, asphyxia and desiccation, the human species is gradually annihilated; humans crumble and peel, falling into pieces at the slightest shock. Nothing any longer remains, to replace vegetables, but a few metallic plants that have been made to grow by irrigating them in vitriol. To slake devouring thirst, to reanimate calcined nervous systems, and to liquefy coagulating albumin, there are no liquids left but sulphuric and nitric acids.

Vain efforts.

With every breath of wind that agitates the anhydrous atmosphere, thousands of human creatures are instantaneously desiccated; the rider of his horse, the advocate at the bar, the judge on his bench, the acrobat on his rope, the seamstress at her window and the king on his throne all come to a stop, mummified.

Then comes the final day.

They are no more than 37, wandering like tinder specters in the midst of a frightful population of mummies, which gaze at them with eyes reminiscent of Corinthian grapes. And they take one another by the hand, and commence a furious round-dance, and with each rotation one of the dancers stumbles and falls down dead, with a dry sound. And when the 26th cycle is over, the survivor remains alone in front of the miserable heap in which the last debris of the human race is assembled.

He darts one last glance at the Earth; he says goodbye to it on behalf of all of us, and a tear falls from his poor scorched eyes—humankind's last tear. He catches it in his hand, drinks it, and dies, gazing at the Heavens. Pouff!

A little blue flame rises up tremulously, then two, then three, then 1000. The entire globe catches fire, burns momentarily, and goes out.

It is all over; the Earth is dead.

Bleak and icy. It rolls sadly through the silent deserts of space; and of so much beauty, so much glory, so much joy, so much love, nothing any longer remains but a little charred stone, wandering miserably through the luminous spheres of new worlds.

Goodbye, Earth! Goodbye, touching memories of our history, of our genius, of our pains and our loves! Goodbye, Nature, whose gentle and serene majesty consoled us so effectively in our suffering! Goodbye, cool and somber woods, where, during the beautiful nights of summer, by the silvery light of the Moon, the song of the nightingale was heard. Goodbye, terrible and charming creatures that guided the world with a tear or a smile, whom we called by such sweet names! Ah, since nothing more remains of you, all is truly finished: THE EARTH IS DEAD.

THE FACTS IN THE CASE OF M. VALDEMAR

Edgar Allan Poe

Of course I shall not pretend to consider it any matter for wonder, that the extraordinary case of M. Valdemar has excited discussion. It would have been a miracle had it not—especially under the circumstances. Through the desire of all parties concerned, to keep the affair from the public, at least for the present, or until we had farther opportunities for investigation—through our endeavors to effect this—a garbled or exaggerated account made its way into society, and became the source of many unpleasant misrepresentations; and, very naturally, of a great deal of disbelief.

It is now rendered necessary that I give the facts—as far as I comprehend them myself. They are, succinctly, these:

My attention, for the last three years, had been repeatedly drawn to the subject of Mesmerism; and, about nine months ago it occurred to me, quite suddenly, that in the series of experiments made hitherto, there had been a very remarkable and most unaccountable omission:—no person had as yet been mesmerized in articulo mortis. It remained to be seen, first, whether, in such condition, there existed in the patient any susceptibility to the magnetic influence; secondly, whether, if any existed, it was impaired or increased by the condition; thirdly, to what extent, or for how long a period, the encroachments of Death might be arrested by the process. There were other points to be ascertained, but these most excited my curiosity—the last in especial, from the immensely important character of its consequences.

In looking around me for some subject by whose means I might test these particulars, I was brought to think of my friend, M. Ernest Valdemar, the well-known compiler of the "Bibliotheca Forensica," and author (under the nom de plume of Issachar Marx) of the Polish versions of "Wallenstein" and "Gargantua." M. Valdemar, who has resided principally at Harlem, N.Y., since the year 1839, is (or was) particularly noticeable for the extreme spareness of his person—his lower limbs much resembling those of John Randolph; and, also, for the whiteness of his whiskers, in violent contrast to the blackness of his hair—the latter, in consequence, being very generally mistaken for a wig. His temperament was markedly nervous, and rendered him a good subject for mesmeric experiment. On two or three occasions I had put him to sleep with little difficulty, but was disappointed in other results which his peculiar constitution had naturally led me to anticipate. His will was at no period positively, or thoroughly, under my control, and in regard to clairvoyance, I could accomplish with him nothing to be relied upon. I always attributed my failure at these points to the disordered state of his health. For some months previous to my becoming acquainted with him, his physicians had declared him in a confirmed phthisis. It was his custom, indeed, to speak calmly of his approaching dissolution, as of a matter neither to be avoided nor regretted.

When the ideas to which I have alluded first occurred to me, it was of course very natural that I should think of M. Valdemar. I knew the steady philosophy of the man too well to apprehend any scruples from him; and he had no relatives in America who would be likely to interfere. I spoke to him frankly upon the subject; and, to my surprise, his interest seemed vividly excited. I say to my surprise, for, although he had always yielded his person freely to my experiments, he had never before given me any tokens of sympathy with what I did. His disease was of that character which would admit of exact calculation in respect to the epoch of its termination in death; and it was finally arranged between us that he would send for me about twenty-four hours before the period announced by his physicians as that of his decease.

It is now rather more than seven months since I received, from M. Valdemar himself, the subjoined note:

MY DEAR P—,

You may as well come now. D—and F—are agreed that I cannot hold out beyond to-morrow midnight; and I think they have hit the time very nearly.

VALDEMAR

I received this note within half an hour after it was written, and in fifteen minutes more I was in the dying man's chamber. I had not seen him for ten days, and was appalled by the fearful alteration which the brief interval had wrought in him. His face wore a leaden hue; the eyes were utterly lustreless; and the emaciation was so extreme that the skin had been broken through by the cheek-bones. His expectoration was excessive. The pulse was barely perceptible. He retained, nevertheless, in a very remarkable manner, both his mental power and a certain degree of physical strength. He spoke with distinctness—took some palliative medicines without aid—and, when I entered the room, was occupied in penciling memoranda in a pocket-book. He was propped up in the bed by pillows. Doctors D—and F—were in attendance.

After pressing Valdemar's hand, I took these gentlemen aside, and obtained from them a minute account of the patient's condition. The left lung had been for eighteen months in a semi-osseous or cartilaginous state, and was, of course, entirely useless for all purposes of vitality. The right, in its upper portion, was also partially, if not thoroughly, ossified, while the lower region was merely a mass of purulent tubercles, running one into another. Several extensive perforations existed; and, at one point, permanent adhesion to the ribs had taken place. These appearances in the right lobe were of comparatively recent date. The ossification had proceeded with very unusual rapidity; no sign of it had been discovered a month before, and the adhesion had only been observed during the three previous days. Independently of the phthisis, the patient was suspected of aneurism of the aorta; but on this point the osseous symptoms rendered an exact diagnosis impossible. It was the opinion of both physicians that M. Valdemar would die about midnight on the morrow (Sunday). It was then seven o'clock on Saturday evening.

On quitting the invalid's bed-side to hold conversation with myself, Doctors D—and F—had bidden him a final farewell. It had not been their intention to return; but, at my request, they agreed to look in upon the patient about ten the next night.

When they had gone, I spoke freely with M. Valdemar on the subject of his approaching dissolution, as well as, more particularly, of the experiment proposed. He still professed himself quite willing and even anxious to have it made, and urged me to commence it at once. A male and a female nurse were in attendance; but I did not feel myself altogether at liberty to engage in a task of this character with no more reliable witnesses than these people, in case of sudden accident, might prove. I therefore postponed operations until about eight the next night, when the arrival of a medical student with whom I had some acquaintance, (Mr. Theodore L—l,) relieved me from farther embarrassment. It had been my design, originally, to wait for the physicians; but I was induced to proceed, first, by the urgent entreaties of M. Valdemar, and secondly, by my conviction that I had not a moment to lose, as he was evidently sinking fast.

Mr. L——l was so kind as to accede to my desire that he would take notes of all that occurred, and it is from his memoranda that what I now have to relate is, for the most part, either condensed or copied verbatim.

It wanted about five minutes of eight when, taking the patient's hand, I begged him to state, as distinctly as he could, to Mr. L——l, whether he (M. Valdemar) was entirely willing that I should make the experiment of mesmerizing him in his then condition.

He replied feebly, yet quite audibly, "Yes, I wish to be. I fear you have mesmerized"—adding immediately afterwards: "I fear you have deferred it too long."

While he spoke thus, I commenced the passes which I had already found most effectual in subduing him. He was evidently influenced with the first lateral stroke of my hand across his forehead; but although I exerted all my powers, no further perceptible effect was induced until some minutes after ten o'clock, when Doctors D——and F——called, according to appointment. I explained to them, in a few words, what I designed, and as they opposed no objection, saying that the patient was already in the death agony, I proceeded without hesitation—exchanging, however, the lateral passes for downward ones, and directing my gaze entirely into the right eye of the sufferer.

By this time his pulse was imperceptible and his breathing was stertorous, and at intervals of half a minute.

This condition was nearly unaltered for a quarter of an hour. At the expiration of this period, however, a natural although a very deep sigh escaped the bosom of the dying man, and the stertorous breathing ceased—that is to say, its stertorousness was no longer apparent; the intervals were undiminished. The patient's extremities were of an icy coldness.

At five minutes before eleven I perceived unequivocal signs of the mesmeric influence. The glassy roll of the eye was changed for that expression of uneasy inward examination which is never seen except in cases of sleep-waking, and which it is quite impossible to mistake. With a few rapid lateral passes I made the lids quiver, as in incipient sleep, and with a few more I closed them altogether. I was not satisfied, however, with this, but continued the manipulations vigorously, and with the fullest exertion of the will, until I had completely stiffened the limbs of the slumberer, after placing them in a seemingly easy position. The legs were at full length; the arms were nearly so, and reposed on the bed at a moderate distance from the loin. The head was very slightly elevated.

When I had accomplished this, it was fully midnight, and I requested the gentlemen present to examine M. Valdemar's condition. After a few experiments, they admitted him to be an unusually perfect state of mesmeric trance. The curiosity of both the physicians was greatly excited. Dr. D—resolved at once to remain with the patient all night, while Dr. F—took leave with a promise to return at daybreak. Mr. L—l and the nurses remained.

We left M. Valdemar entirely undisturbed until about three o'clock in the morning, when I approached him and found him in precisely the same condition as when Dr. F—went away—that is to say, he lay in the same position; the pulse was imperceptible; the breathing was gentle (scarcely noticeable, unless through the application of a mirror to the lips); the eyes were closed naturally; and the limbs were as rigid and as cold as marble. Still, the general appearance was certainly not that of death.

As I approached M. Valdemar I made a kind of half effort to influence his right arm into pursuit of my own, as I passed the latter gently to and fro above his person. In such experiments with this patient, I had never perfectly succeeded before, and assuredly I had little thought of succeeding now; but to my astonishment, his arm very readily, although feebly, followed every direction I assigned it with mine. I determined to hazard a few words of conversation.

"M. Valdemar," I said, "are you asleep?" He made no answer, but I perceived a tremor about the lips, and was thus induced to repeat the question, again and again. At its third repetition, his whole frame was agitated by a very slight shivering; the eyelids unclosed themselves so far as to display a white line of the ball; the lips moved sluggishly, and from between them, in a barely audible whisper, issued the words:

"Yes;—asleep now. Do not wake me!—let me die so!"

I here felt the limbs and found them as rigid as ever. The right arm, as before, obeyed the direction of my hand. I questioned the sleep-waker again:

"Do you still feel pain in the breast, M. Valdemar?"

The answer now was immediate, but even less audible than before:

"No pain—I am dying."

I did not think it advisable to disturb him farther just then, and nothing more was said or done until the arrival of Dr. F—, who came a little before sunrise, and expressed unbounded astonishment at finding the patient still alive. After feeling the pulse and applying a mirror to the lips, he requested me to speak to the sleep-waker again. I did so, saying:

"M. Valdemar, do you still sleep?"

As before, some minutes elapsed ere a reply was made; and during the interval the dying man seemed to be collecting his energies to speak. At my fourth repetition of the question, he said very faintly, almost inaudibly:

"Yes; still asleep—dying."

It was now the opinion, or rather the wish, of the physicians, that M. Valdemar should be suffered to remain undisturbed in his present apparently tranquil condition, until death should supervene—and this, it was generally agreed, must now take place within a few minutes. I concluded, however, to speak to him once more, and merely repeated my previous question.

While I spoke, there came a marked change over the countenance of the sleep-waker. The eyes rolled themselves slowly open, the pupils disappearing upwardly; the skin generally assumed a cadaverous hue, resembling not so much parchment as white paper; and the circular hectic spots which, hitherto, had been strongly defined in the centre of each cheek, went out at once. I use this expression, because the suddenness of their departure put me in mind of nothing so much as the extinguishment of a candle by a puff of the breath. The upper lip, at the same time, writhed itself away from the teeth, which it had previously covered completely; while the lower jaw fell with an audible jerk, leaving the mouth widely extended, and disclosing in full view the swollen and blackened tongue. I presume that no member of the party then present had been unaccustomed to death-bed horrors; but so hideous beyond conception was the appearance of M. Valdemar at this moment, that there was a general shrinking back from the region of the bed.

I now feel that I have reached a point of this narrative at which every reader will be startled into positive disbelief. It is my business, however, simply to proceed.

There was no longer the faintest sign of vitality in M. Valdemar; and concluding him to be dead, we were consigning him to the charge of the nurses, when a strong vibratory motion was observable in the tongue. This continued for perhaps a minute. At the expiration of this period, there issued from the distended and motionless jaws a voice—such as it would be madness in me to attempt describing. There are, indeed, two or three epithets which might be considered as applicable to it in part; I might say, for example, that the sound was harsh, and broken and hollow; but the hideous whole is indescribable, for the simple reason that no similar sounds have ever jarred upon the ear of humanity. There were two particulars, nevertheless, which I thought then, and still think, might fairly be stated as characteristic of the intonation—as well adapted to convey some idea of its unearthly peculiarity. In the first place, the voice seemed to reach our ears—at least mine—from a vast distance, or from some deep cavern within the earth. In the second place, it impressed me (I fear, indeed, that it will be impossible to make myself comprehended) as gelatinous or glutinous matters impress the sense of touch.

I have spoken both of "sound" and of "voice." I mean to say that the sound was one of distinct—of even wonderfully, thrillingly distinct—syllabification. M. Valdemar spoke—obviously in reply to the question I had propounded to him a few minutes before. I had asked him, it will be remembered, if he still slept. He now said:

"Yes;—no;—I have been sleeping—and now—now—I am dead."

No person present even affected to deny, or attempted to repress, the unutterable, shuddering horror which these few words, thus uttered, were so well calculated to convey. Mr. L—l (the student) swooned. The nurses immediately left the chamber, and could not be induced to return. My own impressions I would not pretend to render intelligible to the reader. For nearly an hour, we busied ourselves, silently—without the utterance of a word—in endeavors to revive Mr. L—l. When he came to himself, we addressed ourselves again to an investigation of M. Valdemar's condition.

It remained in all respects as I have last described it, with the exception that the mirror no longer afforded evidence of respiration. An attempt to draw blood from the arm failed. I should mention, too, that this limb was no farther subject to my will. I endeavored in vain to make it follow the direction of my hand. The only real indication, indeed, of the mesmeric influence, was now found in the vibratory movement of the tongue, whenever I addressed M. Valdemar a question. He seemed to be making an effort to reply, but had no longer sufficient volition. To queries put to him by any other person than myself he seemed utterly insensible—although I endeavored to place each member of the company in mesmeric rapport with him. I believe that I have now related all that is necessary to an understanding of the sleep-waker's state at this epoch. Other nurses were procured; and at ten o'clock I left the house in company with the two physicians and Mr. L—l.

In the afternoon we all called again to see the patient. His condition remained precisely the same. We had now some discussion as to the propriety and feasibility of awakening him; but we had little difficulty in agreeing that no good purpose would be served by so doing. It was evident that, so far, death (or what is usually termed death) had been arrested by the mesmeric process. It seemed clear to us all that to awaken M. Valdemar would be merely to insure his instant, or at least his speedy, dissolution.

From this period until the close of last week—an interval of nearly seven months—we continued to make daily calls at M. Valdemar's house, accompanied, now and then, by medical and other friends. All this time the sleeper-waker remained *exactly* as I have last described him. The nurses' attentions were continual.

It was on Friday last that we finally resolved to make the experiment of awakening, or attempting to awaken him; and it is the (perhaps) unfortunate result of this latter experiment which has given rise to so much discussion in private circles—to so much of what I cannot help thinking unwarranted popular feeling.

For the purpose of relieving M. Valdemar from the mesmeric trance, I made use of the customary passes. These, for a time, were unsuccessful. The first indication of revival was afforded by a partial descent of the iris. It was observed, as especially remarkable, that this lowering of the pupil was accompanied by the profuse out-flowing of a yellowish ichor (from beneath the lids) of a pungent and highly offensive odor.

It was now suggested that I should attempt to influence the patient's arm, as heretofore. I made the attempt and failed. Dr. F—then intimated a desire to have me put a question. I did so, as follows:

"M. Valdemar, can you explain to us what are your feelings or wishes now?"

There was an instant return of the hectic circles on the cheeks; the tongue quivered, or rather rolled violently in the mouth (although the jaws and lips remained rigid as before), and at length the same hideous voice which I have already described, broke forth:

"For God's sake!—quick!—quick!—put me to sleep—or, quick!—waken me!—quick!—I say to you that I am dead!"

I was thoroughly unnerved, and for an instant remained undecided what to do. At first I made an endeavor to recompose the patient; but, failing in this through total abeyance of the will, I retraced my steps and as earnestly struggled to awaken him. In this attempt I soon saw that I should be successful—or at least I soon fancied that my success would be complete—and I am sure that all in the room were prepared to see the patient awaken.

For what really occurred, however, it is quite impossible that any human being could have been prepared.

As I rapidly made the mesmeric passes, amid ejaculations of

"dead! dead!" absolutely bursting from the tongue and not from the lips of the sufferer, his whole frame at once—within the space of a single minute, or even less, shrunk—crumbled—absolutely rotted away beneath my hands. Upon the bed, before that whole company, there lay a nearly liquid mass of loathsome—of detestable putrescence.

THE FLYING HEAD

A. Hyatt Verrill

It was indeed strange, Dr. Stokes thought, that his Indian labourers should appear so loath to dig into the mound. They worked half-heartedly, hung back, and appeared nervous and ill at ease. Dr. Stokes had excavated hundreds of burial mounds in Peru and had disinterred countless Inca and pre-Inca mummies; yet never before had the Cholos showed the least hesitation in digging into graves of their forefathers and dragging out their dessicated bodies.

When the archaeologist questioned them they merely muttered and mumbled in their native Quichua, saying something unintelligible about supay, or devil; and when at last the posts and adobe bricks marking a grave were exposed, the men demanded their pay and deserted in a body.

"Looks as if we'd have to do the rest of the work ourselves, Tom," Dr. Stokes said to his assistant.

Presently the last of the bricks were removed, and the scientist uttered an exclamation of delight as he saw the contents of the tomb. The mummy-bundle itself was magnificent with silver and gold ornaments, and grouped about it were splendid specimens of pottery.

"By Jove!" he cried as he examined one of the jars. "An entirely new motif! See here, Tom!"

Painted in black and scarlet upon the cream-coloured surface of the jar was a grotesque, winged figure resembling an owl, with a horribly fiendish expression on its almost-human face. Never before had Dr. Stokes seen anything like it, and his enthusiasm increased when he discovered that every piece of pottery in the tomb bore the same strange design.

All impatience to learn the contents of the mummy-bundle, the two men took it from the grave and packed up the pottery. Loading their discoveries into their ramshackle car, they started on the long drive to San Isidro where, in the scientist's temporary laboratory, the mummy could be unwrapped. It was late when they arrived, but so anxious was the archaeologist to learn what might be hidden under the wrappings of the mummy, that he could not wait until morning and Tom's assistance before getting at it.

With notebook at hand he began removing the layers of coarse cotton cloth, and his enthusiasm increased at the splendid robes and ornate decorations revealed beneath. Never had he seen anything to equal it! Carefully removing and labelling each of the many gold and silver ornaments, folding the delicate robes and making copious notes, Dr. Stokes chuckled with delight at the chased silver mask covering the face of the false head, and mentally preened himself on the turquoise and lapis lazuli beads.

Then, as he lifted the last of the gorgeous robes, an ejaculation of wonder came from the scientist's lips. Resting between the drawn-up knees of the mummy, and clasped in the shrunken hands, was a human head.

"By Jove!" Dr. Stokes exclaimed. "A trophy head, and a marvellously fine one at that!"

Triumphant at having made such a remarkable discovery, he stood gazing admiringly at it. The head was perfectly preserved and the eyes, apparently of some dull green, jade-like material, which had been inserted in the sockets, gave a most lifelike effect. On either side of the skull, long black hair hung from beneath a tightly fitting leather cap with long ears or tabs, and this together with the snaky locks and cold, green staring eyes, lent the mummified head a most horrible and fiendish expression. An expression of unspeakable malevolence and cruelty!

"Whoever you were, you were no beauty," Dr. Stokes muttered to himself a little grimly. "But you're a wonderful specimen, all the same."

Then, as he carefully moved the mummy's shrivelled hands and lifted the head, preparatory to placing it in a case, the scientist almost dropped the gruesome thing in his sudden astonishment. He stood there staring incredulously, dumbfounded with wonder. Attached to the fearsome head was a tiny, shrivelled body! A body no larger than that of a newly born infant, but unspeakably repulsive with its covering of dark, curly hair.

For a brief instant, his first astonishment over, Dr. Stokes thought that the dried body was that of a monkey attached to the trophy head as a decoration; but only a glance was needed to prove this surmise wrong. The body belonged to the head itself. It was the mummy of a strange, horrible freak; a being with the body of a hairy midget, barely a foot in length and with the head of a full-grown man!

Here, indeed, was a momentous discovery. Very carefully placing the unique specimen in a covered tray upon his laboratory table, Dr. Stokes switched out the lights and went to his bedroom, highly elated at the results of his latest excavations.

He was not a nervous or excitable man, and through years of disinterring and handling the earthly remains of human beings he had come to regard bones and mummies merely as specimens. He was not addicted to day-dreaming, and there was not a trace of superstition in his makeup. Otherwise his rest might have been disturbed by most unpleasant dreams; but as it was, he slept soundly until suddenly he found himself awake, fully conscious, listening for some sound which he felt sure had awakened him. Then he heard it. A rustling, scratching noise from his laboratory, followed an instant later by a crash.

"Confound those cats!" the scientist exclaimed, leaping from his bed. "Now one of the beasts has upset something."

Switching on the lights he glanced about him. Upon the table was the overturned tray, the mummy of the freak beside it, and on the floor was the cover where it had fallen.

"Damn!" Dr. Stokes exclaimed aloud. Then, to himself, "Lucky it wasn't the mummy the beast knocked off. Strange I should have forgotten to close the shutters."

Replacing the mummy in the tray, he set it upon a shelf; then armed himself with a stout stick and commenced a hunt for the offending feline. But he could find no trace of a trespassing cat. Satisfied that the creature had been frightened by the crash of the falling tray and had dashed out through the barred window, he closed the wooden shutters, switched off the light and again went to bed.

He did not know how long he had slept when he was awakened. For an instant there was no sound, nothing to have disturbed his slumbers. Then from the darkness came a soft, swishing, fluttering noise, and he felt a breath of air against his face as if some moving object had passed swiftly by.

"Bat," was his mental comment, as he fumbled for his flashlight. As the beam stabbed the darkness he caught a glimpse of a shadowy, indistinct form, two feet or more across the wings, as it flitted through the door leading to the laboratory.

"One of those big fruit-bats," he decided as he rose. "Probably that's the nuisance that knocked over the tray. I'll finish him in short order."

But there was no sign of the bat in the laboratory. Deciding that the creature had found a way out through some aperture under the eaves, Dr. Stokes resumed his interrupted slumbers and slept soundly until aroused by Tom's knocking on the outer door.

"I'll bet you sat up all night working on that mummy," Tom said, as Dr. Stokes, in dressing gown and slippers, admitted him. "Still in bed at this hour and you look all ragged out. Really, you shouldn't—"

"You're wrong, Tom,' the other interrupted. "I went to bed early enough, but I had a bad night. First a dratted cat came in—I'd forgotten to close the shutters in the laboratory; then one of those big fruit-bats, or maybe it was the bat both times. Anyway, cat or bat, the pest made a racket. Knocked over a tray on my table and—

"Great Scott, I'd forgotten you didn't know. Tom, my boy, that mummy we dug up is a most marvellous discovery! Absolutely unique. Magnificent robes and ornaments—but nothing compared to what was buried with him. Another mummy? Why, the most amazing mummy ever found in Peru! Just wait till you see it."

Anxious to witness Tom's astonishment and enthusiasm when he saw the dessicated freak, Dr. Stokes led the way to the laboratory and reached for the tray in which he had placed the mummified midget during the night. As he was on the point of lifting it down, there was an exclamation of surprise from Tom.

"Oh, I say, that is a find! What a magnificent trophy head!" Dr. Stokes wheeled. "Trophy head?" he cried. "What—" His words died on his lips and he stood staring, dumbfounded, incredulous. Resting in the lap of the mummy, just as he had first seen it, was the mummified freak! How had the thing come there? He was positive he had placed it in the tray on the shelf after the trespassing creature of the night had upset it on the table. And he was equally positive he had not replaced it in its original position. Was it possible he had walked in his sleep and, while unconscious, had replaced the shrivelled midget in the mummy's lap? Or had the incidents of the night been merely a dream?

But even so, that would not explain the matter; for he had lifted the supposed trophy head from the mummy's lap and had placed it in the tray on his table before he had retired for the night. Yes, he must have placed it there in his sleep. That was the logical explanation.

All these thoughts flashed through his brain in a fraction of a second. Then, recovering himself with a bit of an effort, he stepped forward with a simulated chuckle.

"Trophy head!" he exclaimed. "Just lift it carefully, Tom, and for heaven's sake don't drop it in your amazement."

Somewhat puzzled, his assistant gingerly lifted the gruesome green-eyed thing, and a long whistle of astonishment came from his lips.

"Good Lord!" he cried. "It's a freak! Ugh!" He shuddered. "It's a perfect horror! I'd hate like blazes to see or meet such a nightmarish thing alive. But it's a marvellous specimen—nothing like it in the world, I suppose. But what do you make of it, Doctor? Why was the other chap buried with this hobgoblin in his lap?"

"I think the explanation is simple enough," replied the scientist. "The other chap, as you term him, was unquestionably a noble of high rank—his robes and wealth of gold prove that; and undoubtedly the malformed midget was his court jester, as you might term him. According to the accounts of Francisco Pizarro, the conqueror of Peru, and his fellows, dwarfs or hunchbacks or human freaks were quite commonly kept by members of the Inca court. But I believe this is the first ever to be disinterred."

Tom had replaced the repulsive thing and was examining the other objects take from the grave and mummy-bundle.

"Gosh!" he exclaimed. "Did you notice the resemblance between these figures on the pottery and that—that beastly midget? See, Doctor, the heads are almost identical; green eyes, hair, painting and all. And the hairy body! All that horrible thing needs is a pair of wings to make the design a perfect likeness."

"Hmm. Yes, there is a striking similarity," agreed the other. "Very likely the designs were intended to portray the creature. Somewhat conventionalized, of course. Wings added for symbolism, perhaps; or possibly, in fact I should say probably, the midget was unable to walk—don't see how he could with the immense head and undeveloped legs—and the artist felt he should be given wings to make up for his handicaps. But just look at this robe, Tom, and start cataloguing the items while I get dressed and run over to Joe's for a cup of coffee."

Throughout the day the two men worked at the specimens, Tom numbering and cataloguing them while Dr. Stokes wrote minute descriptions of each. But busily occupied as he was, a corner of his brain was ceaselessly struggling to straighten out the events of the preceding night. He fought to solve the mystery as to why the mummified freak had been in the mummy's lap, in spite of the fact that he distinctly recalled having placed it on the shelf on the other side of the room.

To Dr. Stokes the only logical explanation appeared to be that he had walked in his sleep, a thing he had never done in his life before, and with the remarkable midget's mummy on his mind he had placed it where it had been found. Yet this seemingly reasonable solution of the matter did not entirely satisfy him.

As there was no other possible way to account for it he finally dismissed the matter for the time being, while he took time off for a good dinner and a pleasant evening at the home of the alcalde, the local mayor. But when he went to bed his thoughts reverted once more to the events of the previous night. But not for long. He was very sleepy. This time he flattered himself that no cats or bats would disturb him, for he had carefully closed and barred the shutters. Presently he was sleeping soundly.

Dr. Stokes awoke from a dreamless slumber to find himself tense, expectant, listening. Something, he couldn't say what, made him feel nervous, apprehensive. Could it be, he wondered, that there had been a slight earthquake shock? Then once again he heard it—the same soft rustling sound of the night before! Something was moving about near him, flitting back and forth in the darkness; and an involuntary shudder passed over the scientist.

But the next instant he was himself again. It was only that confounded fruit-bat, or another one of its tribe. But how the deuce did the thing get in? Probably never went out, Dr. Stokes decided. No doubt the beast had its hideout somewhere in the roof and was trying to get out, but found it impossible with the windows shuttered. Well, he would soon put an end to that nuisance.

Rising, Dr. Stokes fumbled for a stout stick. Grasping the club he snapped on his flashlight and aimed a vicious blow at a flapping shadow. But the weapon swished harmlessly through the air, and the flitting creature vanished in the darkness of the doorway. Intent on knocking the thing down, the scientist shut the door and, flashing his light about the hallway, entered the laboratory and closed the door behind him.

As he did so there was a swish of air past his head. He involuntarily ducked, and the flying creature swept by within an inch of his face. Wheeling, the scientist struck blindly. There was a soft thud, an agonized cry so filled with mingled pain and anger that Dr. Stokes shuddered as he heard the thing striking the floor.

"Got him!" exulted the scientist, and swung the beam of his flashlight in the direction whence had come the sound of the creature's fall. The torch almost dropped from his hand when he staggered back wide-eyed, chills running up and down his spine. On the floor, staring up at him with green eyes ablaze with fiendish fury and hatred, was the horrible mummified freak! The thing was alive!

It was impossible, incredible; and for a brief instant Dr. Stokes felt that he must be in the grip of a horrible nightmare. He must break this unholy spell! Controlling his shaken nerves with a tremendous effort, the scientist raised his stick for the fatal blow. Keeping his light focused upon the fearsome thing on the floor, he took a step forward.

A scream of abject terror came from the man's lips. He sprang back, the stick clattering from his hand. Chilled with horror he stood there, powerless to move. The awful head with its diminutive hairy body was advancing! With terror clutching at his heart, icy cold, while beads of cold perspiration oozed from his forehead, he stood transfixed, powerless to move as if hypnotized by the harsh, malignant green eyes in that demoniacal skull. Dr. Stokes saw the long tabs of the thing's leather cap tremble and— No, not the flaps of the cap but wings—soft, leathery wings that were attached to the nightmarish head of the apparition!

Yet even in his mad, helpless terror the scientist noticed with vast relief that one of the thing's batlike wings was injured, torn, and useless, where the stick had struck. And so this spawn of hell, this awful being, this mummified freak that by some supernatural means had come to life, could no longer fly. But it was creeping toward its attacker!

Uttering strange, uncanny, gibbering sounds, its lips drawn back above sharp, pointed teeth, its baleful green eyes fixed upon the scientist, the loathsome, hideous monstrosity was dragging its attenuated body across the floor; pushing itself forward by its shrunken legs, balancing its great head by its batlike wings and tiny hands; moving slowly, inch by inch, but steadily toward the spot where Dr. Stokes stood back against the wall, gasping, choking, dumb with utter horror.

He strove with all his will power to move, to escape, but not a muscle responded. If only he could recover his stick, could crush this devilish spawn of the nether world to a shapeless pulp! But the scientist's limbs, his arms were nerveless, limp, incapable of control. Within two feet of where he stood, the stick rested where it had fallen from his shaking hand.

At his feet, the torch lay on the floor, its beam still directed at the malignant, awful monstrosity that was moving nearer and nearer. Dr. Stokes, however, was paralyzed, frozen into immobility with hypnotic terror. Yet his brain was active, his mind receptive, functioning sanely enough. Or was he sane? he asked himself.

Did the thing actually exist—or was it but the figment of a disordered mind? His common-sense scientific brain told him it could not be real, that a mummy thousands of years old could not be endowed with life, that a semi-human freak could not possess wings and fly. It was too preposterous, too supernatural to be real. Yet Dr. Stokes' staring, horror-filled eyes contradicted the arguments in his brain. The awful thing was there, and it was alive, and every moment it was dragging its repulsive, fiendish being nearer; a ghastly, demoniacal thing conjured by some black magic back to life.

Nearer and nearer it crept; in the silence of the room, the scraping, shuffling sounds of the thing's movements seemed loud and distinct. It reached the fallen stick and, in a sudden mad fury seized it in its teeth and shook it as a terrier worries a rat, mouthing and growling, biting splinters from the hard, tough wood. Then, dropping the inanimate club, the ghastly thing gathered itself together, bared its needle-pointed teeth and, with a sudden harsh flap of its wings, leaped at the man!

With a shriek of abject terror the scientist came to life and sprang aside. He stepped upon the torch, reeled backward and fell heavily to the floor as the shattered light plunged the room into inky blackness. As he fell he felt the loathsome, horrible thing strike his leg, and there was a sharp stab of pain as the strong keen teeth of the devilish creature bit into his flesh.

Then he was struggling, fighting madly, clawing and striking with his fists at the misshapen, incredible, indescribably vile semi-human monster that clung to him like a leech. Heedless of the frantic blows rained upon it, the thing was crawling, dragging its way across the scientist's chest, closer and closer to his sweating throat and face.

Dr. Stokes' clutching hands grasped a leathery wing, only to release their grip as fanglike teeth bit deeply into his wrists. Screaming with deadly fear, he saw the thing's eyes glowing like green fire in the blackness. In the scientist's nostrils was the musty, fetid odour of ancient, ravaged tombs. His tortured nerves gave way at last. Something seemed to snap within his mind and he sank back limp, inert, unconscious...

There was no response to Tom's repeated knocking on the doctor's door. Wondering, thinking it most strange that his employer should be out so early or should be sleeping so soundly, and vaguely troubled, the young assistant walked around the house. The bedroom windows were tightly shuttered, but to Tom's surprise the shutters on the laboratory windows were ajar. Raising himself on tiptoe he peered between the iron bars into the room, only to reel back, feeling faint and nauseated at what he had seen.

Lying upon the laboratory floor in a great pool of blood was the body of the scientist, an expression of unspeakable terror in his dead, glassy eyes, his head twisted horribly to one side, exposing a fearful, ragged gash in his throat.

Trembling in every limb, Tom rushed to the office of the alcalde and in scarcely coherent Spanish babbled that Dr. Stokes had been brutally murdered. Battering down the heavy doors, the native police, with the alcalde and Tom, dashed through the short hallway to the laboratory.

"Madre de Dios!" exclaimed the first man to reach the room, and crossed himself. "What devil's work is this?"

Steeling himself for the effort, Tom bent over the forlorn body of Dr. Stokes.

"Some savage wild beast did this," he declared, his voice shaky. "It must have entered by the open window. Perhaps it is still here."

Whipping out their revolvers the police began searching the room, but no trace of another living thing could be found.

The alcalde shook his head. "Strange things happen," he said in lowered tones. "The Señor Stokes desecrated the tombs of the ancient ones. Perchance"—he glanced furtively about him—"perchance it was no beast, no creature of flesh and blood that destroyed him. The Indios tell of unholy things, Señor. They tell of captive devils buried with the ancient dead to protect their bodies and their treasures from being disturbed. Perchance—quien sabe?"

"Nonsense!" exclaimed Tom. "You may believe in such occult things, but I don't!"

Involuntarily Tom glanced at the mummy as he spoke. A half-suppressed ejaculation came from his lips and a cold chill ran along his spine. Resting between the knees of the mummy was the horrible mummified freak, its jade-green eyes cold and expressionless—yet with its dead, shrunken face and lips smeared with a moist, dull red!

Whether the alcalde or the police had noticed it, Tom could not tell. He hardly thought so. Stepping forward, breathing hard and holding his nerves under iron control, he gently drew a corner of a robe and covered the horrible, gruesome thing.

Doctor Stokes' mutilated body had been removed and

was resting in its casket, awaiting the aeroplane which had been summoned to carry it to Lima, when Tom re-entered the laboratory. Clenching his teeth, summoning all his self-control, mentally cursing himself for a credulous fool, he hastily gathered the robes and ornaments taken from the mummy, flung them over the shrivelled, dessicated monstrosity, covered it with a blanket and, trembling despite himself, loaded the unwieldy bundle in the ramshackle car. Several hours later he returned, the car empty, with an indefinable feeling of vast relief.

Far out in the desert, amid the crumbling ruins of the forgotten pre-Inca city, the mummy again rested in its ancient tomb.

THE FLYING MAN

H.G. Wells

The Ethnologist looked at the *bhimraj* feather thoughtfully. "They seemed loth to part with it," he said.

"It is sacred to the Chiefs," said the lieutenant; "just as yellow silk, you know, is sacred to the Chinese Emperor."

The Ethnologist did not answer. He hesitated. Then opening the topic abruptly, "What on earth is this cock-and-bull story they have of a flying man?"

The lieutenant smiled faintly. "What did they tell you?"

"I see," said the Ethnologist, "that you know of your fame."

The lieutenant rolled himself a cigarette. "I don't mind hearing about it once more. How does it stand at present?"

"It's so confoundedly childish," said the Ethnologist, becoming irritated. "How did you play it off upon them?"

The lieutenant made no answer, but lounged back in his folding-chair, still smiling.

"Here am I, come four hundred miles out of my way to get what is left of the folk-lore of these people, before they are utterly demoralised by missionaries and the military, and all I find are a lot of impossible legends about a sandy-haired scrub of an infantry lieutenant. How he is invulnerable—how he can jump over elephants—how he can fly. That's the toughest nut. One old gentleman described your wings, said they had black plumage and were not quite as long as a mule. Said he often saw you by moonlight hovering over the crests out towards the Shendu country.—Confound it, man!"

The lieutenant laughed cheerfully. "Go on," he said. "Go on."

The Ethnologist did. At last he wearied. "To trade so," he said, "on these unsophisticated children of the mountains. How could you bring yourself to do it, man?"

"I'm sorry," said the lieutenant, "but truly the thing was forced upon me. I can assure you I was driven to it. And at the time I had not the faintest idea of how the Chin imagination would take it. Or curiosity. I can only plead it was an indiscretion and not malice that made me replace the folk-lore by a new legend. But as you seem aggrieved, I will try and explain the business to you.

"It was in the time of the last Lushai expedition but one, and Walters thought these people you have been visiting were friendly. So, with an airy confidence in my capacity for taking care of myself, he sent me up the gorge—fourteen miles of it—with three of the Derbyshire men and half a dozen Sepoys, two mules, and his blessing, to see what popular feeling was like at that village you visited. A force of ten—not counting the mules—fourteen miles, and during a war! You saw the road?"

"*Road!*" said the Ethnologist.

"It's better now than it was. When we went up we had to wade in the river for a mile where the valley narrows, with a smart stream frothing round our knees and the stones as slippery as ice. There it was I dropped my rifle. Afterwards the Sappers blasted the cliff with dynamite and made the convenient way you came by. Then below, where those very high cliffs come, we had to keep on dodging across the river—I should say we crossed it a dozen times in a couple of miles.

"We got in sight of the place early the next morning. You know how it lies, on a spur halfway between the big hills, and as we began to appreciate how wickedly quiet the village lay under the sunlight, we came to a stop to consider.

"At that they fired a lump of filed brass idol at us, just by way of a welcome. It came twanging down the slope to the right of us where the boulders are, missed my shoulder by an inch or so, and plugged the mule that carried all the provisions and utensils. I never heard such a death-rattle before or since. And at that we became aware of a number of gentlemen carrying matchlocks, and dressed in things like plaid dusters, dodging about along the neck between the village and the crest to the east.

"'Right about face,' I said. 'Not too close together.'

"And with that encouragement my expedition of ten men came round and set off at a smart trot down the valley again hitherward. We did not wait to save anything our dead had carried, but we kept the second mule with us—he carried my tent and some other rubbish—out of a feeling of friendship.

"So ended the battle—ingloriously. Glancing back, I saw the valley dotted with the victors, shouting and firing at us. But no one was hit. These Chins and their guns are very little good except at a sitting shot. They will sit and finick over a boulder for hours taking aim, and when they fire running it is chiefly for stage effect. Hooker, one of the Derbyshire men, fancied himself rather with the rifle, and stopped behind for half a minute to try his luck as we turned the bend. But he got nothing.

"I'm not a Xenophon to spin much of a yarn about my retreating army. We had to pull the enemy up twice in the next two miles when he became a bit pressing, by exchanging shots with him, but it was a fairly monotonous affair—hard breathing chiefly—until we got near the place where the hills run in towards the river and pinch the valley into a gorge. And there we very luckily caught a glimpse of half a dozen round black heads coming slanting-ways over the hill to the left of us—the east that is—and almost parallel with us.

"At that I called a halt. 'Look here,' says I to Hooker and the other Englishmen; 'what are we to do now?' and I pointed to the heads.

"'Headed orf, or I'm a nigger,' said one of the men.

"'We shall be,' said another. 'You know the Chin way, George?'

"'They can pot every one of us at fifty yards,' says Hooker, 'in the place where the river is narrow. It's just suicide to go on down.'

"I looked at the hill to the right of us. It grew steeper lower down the valley, but it still seemed climbable. And all the Chins we had seen hitherto had been on the other side of the stream.

"'It's that or stopping,' says one of the Sepoys.

"So we started slanting up the hill. There was something faintly suggestive of a road running obliquely up the face of it, and that we followed. Some Chins presently came into view up the valley, and I heard some shots. Then I saw one of the Sepoys was sitting down about thirty yards below us. He had simply sat down without a word, apparently not wishing to give trouble. At that I called a halt again; I told Hooker to try another shot, and went back and found the man was hit in the leg. I took him up, carried him along to put him on the mule—already pretty well laden with the tent and other things which we had no time to take off. When I got up to the rest with him, Hooker had his empty Martini in his hand, and was grinning and pointing to a motionless black spot up the valley. All the rest of the Chins were behind boulders or back round the bend. 'Five hundred yards,' says Hooker, 'if an inch. And I'll swear I hit him in the head.'

"I told him to go and do it again, and with that we went on again.

"Now the hillside kept getting steeper as we pushed on, and the road we were following more and more of a shelf. At last it was mere cliff above and below us. 'It's the best road I have seen yet in Chin Lushai land,' said I to encourage the men, though

I had a fear of what was coming.

"And in a few minutes the way bent round a corner of the cliff. Then, finis! the ledge came to an end.

"As soon as he grasped the position one of the Derbyshire men fell a-swearing at the trap we had fallen into. The Sepoys halted quietly. Hooker grunted and reloaded, and went back to the bend.

"Then two of the Sepoy chaps helped their comrade down and began to unload the mule.

"Now, when I came to look about me, I began to think we had not been so very unfortunate after all. We were on a shelf perhaps ten yards across it at widest. Above it the cliff projected so that we could not be shot down upon, and below was an almost sheer precipice of perhaps two or three hundred feet. Lying down we were invisible to anyone across the ravine. The only approach was along the ledge, and on that one man was as good as a host. We were in a natural stronghold, with only one disadvantage, our sole provision against hunger and thirst was one live mule. Still we were at most eight or nine miles from the main expedition, and no doubt, after a day or so, they would send up after us if we did not return.

"After a day or so..."

The lieutenant paused. "Ever been thirsty, Graham?"

"Not that kind," said the Ethnologist.

"H'm. We had the whole of that day, the night, and the next day of it, and only a trifle of dew we wrung out of our clothes and the tent. And below us was the river going giggle, giggle, round a rock in mid stream. I never knew such a barrenness of incident, or such a quantity of sensation. The sun might have had Joshua's command still upon it for all the motion one could see; and it blazed like a near furnace. Towards the evening of the first day one of the Derbyshire men said something—nobody heard what—and went off round the bend of the cliff. We heard shots, and when Hooker looked round the corner he was gone. And in the morning the Sepoy whose leg was shot was in delirium, and jumped or fell over the cliff. Then we took the mule and shot it, and that must needs go over the cliff too in its last struggles, leaving eight of us.

"We could see the body of the Sepoy down below, with the head in the water. He was lying face downwards, and so far as I could make out was scarcely smashed at all. Badly as the Chins might covet his head, they had the sense to leave it alone until the darkness came.

"At first we talked of all the chances there were of the main body hearing the firing, and reckoned whether they would begin to miss us, and all that kind of thing, but we dried up as the evening came on. The Sepoys played games with bits of stone among themselves, and afterwards told stories. The night was rather chilly. The second day nobody spoke. Our lips were black and our throats afire, and we lay about on the ledge and glared at one another. Perhaps it's as well we kept our thoughts to ourselves. One of the British soldiers began writing some blasphemous rot on the rock with a bit of pipeclay, about his last dying will, until I stopped it. As I looked over the edge down into the valley and saw the river rippling I was nearly tempted to go after the Sepoy. It seemed a pleasant and desirable thing to go rushing down through the air with something to drink—or no more thirst at any rate—at the bottom. I remembered in time, though, that I was the officer in command, and my duty to set a good example, and that kept me from any such foolishness.

"Yet, thinking of that, put an idea into my head. I got up and looked at the tent and tent ropes, and wondered why I had not thought of it before. Then I came and peered over the cliff again. This time the height seemed greater and the pose of the

Sepoy rather more painful. But it was that or nothing. And to cut it short, I parachuted.

"I got a big circle of canvas out of the tent, about three times the size of that table-cover, and plugged the hole in the centre, and I tied eight ropes round it to meet in the middle and make a parachute. The other chaps lay about and watched me as though they thought it was a new kind of delirium. Then I explained my notion to the two British soldiers and how I meant to do it, and as soon as the short dusk had darkened into night, I risked it. They held the thing high up, and I took a run the whole length of the ledge. The thing filled with air like a sail, but at the edge I will confess I funked and pulled up.

"As soon as I stopped I was ashamed of myself—as well I might be in front of privates—and went back and started again. Off I jumped this time—with a kind of sob, I remember—clean into the air, with the big white sail bellying out above me.

"I must have thought at a frightful pace. It seemed a long time before I was sure that the thing meant to keep steady. At first it heeled sideways. Then I noticed the face of the rock which seemed to be streaming up past me, and me motionless. Then I looked down and saw in the darkness the river and the dead Sepoy rushing up towards me. But in the indistinct light I also saw three Chins, seemingly aghast at the sight of me, and that the Sepoy was decapitated. At that I wanted to go back again.

"Then my boot was in the mouth of one, and in a moment he and I were in a heap with the canvas fluttering down on the top of us. I fancy I dashed out his brains with my foot. I expected nothing more than to be brained myself by the other two, but the poor heathen had never heard of Baldwin, and incontinently bolted.

"I struggled out of the tangle of dead Chin and canvas, and looked round. About ten paces off lay the head of the Sepoy staring in the moonlight. Then I saw the water and went and drank. There wasn't a sound in the world but the footsteps of the departing Chins, a faint shout from above, and the gluck of the water. So soon as I had drunk my full I started off down the river.

"That about ends the explanation of the flying man story. I never met a soul the whole eight miles of the way. I got to Walters' camp by ten o'clock, and a born idiot of a sentinel had the cheek to fire at me as I came trotting out of the darkness. So soon as I had hammered my story into Winter's thick skull, about fifty men started up the valley to clear the Chins out and get our men down. But for my own part I had too good a thirst to provoke it by going with them.

"You have heard what kind of a yarn the Chins made of it. Wings as long as a mule, eh?—And black feathers! The gay lieutenant bird! Well, well."

The lieutenant meditated cheerfully for a moment. Then he added, "You would scarcely credit it, but when they got to the ridge at last, they found two more of the Sepoys had jumped over."

"The rest were all right?" asked the Ethnologist.

"Yes," said the lieutenant; "the rest were all right, barring a certain thirst, you know."

And at the memory he helped himself to soda and whisky again.

THE TRIUMPHS OF A TAXIDERMIST

H.G. Wells

Here are some of the secrets of taxidermy. They were told me by the taxidermist in a mood of elation. He told me them in the time between the first glass of whisky and the fourth, when a man is no longer cautious and yet not drunk. We sat in his den together; his library it was, his sitting and his eating-room—separated by a bead curtain, so far as the sense of sight went, from the noisome den where he plied his trade.

He sat on a deck chair, and when he was not tapping refractory bits of coal with them, he kept his feet—on which he wore, after the manner of sandals, the holy relics of a pair of carpet slippers—out of the way upon the mantel-piece, among the glass eyes. And his trousers, by-the-by—though they have nothing to do with his triumphs—were a most horrible yellow plaid, such as they made when our fathers wore side-whiskers and there were crinolines in the land. Further, his hair was black, his face rosy, and his eye a fiery brown; and his coat was chiefly of grease upon a basis of velveteen. And his pipe had a bowl of china showing the Graces, and his spectacles were always askew, the left eye glaring nakedly at you, small and penetrating; the right, seen through a glass darkly, magnified and mild. Thus his discourse ran: "There never was a man who could stuff like me, Bellows, never. I have stuffed elephants and I have stuffed moths, and the things have looked all the livelier and better for it. And I have stuffed human beings—chiefly amateur ornithologists. But I stuffed a nigger once.

"No, there is no law against it. I made him with all his fingers out and used him as a hat-rack, but that fool Homersby got up a quarrel with him late one night and spoilt him. That was before your time. It is hard to get skins, or I would have another.

"Unpleasant? I don't see it. Seems to me taxidermy is a promising third course to burial or cremation. You could keep all your dear ones by you. Bric-à-brac of that sort stuck about the house would be as good as most company, and much less expensive. You might have them fitted up with clockwork to do things.

"Of course they would have to be varnished, but they need not shine more than lots of people do naturally. Old Manningtree's bald head... Anyhow, you could talk to them without interruption. Even aunts. There is a great future before taxidermy, depend upon it. There is fossils again..."

He suddenly became silent.

"No, I don't think I ought to tell you that." He sucked at his pipe thoughtfully. "Thanks, yes. Not too much water.

"Of course, what I tell you now will go no further. You know I have made some dodos and a great auk? No! Evidently you are an amateur at taxidermy. My dear fellow, half the great auks in the world are about as genuine as the handkerchief of Saint Veronica, as the Holy Coat of Treves. We make 'em of grebes' feathers and the like. And the great auk's eggs too!"

"Good heavens!"

"Yes, we make them out of fine porcelain. I tell you it is worth while. They fetch—one fetched 300 only the other day. That one was really genuine, I believe, but of course one is never certain. It is very fine work, and afterwards you have to get them dusty, for no one who owns one of these precious eggs has ever the temerity to clean the thing. That's the beauty of the business. Even if they suspect an egg they do not like to examine it too closely. It's such brittle capital at the best.

"You did not know that taxidermy rose to heights like that. My boy, it has risen higher. I have rivalled the hands of Nature herself. One of the *genuine* great auks"—his voice fell to a whisper—"one of the *genuine* great auks *was made by me*."

"No. You must study ornithology, and find out which it is yourself. And what is more, I have been approached by a syndicate of dealers to stock one of the unexplored skerries to the north of Iceland with specimens. I may—some day. But I have another little thing in hand just now. Ever heard of the dinornis?

"It is one of those big birds recently extinct in New Zealand. 'Moa' is its common name, so called because extinct: there is no moa now. See? Well, they have got bones of it, and from some of the marshes even feathers and dried bits of skin. Now, I am going to—well, there is no need to make any bones about it—going to *forge* a complete stuffed moa. I know a chap out there who will pretend to make the find in a kind of antiseptic swamp, and say he stuffed it at once, as it threatened to fall to pieces. The feathers are peculiar, but I have got a simply lovely way of dodging up singed bits of ostrich plume. Yes, that is the new smell you noticed. They can only discover the fraud with a microscope, and they will hardly care to pull a nice specimen to bits for that.

"In this way, you see, I give my little push in the advancement of science.

"But all this is merely imitating Nature. I have done more than that in my time. I have—beaten her."

He took his feet down from the mantel-board, and leant over confidentially towards me. "I have *created* birds," he said in a low voice. "*New* birds. Improvements. Like no birds that was ever seen before."

He resumed his attitude during an impressive silence.

"Enrich the universe; *rath*-er. Some of the birds I made were new kinds of humming birds, and very beautiful little things, but some of them were simply rum. The rummest, I think, was the *Anomalopteryx Jejuna. Jejunus-a-um*—empty—so called because there was really nothing in it; a thoroughly empty bird—except for stuffing. Old Javvers has the thing now, and I suppose he is almost as proud of it as I am. It is a masterpiece, Bellows. It has all the silly clumsiness of your pelican, all the solemn want of dignity of your parrot, all the gaunt ungainliness of a flamingo, with all the extravagant chromatic conflict of a mandarin duck. *Such* a bird. I made it out of the skeletons of a stork and a toucan and a job lot of feathers. Taxidermy of that kind is just pure joy, Bellows, to a real artist in the art.

"How did I come to make it? Simple enough, as all great inventions are. One of those young genii who write us Science Notes in the papers got hold of a German pamphlet about the birds of New Zealand, and translated some of it by means of a dictionary and his mother-wit—he must have been one of a very large family with a small mother—and he got mixed between the living apteryx and the extinct anomalopteryx; talked about a bird five feet high, living in the jungles of the North Island, rare, shy, specimens difficult to obtain, and so on. Javvers, who even for a collector, is a miraculously ignorant man, read these paragraphs, and swore he would have the thing at any price. Raided the dealers with enquiries. It shows what a man can do by persistence—will-power. Here was a bird-collector swearing he would have a specimen of a bird that did not exist, that never had existed, and which for very shame of its own profane ungainliness, probably would not exist now if it could help itself. And he got it. *He got it.*"

"Have some more whisky, Bellows?" said the taxidermist, rousing himself from a transient contemplation of the mysteries of will-power and the collecting turn of mind. And, replenished, he proceeded to tell me of how he concocted a most attractive mermaid, and how an itinerant preacher, who could not get an audience because of it, smashed it because it was idolatry, or worse, at Burslem Wakes. But as the conversation of all the parties to this transaction, creator, would-be preserver, and destroyer, was uniformly unfit for publication, this cheerful incident must still remain unprinted.

The reader unacquainted with the dark ways of the collector may perhaps be inclined to doubt my taxidermist, but so far as great auks' eggs, and the bogus stuffed birds are concerned, I find that he has the confirmation of distinguished ornithological writers. And the note about the New Zealand bird certainly appeared in a morning paper of unblemished reputation, for the Taxidermist keeps a copy and has shown it to me.

THE INSIDE OF THE EARTH

Edward Page Mitchell

A BIG HOLE THROUGH THE PLANET FROM POLE TO POLE

How claltus treats the theory of the open polar sea—what he says about the gulf stream—life of a brooklyn discoverer

He was an elderly man with a beard of grizzled gray unkempt hair, light eyes that shot quick, furtive glances, pale lips that trembled often with weak, uneasy smiles, and hands that restlessly rubbed each other, or else groped unconsciously for some missing tool. His clothes were coarse and in rags, and as he sat on a low upturned box, close before a half-warm stove, he shivered sometimes when a fierce gust of freezing wind rattled the patched and dingy windows. Behind him was a carpenter's bench, with a rack of neatly kept woodworking tools above it; a lathe and a small stock of very handsomely finished library stepladders. A great pile of black walnut chips and lathe dust lay on the floor, and the air was full of the clean, fresh smell of the wood. The room in which he sat was a garret, at the top of two eroded flights of steep and rickety stairs, in a building within three blocks of the southernmost extremity of that Lilliputian railway on which Saratoga trunks, fitted up as horse cars, are run from Fulton ferry to Hamilton ferry.

"Don't mention my name at all, sir," said he to the SUN reporter, who perched upon an unsteady box before him, "nor don't give them the exact place, please, for there are lots about who know me, and who'd be bothering me, and maybe laughing at me. Call me John Claltus. That's the name I was known by down in Charleston and all down South, and it did very well while I was working there, so you can put it in that."

"But why, having a grand scientific idea, and being the originator of novel and bold theories, do you shrink so modestly from public recognition and admiration?"

"I don't want any glory. I've thought out what I have because I felt I had a mission to do it, and maybe mightn't be let live if I didn't; but I'm done now. I can't last much longer. I'm old and poor, and I don't care to have folks bothering me and maybe laughing at me; and you see my brother, my cousins, and sometimes some sailor friends come to see me, and I'd rather you'd let it go as Claltus, sir."

"And as Claltus it shall go. But about your discovery. Was it not Symmes's theory of a hole through the globe that first gave you the idea?"

Remarkable Visions

"Oh, not at all! I was shown it all in a vision years before I ever heard of him. It was more than thirty-eight years ago. I was only a twelve-year-old boy. I was greatly afraid when I saw it; it was so terrible to me. I really think, from what I saw, that the earth was all in a sort of mist or fog once. I felt that I must go to sea and try to find out what I could about it as a poor man; so as a sailor I went for years, always thinking about it and inquiring when I could of them that might have had a chance to know something. About two years ago I went South and tried to establish myself there, and then I saw the vision again, not so terrible as before, and I could understand it better. It came to me like a globe, about two feet through, and a hole through it one third of its diameter in bigness. I told it to people there and they said I was crazy. I told it to two men I was working for—brothers they were and Frenchmen. I built an extension table and raised the roof of their house for them, and they said, 'How can it be that you do our work so well and yet are not in your right mind?' So I quit saying anything about it. This is a model of like what I saw in the vision."

The model of the vision as produced is a ball of black walnut wood, four and a half inches in diameter, traversed by a round aperture whose diameter seemed to be about one third the diameter of the ball or globe. Around the exterior, lines have been traced by a lathe tool, the spaces between them representing ten degrees each. A chalk mark on one side represents New York. This ball is mounted between the points of an inverted U of strong wire, so based upon a little board as to admit of being tipped to change the angle at which the ball is poised. The points of the wire are fastened near the edges of the ends of the hole at opposite sides of the little globe, so as to admit of its turning, and thus alternately raising and depressing, with reference to the false poles, the ends of the hole. As the thing stood on a little stand, where he placed it very carefully, the sunlight poured through the hole, and as he turned it the area covered in the interior of the ball by the sun's direct rays was gradually narrowed, shortened, and finally so diminished as to extend inward only a very little way; then, as he continued turning it, the patch of light once more widened and lengthened until the sun again shone all the way through.

The Lesson of the Model

"There," said he, "that represents a day and a night for the people in the inside of the earth. I'm perfectly satisfied in my own mind that the turn is made on about ten degrees, and about ten degrees from the outside rim of it; them that goes there would get to the flat part on the inside. When they get to the ninetieth degree that's the pole they've always been trying to make. They'll be turning into the inside. Eighty degrees is the furthest they've ever got yet, at least that's the furthest for anyone that has come back to tell about it. Perry's Point is the furthest land northward on this continent that has ever been reached, and Spitsbergen is about as far on the other side. The furtherst they have gone south is Victoria Island, opposite Cape Horn, maybe a thousand miles away from the Cape, and that's only about eighty degrees. I've got a bit of stone here that came from Victoria Island that a sailor man gave me, thinkin', maybe, I might find out something about it from somebody that knew."

The discoverer arose and walked slowly to the further end of his garret, where he took from a shelf a little piece of stone, about three inches in length, two in width, and three quarters in thickness, soft as rotten stone almost, light brown and looking like a bit of petrified wood.

"I don't know what it is. There isn't much curious about it. I've seen bits of stone from the Central Park that looked much like it, but not just the same. I tried to make a whetstone of it, but it was too soft; it wouldn't take any polish."

"In your long sea service did you ever get far enough toward the poles to find anything corroborative of your theories?"

"Not myself, though I've noticed things that confirmed me. Now, there's the Gulf Stream, for instance. They say there's a current from the Gulf of Mexico that goes across to Europe; but I've seen enough myself, in the Indian Ocean, that I've crossed many a time and often, and round to Cape Horn, that I'm convinced it's the polar stream and the action of the sun on the narrow part of the rim there causes it. I studied it in the Gulf of Mexico. They thought the pressure of them big rivers flowing into the gulf made it. Now if that was so it would make a great pressure where it rushes through the narrow place between Florida and the West Indies that would set the stream going away to the other side of the ocean, but I couldn't see any such pressure greater there than anywhere else. Them rivers has no more effect there than a bucket of water poured into the bay down beyond. It's the great heat of the sun at the narrow rim melting the ice, and the current pouring out of that hole, that makes what they call the Gulf Stream in the part of it they've observed."

What a Sailor Said He Saw

"Have you ever met any sailors who knew anything more about it than you did yourself?"

"Yes," the discoverer answered quickly, ceasing to bore bits from the soft stone with his thick thumbnail and looking up with an eager smile, "I met a sailor man in Charleston—Tola or Toland his name was—and he said he had been far enough to see a great, bright arch that rose out of the water like, and I said, 'That's my arch; that's the rim of the hole to the inside of the earth.' He was there in Charleston waiting for a ship, and I was making patterns. We used to meet every night to talk about the thing, for he was a knowledgeable man, and took an interest in it, the same as I did. He saw that arch every night for two weeks while the privateer he was on was in them waters, and all that was with him saw it, but they couldn't make it out. Then they got frightened of it, beating about in strange waters, and at last they got back to parts of the ocean they knew, and so came away as fast as they could. Well," sighing as he spoke, "sailors sometimes make a heap of brag about what they've seen and possibly there's nothing in it, but there may be. I know it's there all the same, for I've seen it in the vision and it stands to reason. I asked him if he could see anything in the daytime, and he said no—nothing, only clouds and mists about him. And that stands to reason, for in the night, you see, the reflected light would shine up the arch and show it, but in daytime it would be so high and so far off that it could not be seen. I had some hopes that he might have got the color of land, but he didn't."

"What do you suppose is the character of the country in there?"

"Oh! I don't know, but it's likely there are mountains and rivers in there. I think it's most likely they have most water in there, but maybe a good deal of land, too; and maybe gold and various kinds of things that's scarce on the outside."

"And people, too?"

"I shouldn't wonder at all if there was people there, driven in there by the storms, and that couldn't find their way out again."

"And how do you suppose they support life?"

"Why shouldn't they the same as people on the outside? Haven't they got air and light and heat and the change of seasons, and water and soil, the same as there is outside? It's a big place in there. The open polar circle, I calculate, is in circumference about the diameter of the earth, and that would give one third of the earth open inside. They get light and heat from the sun, and maybe a good deal of reflected light and heat all the way through from the south end of the hole. That's where it all goes in at."

The Men Who Live Inside

"And what sort of folks do you suppose are in there?"

"Ah! I don't know. There may be Irishmen there, and there may be Dutch there, and there may be Malays there, and other kinds of people, and there may be Danes there, too—they were good smart sailor people, too, in their time, always beating about the waters and they might have got drifted in there and couldn't get out."

"How do you mean 'couldn't get out'?"

"Couldn't find their way. There's no charts of them waters, and maybe the needle won't work the same there, and the place is so big they may go on sailing there and never going straight or finding their way back. Maybe they've been wrecked, and had no means of coming away. Sure there must be mighty storms in there. Great storms come out of that hole in the south. 'Great storms come out of the South,' the Scriptures say. You'll find that in the Book of Job, that and lots more about the earth. He talks about it as if he knew all about it. He knew all about that hole in the inside of the earth, and as he wasn't with the Creator when He made it, he must have seen it to know so much about it as he shows he did.

"And yet—" he murmured in a lower voice, meditatively digging off little bits from a piece of chalk with his fingernails, and touching up the spot representing New York on the wooden ball—"you'll find a good many things in the Scriptures if you search them, about the interior of the earth."

"Have you ever tried to enlist government or private enterprise to prosecute an investigation of the correctness of your theories?"

"No. What could I do? I was always only a poor, hard-working, ignorant man, but I seen it in a vision and I felt it my duty to study on it and make it known. But I think if a good steamship was laid on her course proper from New York, set in the way I know she would have to be, and provided for rightly, in about ten weeks she would get there and into the inside of the earth. Her wheels would never stop until she got there, for there's more than human thought about it. It's Cod's will it should be known, and her machinist couldn't stop her wheels if she was going the right way for it. But she would have to be provided with a good shower bath to keep her wet all the time, for on the rim there, on the narrow part, it will be five times as hot as at the equator. If they get up an expedition to go there, it will have to be well armed, too. If they find them Irish and Danes in there, there will be fighting, for they are hostile people. Yes, and them Malays, too. They know how to navigate ships, too, and they're warlike chaps and they'll give them some trouble. Yes, the expedition will have to be well armed."

Of Light

"Do the inhabitants of the hole see the moon and the stars?"

"Partly, I conceive. They get the good of the moon about nine days in the month, and can see such parts of the heavens as are visible out of the ends of the hole. That's all; but it would never be real night there, for even when the sun would be off on one side its light would be reflected from the walls of the other side. You see the earth is moving about the sun all the time. Not that I think it goes round in the form them astronomers say it does. I think it goes round on the high and low orbit, that is, one side of the circle is raised in coming down from the sun—and always at the same distance from the sun. Any globe working about the sun must have the same force and the same balance all the time to keep face. The theory of the astronomers is that it goes out many millions of miles at certain times of the year and comes back. Now, there would be no order or regularity about that. It isn't reason. It would make a regular hurly-burly of everything if the earth was allowed to run around in that wild way. And there's another thing that goes to show the world is hollow inside. A solid globe you can't make roll of itself in the sunlight but a hollow one will. You go to work and make a globe of fine silk and fill it with gas, or make it of cork and hollow, and put it into a glass jar in the sun, and pump the air out, and raise it up to a certain temperature—about 180 degrees or maybe 200, I think—and it'll roll in the sun, but a solid one won't do it. So it stands to reason the earth is hollow, so it will roll in the sun. I've tried that experiment in my shop during the war. I made it up nice, but I haven't got it now, for my shop was robbed three years ago, and I lost that and a lot more things, and all my tools. The model I had for the Patent Office was carried away, too."

"But let us get back to our hole. Beyond what the sailor told you, you have nothing more than theory?"

"Not altogether. There are signs of life from further to the south than anybody has ever gone yet that we know of. I read in a paper last August that an English captain went far enough south to get into warm water; and there he picked up a log drifting from still further south, with nails in it and marks of an ax on it, and that log he brought back with him to England, and it's there now. Anyway, I read that in the paper—but," speaking in a tone of regretful sadness, "these newspapers start so many curious things and ideas that you can't always be certain about what they say. But other sailor men than that captain have found the water growing warmer, and had reason to know of open seas at the poles. Besides, there's another thing that goes to show that there's life inside the earth, and that is the great bones and tusks of animals, so big that no animals on the earth now can carry them or have such things, that they find away up in Siberia. Them came from the inside of the earth, I've no doubt, drifted out in the ice that was parted there when the sun cracked the floes and set them drifting out in a polar current."

Surely Hollow

"You are, of course, aware that many people have a theory that the interior of the earth is in a state of fusion, and others that there are vast internal seas, whose waves act upon chemical substances in the earth, and produce spontaneous combustion and earthquakes and volcanoes?"

"Yes, and what's to hinder. The crust of the earth, between the hole inside and the outside surface, is nearly three thousand miles thick, and surely in all that there's a heap of room for many strange things. But as sure as you live and I live the earth is hollow inside, and there's a great country there where people can live, and where I've no doubt they do live, and some day it will all be found out about it."

THE MAN IN THE MACHINE

J.D. Beresford

The shock had affected my sensibility. I knew that my right arm had suffered in some way, but I did not realise that the humerus was broken. My first impulse was to reassure my wife. I was immensely elated at having escaped death. I sat up and shouted; and then I tried to raise my arm and wave to her.

She had to make a long detour before she could get down the cliff, and during those ten minutes, I was still almost insensible to pain. I was numbed and yet that sense of elation persisted. A bright little trickle of thought ran clearly through my mind. I had had an amazing escape. I had fallen sixty feet on to the rocks, and I was not dead nor likely to die. I was proud of my adventure and of my immunity.

And when my wife came to me, I began to talk with a high, quick eagerness. I wanted to show her at once that I was not seriously hurt.

"But your arm is broken," she said.

I looked at it stupidly and tried again to raise it. I was annoyed because my control over it was gone. The lever was snapped, and the muscles had no purchase. They had but a single function, and it was dependent upon the rigidity of that lever. I saw that useless arm as something altogether dissociated from me: I saw it as a purely mechanical arrangement of parts.

But even as I turned my mind to the contemplation of the fracture, the arm began to burn me with a white-hot fire. I gasped at the sudden pain, but some controlling sense within me sighed its relief. I was vaguely aware that pain was more endurable than that numbness, that sense of separation...

The nearest doctor lived five miles away. At least an hour must elapse before he could arrive. I had been desperately tried by my walk up to our house. And my wife, who had once been ward-sister at St. Andrew's Hospital, gave me a strong injection of morphia...

I slipped so softly and easily out of pain and distress, and all the harassing expectations of my reality, that I can recall no incident of the passing from my bedroom to the Great Hall of my vision. The past had been taken from me by the power of the drug; and I could no longer check present experience by the thought of anticipations based upon old observation. Surprise had been eliminated from my mind until such time as it could be reconstructed from the elements of new knowledge.

I was not surprised, for example, by the indescribable immensity of the Great Hall; nor by the strange appearance of the machine that was working close at hand; nor by the fact that I had an unknown companion with whom I was, apparently, on terms of reasonable intimacy.

"That machine interests me," I said.

We went a few steps nearer.

"What works it?" I asked.

"The man inside," my companion told me.

I accepted that without demur. The man was invisible, but his existence somewhere in the complicated heart of the machine was a perfectly natural inference.

"It looks an intricate affair," I said.

"Oh! very!" my companion replied carelessly, and then added as an afterthought: "Of course we understand it much better than we used to. The engineers can effect really wonderful repairs in it, nowadays."

We were moving on when a new thought occurred to me.

"I say!" I said. "Doesn't that chap inside there ever come out?"

My companion yawned, and mumbled something about never having taken much interest in mechanics.

I was suddenly annoyed with him. I wanted to hold his attention, to insist upon an answer to my questions; but he was staring abstractedly into the distance. I had an absurd impression that he was many miles away; that I should have to undertake a long and troublesome journey before I could make him listen to me...

I found myself addressing the machine.

"Don't you *want* to get out," I was saying; and the stress I laid upon the important word seemed to imply some earlier, forgotten conversation.

"Why should I?" was the answer I received.

A feeling of profound sadness overtook me. I realised with a deep regret that I could not expect truth from this complicated mechanism. The man inside was so involved in all this fearful arrangement of levers and controls. Both my question and his answer emerged, twisted and altered by the million obstructions through which they had had to trickle. The man himself, invisible and intangible, was so shut out; so hopelessly distant.

I wondered whether if one smashed tremendously through his ingenious machine, one would ultimately find him? Or if with infinite patience one delicately cut and probed...?

I heard an urgent voice calling to me. "Will you come up?" it said.

A hand was clasped about my upper arm; and as I was lifted high in the air, the hand tightened until it gripped me like a ring of iron.

I had a terrifying premonition that I was to be thrust into a machine; to be immured, hidden, cut off from all freedom and immediacy.

I was at once aghast and furious. I began fiercely to explain that the thing was unjust, cruel, utterly undeserved. I tried furiously to struggle; but I was so impotent held there, in mid-air, by one arm. And the grip upon me tightened continually, until the pain of it was unendurable.

I shouted with all my strength and heard my own voice wailing feebly down the immensities of the Great Hall.

Far away another voice made a little hushed announcement. "He's coming, too," it said.

I desired with all my soul to combat that statement, but I was faint with the heat of my impotent struggle and the agony of that gripping hand. I saw a rising drift of blackness and knew that there lay the entrance to confinement.

Then my spirit failed me, and I fell horribly through the darkness, down into the deep, hidden heart of the machine.

Presently, I dared to peer out at the light through two little darkened windows.

"I think he has come to," announced the hushed voice of my wife from the far side of the bed.

THE MAN IN THE MOON

L. Frank Baum

The Man in the Moon came tumbling down,
    And enquired the way to Norwich;
    He went by the south and burned his mouth
    With eating cold pease porridge!

What! Have you never heard the story of the Man in the Moon? Then I must surely tell it, for it is very amusing, and there is not a word of truth in it.

The Man in the Moon was rather lonesome, and often he peeked over the edge of the moon and looked down upon the earth and envied all the people who lived together, for he thought it must be vastly more pleasant to have companions to talk to than to be shut up in a big planet all by himself, where he had to whistle to keep himself company.

One day he looked down and saw an alderman sailing up through the air towards him. This alderman was being translated (instead of being transported, owing to a misprint in the law) and as he came near the Man in the Moon called to him and said,

"How is everything down on the earth?"

"Everything is lovely," replied the alderman, "and I wouldn't leave it if I was not obliged to."

"What's a good place to visit down there?" enquired the Man in the Moon.

"Oh, Norwich is a mighty fine place," returned the alderman, "and it's famous for its pease porridge;" and then he sailed out of sight and left the Man in the Moon to reflect upon what he had said.

The words of the alderman made him more anxious than ever to visit the earth, and so he walked thoughtfully home, and put a few lumps of ice in the stove to keep him warm, and sat down to think how he should manage the trip.

You see, everything went by contraries in the Moon, and when the Man wished to keep warm he knocked off a few chunks of ice and put them in his stove; and he cooled his drinking water by throwing red-hot coals of fire into the pitcher. Likewise, when he became chilly he took off his hat and coat, and even his shoes, and so became warm; and in the hot days of summer he put on his overcoat to cool off.

All of which seems very queer to you, no doubt; but it wasn't at all queer to the Man in the Moon, for he was accustomed to it.

Well, he sat by his ice-cool fire and thought about his journey to the earth, and finally he decided the only way he could get there was to slide down a moonbeam.

So he left the house and locked the door and put the key in his pocket, for he was uncertain how long he should be gone; and then he went to the edge of the moon and began to search for a good strong moonbeam.

At last he found one that seemed rather substantial and reached right down to a pleasant-looking spot on the earth; and so he swung himself over the edge of the moon, and put both arms tight around the moonbeam and started to slide down. But he found it rather slippery, and in spite of all his efforts to hold on he found himself going faster and faster, so that just before he reached the earth he lost his hold and came tumbling down head over heels and fell plump into a river.

The cool water nearly scalded him before he could swim out, but fortunately he was near the bank and he quickly scrambled upon the land and sat down to catch his breath.

By that time it was morning, and as the sun rose its hot

rays cooled him off somewhat, so that he began looking about curiously at all the strange sights and wondering where on earth he was.

By and by a farmer came along the road by the river with a team of horses drawing a load of hay, and the horses looked so odd to the Man in the Moon that at first he was greatly frightened, never before having seen horses except from his home in the moon, from whence they looked a good deal smaller. But he plucked up courage and said to the farmer,

"Can you tell me the way to Norwich, sir?"

"Norwich?" repeated the farmer musingly; "I don't know exactly where it be, sir, but it's somewhere away to the south."

"Thank you," said the Man in the Moon.—But stop! I must not call him the Man in the Moon any longer, for of course he was now out of the moon; so I'll simply call him the Man, and you'll know by that which man I mean.

Well, the Man in the—I mean the Man (but I nearly forgot what I have just said)—the Man turned to the south and began walking briskly along the road, for he had made up his mind to do as the alderman had advised and travel to Norwich, that he might eat some of the famous pease porridge that was made there. And finally, after a long and tiresome journey, he reached the town and stopped at one of the first houses he came to, for by this time he was very hungry indeed.

A good-looking woman answered his knock at the door, and he asked politely,

"Is this the town of Norwich, madam?"

"Surely this is the town of Norwich," returned the woman.

"I came here to see if I could get some pease porridge," continued the Man, "for I hear you make the nicest porridge in the world in this town."

"That we do, sir," answered the woman, "and if you'll step

inside I'll give you a bowl, for I have plenty in the house that is newly made."

So he thanked her and entered the house, and she asked,

"Will you have it hot or cold, sir?"

"Oh, cold, by all means," replied the Man, "for I detest anything hot to eat."

She soon brought him a bowl of cold pease porridge, and the Man was so hungry that he took a big spoonful at once.

But no sooner had he put it into his mouth than he uttered a great yell, and began dancing frantically about the room, for of course the porridge that was cold to earth folk was hot to him, and the big spoonful of cold pease porridge had burned his mouth to a blister!

"What's the matter?" asked the woman.

"Matter!" screamed the Man; "why, your porridge is so hot it has burned me."

"Fiddlesticks!" she replied, "the porridge is quite cold."

"Try it yourself!" he cried. So she tried it and found it very cold and pleasant. But the Man was so astonished to see her eat the porridge that had blistered his own mouth that he became frightened and ran out of the house and down the street as fast as he could go.

The policeman on the first corner saw him running, and promptly arrested him, and he was marched off to the magistrate for trial.

"What is your name?" asked the magistrate.

"I haven't any," replied the Man; for of course as he was the only Man in the Moon it wasn't necessary he should have a name.

"Come, come, no nonsense!" said the magistrate, "you must have some name. Who are you?"

"Why, I'm the Man in the Moon."

"That's rubbish!" said the magistrate, eyeing the prisoner

severely, "you may be a man, but you're not in the moon—you're in Norwich."

"That is true," answered the Man, who was quite bewildered by this idea.

"And of course you must be called something," continued the magistrate.

"Well, then," said the prisoner, "if I'm not the Man in the Moon I must be the Man out of the Moon; so call me that."

"Very good," replied the judge; "now, then, where did you come from?"

"The moon."

"Oh, you did, eh? How did you get here?"

"I slid down a moonbeam."

"Indeed! Well, what were you running for?"

"A woman gave me some cold pease porridge, and it burned my mouth."

The magistrate looked at him a moment in surprise, and then he said, "This person is evidently crazy; so take him to the lunatic asylum and keep him there."

This would surely have been the fate of the Man had there not been present an old astronomer who had often looked at the moon through his telescope, and so had discovered that what was hot on earth was cold in the moon, and what was cold here was hot there; so he began to think the Man had told the truth. Therefore he begged the magistrate to wait a few minutes while he looked through his telescope to see if the Man in the Moon was there. So, as it was now night, he fetched his telescope and looked at the Moon,—and found there was no man in it at all!

"It seems to be true," said the astronomer, "that the Man has got out of the Moon somehow or other. Let me look at your mouth, sir, and see if it is really burned."

Then the Man opened his mouth, and everyone saw plainly

it was burned to a blister! Thereupon the magistrate begged his pardon for doubting his word, and asked him what he would like to do next.

"I'd like to get back to the Moon," said the Man, "for I don't like this earth of yours at all. The nights are too hot."

"Why, it's quite cool this evening!" said the magistrate.

"I'll tell you what we can do," remarked the astronomer; "there's a big balloon in town which belongs to the circus that came here last summer, and was pawned for a board bill. We can inflate this balloon and send the Man out of the Moon home in it."

"That's a good idea," replied the judge. So the balloon was brought and inflated, and the Man got into the basket and gave the word to let go, and then the balloon mounted up into the sky in the direction of the moon.

The good people of Norwich stood on the earth and tipped back their heads, and watched the balloon go higher and higher, until finally the Man reached out and caught hold of the edge of the moon, and behold! the next minute he was the Man in the Moon again!

After this adventure he was well contented to stay at home; and I've no doubt if you look through a telescope you will see him there to this day.

THE MAN WITH THE STRANGE HEAD

Miles J. Breuer

A man in a gray hat stood half way down the corridor, smoking a cigar and apparently interested in my knocking and waiting. I rapped again on the door of Number 216 and waited some more, but all remained silent. Finally my observer approached me.

"I don't believe it will do any good," he said "I've just been trying it. I would like to talk to someone who is connected with Anstruther. Are you?"

"Only this." I handed him a letter out of my pocket without comment, as one is apt to do with a thing that has caused one no little wonderment:

> "Dear Doctor:" it said succinctly: "I have been under the care of Dr. Faubourg who has recently died. I would like to have you take charge of me on a contract basis, and keep me well, instead of waiting till I get sick. I can pay you enough to make you independent, but in return for that, you will have to accept an astonishing revelation concerning me, and keep it to yourself. If this seems acceptable to you, call on me at 9 o'clock, Wednesday evening. Josiah Anstruther, Room 216, Cornhusker Hotel."

"If you have time," said the man in the gray hat, handing me back the letter, "come with me. My name is Jerry Stoner, and I make a sort of living writing for magazines. I live in 316, just above here."

"By some curious architectural accident," he continued, as we reached his room, "that ventilator there enables me to hear minutely everything that goes on in the room below. I haven't ever said any-thing about it during the several months that I've lived here, partly because it does not disturb me, and partly because it has begun to pique my curiosity a writer can confess to that, can he not? The man below is quiet and orderly, but seems to work a good deal on some sort of clockwork; I can hear it whirring and clicking quite often. But listen now!"

Standing within a couple of feet of the opening which was covered with an iron grill, I could hear footsteps. They were regular, and would decrease in intensity as the person walked away from the ventilator opening below, and increase again as he approached it; were interrupted for a moment as he probably stepped on a rug; and were shorter for two or three counts, no doubt as he turned at the end of the room. This was repeated in a regular rhythm as long as I listened.

"Well?" I said.

"You perceive nothing strange about that, I suppose," said Jerry Stoner. "But if you had listened all day long to just exactly that you would begin to wonder. That is the way he was going on when I awoke this morning; I was out from 10 to 11 this forenoon. The rest of the time I have been writing steadily, with an occasional stretch at the window, and all of the time I have heard steadily what you hear now, without interruption or change. It's getting on my nerves.

"I have called him on the phone, and have rung it on and off for twenty minutes; I could hear his bell through the ventilator, but he pays no attention to it. So, a while ago I tried to call on him. Do you know him?"

"I know who he is," I replied, "but do not remember ever having met him."

"If you had ever met him you would remember. He has a queer head. I made my curiosity concerning the sounds from his room an excuse to cultivate his acquaintance. The cultivation was difficult. He is courteous, but seemed afraid of me."

We agreed that there was not much that we could do about it. I gave up trying to keep my appointment, told Stoner that I was glad I had met him, and went home. The next morning at seven he had me on the telephone. "Are you still interested?" he asked, and his voice was nervous. "That bird's been at it all night. Come and help me talk to the hotel management." I needed no urging.

I found Beesley, the hotel manager, with Stoner; he was from St. Louis, and looked French. "He can do it if he wants to," he said, shrugging his shoulders comically; "unless you complain of it as a disturbance."

"It isn't that," said Stoner; "there must be something wrong with the man."

"Some form of insanity—" I suggested; "or a compulsion neurosis."

"That's what I'll be pretty soon," Stoner said. "He is a queer gink anyway. As far as I have been able to find out, he has no close friends. There is something about his appearance that makes me shiver; his face is so wrinkled and droopy, and yet he sails about the streets with an unusually graceful and vigorous step. Loan me your pass key; I think I'm as close a friend of his as anyone."

Beesley lent the key, but Stoner was back in a few minutes, shaking his head. Beesley was expecting that; he told us that when the hotel was built, Anstruther had the doors made of steel with special bars, at his own expense, and the windows shuttered, as though he were afraid for his life.

"His rooms would be as hard to break into as a fort," Beesley said as he left us; "and thus far we do not have sufficient reason for wrecking the hotel."

"Look here!" I said to Stoner; "it will take me a couple of

hours to hunt up the stuff and string up a periscope; it's an old trick I learned as a Boy Scout."

Between us we had it up in about that time; a radio aerial mast clamped on the window sill with mirrors at the top and bottom, and a telescope a tour end of it, gave us a good view of the room below us. It was a sort of living room made by throwing together two of the regular sized hotel rooms. Anstruther was walking across it diagonally, disappearing from our field of view at the further end, and coming back again. His head hung forward on his chest with a ghastly limpness. He was a big, well-built man, with a vigorous stride. Always it was the same path. He avoided the small table in the middle each time with exactly the same sort of side step and swing. His head bumped limply as he turned near the window and started back across the room. For two hours we watched him in shivering fascination, during which he walked with the same hideous uniformity.

"That makes thirty hours of this," said Stoner. "Wouldn't you say that there was something wrong?"

We tried another consultation with the hotel manager. As a physician, I advised that something be done; that he be put in a hospital or something. I was met with another shrug.

"How will you get him? I still do not see sufficient cause for destroying the hotel company's property. It will take dynamite to get at him."

He agreed, however, to a consultation with the" police, and in response to our telephone call, the great, genial chief, Peter John Smith was soon sitting with us. He advised us against breaking in.

"A man has a right to walk that way if he wants to," he said. "Here's this fellow in the papers who played the piano for 49 hours, and the police didn't stop him; and in Germany they practice making public speeches for 18 hours at a stretch. And there was this Olympic dancing fad some months ago, where a couple danced for 57 hours."

"It doesn't look right to me," I said, shaking my head. "There seems to be something wrong with the man's appearance ; some uncanny disease of the nervous system—Lord knows I've never heard of anything that resembles it!"

We decided to keep a constant watch. I had to spend a little time on my patients, but Stoner and the chief stayed, and agreed to call me if occasion arose. I peeped through the periscope at the walking man several times during the next twenty-four hours; and it was always exactly the same, the hanging, bumping head, the uniformity of his course, the uncanny, machine-like exactitude of his movements. I spent an hour at a time with my eye at the telescope studying his movements for some variation, but was unable to be certain of any. That afternoon I looked up my neurology texts, but found no clues. The next day at 4 o'clock in the afternoon, after not less than 55 hours of it, I was there with Stoner to see the end of it; Chief Peter John Smith was out.

As we watched, we saw that he moved more and more slowly, but with otherwise identical motions. It had the effect of the slowed motion pictures of dancers or athletes; or it seemed like some curious dream; for as we watched, the sound of the steps through the ventilator also slowed and weakened. Then we saw him sway a little, and totter, as though his balance were imperfect. He swayed a few times and fell sidewise on the floor; we could see one leg in the field of our periscope moving slowly with the same movements as in walking, a slow, dizzy sort of motion. In five more minutes he was quite still.

The Chief was up in a few moments in response to our telephone call.

"Now we've got to break in," he said. Beesley shrugged his shoulders and said nothing. Stoner came to the rescue of the hotel property.

"A small man could go down this ventilator. This grill can be unscrewed, and the lower one can be knocked out with a hammer; it is cast-iron."

Beesley was gone like a flash, and soon returned with one of his window-washers, who was small and wiry, and also a rope and hammer. We took off the grill and held the rope as the man crawled in. He shouted to us as he hit the bottom. The air drew strongly downwards, but the blows of his hammer on the grill came up to us. We hurried downstairs. Not a sound came through the door of 216, and we waited for some minutes. Then there was a rattle of bars and the door opened, and a gust of cold wind struck us, with a putrid odor that made us gulp. The man had evidently run to open a window before coming to the door.

Anstruther lay on his side, with one leg straight and the other extended forward as in a stride; his face was livid, sunken, hideous. Stoner gave him a glance, and then scouted around the room—looking for the machinery he had been hearing, but finding none. The Chief and I also went over the rooms, but they were just conventional rooms, rather colorless and lacking in personality. The Chief called an undertaker and also the coroner, and arranged for a post-mortem examination. I received permission to notify a number of professional colleagues; I wanted some of them to share in the investigation of this unusual case with me. As I was leaving, I could not help noting the astonished gasps of the undertaker's assistants as they lifted the body; but they were apparently too well trained to say anything.

That evening, a dozen physicians gathered around the figure covered with a white sheet on the table in the center of the undertaker's work room. Stoner was there; a writer may be anywhere he chooses. The coroner was preparing to draw back the sheet.

"The usual medical history is lacking in this case," he said.

"Perhaps an account by Dr. Bor his author friend, of the curious circumtances connected with the death of this man, may take its place."

"I can tell a good deal," said Stoner; "and I think it will bear directly on what you find when you open him up, even though it is not technical medical stuff. Do you care to hear it?"

"Tell it! Go on! Let's have it!"

"I have lived above him in the hotel for several months," Stoner began. "He struck me as a curious person, and as I do some writing, all mankind is my legitimate field for study. I tried to find out all I could about him.

"He has an office in the Little Building, and did a rather curious business. He dealt in vases and statuary, book-ends and chimes, and things you put around in rooms to make them look artistic. He had men out buying the stuff, and others selling it, all by personal contact and on a very exclusive basis. He kept the stock in a warehouse near the Rock Island tracks where they pass the Ball Park; I do not believe that he ever saw any of it. He just sat in the office and signed papers, and the other fellows made the money; and apparently they made a lot of it, for he has swung some big financial deals in this town.

"I often met him in the lobby or the elevator. He was a big, vigorous man and walked with an unusually graceful step and an appearance of strength and vitality. His eyes seemed to light up with recognition when he saw me, but in my company he was always formal and reserved. For such a vigorous looking man, his voice was singularly cracked and feeble, and his head gave an impression of being rather small for him, and his face old and wrinkled.

"He seemed fairly well known about the city. At the Eastridge Club they told me that he plays golf occasionally and excellently, and is a graceful dancer, though somehow not a popular partner.

He was seen frequently at the Y. M. C. A. bowling alleys, and played with an uncanny skill. Men loved to see him bowl for his cleverness with the balls, but wished he were not so formally courteous, and did not wear such an expression of complete happiness over his victories. Eridley, manager of Rudge & Guenzel's book department, was the oldest friend of his that I could find, and he gave me some interesting information. They went to school together, and Anstruther was poor in health as well as in finances. Twenty-five years ago, during the hungry and miserable years after his graduation from the University, Eridley remembered him as saying:

"'My brain needs a body to work with. If I had physical strength, I could do anything. If I find a fellow who can give it to me, I'll make him rich!'

"Eridley also remembers that he was sensitive because girls did not like his debilitated physique. He seems to have found health later, though I can find no one who remembers how or when. About ten years ago he came back from Europe where he had been for several years, in Paris, Eridley thinks; and for several years after this, a French-man lived with him. The city directory of that time has him living in the big stone house at 13th and 'G' streets. I went up there to look around, and found it a double house, Dr. Faubourg having occupied the other half. The present caretaker has been there ever since Anstruther lived in the house, and she says that his French companion must have been some sort of an engineer, and that the two must have been working on an invention, from the sounds she heard and the materials they had about. Some three or four years ago the Frenchman and the machinery vanished, and Anstruther moved to the Cornhusker Hotel. Also at about this time, Dr. Faubourg retired from the practice of medicine. He must have been about 50 years old, and too healthy and vigorous to be retiring on account of old age or ill health.

"Apparently Anstruther never married. His private life was quite obscure, but he appeared much in public. He was always very courtly and polite to the ladies. Outside his business he took a great interest in Y. M. C. A. and Boy Scout camps, in the National Guard, and in fact in everything that stood for an outdoor, physical life, and promoted health. In spite of his oddity he was quite a hero with the small boys, especially since the time of his radium hold-up. This is intimately connected with the story of his radium speculation that caused such a sensation in financial circles a couple of years ago.

"About that time, the announcement appeared of the discovery of new uses for radium; a way had been found to accelerate its splitting and to derive power from it. Its price went up, and it promised to become a scarce article on the market. Anstruther had never been known to speculate, nor to tamper with sensational things like oil and helium; but on this occasion he seemed to go into a panic. He cashed in on a lot of securities and caused a small panic in the city, as he was quite wealthy and had especially large amounts of money in the building loan business. The newspapers told of how he had bought a hundred thousand dollars worth of radium, which was to be delivered right here in Lincoln a curious method of speculating, the editors volunteered.

"It arrived by express one day, and Anstruther rode the express wagon with the driver to the station. I found the driver and he told the story of the hold-up at 8th and 'P' streets at eleven o'clock at night. A Ford car drove up beside them, from which a man pointed a pistol at them and ordered them to stop. The driver stopped.

"'Come across with the radium!' shouted the big black bulk in the Ford, climbing upon the express wagon. Anstruther's fist shot out like a flash of lightning and struck the arm holding the pistol; and the driver states that he heard the pistol crash through the window on the second floor of the Lincoln Hotel. Anstruther pushed the express driver, who was in his way, backwards over the seat among the packages and leaped upon the hold-up man; the driver said he heard Anstruther's muscles crunch savagely, as with little apparent effort he flung the man over the Ford; he fell with a thud on the asphalt and stayed there. Anstruther then launched a kick at the man at the wheel of the Ford, who crumpled up and fell out of the opposite side of the car.

"The police found the pistol inside a room on the second floor of the Lincoln Hotel. The steering post of the Ford car was torn from its fastenings. Both of the hold-up men had ribs and collar-bones broken, and the gunman's forearm was bent double in the middle with both bones broken. These two men agreed later with the express driver that Anstruther's attack, for suddenness, swiftness, and terrific strength was beyond anything they had dreamed possible; he was like a thunderbolt; likesome furious demon. When the two men were huddled in black heaps on the pavement, Anstruther said to the driver, quite impersonally:

"'Drive to the police station; Come on! Wakeup! I've got to get this stuff locked up!'

"One of the hold-up men had lost all his money and the home he was building when Anstruther had foreclosed a loan in his desperate scramble for radium. He was a Greek named Poulos, and has been in prison for two years; just last week he was released—"

Chief Peter John Smith interrupted.

"I've been putting two and two together, and I can shed a little light on this problem. Three days ago, the day before I was called to watch Anstruther pacing his room, we picked up this man Poulos in the alleyway between Rudge & Guenzel's and Miller

& Paine's. He was unconscious, and must have received a terrible licking at somebody's hands; his face was almost unrecognizable; several ribs and several fingers on his right hand were broken. He clutched a pistol fitted with a silencer, and we found that two shots had been fired from it. Here he is—"

A limp, bandaged, plastered man was pushed in between two policemen. He was sullen and apathetic, until he caught sight of Anstruther's face from which the chief had drawn a corner of the sheet. Terror and joy seemed to mingle in his face and in his voice. He raised his bandaged hand with an ineffectual gesture, and started off on some Greek religious expression, and then turned dazedly to us, speaking painfully through his swollen face.

"Glad he dead. I try to kill him. Shoot him two time. No kill. So close—" indicating the distance of a foot from his chest; "then he lick me. He is not man. He is devil. I not kill him, but I glad he dead!"

The Chief hurried him out, and came in with a small, dapper man with a black chin whisker. He apologized to the coroner.

"This is not a frame-up. I am just following out a hunch that I got a few minutes ago while Stoner was talking. This is Mr. Fournier. I found his address in Anstruther's room, and dug him up. I think he will be more important to you doctors than he will in a court. Tell 'em what you told me!"

While the little Frenchman talked, the undertaker's assistant jerked off the sheet. The undertaker's work had had its effect in getting rid of the frightful odor, and in making Anstruther's face presentable. The body, however, looked for all the world as though it were alive, plump, powerful, pink. In the chest, over the heart, were two bullet holes, not bloody, but clean-cut and black. The Frenchman turned to the body and worked on it with a little screw-driver as he talked.

"Mr. Anstruther came to me ten years ago, when I was a poor

mechanic. He had heard of my automatic chess-player, and my famous animated show-window models; and he offered me time and money to find him a mechanical relief for his infirmity. I was an assistant at a Paris laboratory, where they had just learned to split radium and get a hundred horse-power from a pinch of powder. Anstruther was weak and thin, but ambitious."

The Frenchman lifted off two plates from the chest and abdomen of the body, and the flanks swung outward as though on hinges. He removed a number of packages that seemed to fit carefully within, and which were on the ends of cables and chains.

"Now—" he said to the assistants, who held the feet. He put his hands into the chest cavity, and as the assistants pulled the feet away, he lifted out of the shell a small, wrinkled, emaciated body; the body of an old man, which now looked quite in keeping with the well-known Anstruther head. Its chest was covered with dried blood, and there were two bullet holes over the heart. The undertaker's assistants carried it away while we crowded around to inspect the mechanism within the arms and legs of the pink and live-looking shell, headless, gaping at the chest and abdomen, but uncannily like a healthy, powerful man.

THE MAN WITHOUT A BODY

Edward Page Mitchell

On a shelf in the old Arsenal Museum, in the Central Park, in the midst of stuffed hummingbirds, ermines, silver foxes, and bright-colored parakeets, there is a ghastly row of human heads. I pass by the mummied Peruvian, the Maori chief, and the Flathead Indian to speak of a Caucasian head which has had a fascinating interest to me ever since it was added to the grim collection a little more than a year ago.

I was struck with the Head when I first saw it. The pensive intelligence of the features won me. The face is remarkable, although the nose is gone, and the nasal fossae are somewhat the worse for wear. The eyes are likewise wanting, but the empty orbs have an expression of their own. The parchmenty skin is so shriveled that the teeth show to their roots in the jaws. The mouth has been much affected by the ravages of decay, but what mouth there is displays character. It seems to say: "Barring certain deficiencies in my anatomy, you behold a man of parts!" The features of the Head are of the Teutonic cast, and the skull is the skull of a philosopher. What particularly attracted my attention, however, was the vague resemblance which this dilapidated countenance bore to some face which had at some time been familiar to me—some face which lingered in my memory, but which I could not place.

After all, I was not greatly surprised, when I had known the Head for nearly a year, to see it acknowledge our acquaintance and express its appreciation of friendly interest on my part by deliberately winking at me as I stood before its glass case.

This was on a Trustees' Day, and I was the only visitor in the hall. The faithful attendant had gone to enjoy a can of beer with his friend, the superintendent of the monkeys.

The Head winked a second time, and even more cordially than before. I gazed upon its efforts with the critical delight of an anatomist. I saw the masseter muscle flex beneath the leathery skin. I saw the play of the glutinators, and the beautiful lateral movement of the internal playtsyma. I knew the Head was trying to speak to me. I noted the convulsive twitchings of the risorius and the zygomatie major, and knew that it was endeavoring to smile.

"Here," I thought, "is either a case of vitality long after decapitation, or, an instance of reflex action where there is no diastaltic or excitor-motory system. In either case the phenomenon is unprecedented, and should be carefully observed. Besides, the Head is evidently well disposed toward me." I found a key on my bunch which opened the glass door.

"Thanks," said the Head. "A breath of fresh air is quite a treat."

"How do you feel?" I asked politely. "How does it seem without a body?"

The Head shook itself sadly and sighed. "I would give," it said, speaking through its ruined nose, and for obvious reasons using chest tones sparingly, "I would give both ears for a single leg. My ambition is principally ambulatory, and yet I cannot walk. I cannot even hop or waddle. I would fain travel, roam, promenade, circulate in the busy paths of men, but I am chained to this accursed shelf. I am no better off than these barbarian heads—I, a man of science! I am compelled to sit here on my neck and see sandpipers and storks all around me, with legs and to spare. Look at that infernal little Oedieneninus longpipes over there. Look at that miserable gray-headed porphyric. They have no brains, no ambition, no yearnings. Yet they have legs, legs, legs, in profusion." He cast an envious glance across the alcove at the tantalizing limbs of the birds in question and added gloomily, "There isn't even enough of me to make a hero for one of Wilkie Collins's novels."

I did not exactly know how to console him in so delicate a manner, but ventured to hint that perhaps his condition had its compensations in immunity from corns and the gout.

"And as to arms," he went on, "there's another misfortune for you! I am unable to brush away the flies that get in here—Lord knows how—in the summertime. I cannot reach over and cuff that confounded Chinook mummy that sits there grinning at me like a jack-in-the-box. I cannot scratch my head or even blow my nose (his nose!) decently when I get cold in this thundering draft. As to eating and drinking, I don't care. My soul is wrapped up in science. Science is my bride, my divinity. I worship her footsteps in the past and hail the prophecy of her future progress. I—"

I had heard these sentiments before. In a flash I had accounted for the familiar look which had haunted me ever since I first saw the Head. "Pardon me," I said, "you are the celebrated Professor Dummkopf?"

"That is, or was, my name," he replied, with dignity.

"And you formerly lived in Boston, where you carried on scientific experiments of startling originality. It was you who first discovered how to photograph smell, how to bottle music, how to freeze the aurora borealis. It was you who first applied spectrum analysis to Mind."

"Those were some of my minor achievements," said the Head, sadly nodding itself—"small when compared with my final invention, the grand discovery which was at the same time my greatest triumph and my ruin. I lost my Body in an experiment."

"How was that?" I asked. "I had not heard."

"No," said the Head. "I being alone and friendless, my disappearance was hardly noticed. I will tell you."

There was a sound upon the stairway. "Hush!" cried the Head. "Here comes somebody. We must not be discovered. You must dissemble."

I hastily closed the door of the glass case, locking it just in time to evade the vigilance of the returning keeper, and dissembled by pretending to examine, with great interest, a nearby exhibit.

On the next Trustees' Day I revisited the museum and gave the keeper of the Head a dollar on the pretense of purchasing information in regard to the curiosities in his charge. He made the circuit of the hall with me, talking volubly all the while.

"That there," he said, as we stood before the Head, "is a relic of morality presented to the museum fifteen months ago. The head of a notorious murderer guillotined at Paris in the last century, sir."

I fancied that I saw a slight twitching about the corners of Professor Dummkopf's mouth and an almost imperceptible depression of what was once his left eyelid, but he kept his face remarkably well under the circumstances. I dismissed my guide with many thanks for his intelligent services, and, as I had anticipated, he departed forthwith to invest his easily earned dollar in beer, leaving me to pursue my conversation with the Head.

"Think of putting a wooden-headed idiot like that," said the professor, after I had opened his glass prison, "in charge of a portion, however small, of a man of science—of the inventor of the Telepomp! Paris! Murderer! Last century, indeed!" and the Head shook with laughter until I feared that it would tumble off the shelf.

"You spoke of your invention, the Telepomp," I suggested.

"Ah, yes," said the Head, simultaneously recovering its gravity and its center of gravity; "I promised to tell you how I happen to be a Man without a Body. You see that some three or four years ago I discovered the principle of the transmission of sound by electricity. My telephone, as I called it, would have been an invention of great practical utility if I had been spared to introduce it to the public. But, alas—"

"Excuse the interruption," I said, "but I must inform you that somebody else has recently accomplished the same thing. The telephone is a realized fact."

"Have they gone any further?" he eagerly asked. "Have they discovered the great secret of the transmission of atoms? In other words, have they accomplished the Telepomp?"

"I have heard nothing of the kind," I hastened to assure him, "but what do you mean?"

"Listen," he said. "In the course of my experiments with the telephone I became convinced that the same principle was capable of indefinite expansion. Matter is made up of molecules, and molecules, in their turn, are made up of atoms. The atom, you know, is the unit of being. The molecules differ according to the number and the arrangement of their constituent atoms. Chemical changes are effected by the dissolution of the atoms in the molecules and their rearrangements into molecules of another kind. This dissolution may be accomplished by chemical affinity or by a sufficiently strong electric current. Do you follow me?"

"Perfectly."

"Well, then, following out this line of thought, I conceived a great idea. There was no reason why matter could not be telegraphed, or, to be etymologically accurate, 'telepomped.' It was only necessary to effect at one end of the line the disintegration of the molecules into atoms and to convey the vibrations of the chemical dissolution by electricity to the other pole, where a corresponding reconstruction could be effected from other atoms. As all atoms are alike, their arrangement into molecules of the same order, and the arrangement of those molecules into an organization similar to the original organization, would be practically a reproduction of the original. It would be a materialization—not in the sense of the spiritualists' cant, but in all the truth and logic of stern science. Do you still follow me?"

"It is a little misty," I said, "but I think I get the point. You would telegraph the Idea of the matter, to use the word Idea in Plato's sense."

"Precisely. A candle flame is the same candle flame although the burning gas is continually changing. A wave on the surface of water is the same wave, although the water composing it is shifting as it moves. A man is the same man although there is not an atom in his body which was there five years before. It is the form, the shape, the Idea, that is essential. The vibrations that give individuality to matter may be transmitted to a distance by wire just as readily as the vibrations that give individuality to sound. So I constructed an instrument by which I could pull down matter, so to speak, at the anode and build it up again on the same plan at the cathode. This was my Telepomp."

"But in practice—how did the Telepomp work?"

"To perfection! In my rooms on Joy Street, in Boston, I had about five miles of wire. I had no difficulty in sending simple compounds, such as quartz, starch, and water, from one room to another over this five-mile coil. I shall never forget the joy with which I disintegrated a three-cent postage stamp in one room and found it immediately reproduced at the receiving instrument in another. This success with inorganic matter emboldened me to attempt the same thing with a living organism. I caught a cat—a black and yellow cat—and I submitted him to a terrible current from my two-hundred-cup battery. The cat disappeared in a twinkling. I hastened to the next room and, to my immense satisfaction, found Thomas there, alive and purring, although somewhat astonished. It worked like a charm."

"This is certainly very remarkable."

"Isn't it? After my experiment with the cat, a gigantic idea took possession of me. If I could send a feline being, why not send a human being? If I could transmit a cat five miles by wire in an instant by electricity, why not transmit a man to London by Atlantic cable and with equal dispatch? I resolved to strengthen my already powerful battery and try the experiment. Like a thorough votary of science, I resolved to try the experiment on myself.

"I do not like to dwell upon this chapter of my experience," continued the Head, winking at a tear which had trickled down on to his cheek and which I gently wiped away for him with my own pocket handkerchief. "Suffice it that I trebled the cups in my battery, stretched my wire over housetops to my lodgings in Phillips Street, made everything ready, and with a solemn calmness born of my confidence in the theory, placed myself in the receiving instrument of the Telepomp at my Joy Street office. I was as sure that when I made the connection with the battery I would find myself in my rooms in Phillips Street as I was sure of my existence. Then I touched the key that let on the electricity. Alas!"

For some moments my friend was unable to speak. At last, with an effort, he resumed his narrative.

"I began to disintegrate at my feet and slowly disappeared under my own eyes. My legs melted away, and then my trunk and arms. That something was wrong, I knew from the exceeding slowness of my dissolution, but I was helpless. Then my head went and I lost all consciousness. According to my theory, my head, having been the last to disappear, should have been the first to materialize at the other end of the wire. The theory was confirmed in fact. I recovered consciousness. I opened my eyes in my Phillips Street apartments. My chin was materializing, and with great satisfaction I saw my neck slowly taking shape. Suddenly, and about at the third cervical vertebra, the process stopped. In a flash I knew the reason. I had forgotten to replenish the cups of my battery with fresh sulphuric acid, and there was not electricity enough to materialize the rest of me. I was a Head, but my body was Lord knows where."

I did not attempt to offer consolation. Words would have been mockery in the presence of Professor Dummkopf's grief.

"What matters it about the rest?" he sadly continued. "The house in Phillips Street was full of medical students. I suppose that some of them found my head, and knowing nothing of me or of the Telepomp, appropriated it for purposes of anatomical study. I suppose that they attempted to preserve it by means of some arsenical preparation. How badly the work was done is shown by my defective nose. I suppose that I drifted from medical student to medical student and from anatomical cabinet to anatomical cabinet until some would-be humorist presented me to this collection as a French murderer of the last century. For some months I knew nothing, and when I recovered consciousness I found myself here.

"Such," added the Head, with a dry, harsh laugh, "is the irony of fate!"

"Is there nothing I can do for you?" I asked, after a pause.

"Thank you," the Head replied; "I am tolerably cheerful and resigned. I have lost pretty much all interest in experimental science. I sit here day after day and watch the objects of zoological, ichthyological, ethnological, and conchological interest with which this admirable museum abounds. I don't know of anything you can do for me.

"Stay," he added, as his gaze fell once more upon the

exasperating legs of the Oedienenius longpipes opposite him. "If there is anything I do feel the need of, it is outdoor exercise. Couldn't you manage in some way to take me out for a walk?"

I confess that I was somewhat staggered by this request, but promised to do what I could. After some deliberation, I formed a plan, which was carried out in the following manner:

I returned to the museum that afternoon just before the closing hour, and hid myself behind the mammoth sea cow, or Manatus Americanus. The attendant, after a cursory glance through the hall, locked up the building and departed. Then I came boldly forth and removed my friend from his shelf. With a piece of stout twine, I lashed his one or two vertebrae to the headless vertebrae of a skeleton moa. This gigantic and extinct bird of New Zealand is heavy-legged, full-breasted, tall as a man, and has huge, sprawling feet. My friend, thus provided with legs and arms, manifested extraordinary glee. He walked about, stamped his big feet, swung his wings, and occasionally broke forth into a hilarious shuffle. I was obliged to remind him that he must support the dignity of the venerable bird whose skeleton he had borrowed. I despoiled the African lion of his glass eyes, and inserted them in the empty orbits of the Head. I gave Professor Dummkopf a Fiji war lance for a walking stick, covered him with a Sioux blanket, and then we issued forth from the old arsenal into the fresh night air and the moonlight, and wandered arm in arm along the shores of the quiet lake and through the mazy paths of the Ramble.

THE MISANTHROPE

J.D. Beresford

Since I have returned from the rock and discussed the story in all its bearings, I have begun to wonder if the man made a fool of me. In the deeps of my consciousness I feel that he did not.

Nevertheless, I cannot resist the effect of all the laughter that has been evoked by my narrative.

Here on the mainland the whole thing seems unlikely, grotesque, foolish. On the rock the man's confession carried absolute conviction. The setting is everything; and I am, perhaps, thankful that my present circumstances are so beautifully conducive to sanity. No one appreciates the mystery of life more than I do; but when the mystery involves such a doubt of oneself, I find it pleasanter to forget. Naturally, I do not want to believe the story. If I did I should know myself to be some kind of human horror. And the terror of it all lies in the fact that I may never know precisely what kind...

Before I went we had eliminated the facile and banal explanation that the man was mad, and had fallen back upon the two inevitable alternatives: Crime and Disappointed Love. We were human and romantic, and we tried desperately hard not to be too obvious.

Once before a man had made the same attempt and had built or tried to build a house on the Gulland rock; but he had been defeated within a fortnight, and what was left of his building was taken off the island and turned into a tin church. It is there still. We all went to Trevone and ruminated over and round it, perhaps with some faint hope that one of us might, all-unknowing, have the abilities of a psychometrist.

Nothing came of that visit but a slight intensification of those theories that were already becoming a little stale. We compared the early failure of thirty years ago, the attempt that was baffled, with the present success. For this new misanthrope had lived on the Gulland through the whole winter—and still lived. Indeed, the fact of his presence on that awful lump of rock was now accepted by the country people; to them he was scarcely a shade madder than the other visitors; that remunerative, recurrent host that this year broke their journey to Bedruthan in order to stand on Trevone beach and stare foolishly at the just visible hut that stuck like a cubical gall on the landward face of that humped, desolate island.

We all did that; stared at nothing in particular and meditated enormously; but in what I felt at the time was a wild spirit of adventure, I went out one night to the point of Gunver Head and saw an actual light within that distant hut; a patch of golden lichen on the mother parasite.

Some aspect of humanity I found in that light it was that finally decided me; that and some quality of sympathy, perhaps with the hermit—mad, criminal, or lovelorn?—who had found sanctuary from the pestilent touch of the encroaching crowd. It was, in fact, a wildish night, and I stayed until the little yellow speck went out, and all I could see through the murk was an occasional canopy of curving spray when the elbow of the Trevone Light touched a bare corner of that black Gulland.

The making of a decision was no difficult matter, but while I waited for the necessary calm that would permit the occasional boat to land provisions on the island two miles out from the mainland, I suffered qualms of doubt and nervousness. And I suffered them alone, for I had determined that no hint of my adventure should be given to anyone of our party until the voyage had been made. They might think that I had gone fishing, an excuse which had all the air of probability given to it by the coming of the boatman to say that the tide and wind would serve that morning. I had warned—and bribed—him to give no clue to my friends of the goal of my proposed excursion.

My nervousness suffered no decrease as we approached the rock and saw the authentic figure of its single inhabitant awaiting our arrival. I had some consolation in the thought that he would be in some way prepared by the sight of our surprisingly passengered boat; but my mind shuddered at the necessity for using some conventional form of address if I would make at once my introduction and excuse. The civilised opening was so hopelessly incapable of expressing my sympathy, presenting instead so unmistakably, it seemed to me, the single solution of common curiosity. I wondered that he had not—as the boatman so clearly assured me was the case—had other prying visitors before me.

My self-consciousness increased as we came nearer to the single opening among the spiked rocks, that served as a miniature harbour at half-tide. I felt that I was being watched by the man who now stood awaiting us at the water's edge. And suddenly my spirit broke, I decided that I could not force myself upon him, that I would remain in the boat while its cargo was delivered, and then return with the boatmen to Trevone. So resolute was I in this plan that when we had pulled in to the tiny landing-place, I kept my gaze steadfastly averted from the man I had come to see, and stared solemnly out at the humped back of Trevone, seen now in an entirely new aspect.

The sound of the hermit's voice startled me from a perfectly genuine abstraction.

"Fairly decent weather to-day," he remarked with, I thought, a touch of nervousness. He had, I remembered, addressed the same remark to the boatmen, who were now conveying their cargo up to the hut.

I looked up and met his stare. He was, indeed, regarding me with a curious effect of concentration, as if he were eager to note every detail of my expression.

"Jolly," I replied. "Been pretty beastly the last day or two. Kept you rather short, hasn't it?"

"I make allowances for that," he said. "Keep a reserve, you know. Are you l staying over there?" He nodded towards the bay.

"For a week or two," I told him, and we began to discuss the country around Harlyn with the eagerness of two strangers who find a common topic at a dull reception.

"Never been on the Gulland before, I suppose?" he ventured at last, when the boatmen had discharged their load and were evidently ready to be off.

"No, no, I haven't," I said, and hesitated. I felt that the invitation must come from him.

He boggled over it by saying, "Dashed awkward place to get to, and nothing to see, of course. I don't know if you're at all keen on fishing?"

"Rather," I said with enthusiasm. "There's deep water on the other side of the rock," he went on. "In the right weather you get splendid bass there." He stopped and then added, "It'll be absolutely top hole for 'em, this afternoon."

"Perhaps I could come back..." I began; but the boatman interrupted me at once.

"Yew can coom back to-morrow, sure 'nough," he said. "Tide only serves wance avery twalve hours."

"If you'd care to stay, now..." began the hermit.

"Thanks! it's awfully good of you. I should like to of all things," I said. I stayed on the clear understanding that the boatmen were to fetch me the next morning. At first there was really very little that seemed in any way strange about the man on the Gulland.

His name, he told me, was William Copley, but it appeared that he was no relation to the Copleys I knew. And if he had shaved he would have looked a very ordinary type of Englishman roughing it on a holiday. His age I judged to be between thirty and forty.

Only two things about him struck me as a little queer during our very successful afternoon's fishing. The first was that intense appraising stare of his, as if he tried to fathom the very depths of one's being. The second was an inexplicable devotion to one particular form of ceremony. As our intimacy grew, he dropped the ordinary formal politeness of a host; but he insisted always on one observance that I supposed at first to be the merely conventional business of giving precedence.

Nothing would induce him to go in front of me. He sent me ahead even as we explored the little purlieus of his rock—the only level square yard on the whole island was in the floor of the hut. But presently I noticed that this peculiarity went still further, and that he would not turn his back on me for a single moment.

That discovery intrigued one. I still excluded the explanation of madness—Copley's manner and conversation were so convincingly sane. But I reverted to and elaborated those other two suggestions that had been made. I could not avoid the inference that the man must in some strange way be afraid of me; and I hesitated as to whether he were flying from some form of justice or from revenge, perhaps a vendetta. Either theory seemed to account for his intense, ap-praising stare. I inferred that his longing for companionship had grown so strong that he had determined to risk the possibility of my being an emissary, sent by some—to me—exquisitely romantic person or persons who desired Copley's death. I recalled, and wallowed in, some of the marvellous imaginings of the novelist. I wondered if I could make Copley speak by convincing him of my innocent identity. How I thrilled at the prospect!

But the explanation of it all came without any effort on my part.

He sent me out of the hut while he prepared our supper—quite a magnificent meal, by the way.

I saw his reason at once; he could not manage all that business of cooking and laying the table without turning his back on me. One thing, however, puzzled me a little; he drew down the blind of the little square window as soon as I had gone outside.

Naturally, I made no demur. I climbed down to the edge of the sea—it was a glorious evening—and waited until he called me. He stood at the door of the hut until I was within a few feet of him, and then retreated into the room and sat down with his back to the wall.

We discussed our afternoon's sport as we had supper, but when we had finished and our pipes were going, he said, suddenly:

"I don't see why I shouldn't tell you."

Like a fool, I agreed eagerly, when I might so easily have stopped him...

"It began when I was quite a kid," he said. "My mother found me crying in the garden; and all I could tell her was that Claude, my elder brother, looked 'horrid.' I couldn't bear the sight of him for days afterwards, either; but I was such a perfectly normal child that they weren't seriously perturbed about this one idiosyncrasy of mine. They thought that Claude had 'made a face' at me, and frightened me. My father whacked me for it eventually.

"Perhaps that whacking stuck in my mind. Anyway, I didn't confide my peculiarity to anyone until I was nearly seventeen. I was ashamed of it, of course. I am still—in a way." He stopped and looked down, pushed his plate away from him, and folded his arms on the table. I was pining to ask a question, but I was afraid to interrupt. And after a moment's hesitation he looked up and held my gaze again, but now without that inquiring look of his.

Rather, he seemed to be looking for sympathy.

"I told my house-master," he said. "He was a splendid chap, and he was very decent about it; took it all quite seriously and advised me to consult an oculist, which I did. I went in the holidays with the pater—I had given him a more reasonable account of my trouble—and he took me to the best man in London. He was tremendously interested, and it proves that there must be something in it, that it can't be imagination, because he really found a defect in my eyes, something quite new to him, he said. He called it a new form of astigmatism; but, of course, as he pointed out, no glasses would be any use to me."

"But what...?" I began, unable to keep down my curiosity any longer.

Copley hesitated, and dropped his eyes. "Astigmatism, you know," he said, "is a defect—I quote the dictionary, I learned that definition by heart; I often puzzle over it still—'causing images of lines having a certain direction to be indistinctly seen, while those of lines transverse to the former are distinctly seen.' Only mine is peculiar in the fact that my sight is perfectly normal except when I look back at anyone over my shoulder." He looked up, almost pathetically.

I could see that he hoped I might understand without further explanation.

I had to confess myself utterly mystified. What had this trifling defect of vision to do with his coming to live on the Gulland, I wondered.

I frowned my perplexity. "But I don't see..." I said.

He knocked out his pipe and began to scrape the bowl with his pocket-knife. "Well, mine is a kind of moral astigmatism, too," he said. "At least, it gives me a kind of moral insight. I'm afraid I must call it insight. I've proved in some cases that..." He dropped his voice. He was apparently deeply engrossed in the scraping out of his pipe. He kept his eyes on it as he continued.

"Normally, you understand, when I look at people straight in the face, I see them as anybody else sees them. But when I look back at them over my shoulder I see...oh! I see all their vices and defects. Their faces remain, in a sense, the same, perfectly recognisable, I mean, but distorted—beastly...There was my brother Claude—good-looking chap, he was—but when I saw him...that way...he had a nose like a parrot, and he looked sort of weakly voracious...and vicious." He stopped and shuddered slightly, and then added: "And one knows, now, that he is like that, too. He's just been hammered on the Stock Exchange. Rotten sort of failure it was..."

"And then Denison, my house-master, you know; such a decent chap. I never looked at him, that way, until the end of my last term at school. I had got into the habit, more or less, of never looking over my shoulder, you see. But I was always getting caught. That was an instance. I was playing for the School against the Old Boys. Denison called out, 'Good luck, old chap,' just as I was going in, and I forgot and looked back at him..."

I waited, breathless, and as he did not go on, I prompted him with "Was he...'wrong,' too?"

Copley nodded. "Weak, poor devil. His eyes were all right, but they were fighting his mouth, if you know what I mean. There would have been an awful scandal at the school there, four years after I left, if they hadn't hushed it up and got Denison out of the country.

"Then, if you want any more instances, there was the oculist—big, fine chap, he was. Of course, he made me look at him over my shoulder, to test me. He asked me what I saw, and

I told, more or less. He was simply livid for a moment. He was a sensualist, you see; and when I saw him that way he looked like some filthy old hog.

"The thing that really finished me," he went on, after a long interval, "was the breaking off of my engagement to Helen. We were frightfully in love with one another, and I told her about my trouble. She was very sympathetic, and I suppose rather sentimentally romantic, too. She believed it was some sort of spell that had been put on me. I think, anyway, she had a theory that if I once saw anybody truly and ordinarily over my shoulder, I should never have any more trouble—the spell-would-be-broken sort of thing. And, of course, she wanted to be the person. I didn't resist her much. I was infatuated, I suppose. Anyway, I thought she was perfection and that it was simply impossible that I could find any defect in her. So I agreed, and looked—that way..."

His voice had fallen to an even note of despondency, as though the telling of this final tragedy in his life had brought him to the indifference of despair. "I looked," he continued, "and saw a creature with no chin and watery, doting eyes; a faithful, slobbery thing—eugh! I can't...I never spoke to her again...

"That broke me, you know," he said presently. "After that I didn't care. I used to look at everyone that way, until I had to get away from humanity. I was living in a world of beasts. Most of them looked like some beast or bird or other. The strong were vicious and criminal; and the weak were loathsome. I couldn't stick it. In the end—I had to come here away from them all."

A thought occurred to me. "Have you ever looked at yourself in the glass?" I asked.

He nodded. "I'm no better than the rest of them," he said. "That's why I grew this rotten beard. I hadn't got a looking-glass here."

"And you can't keep a stiff neck, as it were," I asked, "going about looking humanity straight in the face?"

"The temptation is too strong," Copley said. "And it gets stronger. Curiosity, partly, I suppose; but partly it's the momentary sense of superiority it gives you. You see them like that, you know, and forget how you look yourself. And then after a bit it sickens you."

"You haven't..." I said, and hesitated. I wanted to know and yet I was horribly afraid. "You haven't," I began again, "er—you haven't—er—looked at me yet...that way?"

"Not yet," he said.

"Do you suppose..."

"Probably. You look all right, of course. But then so did heaps of the others."

"You've no idea how I should look to you, that way?"

"Absolutely none. I've been trying to guess, but I can't."

"You wouldn't care...?"

"Not now," he said sharply. "Perhaps, just before you go."

"You feel fairly certain, then...?"

He nodded with disgusting conviction.

I went to bed, wondering whether Helen's theory wasn't a true one; and if I might not break the spell for poor Copley.

The boatmen came for me soon after eleven next morning.

I had shaken off some of the feeling of superstitious horror that had held me overnight, and I had not repeated my request to Copley; nor had he offered to look into the dark places of my soul.

He came down after me to the landing-place and we shook hands warmly, but he said nothing about my revisiting him.

And then, just as we were putting off, he turned back towards the hut and looked at me over his shoulder—just one quick glance.

"Wait," I commanded the boatmen, and I stood up and called to him.

"I say, Copley," I shouted.

He turned and looked at me, and I saw that his face was transfigured. He wore an expression of foolish disgust and loathing. I had seen something like it on the face of an idiot child who was just going to be sick.

I dropped down into the boat and turned my back on him.

I wondered then if that was how he had seen himself in the glass.

But since I have only wondered what it was he saw in me...

And I can never go back to ask him.

THE MONARCH OF DREAMS

Thomas Wentworth Higginson

He who forsakes the railways and goes wandering through the hill-country of New England, must adopt one rule as invariable. When he comes to a fork in the road, and is assured that both ways lead to the desired point, he must simply ask which road is the best; and, on its being pointed out, must at once take the other. Nothing can be easier than the explanation of this method. The passers-by will always recommend the new road, which keeps to the valley and avoids the hills; but the old road, deserted by the general public, ascends the steeper grades, and has a monopoly of the wider views.

Turning to the old road, you soon feel that both houses and men are, in a manner, stranded. They see very little of the world, and are under no stimulus to keep themselves in repair. You are wholly beyond the dreary sway of French roofs; and the caricatures of good Queen Anne's day are far from you. If any farm-house on the hill-road was really built within the reign of that much-abused potentate, it is probably a solid, square mansion of brick, three stories high, blackened with time, and frowning rather gloomily from some hilltop,—as essentially a part of the past as an Irish round-tower or a Scotch border-fortress...

It was in such a house that Francis Ayrault had finally taken up his abode, leaving behind him the old family homestead in a Rhode Island seaside town. A series of domestic cares and watchings had almost broken him down: nothing debilitates a man of strong nature like the too prolonged and exclusive exercise of the habit of sympathy. At last, when the very spot where he was born had been chosen as a site for a new railway-station, there seemed nothing more to retain him. He needed utter rest and change; and there was no one left on earth whom he profoundly loved, except a little sunbeam of a sister, the child of his father's second marriage. This little five-year-old girl, of whom he was sole guardian, had been christened by the quaint name of Hart, after an ancestor, Hart Ayrault, whose moss-covered tombstone the child had often explored with her little fingers, to trace the vanishing letters of her own name.

The two had arrived one morning from the nearest railway station to take possession of the old brick farm-house. Ayrault had spent the day in unpacking and in consultations with Cyrus Gerry,—the farmer from whom he had bought the place, and who was still to conduct all outdoor operations. The child, for her part, had compelled her old nurse to follow her through every corner of the buildings. They were at last seated at an early supper, during which little Hart was too much absorbed in the novelty of wild red raspberries to notice, even in the most casual way, her brother's worn and exhausted look.

"Brother Frank," she incidentally remarked, as she began upon her second saucerful of berries, "I love you!"

"Thank you, darling," was his mechanical reply to the customary ebullition. She was silent for a time, absorbed in her pleasing pursuit, and then continued more specifically, "Brother Frank, you are the kindest person in the whole world! I am so glad we came here! May we stay here all winter? It must be lovely in the winter; and in the barn there is a little sled with only one runner gone. Brother Frank, I love you so much, I don't know what I shall do! I love you a thousand pounds, and fifteen, and eleven and a half, and more than tongue can tell besides! And there are three gray kittens,—only one of them is almost all white,—and Susan says I may bring them for you to see in the morning."

Half an hour later, the brilliant eyes were closed in slumber; the vigorous limbs lay in perfect repose; and the child slept that night in the little room inside her brother's, on the same bed that she had occupied ever since she had been left motherless. But her brother lay awake, absorbed in a project too fantastic to be talked about, yet which had really done more than anything else to bring him to that lonely house.

There has belonged to Rhode Islanders, ever since the days of Roger Williams, a certain taste for the ideal side of existence. It is the only State in the American Union where chief justices habitually write poetry, and prosperous manufacturers print essays on the Freedom of the Will. Perhaps, moreover, Francis Ayrault held something of these tendencies from a Huguenot ancestry, crossed with a strain of Quaker blood. At any rate it was there, and asserted itself at this crisis of his life. Being in a manner detached from almost all ties, he resolved to use his opportunity in a direction yet almost unexplored by man. His earthly joys being prostrate, he had resolved to make a mighty effort at self-concentration, and to render himself what no human being bad ever yet been—the ruler of his own dreams.

Coming from a race of day-dreamers, Ayrault had inherited an unusual faculty of dreaming also by night; and, like all persons having an especial gift, he perhaps overestimated its importance. He easily convinced himself that no exertion of the intellect during wakeful hours can for an instant be compared with that we employ in dreams. The finest brain-structures of Shakespeare or Dante, he reasoned, are yet but such stuff as dreams are made of; and the stupidest rustic, the most untrained mind, will sometimes have, could they be but written out, visions that surpass those of these masters...

But Ayrault had been vexed, like all others, by the utter incongruity of successive dreams. This sublime navigation still waited, like that of balloon voyages, for a rudder. Dreams, he reasoned, plainly try to connect themselves. We all have the frequent experience of half-recognizing new situations or even whole trains of ideas. We have seen this view before; reached this point; struck in some way the exquisite chord of memory. When half-aroused, or sometimes even long after clear consciousness, we seem to draw a half-drowned image of association from the deep waters of the mind; then another, then another, until dreaming seems inseparably entangled with waking. Again, over nightly dreams we have at least a certain amount of negative control, sufficient to bring them to an end...

The thought had occurred to him, long since, at what point to apply his efforts for the control of his dreams. He had been quite fascinated, some time before, by a large photograph in a shop window, of the well-known fortress known as Mont Saint Michel, in Normandy. Its steepness, its airy height, its winding and returning stairways, its overhanging towers and machicolations, had struck him as appealing powerfully to that sense of the vertical, which is, for some reason or other, so peculiarly strong in dreams. We are rarely haunted by visions of plains; often of mountains. The sensation of uplifting or downlooking is one of our commonest nightly experiences. It seemed to Ayrault that by going to sleep with the vivid mental image in his brain of a sharp and superb altitude like that of Mont Saint Michel, he could avail himself of this magic, whatever it was, that lay in the vertical line. Casting himself off into the vast sphere of dreams, with the thread of his fancy attached to this fine image, he might risk what would next come to him; as a spider anchors his web and then floats away on it. In the silence of the first night at the farmhouse,—a stillness broken only by the answering cadence of two whippoorwills in the neighboring pine-wood,—Ayrault pondered long over the beautiful details of the photograph, and then went to sleep.

That night he was held, with the greatest vividness and mastery, in the grasp of a dream such as he had never before experienced. He found himself on the side of a green hill, so precipitous that he could only keep his position by lying at full length, clinging to the short soft grass, and imbedding his feet in the turf. There were clouds about him: he could see but a short distance in any direction, nor was any sign of a human being within sight. He was absolutely alone upon the dizzy slope, where he hardly dared to look up or down, and where it took all his concentration of effort to keep a position at all. Yet there was a kind of friendliness in the warm earth; a comfort and fragrance in the crushed herbage. The vision seemed to continue indefinitely; but at last he waked and it was clear day. He rose with a bewildered feeling, and went to little Hart's room. The child lay asleep, her round face tangled in her brown curls, and one plump, tanned arm stretched over her eyes. She waked at his step, and broke out into her customary sweet asseveration, "Brother Frank, I love you!"

Dismissing the child, he pondered on his first experiment. It had succeeded, surely, in so far as he had given something like a direction to his nightly thought. He could not doubt that it was the picture of Mont Saint Michel which had transported him to the steep hillside. That day he spent in the most restless anxiety to see if the dream would come again. Writing down all that he could remember of the previous night's vision, he studied again the photograph that had so touched his fancy, and then he closed his eyes. Again he found himself—at some time between night and morning—on the same high elevation, with the clouds around him. But this time the vapors lifted, and he could see that the hill stretched for an immeasurable distance on each side, always at the same steep slope. Everywhere it was covered with human beings—men, women, and children,—all trying to pursue various semblances of occupations; but all clinging to the short grass. Sometimes, he thought—but this was not positive—that he saw one of them lose his hold and glide downwards. For this he cared strangely little; but he waked feverish, excited, trembling. At last his effort had succeeded: he had, by an effort of will, formed a connection between two dreams...

On the following night he grasped his dream once more. Again he found himself on the precipitous slope, this time looking off through clear air upon that line of detached mountain peaks, Wachusett, Monadnock, Moosilauke, which make the southern outposts of New England hills. In the valley lay pellucid lakes, set in summer beauty,—while he clung to his perilous hold. Presently there came a change; the mountain sank away softly beneath him, and the grassy slope remained a plain. The men and women, his former companions, had risen from their reclining postures and were variously busy; some of them even looked at him, but there was nothing said. Great spaces of time appeared to pass: suns rose and set. Sometimes one of the crowd would throw down his implements of labor, turn his face to the westward, walk swiftly away, and disappear. Yet some one else would take his place, so that the throng never perceptibly diminished. Ayrault began to feel rather unimportant in all this gathering, and the sensation was not agreeable.

On the succeeding night the hillside vanished, never to recur; but the vast plain remained, and the people. Over the wide landscape the sunbeams shed passing smiles of light, now here, now there. Where these shone for a moment, faces looked joyous, and Ayrault found, with surprise, that he could control the distribution of light and shade. This pleased him; it lifted him into conscious importance. There was, however, a singular want of all human relation in the tie between himself and all these people. He felt as if he had called them into being, which indeed he had; and could annihilate them at pleasure, which perhaps could not be so easily done. Meanwhile, there was a certain hardness in his state of mind toward them; indeed, why should a dreamer feel patience or charity or mercy toward those who exist but in his mind? Ayrault at any rate felt none; the sole thing which disturbed him was that they sometimes grew a little dim, as if they might vanish and leave him unaccompanied. When this happened, he drew with conscious volition a gleam of light over them, and thereby refreshed their life. They enhanced his weight in the universe: he would no more have parted with them than a Highland chief with his clansmen.

For several nights after this he did not dream. Little Hart became ill and his mind was preoccupied. He had to send for physicians, to give medicine, to be up with the child at night... Then, with the rapidity of childish convalescence, she grew well again; and he found with joy that he could resume the thread of his dream-life.

Again he was on his boundless plain, with his circle of silent allies around him. Suddenly they all vanished, and there rose before him, as if built out of the atmosphere, a vast building, which he entered. It included all structures in one,—legislative halls where men were assembled by hundreds, waiting for him: libraries, where all the books belonged to him, and whole alcoves were filled with his own publications; galleries of art, where he had painted many of the pictures, and selected the rest. Doors and corridors led to private apartments; lines of obsequious servants stood for him to pass. There seemed no other proprietor, no guests; all was for him; all flattered his individual greatness. Suddenly it occurred to him that he was painfully alone. Then he began to pass eagerly from hall to hall, seeking an equal companion, but in vain. Wherever he went, there was a trace of some one just vanished,—a book laid down, a curtain still waving. Once he fairly came, he thought, upon the object of his pursuit; all retreat was cut off, and he found himself face to face with a mirror that reflected back to him only his own features. They had never looked to him less attractive.

Ayrault's control of his visions became plainly more complete with practice, at least as to their early stages. He could lie down to sleep with almost a perfect certainty that he should begin where he left off. Beyond this, alas! he was powerless. Night after night he was in the same palace, but always differently occupied, and always pursuing, with unabated energy, some new vocation. Sometimes the books were at his command, and he grappled with whole alcoves; sometimes he ruled a listening senate in the halls of legislation; but the peculiarity was, that there were always menials and subordinates about him, never an equal. One night, in looking over these obsequious crowds, he made a startling discovery. They either had originally, or were acquiring, a strange resemblance to one another, and to some person whom he had somewhere seen. All the next day, in his waking hours, this thought haunted him. The next night it flashed upon him that the person whom they all so closely resembled, with a likeness that now amounted to absolute identity, was himself.

From the moment of this discovery, these figures multiplied; they assumed a mocking, taunting, defiant aspect. The thought was almost more than he could bear, that there was around him a whole world of innumerable and uncontrollable beings, every one of whom was Francis Ayrault. As if this were not sufficient, they all began visibly to duplicate themselves before his eyes. The confusion was terrific. Figures divided themselves into twins, laughing at each other, jeering, running races, measuring heights, actually playing leap-frog with one another. Worst of all, each one of these had as much apparent claim to his personality as he himself possessed. He could no more retain his individual hold upon his consciousness than the infusorial animalcule in a drop of water can know to which of its subdivided parts the original individuality attaches. It became insufferable, and by a mighty effort he waked.

The next day, after breakfast, old Susan sought an interview with Ayrault, and taxed him roundly with neglect of little Hart's condition. Since her former illness she never had been quite the same; she was growing pale and thin. As her brother no longer played with her, she only moped about with her kitten, and talked to herself. It touched Ayrault's heart. He took pains to be with the child that day, carried her for a long drive, and went to see her Guinea hen's eggs. That night he kept her up later than usual, instead of hurrying her off as had become his wont; he really found himself shrinking from the dream-world he had with such effort created. The most timid and shy person can hardly hesitate more about venturing among a crowd of strangers than Francis Ayrault recoiled, that evening, from the thought of this mob of intrusive persons, every one of whom reflected his own image. Gladly would he have undone the past, and swept them all away forever. But the shrinking was all on one side: the moment he sank to sleep, they all crowded upon him, laughing, frolicking, claiming detestable intimacy. No one among strangers ever longed for a friendly face, as he, among these intolerable duplicates, longed for the sight of a stranger. It was worse yet when the images grew smaller and smaller, until they had shrunk to a pin's length. He found himself trying with all his strength of will to keep them at their ampler size, with only the effect that they presently became no larger than the heads of pins. Yet his own individuality was still so distributed among them that it could not be distinguished from them; but he found himself merged in this crowd of little creatures an eighth of an inch long...

Having long since fallen out of the way of action, or at best grown satisfied to imagine enterprises and leave others to execute them, he now, more than ever, drifted on from day to day. There had been a strike at the neighboring manufacturing village, and there was to be a public meeting, at which he was besought, as a person not identified with either party, to be present, and throw his influence for peace. It touched him, and he meant to attend. He even thought of a few things, which, if said, might do good; then forgot the day of the meeting, and rode ten miles in another direction. Again, when at the little post-office one day, he was asked by the postmaster to translate several letters in the French language, addressed to that official, and coming from an unknown village in Canada. They proved to contain anxious inquiries as to the whereabouts of a handsome young French girl, whom Ayrault had occasionally met driving about in what seemed doubtful company. His sympathy was thoroughly aroused by the anxiety of the poor parents, from whom the letters came. He answered them himself, promising to interfere in behalf of the girl; delayed, day by day, to fulfil the promise; and, when he at last looked for her, she was not to be found. Yet, while his power of efficient action waned, his dream-power increased. His little people were busier about him than ever, though he controlled them less and less. He was Gulliver bound and fettered by Lilliputians.

But a more stirring appeal was on its way to him. The storm of the Civil War began to roll among the hills; regiments were recruited, camps were formed. The excitement reached the benumbed energies of Ayrault. Never, indeed, had he felt such a thrill. The old Huguenot pulse beat strongly within him. For days, and even nights, these thoughts possessed his mind, and his dreams utterly vanished. Then there was a lull in the excitement; recruiting stopped, and his nightly habit of confusing visions set in again with dreary monotony. Then there was a fresh call for troops. An old friend of Ayrault's came to a neighboring village, and held a noonday meeting in one of the churches to recruit a company. Ayrault listened with absorbed interest to the rousing appeal, and, when recruits were called for, was the first to rise. It turned out that the matter could not be at once consummated, as the proper papers were not there. Other young men from the neighborhood followed Ayrault's example, and it was arranged that they should all go to the city for regular enlistment the next day. All that afternoon was spent in preparations, and in talking with other eager volunteers, who seemed to look to Ayrault as their head. It was understood, they told him, that he would probably be an officer in the company. He felt himself a changed being; he was as if floating in air, and ready to swim off to some new planet. What had he now to do with that pale dreamer who had nourished his absurd imaginings until he had barely escaped being controlled by them? When they crossed his mind it was only to make him thank God for his escape. He flung wide the windows of his chamber. He hated the very sight of the scene where his proud vision had been fulfilled, and he had been Monarch of Dreams. No matter: he was now free, and the spell was broken. Life, action, duty, honor, a redeemed nation, lay before him; all entanglements were cut away.

That evening there went through the little village a summons that opened the door of every house. A young man galloped out from the city, waking the echoes of the hills with his somewhat untutored bugle-notes, as he dashed along. Riding from house to house of those who had pledged themselves, he told the news. There had been a great defeat; reinforcements had been summoned instantly; and the half-organized regiment, undrilled, unarmed, not even uniformed, was ordered to proceed that night to the front, and replace in the forts round Washington other levies that were a shade less raw. Every man desiring to enlist must come instantly; yet, as before daybreak the regiment would pass by special train on the railway that led through the village, those in that vicinity might join it at the station, and have still a few hours at home. They were hurried hours for Ayrault, and toward midnight he threw himself on his bed for a moment's repose, having left strict orders for his awakening. He gave not one thought to his world of visions; had he done so, it would have only been to rejoice that he had eluded them forever.

Let a man at any moment attempt his best, and his life will still be at least half made up of the accumulated results of past action. Never had Ayrault seemed so absolutely safe from the gathered crowd of his own delusions: never had they come upon him with a power so terrific. Again he was in those stately halls which his imagination had so laboriously built up; again the mob of unreal beings came around him, each more himself than he was. Ayrault was beset, encircled, overwhelmed; he was in a manner lost in the crowd of himself...

In the midst of this tumultuous dreaming, came confused sounds from without. There was the rolling of railway wheels, the scream of locomotive engines, the beating of drums, the cheers of men, the report and glare of fireworks. Mingled with all, there came the repeated sound of knocking at his own door, which he had locked, from mere force of habit, ere he lay down. The sounds seemed only to rouse into new tumult the figures of his dream. These suddenly began to increase steadily in size, even as they had before diminished; and the waxing was more fearful than the waning. From being Gulliver among the Lilliputians, Ayrault was Gulliver in Brobdingnag. Each image of himself, before diminutive, became colossal: they blocked his path; he actually could not find himself, could not tell which was he that should arouse himself in their vast and endless self-multiplication.

He became vaguely conscious, amidst the bewilderment, that the shouts in the village were subsiding, the illuminations growing dark; and the train with its young soldiers was again in motion, throbbing and resounding among the hills, and bearing the lost opportunity of his life away—away—away.

THE MONSTER OF LAKE LAMETRIE

Wardon Allan Curtis
Being the narration of James McLennegan,
M.D., Ph.D.
Prof. Wilhelm G. Breyfogle.
University of Taychobera.

Dear Friend,

Inclosed you will find some portions of the diary it has been my life-long custom to keep, arranged in such a manner as to narrate connectedly the history of some remarkable occurrences that have taken place here during the last three years. Years and years ago, I heard vague accounts of a strange lake high up in an almost inaccessible part of the mountains of Wyoming. Various incredible tales were related of it, such as that it was inhabited by creatures which elsewhere on the globe are found only as fossils of a long vanished time.

The lake and its surroundings are of volcanic origin, and not the least strange thing about the lake is that it is subject to periodic disturbances, which take the form of a mighty boiling in the centre, as if a tremendous artesian well were rushing up there from the bowels of the earth. The lake rises for a time, almost filling the basin of black rocks in which it rests, and then recedes, leaving on the shores mollusks and trunks of strange trees and bits of strange ferns which no longer grow—on the earth, at least—and are to be seen elsewhere only in coal measures and beds of stone. And he who casts hook and line into the dusky waters, may haul forth, ganoid fishes completely covered with bony plates.

All of this is described in the account written by Father LaMetrie years ago, and he there advances the theory that the earth is hollow, and that its interior is inhabited by the forms of plant and animal life which disappeared from its surface ages ago, and that the lake connects with this interior region. Symmes' theory of polar orifices is well known to you. It is amply corroborated. I know that it is true now. Through the great holes at the poles, the sun sends light and heat into the interior.

Three years ago this month, I found my way through the mountains here to Lake LaMetrie accompanied by a single companion, our friend, young Edward Framingham. He was led to go with me not so much by scientific fervor, as by a faint hope that his health might be improved by a sojourn in the mountains, for he suffered from an acute form of dyspepsia that at times drove him frantic.

Beneath an overhanging scarp of the wall of rock surrounding the lake, we found a rudely-built stone-house left by the old cliff dwellers. Though somewhat draughty, it would keep out the infrequent rains of the region, and serve well enough as a shelter for the short time which we intended to stay.

The extracts from my diary follow:

APRIL 29TH, 1896.

I have been occupied during the past few days in gathering specimens of the various plants which are cast upon the shore by the waves of this remarkable lake. Framingham does nothing but fish, and claims that he has discovered the place where the lake communicates with the interior of the earth, if, indeed, it does, and there seems to be little doubt of that. While fishing at a point near the centre of the lake, he let down three pickerel lines tied together, in all nearly three hundred feet, without finding bottom.

Coming ashore, he collected every bit of line, string, strap, and rope in our possession, and made a line five hundred feet long, and still he was unable to find the bottom.

MAY 2ND, EVENING.

The past three days have been profitably spent in securing specimens, and mounting and pickling them for preservation. Framingham has had a bad attack of dyspepsia this morning and is not very well. Change of climate had a brief effect for the better upon his malady, but seems to have exhausted its force much sooner than one would have expected, and he lies on his couch of dry water-weeds, moaning piteously. I shall take him back to civilisation as soon as he is able to be moved.

It is very annoying to have to leave when I have scarcely begun to probe the mysteries of the place. I wish Framingham had not come with me. The lake is roaring wildly without, which is strange, as it has been perfectly calm hitherto, and still more strange because I can neither feel nor hear the rushing of the wind, though perhaps that is because it is blowing from the south, and we are protected from it by the cliff. But in that case there ought to be no waves on this shore. The roaring seems to grow louder momentarily. Framingham—

MAY 3RD, MORNING.

Such a night of terror we have been through. Last evening, as I sat writing in my diary, I heard a sudden hiss, and, looking down, saw wriggling across the earthen floor what I at first took to be a serpent of some kind, and then discovered was a stream of water which, coming in contact with the fire, had caused the startling hiss. In a moment, other streams had darted in, and before I had collected my senses enough to move, the water was two inches deep everywhere and steadily rising.

Now I knew the cause of the roaring, and, rousing Framingham, I half dragged him, half carried him to the door, and digging our feet into the chinks of the wall of the house, we climbed up to its top. There was nothing else to do, for above us and behind us was the unscalable cliff, and on each side the ground sloped away rapidly, and it would have been impossible to reach the high ground at the entrance to the basin.

After a time we lighted matches, for with all this commotion there was little air stirring, and we could see the water, now half-way up the side of the house, rushing to the west with the force and velocity of the current of a mighty river, and every little while it hurled tree-trunks against the house-walls with a terrific shock that threatened to batter them down. After an hour or so, the roaring began to decrease, and finally there was an absolute silence. The water, which reached to within a foot of where we sat, was at rest, neither rising nor falling.

Presently a faint whispering began and became a stertorous breathing, and then a rushing like that of the wind and a roaring rapidly increasing in volume, and the lake was in motion again, but this time the water and its swirling freight of tree-trunks flowed by the house toward the east, and was constantly falling, and out in the centre of the lake the beams of the moon were darkly reflected by the sides of a huge whirlpool, streaking the surface of polished blackness down, down, down the vortex into the beginning of whose terrible depths we looked from our high perch.

This morning the lake is back at its usual level. Our mules are drowned, our boat destroyed, our food damaged, my specimens and some of my instruments injured, and Framingham is very ill. We shall have to depart soon, although I dislike exceedingly to do so, as the disturbance of last night, which is clearly like the one described by Father LaMetrie, has undoubtedly brought up from the bowels of the earth some strange and interesting things. Indeed, out in the middle of the lake where the whirlpool subsided, I can see a large quantity of floating things; logs and branches, most of them probably, but who knows what else?

Through my glass I can see a tree-trunk, or rather stump, of enormous dimensions. From its width I judge that the whole tree must have been as large as some of the Californian big trees. The main part of it appears to be about ten feet wide and thirty feet long. Projecting from it and lying prone on the water is a limb, or root, some fifteen feet long, and perhaps two or three feet thick. Before we leave, which will be as soon as Framingham is able to go, I shall make a raft and visit the mass of driftwood, unless the wind providentially sends it ashore.

MAY 4TH, EVENING.

A day of most remarkable and wonderful occurrences. When I arose this morning and looked through my glass, I saw that the mass of driftwood still lay in the middle of the lake, motionless on the glassy surface, but the great black stump had disappeared. I was sure it was not hidden by the rest of the driftwood, for yesterday it lay some distance from the other logs, and there had been no disturbance of wind or water to change its position. I therefore concluded that it was some heavy wood that needed to become but slightly waterlogged to cause it to sink.

Framingham having fallen asleep at about ten, I sallied forth to look along the shores for specimens, carrying with me a botanical can, and a South American machete, which I have possessed since a visit to Brazil three years ago, where I learned the usefulness of this sabre-like thing. The shore was strewn with bits of strange plants and shells, and I was stooping to pick one up, when suddenly I felt my clothes plucked, and heard a snap behind me, and turning about I saw—but I won't describe it until I tell what I did, for I did not fairly see the terrible creature until I had swung my machete round and sliced off the top of its head, and then tumbled down into the shallow water where I lay almost fainting.

Here was the black log I had seen in the middle of the lake, a monstrous elasmosaurus, and high above me on the heap of rocks lay the thing's head with its long jaws crowded with sabre-like teeth, and its enormous eyes as big as saucers. I wondered that it did not move, for I expected a series of convulsions, but no sound of a commotion was heard from the creature's body, which lay out of my sight on the other side of the rocks. I decided that my sudden cut had acted like a stunning blow and produced a sort of coma, and fearing lest the beast should recover the use of its muscles before death fully took place, and in its agony roll away into the deep water where I could not secure it, I hastily removed the brain entirely, performing the operation neatly, though with some trepidation, and restoring to the head the detached segment cut off by my machete, I proceeded to examine my prize.

In length of body, it is exactly twenty-eight feet. In the widest part it is eight feet through laterally, and is some six feet through from back to belly. Four great flippers, rudimentary arms and feet, and an immensely long, sinuous, swan-like neck, complete the creature's body. Its head is very small for the size of the body and is very round and a pair of long jaws project in front much like a duck's bill. Its skin is a leathery integument of a lustrous black, and its eyes are enormous hazel optics with a soft, melancholy stare in their liquid depths. It is an elasmosaurus, one of the largest of antediluvian animals. Whether of the same species as those whose bones have been discovered, I cannot say.

My examination finished, I hastened after Framingham, for I was certain that this waif from a long past age would arouse almost any invalid. I found him somewhat recovered from his attack of the morning, and he eagerly accompanied me to the elasmosaurus. In examining the animal afresh, I was astonished to find that its heart was still beating and that all the functions of the body except thought were being performed one hour after the thing had received its death blow, but I knew that the hearts of sharks, have been known to beat hours after being removed from the body, and that decapitated frogs live, and have all the powers of motion, for weeks after their heads have been cut off.

I removed the top of the head to look into it and here another surprise awaited me, for the edges of the wound were granulating and preparing to heal. The colour of the interior of the skull was perfectly healthy and natural, there was no undue flow of blood, and there was every evidence that the animal intended to get well and live without a brain. Looking at the interior of the skull, I was struck by its resemblance to a human skull; in fact, it is, as nearly as I can judge, the size and shape of the brain-pan of an ordinary man who wears a seven and an eighth hat. Examining the brain itself, I found it to be the size of an ordinary human brain, and singularly like it in general contour, though it is very inferior in fibre and has few convolutions.

MAY 5TH, MORNING.

Framingham is exceedingly ill and talks of dying, declaring that if a natural death does not put an end to his sufferings, he will commit suicide. I do not know what to do. All my attempts to encourage him are of no avail, and the few medicines I have no longer fit his case at all.

MAY 5TH, EVENING.

I have just buried Framingham's body in the sand of the lake shore. I performed no ceremonies over the grave, for perhaps the real Framingham is not dead, though such speculation seems utterly wild. To-morrow I shall erect a cairn upon the mound, unless indeed there are signs that my experiment is successful, though it is foolish to hope that it will be.

At ten this morning, Framingham's qualms left him, and he set forth with me to see the elasmosaurus. The creature lay in the place where we left it yesterday, its position unaltered, still breathing, all the bodily functions performing themselves. The wound in its head had healed a great deal during the night, and I daresay will be completely healed within a week or so, such is the rapidity with which these reptilian organisms repair damages to themselves. Collecting three or four bushels of mussels, I shelled them and poured them down the elasmosaurus's throat. With a convulsive gasp, they passed down and the great mouth slowly closed.

"How long do you expect to keep the reptile alive?" asked Framingham.

"Until I have gotten word to a number of scientific friends, and they have come here to examine it. I shall take you to the nearest settlement and write letters from there. Returning, I shall feed the elasmosaurus regularly until my friends come, and we decide what final disposition to make of it. We shall probably stuff it."

"But you will have trouble in killing it, unless you hack it to pieces, and that won't do. Oh, if I only had the vitality of that animal. There is a monster whose vitality is so splendid that the removal of its brain does not disturb it. I should feel very happy if someone would remove my body. If I only had some of that beast's useless strength."

"In your case, the possession of a too active brain has injured the body," said I. "Too much brain exercise and too little bodily exercise are the causes of your trouble. It would be a pleasant thing if you had the robust health of the elasmosaurus, but what a wonderful thing it would be if that mighty engine had your intelligence."

I turned away to examine the reptile's wounds, for I had brought my surgical instruments with me, and intended to dress them. I was interrupted by a burst of groans from Framingham and turning, beheld him rolling on the sand in an agony. I hastened to him, but before I could reach him, he seized my case of instruments, and taking the largest and sharpest knife, cut his throat from ear to ear.

"Framingham, Framingham," I shouted and, to my astonishment, he looked at me intelligently. I recalled the case of the French doctor who, for some minutes after being guillotined, answered his friends by winking.

"If you hear me, wink," I cried. The right eye closed and opened with a snap. Ah, here the body was dead and the brain lived. I glanced at the elasmosaurus. Its mouth, half closed over its gleaming teeth, seemed to smile an invitation. The intelligence of the man and the strength of the brain. The living body and the living brain. The curious resemblance of the reptile's brain-pan to that of a man flashed across my mind.

"Are you still alive, Framingham?"

The right eye winked. I seized my machete, for there was no time for delicate instruments. I might destroy all by haste and roughness, I was sure to destroy all by delay. I opened the skull and disclosed the brain. I had not injured it, and breaking the wound of the elasmosaurus's head, placed the brain within. I dressed the wound and, hurrying to the house, brought all my store of stimulants and administered them.

For years the medical fraternity has been predicting that brain-grafting will some time be successfully accomplished. Why has it never been successfully accomplished? Because it has not been tried. Obviously, a brain from a dead body cannot be used and what living man would submit to the horrible process of having his head opened, and portions of his brain taken for the use of others?

The brains of men are frequently examined when injured and parts of the brain removed, but parts of the brains of other men have never been substituted for the parts removed. No uninjured man has ever been found who would give any portion of his brain for the use of another. Until criminals under sentence of death are handed over to science for experimentation, we shall not know what can be done in the way of brain-grafting. But public opinion would never allow it.

Conditions are favourable for a fair and thorough trial of my experiment. The weather is cool and even, and the wound in the head of the elasmosaurus has every chance for healing. The animal possesses a vitality superior to any of our later day animals, and if any organism can successfully become the host of a foreign brain, nourishing and cherishing it, the elasmosaurus with its abundant vital forces can do it. It may be that a new era in the history of the world will begin here.

MAY 6TH, NOON.

I think I will allow my experiment a little more time.

MAY 7TH, NOON.

It cannot be imagination. I am sure that as I looked into the elasmosaurus's eyes this morning there was expression in them. Dim, it is true, a sort of mistiness that floats over them like the reflection of passing clouds.

MAY 8TH, NOON.

I am more sure than yesterday that there is expression in the eyes, a look of troubled fear, such as is seen in the eyes of those who dream nightmares with unclosed lids.

MAY 11TH, EVENING.

I have been ill, and have not seen the elasmosaurus for three days, but I shall be better able to judge the progress of the experiment by remaining away a period of some duration.

MAY 12TH, NOON.

I am overcome with awe as I realise the success that has so far crowned my experiment. As I approached the elasmosaurus this morning, I noticed a faint disturbance in the water near its flippers. I cautiously investigated, expecting to discover some fishes nibbling at the helpless monster, and saw that the commotion was not due to fishes, but to the flippers themselves, which were feebly moving.

"Framingham, Framingham," I bawled at the top of my voice. The vast bulk stirred a little, a very little, but enough to notice. Is the brain, or Framingham, it would perhaps be better to say, asleep, or has he failed to establish connection with the body? Undoubtedly he has not yet established connection with the body, and this of itself would be equivalent to sleep, to unconsciousness. As a man born with none of the senses would be unconscious of himself, so Framingham, just beginning to establish connections with his new body, is only dimly conscious of himself and sleeps. I fed him, or it—which is the proper designation will be decided in a few days—with the usual allowance.

MAY 17TH, EVENING.

I have been ill for the past three days, and have not been out of doors until this morning. The elasmosaurus was still motionless when I arrived at the cove this morning. Dead, I thought; but I soon detected signs of breathing, and I began to prepare some mussels for it, and was intent upon my task, when I heard a slight, gasping sound, and looked up. A feeling of terror seized me. It was as if in response to some doubting incantations there had appeared the half-desired, yet wholly-feared and unexpected apparition of a fiend. I shrieked, I screamed, and the amphitheatre of rocks echoed and re-echoed my cries, and all the time the head of the elasmosaurus raised aloft to the full height of its neck, swayed about unsteadily, and its mouth silently struggled and twisted, as if in an attempt to form words, while its eyes looked at me now with wild fear and now with piteous intreaty.

"Framingham," I said.

The monster's mouth closed instantly, and it looked at me attentively, pathetically so, as a dog might look.

"Do you understand me?"

The mouth began struggling again, and little gasps and moans issued forth.

"If you understand me, lay your head on the rock."

Down came the head. He understood me. My experiment was a success. I sat for a moment in silence, meditating upon the wonderful affair, striving to realise that I was awake and sane, and then began in a calm manner to relate to my friend what had taken place since his attempted suicide.

"You are at present something in the condition of a partial paralytic, I should judge," said I, as I concluded my account. "Your mind has not yet learned to command your new body. I see you can move your head and neck, though with difficulty. Move your body if you can. Ah, you cannot, as I thought. But it will all come in time. Whether you will ever be able to talk or not, I cannot say, but I think so, however. And now if you cannot, we will arrange some means of communication. Anyhow, you are rid of your human body and possessed of the powerful vital apparatus you so much envied its former owner. When you gain control of yourself, I wish you to find the communication between this lake and the under-world, and conduct some explorations. Just think of the additions to geological knowledge you can make. I will write an account of your discovery, and the names of Framingham and McLennegan will be among those of the greatest geologists."

I waved my hands in my enthusiasm, and the great eyes of my friend glowed with a kindred fire.

JUNE 2ND, NIGHT.

The process by which Framingham has passed from his first powerlessness to his present ability to speak, and command the use of his corporeal frame, has been so gradual that there has been nothing to note down from day to day. He seems to have all the command over his vast bulk that its former owner had, and in addition speaks and sings. He is singing now. The north wind has risen with the fall of night, and out there in the darkness I hear the mighty organ pipe-tones of his tremendous, magnificent voice, chanting the solemn notes of the Gregorian, the full throated Latin words mingling with the roaring of the wind in a wild and weird harmony.

To-day he attempted to find the connection between the lake and the interior of the earth, but the great well that sinks down in the centre of the lake is choked with rocks and he has discovered nothing. He is tormented by the fear that I will leave him, and that he will perish of loneliness. But I shall not leave him. I feel too much pity for the loneliness he would endure, and besides, I wish to be on the spot should another of those mysterious convulsions open the connection between the lake and the lower world.

He is beset with the idea that should other men discover him, he may be captured and exhibited in a circus or museum, and declares that he will fight for his liberty even to the extent of taking the lives of those attempting to capture him. As a wild animal, he is the property of whomsoever captures him, though perhaps I can set up a title to him on the ground of having tamed him.

JULY 6TH.

One of Framingham's fears has been realised. I was at the pass leading into the basin, watching the clouds grow heavy and pendulous net appear over a knoll in the pass, followed by its bearer, a small man, unmistakably a scientist, but I did not note him well, for as he looked down into the valley, suddenly there burst forth with all the power and volume of a steam calliope, the tremendous voice of Framingham, singing a Greek song of Anacreon to the tune of "Where did you get that hat?" and the singer appeared in a little cove, the black column of his great neck raised aloft, his jagged jaws wide open.

That poor little scientist. He stood transfixed, his butterfly net dropped from his hand, and as Framingham ceased his singing, curvetted and leaped from the water and came down with a splash that set the whole cove swashing, and laughed a guffaw that echoed among the cliffs like the laughing of a dozen demons, he turned and sped through the pass at all speed.

I skip all entries for nearly a year. They are unimportant.

JUNE 30TH, 1897.

A change is certainly coming over my friend. I began to see it some time ago, but refused to believe it and set it down to imagination. A catastrophe threatens, the absorption of the human intellect by the brute body. There are precedents for believing it possible. The human body has more influence over the mind than the mind has over the body. The invalid, delicate Framingham with refined mind, is no more. In his stead is a roistering monster, whose boisterous and commonplace conversation betrays a constantly growing coarseness of mind.

No longer is he interested in my scientific investigations, but pronounces them all bosh. No longer is his conversation such as an educated man can enjoy, but slangy and diffuse iterations concerning the trivial happenings of our uneventful life. Where will it end? In the absorption of the human mind by the brute body? In the final triumph of matter over mind and the degradation of the most mundane force and the extinction of the celestial spark? Then, indeed, will Edward Framingham be dead, and over the grave of his human body can I fittingly erect a headstone, and then will my vigil in this valley be over.
FORT D. A. RUSSELL, WYOMING.

APRIL 15TH, 1899.

Prof. William G. Breyfogle.

Dear Sir,

The inclosed intact manuscript and the fragments which accompany it, came into my possession in the manner I am about to relate and I inclose them to you, for whom they were intended by their late author. Two weeks ago, I was dispatched into the mountains after some Indians who had left their reservation, having under my command a company of infantry and two squads of cavalrymen with mountain howitzers. On the seventh day of our pursuit, which led us into a wild and unknown part of the mountains, we were startled at hearing from somewhere in front us a succession of bellowings of a very unusual nature, mingled with the cries of a human being apparently in the last extremity, and rushing over a rise before us, we looked down upon a lake and saw a colossal, indescribable thing engaged in rending the body of a man.

Observing us, it stretched its jaws and laughed, and in saying this, I wish to be taken literally. Part of my command cried out that it was the devil, and turned and ran. But I rallied them, and thoroughly enraged at what we had witnessed, we marched down to the shore, and I ordered the howitzers to be trained upon the murderous creature. While we were doing this, the thing kept up a constant blabbing that bore a distinct resemblance to human speech, sounding very much like the jabbering of an imbecile, or a drunk trying to talk. I gave the command to fire and to fire again, and the beast tore out into the lake in its death-agony, and sank.

With the remains of Dr. McLennegan, I found the foregoing manuscript intact, and the torn fragments of the diary from which it was compiled, together with other papers on scientific subjects, all of which I forward. I think some attempt should be made to secure the body of the elasmosaurus. It would be a priceless addition to any museum.

Arthur W. Fairchild.
Captain U.S.A.

THE POOL OF THE STONE GOD

Abraham Merritt

This is Professor James Marston's story. A score of learned bodies have courteously heard him tell it, and then among themselves have lamented that so brilliant a man should have such an obsession. Professor Marston told it to me in San Francisco, just before he started to find the island that holds his pool of the stone god and—the wings that guard it. He seemed to me very sane. It is true that the equipment of his expedition was unusual, and not the least curious part of it are the suits of fine chain mail and masks and gauntlets with which each man of the party is provided.

The Five of us, said Professor Marston, sat side by side on the beach. There was Wilkinson the first officer, Bates and Cassidy the two seamen, Waters the pearler and myself. We had all been on our way to New Guinea, I to study the fossils for the Smithsonian. The *Moranus* had struck the hidden reef the night before and had sunk swiftly. We were then, roughly, about five hundred miles northeast of the Guinea coast. The five of us had managed to drop a lifeboat and get away. The boat was well stocked with water and provisions. Whether the rest of the crew had escaped we did not know. We had sighted the island at dawn and had made for her. The lifeboat was drawn safely up on the sands.

"We'd better explore a bit, anyway," said Waters. "This may be a perfect place for us to wait rescue. At least until the typhoon season is over. We've our pistols. Let's start by following this brook to its source, look over the place and then decide what we'll do."

The trees began to thin out. We saw ahead an open space. We reached it and stopped in sheer amazement. The clearing was perfectly square and about five hundred feet wide. The trees stopped abruptly at its edges as though held back by something unseen.

But it was not this singular impression that held us. At the far end of the square were a dozen stone huts clustered about one slightly larger. They reminded me powerfully of those prehistoric structures you see in parts of England and France. I approach now the most singular thing about this whole singular and sinister place. In the center of the space was a pool walled about with huge blocks of cut stone. At the side of the pool rose a great stone figure, carved in the semblance of a man with outstretched hands. It was at least twenty feet high and was extremely well executed. At the distance the statue seemed nude and yet it had a peculiar effect of drapery about it. As we drew nearer we saw that it was covered from ankles to neck with the most extraordinary carved wings. They looked exactly like bat wings when they were folded.

There was something extremely disquieting about this figure. The face was inexpressibly ugly and malignant. The eyes, Mongol-shaped, slanted evil. It was not from the face, though, that this feeling seemed to emanate. It was from the body covered with wings—and especially from the wings. They were part of the idol and yet they gave one the idea that they were clinging to it.

Cassidy, a big brute of a man, swaggered up to the idol and laid his hand on it. He drew it away quickly, his face white, his mouth twitching. I followed him and conquering my unscientific repugnance, examined the stone. It, like the huts and in fact the whole place, was clearly the work of that forgotten race whose monuments are scattered over the Southern Pacific. The carving of the wings was wonderful. They were batlike, as I have said, folded and each ended in a little ring of conventionalized feathers.

They ranged in size from four to ten inches. I ran my fingers over one. Never have I felt the equal of the nausea that sent me to my knees before the idol. The wing had felt like smooth, cold stone, but I had the sensation of having touched back of the stone some monstrous obscene creature of a lower world. The sensation came of course, I reasoned, only from the temperature and texture of the stone—and yet this did not really satisfy me.

Dusk was soon due. We decided to return to the beach and examine the clearing further on the morrow. I desired greatly to explore the stone huts.

We started back through the forest. We walked some distance and then night fell. We lost the brook. After a half hour's wandering we heard it again. We started for it. The trees began to thin out and we thought we were approaching the beach. Then Waters clutched my arm. I stopped. Directly in front of us was the open space with the stone god leering under the moon and the green water shining at his feet!

We had made a circle. Bates and Wilkinson were exhausted. Cassidy swore that devils or no devils he was going to camp that night beside the pool!

The moon was very bright. And it was so very quiet. My scientific curiosity got the better of me and I thought I would examine the huts. I left Bates on guard and walked over to the largest. There was only one room and the moonlight shining through the chinks in the wall illuminated it clearly. At the back were two small basins set in the stone. I looked in one and saw a faint reddish gleam reflected from a number of globular objects. I drew a half dozen of them out. They were pearls, very wonderful pearls of a peculiarly rosy hue. I ran toward the door to call Bates—and stopped!

My eyes had been drawn to the stone idol. Was it an effect of the moonlight or did it move? No, it was the wings! They stood out from the stone and waved—they waved, I say, from the ankles to the neck of that monstrous statue.

Bates had seen them, too. He was standing with his pistol raised. Then there was a shot. And after that the air was filled with a rushing sound like that of a thousand fans. I saw the wings loose themselves from the stone god and sweep down in a cloud upon the four men. Another cloud raced up from the pool and joined them. I could not move. The wings circled swiftly around and about the four. All were now on their feet and I never saw such horror as was in their faces.

Then the wings closed in. They clung to my companions as they had clung to the stone.

I fell back into the hut. I lay there through the night insane with terror. Many times I heard the fan-like rushing about the enclosure, but nothing entered my hut. Dawn came, and silence, and I dragged myself to the door. There stood the stone god with the wings carved upon him as we had seen him ten hours before!

I ran over to the four lying on the grass. I thought that perhaps I had had a nightmare. But they were dead. That was not the worst of it. Each man was shrunken to his bones! They looked like collapsed white balloons. There was not a drop of blood in them. They were nothing but bones wrapped around in thin skin!

Mastering myself, I went close to the idol. There was something different about it. It seemed larger—as though, the thought went through my mind, as though it had eaten. Then I saw that it was covered with tiny drops of blood that had dropped from the ends of the wings that clothed it!

I do not remember what happened afterward. I awoke on the pearling schooner *Luana* which had picked me up, crazed with thirst as they supposed in the boat of the *Moranus*.

THE ROCKET OF 1955

C.M. Kornbluth

The scheme was all Fein's, but the trimmings that made it more than a pipe dream and its actual operation depended on me. How long the plan had been in incubation I do not know, but Fein, one spring day, broke it to me in crude form. I pointed out some errors, corrected and amplified on the thing in general, and told him that I'd have no part of it—and changed my mind when he threatened to reveal certain indiscretions committed by me some years ago.

It was necessary that I spend some months in Europe, conducting research work incidental to the scheme. I returned with recorded statements, old newspapers, and photostatic copies of certain documents. There was a brief, quiet interview with that old, bushy-haired Viennese worshipped incontinently by the mob; he was convinced by the evidence I had compiled that it would be wise to assist us.

You all know what happened next—it was the professor's historic radio broadcast. Fein had drafted the thing, I had rewritten it, and told the astronomer to assume a German accent while reading. Some of the phrases were beautiful: "American dominion over the very planets!...veil at last ripped aside...man defies gravity...travel through limitless space...plant the red-white-and-blue banner in the soil of Mars!"

The requested contributions poured in. Newspapers and magazines ostentatiously donated yard-long checks of a few thousand dollars; the government gave a welcome half-million; heavy sugar came from the "Rocket Contribution Week" held in the nation's public schools; but independent contributions were the largest. We cleared seven million dollars, and then started to build the spaceship.

The virginium that took up most of the money was tin plate; the monoatomic fluorine that gave us our terrific speed was hydrogen. The take-off was a party for the newsreels: the big, gleaming bullet extravagant with vanes and projections; speeches by the professor; Farley, who was to fly it to Mars, grinning into the cameras. He climbed an outside ladder to the nose of the thing, then dropped into the steering compartment. I screwed down the sound-proof door, smiling as he hammered to be let out. To his surprise, there was no duplicate of the elaborate dummy controls he had been practicing on for the past few weeks.

I cautioned the pressmen to stand back under the shelter, and gave the professor the knife switch that would send the rocket on its way. He hesitated too long—Fein hissed into his ear: "Anna Pareloff of Cracow, Herr Professor.

The triple blade clicked into the sockets. The vaned projectile roared a hundred yards into the air with a wobbling curve—then exploded.

A photographer, eager for an angle shot, was killed; so were some kids. The steel roof protected the rest of us. Fein and I shook hands, while the pressmen screamed into the telephones which we had provided.

But the professor got drunk, and, disgusted with the part he had played in the affair, told all and poisoned himself. Fein and I left the cash behind and hopped a freight. We were picked off it by a vigilance committee (headed by a man who had lost fifty cents in our rocket). Fein was too frightened to talk or write so they hanged him first, and gave me a paper and pencil to tell the story as best I could.

Here they come, with an insulting thick rope.

THE SCIENTIFIC APE

Robert Louis Stevenson

In a certain West Indian Isle, there stood a house and hard by a grove of trees. In the house there dwelt a vivisectionist, and on the trees a clan of anthropoid apes. It chanced that one of these was caught by the vivisectionist and kept some time in a cage in the laboratory. There he was much terrified by what he saw, deeply interested in all he heard; and as he had the fortune to escape at an early period of his case (which was numbered 701) and to return to his family with only a trifling lesion of one foot, he thought himself on the whole the gainer.

He was no sooner back than he dubbed himself doctor and began to trouble his neighbours with the question: Why are not apes progressive?

"I do not know what progressive means," said one, and threw a cocoanut at his grandmother.

"I neither know nor care," said another, and swung himself into a neighbouring tree.

"O stow that!" cried a third.

"Damn progress!" said the chief, who was an old physical-force tory. "Try and behave yourselves better the way you are."

But when the scientific ape got the younger males alone, he was heard with more attention. "Man is only a promoted ape," said he, hanging his tail from a high branch. "The geological record being incomplete, it is impossible to say how long he took to rise, and how long it might take us to follow in his steps. But by plunging vigorously in medias res on a system of my own, I believe we shall astonish everyone. Man lost centuries over religion, morals, poetry and other fudge; it was centuries before he got properly to science, and only the other day that he began to vivisect. We shall go the other way about, and begin with vivisection."

"What in the name of cocoanuts is vivisection?" asked an ape.

The doctor explained at great length what he had seen in the laboratory; and some of his hearers were delighted, but not all.

"I never heard of anything so beastly!" cried an ape who had lost one ear in quarrel with his aunt.

"And what is the good of it?" asked another.

"Don't you see?" said the doctor. "By vivisecting men, we find out how apes are made, and so we advance."

"But why not vivisect each other?" asked one of his disciples who was disputatious.

"O, fie!" said the doctor. "I will not sit and listen to such talk; or at least not in public."

"But criminals?" inquired the disputant.

"It is highly doubtful if there be such a thing as right or wrong: then, where's your criminal?" replied the doctor. "And besides the public would not stand it. And men are just as good; it's all the same genus." "It seems rough on the men," said the ape with one ear.

"Well, to begin with," said the doctor, "they say that we don't suffer and are what they call automata; so I have a perfect right to say the same of them."

"That must be nonsense," said the disputant; "and besides it's self-destructive. If they are only automata, they can teach us nothing of ourselves; and if they can teach us anything of ourselves, by cocoanuts! they have to suffer."

"I am much of your way of thinking," said the doctor, "and indeed that argument is only fit for the monthly magazines. Say that they do suffer. Well, they suffer in the interest of a lower race, which requires help: there can be nothing fairer than that. And besides we shall doubtless make discoveries which will prove useful to themselves."

"But how are we to make discoveries," inquired the disputant, "when we don't know what to look for?"

"God bless my tail!" cried the Doctor, nettled out of his dignity, "I believe you have the least scientific mind of any ape in the Windward Islands! Know what to look for indeed! True science has nothing to do with that. You just vivisect along, upon the chance; and if you do discover anything, who is so surprised as you?"

"I see one more objection," said the disputant, "though, mind you, I am far from denying it would be capital fun. But men are so strong, and then they have these guns."

"And therefore we shall take babies," concluded the doctor.

That same afternoon, the doctor returned to the vivisectionist's garden, purloined one of his razors through the dressing room window, and on a second trip, removed his baby from the nursery basinette.

There was a great to-do in the tree tops. The ape with the one ear, who was a good natured fellow, nursed the baby in his arms; another stuffed nuts in its mouth, and was aggrieved because it would not eat them. "It has no sense," said he.

"But I wish it would not cry," said the ape with the one ear, "it looks so horribly like a monkey!" "This is childish," said the doctor. "Give me the razor."

But at this the ape with one ear lost heart, spat at the doctor, and fled with the baby into the next tree top.

"Yah!" cried the ape with the one ear, "vivisect yourself!"

At this the whole crew began chasing and screaming; and the noise called up the chief, who was in the neighbourhood, killing fleas.

"What is all this about?" cried the chief. And when they had told him, he wiped his brow. "Great cocoanuts!" cried he, "is this a nightmare? Can apes descend to such barbarity? Take back that baby where it came from."

"You have not a scientific mind," said the doctor.

"I do not know if I have a scientific mind or not," replied the chief; "but I have a very thick stick, and if you lay one claw upon that baby, I will break your head with it."

So they took the baby to the front garden plot. The vivisectionist (who was an estimable family man) was overjoyed, and in the lightness of his heart, began three more experiments in his laboratory before the day was done.

THE STAR

H.G. Wells

It was on the first day of the new year that the announcement was made, almost simultaneously from three observatories, that the motion of the planet Neptune, the outermost of all the planets that wheeled about the sun, had become erratic. Ogilvy had already called attention to a suspected retardation in its velocity in December. Such a piece of news was scarcely calculated to interest the world the greater portion of whose inhabitants were unaware of the existence of the planet Neptune, nor outside the astronomical profession did the subsequent discovery of a faint remote speck of light in the region of the perturbed planet cause any great excitement

Scientific people, however, found the intelligence remarkable enough, even before it became known that the new body was rapidly growing larger and brighter, that its motion was quite different from the orderly progress of the planets, and that the deflection of Neptune and its satellite was becoming now of an unprecedented kind.

Few people without training in science can realize the huge isolation of the solar system. The sun with its specks of planets, its dust of planetoids, and its impalpable comets swims in vacant immensity that almost defeats the imagination. Beyond the orbit of Neptune there is space, vacant so far as human observation has penetrated, without warmth or light or sound, blank emptiness, for twenty billion times a million miles. That is the smallest estimate of the distance to be traversed before the nearest of the stars is attained. And, saving a few comets, more unsubstantial than the thinnest flame, no matter had ever to human knowledge crossed the gulf of space, until early in the twentieth century this wanderer appeared.

A vast mass of matter it was, bulky, heavy, rushing without warning out of the black mystery of the sky into the radiance of the sun. By the second day it was clearly visible to any decent instrument, as a speck with a barely sensible diameter, in the constellation. Leo near Regulus. In a little while an opera glass could attain it.

On the third day of the new year the newspaper readers of two hemispheres were made aware for the first time of the real importance of this unusual apparition in the heavens. "A Planetary Collision," one London paper headed the news, and proclaimed Duchine's opinion that this strange new planet would probably collide with Neptune. The leader writers enlarged upon the topic. So that in most of the capitals of the world, on Jan. 3, there was an expectation, however vague, of some eminent phenomenon in the sky; and as the night followed the sunset round the globe thousands of men turned their eyes skyward, to see—the old familiar stars just as they had always been.

Until it was dawn in London and Pollux setting, and the stars overhead grown pale. The winters dawn it was, a sickly filtering accumulation of daylight, and the light of gas and candles shone yellow in the windows to show where people were astir. But the yawning policeman saw the thing, the busy crowds in the market stopped agape, workmen going to their work betimes, milkmen, the drivers of news carts, dissipation going home jaded and pale, homeless wanderers, sentinels on their beats, and in the country, laborers trudging afield, poachers slinking home, all over the dusky quickening country it would be seen—and out at sea by seamen watching for the day—a great white star, come suddenly into the westward sky!

Brighter it was than any star in our skies; brighter than the evening star at its brightest. It still glowed out white and large, no mere twinkling spot of light but a small round clear shining disk, an hour after the day had come. And where science has not reached, men stared and feared, telling one another of the wars and pestilences that are foreshadowed by these fiery signs in the heavens. Sturdy Boers, dusky Hottentots, Gold Coast negroes, Frenchmen, Spaniards, Portuguese, stood in the glow of the sunrise watching the setting of this strange new star.

And in a hundred observatories there had been suppressed excitement, rising almost to shouting pitch, as the two remote bodies had rushed together. There had been a hurrying to and fro to gather photographic apparatus and spectroscope; to gather this appliance and that, to record the novel astonishing sight, the destruction of a world,—for it was a world, a sister planet of our earth, far greater than our earth indeed, that had so suddenly flashed into flaming death. Neptune it was, which had been struck, fairly, and squarely, by the planet from outer space and the heat of concussion had incontinently turned two solid globes into one vast mass of incandescence.

Round the world that day, two hours before the dawn, went the pallid great white star, fading only as it sank westward and the sun mounted above it. Everywhere man marveled at it, but of all those who saw it none could have marveled more than those sailors, habitual watchers of the stars, who far away at sea had heard nothing of its advent and saw it now rise like a pigmy moon and climb zenithward and hang overhead and sink westward with the passing of the night.

And when next it rose over Europe everywhere were crowds of watchers on hilly slopes, on house roofs, in open spaces, staring eastward, waiting for the rising of the new star. It rose with a white glow in front, like the glare of a white fire, and those who had seen it come into existence the night before cried out at the sight of it. "It is larger," they cried. "It is brighter!" And, indeed, the moon a quarter full and sinking in the west was in its apparent size beyond comparison, but scarcely in all its breadth had it as much brightness now as the little circle of the strange new star.

"It is brighter!" cried the people clustering in the streets. But in the dim observatories the watchers held their breath and peered at one another. "It is nearer," they said. "Nearer!"

And voice after voice repeated. "It is nearer," and the clicking telegraph took that up, and it trembled along telephone wires, and in a thousand cities grimy compositors fingered the type. "It is nearer." Men writing in offices, struck with strange realization, flung down their pens, men talking in a thousand places suddenly came upon a grotesque possibility in those words, "It is nearer." It hurried along awakening streets, it was shouted down the frost-stilled ways of quiet villages, men who had read these things, from the throbbing tape stood in yellow-lit doorways shouting the news to the passers-by. "It is nearer." Pretty women flushed and glittering, heard the news told jestingly between dances, and feigned an intelligent interest they did not feel. "Nearer! Indeed. How curious! How clever people must be to find out things like that!"

Lonely tramps faring through the wintry night murmured those words to comfort themselves—looking skyward. "It has need to be nearer, for the night's as cold as charity. Don't seem much warmth from it if it is nearer, all the same."

"What is a new star to me?" cried the weeping woman kneeling beside her dead.

The schoolboy, rising early for his examination work, puzzled it out for himself—with the great white star shining broad and bright through the frost-flowers of his window. "Centrifugal, centripetal," he said, with his chin on his fist, "Stop a planet in its flight, rob it of its centrifugal force, what then? Centripetal has it, and down it falls into the sun! And this—!"

"Do we come in the way? I wonder—"

The light of that day went the way of its brethren, and with the later watches of the frosty darkness rose the strange star again. And it was now so bright that the waxing moon seemed but a pale yellow ghost of itself, rising huge in the sunset hour. In a South African city a great man had married, and the streets were alight to welcome his return with his bride. "Even the skies have illuminated," said the flatterer. Under Capricorn, two negro lovers, daring the wild beasts and evil spirits, for love of one another, crouched together in a cane brake where the fireflies hovered. "That is our star," they whispered, and felt strangely comforted by the sweet brilliancy of its light.

The master mathematician sat in his private room and pushed the papers from him. His calculations were already finished. In a small white phial there still remained a little of the drug that had kept him awake and active for four long nights. Each day, serene, explicit, patient as ever, he had given his lecture to his students, and then had come back at once to this momentous calculation. His face was grave, a little drawn, and hectic from his drugged activity. For some time he seemed lost in thought. Then he went to the window, and the blind went up with a click. Half way up the sky, over the clustering roofs, chimneys, and steeples of the city, hung the star.

He looked at it as one might look into the eye of a brave enemy, "You may kill me," he said after a silence. "But I can hold you—and all the universe for that matter—in the grip of this little brain. I would not change even now."

He looked at the little phial. "There will be no need of sleep again," he said. The next day at noon, punctual to the minute, he entered his lecture theater, put his hat on the end of the table as his habit was, and carefully selected a large piece of chalk. It was a joke among his students that he could not lecture without that piece of chalk to fumble in his fingers, and once he had been stricken to impotence by their hiding his supply. He came and looked under his gray eyebrows at the rising tiers of young fresh faces, and spoke with his accustomed studied commonness of phrasing. "Circumstances have arisen—circumstances beyond my control," he said and paused, "which will debar me from completing the course I had designed. It would seem, gentlemen, if I may put the thing clearly and briefly, that—man has lived in vain."

The students glanced at one another. Had they heard aright? Mad? Raised eyebrows and grinning lips there were, but one or two faces remained intent upon his calm gray-fringed face. "It will be interesting," he was saying, "to devote this morning to an exposition, so far as I can make it clear to you, of the calculations that have led me to this conclusion. Let us assume—"

He turned toward the blackboard, meditating a diagram in the way that was usual to him. "What was that about 'lived in vain'?" whispered one student to another. "Listen," said the other, nodding toward the lecturer.

And presently they began to understand.

That night the star rose later, for its proper eastward motion had carried it some way across Leo toward Virgo, and its brightness was so great that the sky became a luminous blue as it rose, and every star and planet was hidden, save only Jupiter near the zenith, Capella, Aldebaran, Sirius, and the pointers of the Bear. It was white and beautiful. In many parts of the world that night a pallid halo encircled it about. It was perceptibly larger; in the clear refractive sky of the tropics it seemed as if it were nearly a quarter of the size of the moon. The frost was still on the ground in England, but the world was as brightly lit as if it were midsummer moonlight. One could see to read quite ordinary print by that cold clear light, and in the cities the lamps burnt yellow and wan.

And everywhere the world was awake that night, and throughout Christendom a somber murmur hung in the keen air over the countryside like the buzzing of the bees in the heather, and this murmurous tumult grew to a clangor in the cities. It was the tolling of the bells in a million belfry towers and steeples, summoning the people to sleep no more, to sin no more, but to gather in their churches and pray. And overhead, growing larger and brighter, as the earth rolled on its way and the night passed, rose the dazzling star.

And the streets and houses were alight in all the cities, the shipyards glared, and whatever roads led to high country were lit and crowded all night long. And in all the seas about the civilized lands ships with throbbing engines, and ships with bellying sails, crowded with men and living creatures, were standing out to ocean and the north. For already the warning of the master mathematician had been telegraphed over the world, and translated into a hundred tongues. The new planet and Neptune, locked in a fiery embrace, were whirling headlong, ever faster and faster, toward the sun. Already every second this blazing mass flew a hundred miles, and every second its terrific velocity increased. As it flew its course, it must pass a hundred million of miles wide of the earth and scarcely affect it.

But near its destined path, as yet only slightly perturbed, spun the mighty planet Jupiter and his moons sweeping splendid around the sun. Every moment now the attraction between the fiery star and the greatest of the planets grew stronger. And the result of that attraction? Inevitably Jupiter, would be deflected from its orbit to a new elliptical path, and the burning star, swung by his attraction wide of its sunward rush, would "describe a curved path" and perhaps collide with and certainly pass close to, our earth. "Earthquakes, volcanic outbreaks, cyclones, sea waves, floods, and a steady rise in temperature to I know not what limit"—so prophesied the master mathematician.

And overhead, to carry out his words, lonely and cold and livid, blazed the star of the coming doom.

To many who stared at it that night until their eyes ached, it seemed that it was visibly approaching. And that night, too, the weather changed, and the frost that had gripped all Central Europe and France and England softened towards a thaw.

But you must not imagine because I have spoken of people praying through the night and people going aboard ships and people fleeing towards mountainous country that the whole world was already in a terror because of the star. As a matter of fact, use and wont still ruled the world, and save for the talk of idle moments and the splendor of the night, nine human beings out of ten were still busy at their common occupations. In all the cities the shops, save one here and there, opened and closed at their proper hours, the doctor and the undertaker plied their trades, and workers gathered in the factories, soldiers drilled, scholars studied, lovers sought one another, thieves lurked and fled, politicians planned their schemes. The presses of the newspapers roared through the nights, and many a priest of this church and that would not open his holy building to further what he considered a foolish panic.

The newspapers insisted on the lesson of the year 1000—for then, too, people had anticipated the end. The star was no star—mere gas—a comet; and were it a star it could not possibly strike the earth. There was no precedent for such a thing. Common sense was sturdy everywhere, scornful, jesting, a little inclined to persecute the obdurate fearful. That night at 7:15 by Greenwich time the star would be at its nearest, to Jupiter. Then the world would see the turn things would take. The master mathematician's grim warnings were treated by many as so much mere elaborate self-advertisement. Common sense at last, a little heated, by argument, signified its unalterable convictions by going to bed. So, too, barbarism and savagery, already tired of the novelty, went about their nightly business, and save for a howling dog here and there the beast-world left the star unheeded.

And yet, when at last the watchers in the European states saw the star rise, an hour later, it is true, but no larger than it had been the night before, there were still plenty awake to laugh at the master mathematician—to take the danger as if it had passed.

But hereafter the laughter ceased. The star grew—it grew with a terrible steadiness hour after hour, a little larger each hour, a little nearer the midnight zenith, and brighter and brighter, until it had turned night into day. Had it come straight to the earth instead of in a curved path, had it lost no velocity to Jupiter, it must have leapt the intervening gulf in a day; but as it was it took five days altogether to come by our planet. The next night it had become a third the size of the moon before it set to English eyes, and the thaw was assured.

It rose over America nearly the size of the moon, but blinding white to look at, and hot; and a breath of hot wind blew now with its rising and gathering strength, and in Virginia and Brazil and down the St. Lawrence valley it shone intermittently through a driving reek of thunder clouds, flickering violet lightning, and hail unprecedented. In Manitoba were a thaw and devastating floods. And upon all the mountains of the earth the snow and ice began to melt that night, and all the rivers coming out of high country flowed thick and turbid, and soon—in their upper reaches—with swirling trees and the bodies of beasts and men. They rose steadily, steadily in the ghostly brilliance, and came trickling over their banks at last, behind the flying population of their valleys.

And along the coast of Argentina and up the South Atlantic tides were higher than the had ever been in the memory of man, and the storms drove the waters in many cases scores of miles inland drowning whole cities. And so great grew the heat during the night that the rising of the sun was like the coming of a shadow. The earthquakes began and grew until all down America from the Arctic Circle to Cape Horn hillsides were sliding, fissures were opening, and houses and walls crumbling to destruction.

China was lit glowing white, but over Japan and Java and all the islands of eastern Asia the great star was a ball of dull red fire because of the steam and smoke and ashes the volcanoes were spouting forth to salute its coming. Above were the lava, hot gases, and ash, and below the seething floods, and the whole earth swayed and rumbled with the earthquake shocks. Soon the immemorial snows of Tibet and the Himalayas were melting and pouring down by ten million deepening converging channels upon the plains of Burma and Hindustan. The tangled summits of the Indian jungles were aflame in a thousand places, and below the hurrying waters around the stems were dark objects that struggled feebly and reflected the blood red tongues of fire. And in ungovernable confusion a multitude of men and women fled down the broad riverways to that one last hope of men—the open sea.

Larger grew the star, and larger, hotter, and brighter with a terrible swiftness now. The tropical ocean had lost its phosphorescence, and the whirling steam rose in ghostly wreaths from the black waves that plunged incessantly, speckled with storm-tossed ships.

And then came a wonder. It seemed to those who in Europe watched for the rising of the star that the world must have ceased its rotation. In a thousand open spaces of down and upland the people who had fled thither from the floods and the falling houses and sliding slopes of hill watched for that rising in vain. Hour followed hour through a terrible suspense, and the star rose not. Once again men set their eyes upon the old constellations they had counted lost to them forever. In England it was hot and clear overhead, though the ground quivered perpetually; but in the tropics Sirius and Capella and Aldebaran showed through a veil of steam. And when at last the great star rose, near ten hours late, the sun rose close upon it, and in the center of its white heart was a disk of black.

Over Asia the star had begun to fall behind the movement of the sky, and then suddenly, as it hung over India, its light had been veiled. All the plain of India from the mouth of the Indus to the mouths of the Ganges was a shallow waste of shining water that night, out of which rose temples and palaces, mounds and hills, black with people. Every minaret was a clustering mass of people, who fell one by one into the turbid waters as heat and terror overcame them. The whole land seemed a-wailing, and suddenly there swept a shadow across that furnace of despair, and a breath of cold wind, and a gathering of clouds out of the cooling air. Men looking up, nearly blinded, at the star, and saw that black disk creeping across the light. It was the moon, coming between the star and the earth. And even as men cried to God at this respite, out of the east with a strange, inexplicable swiftness sprang the sun. And then star, sun, and moon rushed together across the heavens.

So it was that presently, to the European watchers, star and sun rose close upon each other, drove headlong for a space, and then slower, and at last came to rest, star and sun merged into one glare of flame at the zenith of the sky. The moon no longer eclipsed the star, but was lost to sight in the brilliance of the sky. And though those who were still alive regarded it for the most part with that dull stupidity that hunger, fatigue, heat, and despair engender, there were still men who could perceive the meaning of these signs. Star and earth had been at their nearest, had swung about one another, and the star had passed. Already it was receding, swifter and swifter, in the last stage of its headlong journey downward into the sun.

And then the clouds gathered, blotting out the vision of the sky; the thunder and lightning wove a garment around the world; all over the earth was such a downpour of rain as men had never seen before; and where the volcanoes flared red against the cloud canopy there descended torrents of mud. Everywhere the waters were pouring off the land, leaving mud stilted ruins, and the earth littered like a storm-worn beach with all that had floated, and the dead bodies of the men and brutes, its children.

For days the water streamed off the land, sweeping away soil and trees and houses in the way and piling huge dikes and scooping out titanic gullies over the countryside. Those were the days of darkness that followed the star and the heat. All through them, and for many weeks and months, the earthquakes continued.

But the star had passed, and men, hunger-driven and gathering courage only slowly, might creep back to their ruined cities, buried granaries, and sodden fields. Such few ships as had escaped the storms of that time came stunned and shattered and sounding their way cautiously through the new marks and shoals of once familiar ports. And as the storms subsided men perceived that everywhere the days were hotter than of yore, and the sun larger, and the moon, shrunk to a third of its former size, took now fourscore days between its new and new.

But of the new brotherhood that grew presently among men, of the saving of laws and books and machines, of the strange change that had come over Iceland and Greenland the shores of Baffin's Bay, so that the sailors coming there presently found them green and gracious, and could scarce believe their eyes, this story does not tell. Nor of the movement of mankind, now that the earth was hotter, northward and southward towards the poles of the earth. It concerns itself only with the coming and the passing of the star.

The Martian astronomers—for there are astronomers on Mars, although they are different beings from men—were naturally profoundly interested by these things. They saw them from their own standpoint, of course. "Considering the mass and temperature of the missile that was flung through our solar system into the sun," one wrote, "it is astonishing what little damage the earth, which it missed so narrowly, has sustained. All the familiar continental markings and the masses of the seas remain intact, and indeed the only difference seems to be a shrinkage of the white discoloration (supposed to be frozen water) round either pole." Which only shows how small the vastest of human catastrophisa may seem at a distance of a few million miles.

THE STOLEN BACILLUS

H.G. Wells

"This again," said the Bacteriologist, slipping a glass slide under the microscope, "is a preparation of the celebrated Bacillus of cholera—the cholera germ."

The pale-faced man peered down the microscope. He was evidently not accustomed to that kind of thing, and held a limp white hand over his disengaged eye. "I see very little," he said.

"Touch this screw," said the Bacteriologist; "perhaps the microscope is out of focus for you. Eyes vary so much. Just the fraction of a turn this way or that."

"Ah! now I see," said the visitor. "Not so very much to see after all. Little streaks and shreds of pink. And yet those little particles, those mere atomies, might multiply and devastate a city! Wonderful!"

He stood up, and releasing the glass slip from the microscope, held it in his hand towards the window. "Scarcely visible," he said, scrutinising the preparation. He hesitated. "Are these—alive? Are they dangerous now?"

"Those have been stained and killed," said the Bacteriologist. "I wish, for my own part, we could kill and stain every one of them in the universe."

"I suppose," the pale man said with a slight smile, "that you scarcely care to have such things about you in the living—in the active state?"

"On the contrary, we are obliged to," said the Bacteriologist. "Here, for instance—" He walked across the room and took up one of several sealed tubes. "Here is the living thing. This is a cultivation of the actual living disease bacteria." He hesitated, "Bottled cholera, so to speak."

A slight gleam of satisfaction appeared momentarily in the face of the pale man.

"It's a deadly thing to have in your possession," he said, devouring the little tube with his eyes. The Bacteriologist watched the morbid pleasure in his visitor's expression. This man, who had visited him that afternoon with a note of introduction from an old friend, interested him from the very contrast of their dispositions. The lank black hair and deep grey eyes, the haggard expression and nervous manner, the fitful yet keen interest of his visitor were a novel change from the phlegmatic deliberations of the ordinary scientific worker with whom the Bacteriologist chiefly associated. It was perhaps natural, with a hearer evidently so impressionable to the lethal nature of his topic, to take the most effective aspect of the matter.

He held the tube in his hand thoughtfully. "Yes, here is the pestilence imprisoned. Only break such a little tube as this into a supply of drinking-water, say to these minute particles of life that one must needs stain and examine with the highest powers of the microscope even to see, and that one can neither smell nor taste—say to them, 'Go forth, increase and multiply, and replenish the cisterns,' and death—mysterious, untraceable death, death swift and terrible, death full of pain and indignity—would be released upon this city, and go hither and thither seeking his victims. Here he would take the husband from the wife, here the child from its mother, here the statesman from his duty, and here the toiler from his trouble. He would follow the water-mains, creeping along streets, picking out and punishing a house here and a house there where they did not boil their drinking-water, creeping into the wells of the mineral-water makers, getting washed into salad, and lying dormant in ices. He would wait ready to be drunk in the horse-troughs, and by unwary children in the public fountains. He would soak into the soil, to reappear in springs and wells at a thousand unexpected places. Once start him at the water supply, and before we could ring him in, and catch him again, he would have decimated the metropolis."

He stopped abruptly. He had been told rhetoric was his weakness.

"But he is quite safe here, you know—quite safe."

The pale-faced man nodded. His eyes shone. He cleared his throat. "These Anarchist—rascals," said he, "are fools, blind fools—to use bombs when this kind of thing is attainable. I think—"

A gentle rap, a mere light touch of the finger-nails was heard at the door. The Bacteriologist opened it. "Just a minute, dear," whispered his wife.

When he re-entered the laboratory his visitor was looking at his watch. "I had no idea I had wasted an hour of your time," he said. "Twelve minutes to four. I ought to have left here by half-past three. But your things were really too interesting. No, positively I cannot stop a moment longer. I have an engagement at four."

He passed out of the room reiterating his thanks, and the Bacteriologist accompanied him to the door, and then returned thoughtfully along the passage to his laboratory. He was musing on the ethnology of his visitor. Certainly the man was not a Teutonic type nor a common Latin one. "A morbid product, anyhow, I am afraid," said the Bacteriologist to himself. "How he gloated on those cultivations of disease-germs!" A disturbing thought struck him. He turned to the bench by the vapour-bath, and then very quickly to his writing-table. Then he felt hastily in his pockets, and then rushed to the door. "I may have put it down on the hall table," he said.

"Minnie!" he shouted hoarsely in the hall.

"Yes, dear," came a remote voice.

"Had I anything in my hand when I spoke to you, dear, just now?"

Pause.

"Nothing, dear, because I remember—"

"Blue ruin!" cried the Bacteriologist, and incontinently ran to the front door and down the steps of his house to the street.

Minnie, hearing the door slam violently, ran in alarm to the window. Down the street a slender man was getting into a cab. The Bacteriologist, hatless, and in his carpet slippers, was running and gesticulating wildly towards this group. One slipper came off, but he did not wait for it. "He has gone *mad*!" said Minnie; "it's that horrid science of his"; and, opening the window, would have called after him. The slender man, suddenly glancing round, seemed struck with the same idea of mental disorder. He pointed hastily to the Bacteriologist, said something to the cabman, the apron of the cab slammed, the whip swished, the horse's feet clattered, and in a moment cab, and Bacteriologist hotly in pursuit, had receded up the vista of the roadway and disappeared round the corner.

Minnie remained straining out of the window for a minute. Then she drew her head back into the room again. She was dumbfounded. "Of course he is eccentric," she meditated. "But running about London—in the height of the season, too—in his socks!" A happy thought struck her. She hastily put her bonnet on, seized his shoes, went into the hall, took down his hat and light overcoat from the pegs, emerged upon the doorstep, and hailed a cab that opportunely crawled by. "Drive me up the road and round Havelock Crescent, and see if we can find a gentleman running about in a velveteen coat and no hat."

"Velveteen coat, ma'am, and no 'at. Very good, ma'am." And

the cabman whipped up at once in the most matter-of-fact way, as if he drove to this address every day in his life.

Some few minutes later the little group of cabmen and loafers that collects round the cabmen's shelter at Haverstock Hill were startled by the passing of a cab with a ginger-coloured screw of a horse, driven furiously.

They were silent as it went by, and then as it receded—"That's 'Arry 'Icks. Wot's *he* got?" said the stout gentleman known as Old Tootles.

"He's a-using his whip, he is, *to* rights," said the ostler boy.

"Hullo!" said poor old Tommy Byles; "here's another bloomin' loonatic. Blowed if there aint."

"It's old George," said old Tootles, "and he's drivin' a loonatic, *as* you say. Aint he a-clawin' out of the keb? Wonder if he's after 'Arry 'Icks?"

The group round the cabmen's shelter became animated. Chorus: "Go it, George!" "It's a race." "You'll ketch 'em!" "Whip up!"

"She's a goer, she is!" said the ostler boy.

"Strike me giddy!" cried old Tootles. "Here! *I'm* a-going' to begin in a minute. Here's another comin'. If all the kebs in Hampstead aint gone mad this morning!"

"It's a fieldmale this time," said the ostler boy.

"She's a followin' *him*," said old Tootles. "Usually the other way about."

"What's she got in her 'and?"

"Looks like a 'igh 'at."

"What a bloomin' lark it is! Three to one on old George," said the ostler boy. "Nexst!"

Minnie went by in a perfect roar of applause. She did not like it but she felt that she was doing her duty, and whirled on down Haverstock Hill and Camden Town High Street with her eyes ever intent on the animated back view of old George, who was driving her vagrant husband so incomprehensibly away from her.

The man in the foremost cab sat crouched in the corner, his arms tightly folded, and the little tube that contained such vast possibilities of destruction gripped in his hand. His mood was a singular mixture of fear and exultation. Chiefly he was afraid of being caught before he could accomplish his purpose, but behind this was a vaguer but larger fear of the awfulness of his crime. But his exultation far exceeded his fear. No Anarchist before him had ever approached this conception of his. Ravachol, Vaillant, all those distinguished persons whose fame he had envied dwindled into insignificance beside him. He had only to make sure of the water supply, and break the little tube into a reservoir. How brilliantly he had planned it, forged the letter of introduction and got into the laboratory, and how brilliantly he had seized his opportunity! The world should hear of him at last. All those people who had sneered at him, neglected him, preferred other people to him, found his company undesirable, should consider him at last. Death, death, death! They had always treated him as a man of no importance. All the world had been in a conspiracy to keep him under. He would teach them yet what it is to isolate a man. What was this familiar street? Great Saint Andrew's Street, of course! How fared the chase? He craned out of the cab. The Bacteriologist was scarcely fifty yards behind. That was bad. He would be caught and stopped yet. He felt in his pocket for money, and found half-a-sovereign. This he thrust up through the trap in the top of the cab into the man's face. "More," he shouted, "if only we get away."

The money was snatched out of his hand. "Right you are," said the cabman, and the trap slammed, and the lash lay along the glistening side of the horse. The cab swayed, and the Anarchist, half-standing under the trap, put the hand containing the little glass tube upon the apron to preserve his balance. He felt the brittle thing crack, and the broken half of it rang upon the floor of the cab. He fell back into the seat with a curse, and stared dismally at the two or three drops of moisture on the apron.

He shuddered.

"Well! I suppose I shall be the first. *Phew*! Anyhow, I shall be a Martyr. That's something. But it is a filthy death, nevertheless. I wonder if it hurts as much as they say."

Presently a thought occurred to him—he groped between his feet. A little drop was still in the broken end of the tube, and he drank that to make sure. It was better to make sure. At any rate, he would not fail.

Then it dawned upon him that there was no further need to escape the Bacteriologist. In Wellington Street he told the cabman to stop, and got out. He slipped on the step, and his head felt queer. It was rapid stuff this cholera poison. He waved his cabman out of existence, so to speak, and stood on the pavement with his arms folded upon his breast awaiting the arrival of the Bacteriologist. There was something tragic in his pose. The sense of imminent death gave him a certain dignity. He greeted his pursuer with a defiant laugh.

"Vive l'Anarchie! You are too late, my friend. I have drunk it. The cholera is abroad!"

The Bacteriologist from his cab beamed curiously at him through his spectacles. "You have drunk it! An Anarchist! I see now." He was about to say something more, and then checked himself. A smile hung in the corner of his mouth. He opened the apron of his cab as if to descend, at which the Anarchist waved him a dramatic farewell and strode off towards Waterloo Bridge, carefully jostling his infected body against as many people as possible. The Bacteriologist was so preoccupied with the vision of him that he scarcely manifested the slightest surprise at the appearance of Minnie upon the pavement with his hat and shoes and overcoat. "Very good of you to bring my things," he said, and remained lost in contemplation of the receding figure of the Anarchist.

"You had better get in," he said, still staring. Minnie felt absolutely convinced now that he was mad, and directed the cabman home on her own responsibility. "Put on my shoes? Certainly dear," said he, as the cab began to turn, and hid the strutting black figure, now small in the distance, from his eyes. Then suddenly something grotesque struck him, and he laughed. Then he remarked, "It is really very serious, though."

"You see, that man came to my house to see me, and he is an Anarchist. No—don't faint, or I cannot possibly tell you the rest. And I wanted to astonish him, not knowing he was an Anarchist, and took up a cultivation of that new species of Bacterium I was telling you of, that infest, and I think cause, the blue patches upon various monkeys; and like a fool, I said it was Asiatic cholera. And he ran away with it to poison the water of London, and he certainly might have made things look blue for this civilised city. And now he has swallowed it. Of course, I cannot say what will happen, but you know it turned that kitten blue, and the three puppies—in patches, and the sparrow—bright blue. But the bother is, I shall have all the trouble and expense of preparing some more.

"Put on my coat on this hot day! Why? Because we might meet Mrs Jabber. My dear, Mrs Jabber is not a draught. But why should I wear a coat on a hot day because of Mrs—? Oh! *very* well."

THE STONE CAT

Miles J. Breuer

Investigation showed that I was the last person to see young Brian before his sudden and mysterious disappearance. I saw him on the day that my remarkable friend, Doctor Fleckinger showed the two of us the stone cat. We found the doctor working in his laboratory, a big, airy room with the sunlight gleaming brightly on the myriad things of glass and polished metal. As usual, Miss Lila was there, busy at some of the doctor's scientific tasks.

Brian had eyes only for the demure young lady in the white apron and rolled-up sleeves. As we came in, she looked up and saw him, and nodded her head to him with a smile in her deep, dark eyes. Brian wished the doctor good morning, and then went over to where she sat cutting sections on a microtome, handling the gossamer-like paraffin ribbons with a consummately delicate touch. I walked over to the other side of the room where the doctor was working with some Petri dishes and a microscope, and exchanged greetings with him.

Dr. Fleckinger went on with his work, and such was his concentration that in a few moments he had forgotten about me. He was pouring a black liquid on some lumps of flesh in the Petri dishes and watching them blacken and crinkle; and then he teased out pieces to examine under the microscope. For a while he gazed abstractedly at his notebook. Then came the uncouth thing that makes me shiver when I think of it. Suddenly he jerked up his cuff and bared his arm, and poured some of the greenish-black stuff on one spot. The effect was hideous. The flesh blackened and shriveled, and his arm shuddered. He regarded it for a while; then, seizing a scalpel, he passed it quickly through a flame, and with one sweep cut off the blackened skin and flesh. He put on a compress-dressing to stop the bleeding, and went on unconcernedly with his work, totally oblivious of me standing there and shuddering.

That was the kind of man he was. I was afraid of him. The friendship that I continued with him was one of those things that we do against the protests of our better judgment. I envied him his comfortable wealth, his astonishing intellect, and his beautiful daughter; for I had to work hard for a living with just a mediocre equipment of brains, and all I had to love and worry about was a nephew who could take better care of himself than I could. I enjoyed Dr. Fleckinger's society during his amiable intervals, and delighted in his wonderful private collection of marble and bronze statuary. But, at other times I was uncomfortable in his society. Though I was his oldest and best friend, I had a feeling that he would cut me in pieces did the conditions of an experiment demand it, with the same unfeeling precision with which he had whirled guinea-pigs in a centrifuge during our college days, to determine the effect on the circulation.

Miss Lila and Brian were so interested in some mutual matter that they had not noticed the uncanny performance. In a quarter of an hour the doctor seemed to have come to a stopping place in his work, for he put it aside and entertained me so pleasantly that I forgot and forgave his previous abstraction. It was when Brian and I were taking our departure that he showed us the stone cat. It was on a low pillar, in a room with a lot of small sculptured figures. I did not look at it much, yet it stuck in my memory, and sticks there yet, haunting me when I try to think of pleasanter things. It was natural size, of some black stone, and was no doubt an admirable piece of sculptural art, with its arched back, straight tail, and angry appearance.

But I didn't like it. Brian hardly noticed it, but Miss Lila stood on the stairs and shuddered. The three year old girl of Dr. Fleckinger's housekeeper was toddling around the room after her mother who was dusting the statuary; and seeing us looking at the cat, came over to join us in her small, sociable way. Spying the cat, she stopped suddenly, looked at it a moment, and let out a wail of lamentation. She continued to weep piteously until she was carried out, crying something about her "kitty." As I went out, I wondered why the stone figure of a cat should make me feel so creepy and cause Miss Lila to shudder, and the child to cry.

Brian and I parted at the corner of the block, and that was the last time anybody saw him. He was missed from his office and his rooms, and the places he usually frequented. His affairs hung in suspense; a case which he was to try the following day had to be put off, and in the evening an opera party with whom he and Miss Lila had engaged a box, waited for him in vain. The newspapers blazed out in big headlines about the utter and untraceable disappearance of the prominent young lawyer.

I had never taken any particular interest in him. That was to come now, for the responsibility of investigating his case would devolve on my department. One thing about him, perhaps held my attention, and that of many others: he was the successful suitor of Dr. Fleckinger's daughter, Lila. The list of young men who had unsuccessfully aspired for this honor was large, and my own nephew, Richard, was among them. It was pretty generally known that it was the doctor himself who stood in the way; he made it so uncomfortable for the young fellows who tried to get acquainted with the girl that they desisted. Richard, who was pretty hard hit, and spent a good many despondent months after his defeat, told me that the "selfish old devil cared less about his daughter's future than he did about his own whims." So, when young Brian, by his persistence and his gracious ways, continued not only in the favor of the young lady, but also in the good graces of her eccentric father, there was a good deal of speculation as to why he, particularly, had been selected.

My nephew, Richard, who is a sergeant in my department of the detective bureau, came to me and asked me to assign him specially to the investigation of Brian's disappearance. I did so gladly, for I had to admit that he was clever, even if most of the time it was difficult for me to believe that the golden-haired lad was really grown up.

"I am looking up Brian's contacts," he reported. "His own record is an easy job; his life is an open book. Miss Fleckinger I know pretty well myself. But, her father seems to be a sort of mystery. You know him intimately. Tell me about him." His brows were dark with angry suspicion.

"Well," I mused; "he and I went to school together. We were drawn together and apart from others by a common streak of intellect, a sort of analytical and investigative faculty that would give us no rest. Out of me, it made a detective, out of him a research scientist. He inherited enough money to make that possible. He keeps to himself, and does not even publish the results of very much of his work. What he is working on, is as profound a riddle to the rest of the scientific world as the secret of the Sphinx. However, I can make my surmises, if he does things like those he used to do. I remember once that he blew a steam whistle for ten days close to a rabbit's ear, and then killed it and made microscopic sections to see the effects on the nerves of hearing."

Richard shut his teeth with a click and said nothing. "I saw the doctor this afternoon," I continued. "He takes a queer attitude toward this affair. His daughter is all broken up about it, but he acts as though he were relieved. He remarked something to the effect that he was glad that he wouldn't lose his daughter after all. Then he had the nerve to ask me if I wouldn't come in to see a new statue which had just arrived. He was all enthused about the statue, and I left in disgust."

"He's a smooth brute," Richard said.

HE worked hard on the case. I saw him seldom, but when I did, I noted that he was losing weight and growing haggard. He was taking it seriously, because he had not lost his old affection for Miss Lila, who was so intimately connected with the case. Perhaps his motive was to make her happy, even though he knew he had to give her up to his rival if he ever succeeded in finding Brian; or perhaps some deeper suspicion drove him on through those long, discouraging weeks. A number of other good men on the force spent a great deal of effort in going over the problem; but no light was shed on Brian's disappearance.

Then one day a young Frenchman was admitted to my office.

"I would wish that you speak French," he said politely.

"I'm sorry," I said. "What can I do for you?"

"You desire to know where is the Monsieur Brian?" he asked, speaking slowly, and finding each word with evident effort.

"There's a big reward out, and it's yours if you tell us," I said shortly.

"I have hopes, uncle, old dear," he said, with an astonishing change in voice and manner, breaking out into Richard's well known grin. With a hat on and a change in expression, it was really Richard.

"You old rascal!" I shouted. "You certainly fooled me!"

"It wasn't easy, uncle, I dye the hair and mustache twice a week, and practice French all night. But, it has fooled all my friends.

Well, I need it. I am Dr. Fleckinger's laboratory assistant now, and we talk French most of the time. You can see that I've learned something about him, because you all thought he was

German. Now I am cataloguing his collection of sculptures, too."

"You're actually in that house?" I demanded in alarm. Some nameless fear for the boy's safety possessed me. Yet, my reason could not tell me what I feared.

"I'm learning all the time," he replied jocularly. Then he gritted his teeth and his face took on a grim look. "Uncle, someone's got to take Lila out of that devil's clutches. Of course he's her father, but—"

"What's the matter?"

"She's wasting away under my very eyes. Every day she is thinner. She goes about and trembles at every shadow; and every now and then bursts into a fit of weeping without any provocation. Something is driving her distracted, and I can see the terrible effort she makes to conceal it. It isn't sorrow that I see in her face; it's horror!"

"What has that to do with Brian's disappearance?"

"I don't know. In order to find out, I've been trying to learn from Lila and the servants what his motive is for refusing to let her have suitors. Apparently there is no real reason for it; it is rather a monomania, a form of insanity on his part."

"One would think you suspected him of having made away with Brian," I hinted.

"Easy to conjecture, hard to prove," he answered enigmatically. "But if you want to see the wind-up, wait until I run a couple of errands, and I'll take you along with me. I think I've figured the thing out."

You could have knocked me over with a feather. Here was a man's job worked out by this boy who still seemed a child to me. He came for me at seven o'clock, carrying some packages. Unwrapping them, he slipped a photograph into an inside pocket, and a couple of live frogs into the pocket of his coat. I stared in astonishment.

"Take your thirty-two automatic along," he suggested. I patted the pocket where it reposed.

We drove to Fleckinger's house in a car with three officers from the station, and stopped at some distance from the house. We walked separately into the yard, and Richard signalled to the officers to wait outside. I was surprised to see him pull out a latchkey and open the door, until I remembered that he was a member of the household.

On the stair-landing in the lower hall stood a statue. Richard pointed to it.

"The one you were invited to see and refused," he commented. "Oh, he's a cool customer!"

He switched on the light in front of it, and asked me to regard it closely. It was of some dull, black, rough material, and represented a young man, almost nude, seated, with his chin leaning against one hand in deep meditation. The face was suggestive of profound concentration like that of a hypnotized man. The statue looked a little larger than life-size. It was set back in a niche so that the light fell on it obliquely, heightening the furrowed effect of the face. There was something about the appearance of it that I did not like, as it stood there with the shadows of the balusters falling on it. It gave me the same sort of creeps that the stone cat had imparted.

"It is really exactly life-size," Richard informed me. "I have measured it."

I gave him an impatient glare, for I did not see what that had to do with Brian's disappearance. "Then," he continued, "look at the features closely!" And he jerked the photograph out of his pocket and held it before me. It was a portrait of Brian, done very dark by the photographer; a duplicate of which I had at the office.

I looked from the picture to the face of the statue and back again, and an icy chill shot through me. But, Richard started suddenly, for the bobbing figure of Doctor Fleckinger appeared at the head of the stairs above us. Obviously that was not on the program.

"Put it away," he whispered. Then he went on slowly and loudly: "He is in the laboratoire. I am certain it will make him much pleasure if you come above—ah, there is Monsieur the doctor now."

Doctor Fleckinger came down and greeted me pleasantly, and shook my hand. My head hummed and whirled; I could scarcely gather my senses enough to answer the platitudes addressed to me as we walked upstairs at the doctor's invitation to the laboratory, where he usually received me.

UP in the laboratory we began a rather lame conversation, and the incongruity of the situation jarred my nerves. The doctor knew that something suspicious was up, and did not trust me. I knew that his cordiality was feigned, and yet I was cordial in response. If I had known Richard's plans, I might have known what to do. The electric light was reflected in a million spots from the glass and polished metal; pieces of apparatus assumed strange shapes, and grotesque shadows stretched dizzily off into corners and dark places.

At the far end of the room, the black depths of a recess yawned at us, with a curtain stretched partly across it. Near it, Richard was busy at a sink in the corner. He paused and stood in front of a window to light a cigarette, and the action had all the appearance of being a preconcerted signal to the policemen below. His face was set, and I knew he was thinking hard. Apparently his plans had been somewhat interfered with by the doctor's unexpected presence.

I also thought hard, as I talked with the doctor, wondering how I could help Richard. Finally, it occurred to me that his inviting me along must have been an afterthought. Evidently he had planned things to carry out alone. Therefore, if I left he would have a clear field. I dreaded to do so, for now I was sure that some danger lurked in wait for him. But, duty is duty. I suggested that I had dropped in for a moment, and had to be moving on. I read approval in Richard's eyes.

As Doctor Fleckinger turned his back for a moment to go to the door with me, Richard darted to the curtain across the black recess and dipped out a ladleful of something from behind it. I could see him fish a frog out of his pocket and drop it into the ladle. Then he set the whole into the sink, at the same time that I walked out into the hall. I did not go away, however; I dodged behind the door, and watched through the crack.

The doctor whirled suddenly about and walked with a queer, tense swiftness toward the curtained recess. He crossed the room and reached it before I realized what he was about; and with the suddenness of a wildcat he leaped upon Richard, caught him around the body, and lifted him off his feet. He began to shove the body into the darkness of the recess.

What fiendish fate awaited him there, I could only gather from the scream of dismay that broke from Richard's throat. The lad had been taken completely by surprise, and was helpless. His face was ghastly white, and paralyzed with terror. I stood rooted to the spot for a valuable moment, trying to realize what was happening, and then started toward them.

Suddenly, a piercing scream broke upon my ears, and turning around, I saw Miss Lila's pale figure for an instant in the doorway. Then she fell backwards in a faint. This startled the doctor only a little, but enough to enable Richard to get a hold and make the game a little less one-sided. For another moment I watched, and then my mind was at rest concerning the outcome, for the doctor's sedentary muscles were no match for Richard's splendid training. While I stood there, with Miss Lila's unconscious form lying in the doorway, and the two men locked in reeling, swaying embrace at the end of the room, there was a hurried trampling on the stairs, and the officers who had been waiting below, swarmed into the room.

They stopped an instant in surprise. Then, as one of them picked up Miss Lila and carried her to a sofa, the others hurried toward the combatants in front of the curtained recess. For a moment my heart jumped into my mouth, and I thought they would be too late. In some way the doctor had gained an advantage and was pushing Richard behind the curtain. Again a cry broke from Richard's throat, something between a gulp and a shout of "Help!" Then Richard made a mighty effort and with a clever twist, had hurled the doctor bodily into the shadow behind the curtain. As the doctor's wriggling body suddenly grew limp. Richard jumped quickly backwards, and as I approached on the run, I heard a splash, and saw drops of a thick, foul-smelling liquid spatter out from the gloom. Richard looked hurriedly at us and himself, to see if anyone had been touched.

He was trembling as though from the ague, and his breath came in gasps.

"It was a barbarous thing to do," he panted. "But I had to do it, or I would be there myself—where Brian is now."

We approached the curtain. "Stay away from the vat!" Richard commanded anxiously. "The stuff may do you harm. I don't know just how to handle it. If you want to know what has happened, look here!"

He stepped to the sink and poured out the ladleful of black, heavy liquid. The frog tumbled out into the sink, and Richard pushed it under a stream of water from the tap. Washing it thoroughly, he handed it to me.

"You saw me put it in—alive?" he asked significantly.

Now it was hard as stone, and heavy—petrified.

It looked for all the world like the little stone frogs in the Pompeiian collection at the Metropolitan Museum.

Richard explained.

"The first thing that struck my attention," he began, "was the sorrow of the housekeeper's child for her missing cat. The baby recognized the figure on the pedestal, where our acquired conventional associations of statuary put us off the track. Then, gradually, the fearful resemblance of the statue in the lower hall to the missing lawyer, broke upon me."

His face took on a hard look as he turned toward the vat behind the curtain.

"He ought to be set up in some museum," he said grimly. "But, for God's sake, don't make it too sudden for Lila!"

THE UNPARALLELED INVASION

Jack London

It was in the year 1976 that the trouble between the world and China reached its culmination. It was because of this that the celebration of the Second Centennial of American Liberty was deferred. Many other plans of the nations of the earth were twisted and tangled and postponed for the same reason. The world awoke rather abruptly to its danger; but for over seventy years, unperceived, affairs had been shaping toward this very end.

The year 1904 logically marks the beginning of the development that, seventy years later, was to bring consternation to the whole world. The Japanese-Russian War took place in 1904, and the historians of the time gravely noted it down that that event marked the entrance of Japan into the comity of nations. What it really did mark was the awakening of China. This awakening, long expected, had finally been given up. The Western nations had tried to arouse China, and they had failed. Out of their native optimism and race-egotism they had therefore concluded that the task was impossible, that China would never awaken.

What they had failed to take into account was this: *that between them and China was no common psychological speech.* Their thought-processes were radically dissimilar. There was no intimate vocabulary. The Western mind penetrated the Chinese mind but a short distance when it found itself in a fathomless maze. The Chinese mind penetrated the Western mind an equally short distance when it fetched up against a blank, incomprehensible wall. It was all a matter of language. There was no way to communicate

Western ideas to the Chinese mind. China remained asleep. The material achievement and progress of the West was a closed book to her; nor could the West open the book. Back and deep down on the tie-ribs of consciousness, in the mind, say, of the English-speaking race, was a capacity to thrill to short, Saxon words; back and deep down on the tie-ribs of consciousness of the Chinese mind was a capacity to thrill to its own hieroglyphics; but the Chinese mind could not thrill to short, Saxon words; nor could the English-speaking mind thrill to hieroglyphics. The fabrics of their minds were woven from totally different stuffs. They were mental aliens. And so it was that Western material achievement and progress made no dent on the rounded sleep of China.

Came Japan and her victory over Russia in 1904. Now the Japanese race was the freak and paradox among Eastern peoples. In some strange way Japan was receptive to all the West had to offer. Japan swiftly assimilated the Western ideas, and digested them, and so capably applied them that she suddenly burst forth, full-panoplied, a world-power. There is no explaining this peculiar openness of Japan to the alien culture of the West. As well might be explained any biological sport in the animal kingdom.

Having decisively thrashed the great Russian Empire, Japan promptly set about dreaming a colossal dream of empire for herself. Korea she had made into a granary and a colony; treaty privileges and vulpine diplomacy gave her the monopoly of Manchuria. But Japan was not satisfied. She turned her eyes upon China. There lay a vast territory, and in that territory were the hugest deposits in the world of iron and coal—the backbone of industrial civilization. Given natural resources, the other great factor in industry is labour. In that territory was a population of 400,000,000 souls—one quarter of the then total population of the earth. Furthermore, the Chinese were excellent workers, while their fatalistic philosophy (or religion) and their stolid nervous organization constituted them splendid soldiers—if they were properly managed. Needless to say, Japan was prepared to furnish that management.

But best of all, from the standpoint of Japan, the Chinese was a kindred race. The baffling enigma of the Chinese character to the West was no baffling enigma to the Japanese. The Japanese understood as we could never school ourselves or hope to understand. Their mental processes were the same. The Japanese thought with the same thought-symbols as did the Chinese, and they thought in the same peculiar grooves. Into the Chinese mind the Japanese went on where we were balked by the obstacle of incomprehension. They took the turning which we could not perceive, twisted around the obstacle, and were out of sight in the ramifications of the Chinese mind where we could not follow. They were brothers. Long ago one had borrowed the other's written language, and, untold generations before that, they had diverged from the common Mongol stock. There had been changes, differentiations brought about by diverse conditions and infusions of other blood; but down at the bottom of their beings, twisted into the fibres of them, was a heritage in common, a sameness in kind that time had not obliterated.

And so Japan took upon herself the management of China. In the years immediately following the war with Russia, her agents swarmed over the Chinese Empire. A thousand miles beyond the last mission station toiled her engineers and spies, clad as coolies, under the guise of itinerant merchants or proselytizing Buddhist priests, noting down the horse-power of every waterfall, the likely sites for factories, the heights of mountains and passes, the strategic advantages and weaknesses, the wealth of the farming valleys, the number of bullocks in a district or the number of labourers that could be collected by forced levies. Never was there such a census, and it could have been taken by no other people than the dogged, patient, patriotic Japanese.

But in a short time secrecy was thrown to the winds. Japan's officers reorganized the Chinese army; her drill sergeants made the mediæval warriors over into twentieth century soldiers, accustomed to all the modern machinery of war and with a higher average of marksmanship than the soldiers of any Western nation. The engineers of Japan deepened and widened the intricate system of canals, built factories and foundries, netted the empire with telegraphs and telephones, and inaugurated the era of railroad-building. It was these same protagonists of machine-civilization that discovered the great oil deposits of Chunsan, the iron mountains of Whang-Sing, the copper ranges of Chinchi, and they sank the gas wells of Wow-Wee, that most marvellous reservoir of natural gas in all the world.

In China's councils of empire were the Japanese emissaries. In the ears of the statesmen whispered the Japanese statesmen. The political reconstruction of the Empire was due to them. They evicted the scholar class, which was violently reactionary, and put into office progressive officials. And in every town and city of the Empire newspapers were started. Of course, Japanese editors ran the policy of these papers, which policy they got direct from Tokio. It was these papers that educated and made progressive the great mass of the population.

China was at last awake. Where the West had failed, Japan succeeded. She had transmuted Western culture and achievement into terms that were intelligible to the Chinese understanding. Japan herself, when she so suddenly awakened, had astounded the world. But at the time she was only forty millions strong. China's awakening, with her four hundred millions and the scientific advance of the world, was frightfully astounding. She was the colossus of the nations, and swiftly her voice was heard in no uncertain tones in the affairs and councils of the nations.

Japan egged her on, and the proud Western peoples listened with respectful ears.

China's swift and remarkable rise was due, perhaps more than to anything else, to the superlative quality of her labour. The Chinese was the perfect type of industry. He had always been that. For sheer ability to work no worker in the world could compare with him. Work was the breath of his nostrils. It was to him what wandering and fighting in far lands and spiritual adventure had been to other peoples. Liberty, to him, epitomized itself in access to the means of toil. To till the soil and labour interminably was all he asked of life and the powers that be. And the awakening of China had given its vast population not merely free and unlimited access to the means of toil, but access to the highest and most scientific machine-means of toil.

China rejuvenescent! It was but a step to China rampant. She discovered a new pride in herself and a will of her own. She began to chafe under the guidance of Japan, but she did not chafe long. On Japan's advice, in the beginning, she had expelled from the Empire all Western missionaries, engineers, drill sergeants, merchants, and teachers. She now began to expel the similar representatives of Japan. The latter's advisory statesmen were showered with honours and decorations, and sent home. The West had awakened Japan, and, as Japan had then requited the West, Japan was not requited by China. Japan was thanked for her kindly aid and flung out bag and baggage by her gigantic protégé. The Western nations chuckled. Japan's rainbow dream had gone glimmering. She grew angry. China laughed at her. The blood and the swords of the Samurai would out, and Japan rashly went to war. This occurred in 1922, and in seven bloody months Manchuria, Korea, and Formosa were taken away from her and she was hurled back, bankrupt, to stifle in her tiny, crowded islands. Exit Japan from the world drama. Thereafter she devoted herself to art, and her task became to please the world greatly with her creations of wonder and beauty.

Contrary to expectation, China did not prove warlike. She had no Napoleonic dream, and was content to devote herself to the arts of peace. After a time of disquiet, the idea was accepted that China was to be feared, not in war, but in commerce. It will be seen that the real danger was not apprehended. China went on consummating her machine-civilization. Instead of a large standing army, she developed an immensely larger and splendidly efficient militia. Her navy was so small that it was the laughing stock of the world; nor did she attempt to strengthen her navy. The treaty ports of the world were never entered by her visiting battleships.

The real danger lay in the fecundity of her loins, and it was in 1970 that the first cry of alarm was raised. For some time all territories adjacent to China had been grumbling at Chinese immigration; but now it suddenly came home to the world that China's population was 500,000,000. She had increased by a hundred millions since her awakening. Burchaldter called attention to the fact that there were more Chinese in existence than white-skinned people. He performed a simple sum in arithmetic. He added together the populations of the United States, Canada, New Zealand, Australia, South Africa, England, France, Germany, Italy, Austria, European Russia, and all Scandinavia. The result was 495,000,000. And the population of China overtopped this tremendous total by 5,000,000. Burchaldter's figures went round the world, and the world shivered.

For many centuries China's population had been constant. Her territory had been saturated with population; that is to say, her territory, with the primitive method of production, had supported the maximum limit of population. But when she awoke and inaugurated the machine-civilization, her productive power had been enormously increased. Thus, on the same territory, she was able to support a far larger population. At once the birth rate began to rise and the death rate to fall. Before, when population pressed against the means of subsistence, the excess population had been swept away by famine. But now, thanks to the machine-civilization, China's means of subsistence had been enormously extended, and there were no famines; her population followed on the heels of the increase in the means of subsistence.

During this time of transition and development of power, China had entertained no dreams of conquest. The Chinese was not an imperial race. It was industrious, thrifty, and peace-loving. War was looked upon as an unpleasant but necessary task that at times must be performed. And so, while the Western races had squabbled and fought, and world-adventured against one another, China had calmly gone on working at her machines and growing. Now she was spilling over the boundaries of her Empire—that was all, just spilling over into the adjacent territories with all the certainty and terrifying slow momentum of a glacier.

Following upon the alarm raised by Burchaldter's figures, in 1970 France made a long-threatened stand. French Indo-China had been overrun, filled up, by Chinese immigrants. France called a halt. The Chinese wave flowed on. France assembled a force of a hundred thousand on the boundary between her unfortunate colony and China, and China sent down an army of militia-soldiers a million strong. Behind came the wives and sons and daughters and relatives, with their personal household luggage, in a second army. The French force was brushed aside like a fly. The Chinese militia-soldiers, along with their families, over five millions all told, coolly took possession of French Indo-China and settled down to stay for a few thousand years.

Outraged France was in arms. She hurled fleet after fleet against the coast of China, and nearly bankrupted herself by the effort. China had no navy. She withdrew like a turtle into her shell. For a year the French fleets blockaded the coast and bombarded exposed towns and villages. China did not mind. She did not depend upon the rest of the world for anything. She calmly kept out of range of the French guns and went on working. France wept and wailed, wrung her impotent hands and appealed to the dumfounded nations. Then she landed a punitive expedition to march to Peking. It was two hundred and fifty thousand strong, and it was the flower of France. It landed without opposition and marched into the interior. And that was the last ever seen of it. The line of communication was snapped on the second day. Not a survivor came back to tell what had happened. It had been swallowed up in China's cavernous maw, that was all.

In the five years that followed, China's expansion, in all land directions, went on apace. Siam was made part of the Empire, and, in spite of all that England could do, Burma and the Malay Peninsula were overrun; while all along the long south boundary of Siberia, Russia was pressed severely by China's advancing hordes. The process was simple. First came the Chinese immigration (or, rather, it was already there, having come there slowly and insidiously during the previous years). Next came the clash of arms and the brushing away of all opposition by a monster army of militia-soldiers, followed by their families and household baggage. And finally came their settling down as colonists in the conquered territory. Never was there so strange and effective a method of world conquest.

Napal and Bhutan were overrun, and the whole northern boundary of India pressed against by this fearful tide of life. To the west, Bokhara, and, even to the south and west, Afghanistan, were swallowed up. Persia, Turkestan, and all Central Asia felt the pressure of the flood. It was at this time that Burchaldter revised his figures. He had been mistaken. China's population must be seven hundred millions, eight hundred millions, nobody knew how many millions, but at any rate it would soon be a billion. There were two Chinese for every white-skinned human in the world, Burchaldter announced, and the world trembled. China's increase must have begun immediately, in 1904. It was remembered that since that date there had not been a single famine. At 5,000,000 a year increase, her total increase in the intervening seventy years must be 350,000,000. But who was to know? It might be more. Who was to know anything of this strange new menace of the twentieth century—China, old China, rejuvenescent, fruitful, and militant!

The Convention of 1975 was called at Philadelphia. All the Western nations, and some few of the Eastern, were represented. Nothing was accomplished. There was talk of all countries putting bounties on children to increase the birth rate, but it was laughed to scorn by the arithmeticians, who pointed out that China was too far in the lead in that direction. No feasible way of coping with China was suggested. China was appealed to and threatened by the United Powers, and that was all the Convention of Philadelphia came to; and the Convention and the Powers were laughed at by China. Li Tang Fwung, the power behind the Dragon Throne, deigned to reply.

"What does China care for the comity of nations?" said Li Tang Fwung. "We are the most ancient, honourable, and royal of races. We have our own destiny to accomplish. It is unpleasant that our destiny does not tally with the destiny of the rest of the world, but what would you? You have talked windily about the royal races and the heritage of the earth, and we can only reply that that remains to be seen. You cannot invade us. Never mind about your navies. Don't shout. We know our navy is small. You see we use it for police purposes. We do not care for the sea. Our strength is in our population, which will soon be a billion. Thanks to you, we are equipped with all modern war-machinery. Send your navies. We will not notice them. Send your punitive expeditions, but first remember France. To land half a million soldiers on our shores would strain the resources of any of you. And our thousand millions would swallow them down in a mouthful. Send a million; send five millions, and we will swallow them down just as readily. Pouf! A mere nothing, a meagre morsel. Destroy, as you have threatened, you United States, the ten million coolies we have forced upon your shores—why, the amount scarcely equals half of our excess birth rate for a year."

So spoke Li Tang Fwung. The world was nonplussed, helpless, terrified. Truly had he spoken. There was no combating China's amazing birth rate. If her population was a billion, and was increasing twenty millions a year, in twenty-five years it would be a billion and a half—equal to the total population of the world in 1904. And nothing could be done. There was no way to dam up the over-spilling monstrous flood of life. War was futile. China laughed at a blockade of her coasts. She welcomed invasion. In her capacious maw was room for all the hosts of earth that could be hurled at her. And in the meantime her flood of yellow life poured out and on over Asia. China laughed and read in their magazines the learned lucubrations of the distracted Western scholars.

But there was one scholar China failed to reckon on—Jacobus Laningdale. Not that he was a scholar, except in the widest sense. Primarily, Jacobus Laningdale was a scientist, and, up to that time, a very obscure scientist, a professor employed in the laboratories of the Health Office of New York City. Jacobus Laningdale's head was very like any other head, but in that head was evolved an idea. Also, in that head was the wisdom to keep that idea secret. He did not write an article for the magazines. Instead, he asked for a vacation. On September 19, 1975, he arrived in Washington.

It was evening, but he proceeded straight to the White House, for he had already arranged an audience with the President. He was closeted with President Moyer for three hours. What passed between them was not learned by the rest of the world until long after; in fact, at that time the world was not interested in Jacobus Laningdale. Next day the President called in his Cabinet. Jacobus Laningdale was present. The proceedings were kept secret. But that very afternoon Rufus Cowdery, Secretary of State, left Washington, and early the following morning sailed for England. The secret that he carried began to spread, but it spread only among the heads of Governments. Possibly half-a-dozen men in a nation were entrusted with the idea that had formed in Jacobus Laningdale's head. Following the spread of the secret, sprang up great activity in all the dockyards, arsenals, and navy-yards. The people of France and Austria became suspicious, but so sincere were their Governments' calls for confidence that they acquiesced in the unknown project that was afoot.

This was the time of the Great Truce. All countries pledged themselves solemnly not to go to war with any other country. The first definite action was the gradual mobilization of the armies of Russia, Germany, Austria, Italy, Greece, and Turkey. Then began the eastward movement. All railroads into Asia were glutted with troop trains. China was the objective, that was all that was known. A little later began the great sea movement. Expeditions of warships were launched from all countries. Fleet followed fleet, and all proceeded to the coast of China. The nations cleaned out their navy-yards. They sent their revenue cutters and dispatch boats and lighthouse tenders, and they sent their last antiquated cruisers and battleships. Not content with this, they impressed the merchant marine. The statistics show that 58,640 merchant steamers, equipped with searchlights and rapid-fire guns, were despatched by the various nations to China.

And China smiled and waited. On her land side, along her boundaries, were millions of the warriors of Europe. She mobilized five times as many millions of her militia and awaited the invasion. On her sea coasts she did the same. But China was puzzled. After all this enormous preparation, there was no invasion. She could not understand. Along the great Siberian frontier all was quiet. Along her coasts the towns and villages were not even shelled. Never, in the history of the world, had there been so mighty a gathering of war fleets. The fleets of all the world were there, and day and night millions of tons of battleships ploughed the brine of her coasts, and nothing happened. Nothing was attempted. Did they think to make her emerge from her shell? China smiled. Did they think to tire her out, or starve her out? China smiled again.

But on May 1, 1976, had the reader been in the imperial city of Peking, with its then population of eleven millions, he would have witnessed a curious sight. He would have seen the streets filled with the chattering yellow populace, every queued head tilted back, every slant eye turned skyward. And high up in the blue he would have beheld a tiny dot of black, which, because of its orderly evolutions, he would have identified as an airship. From this airship, as it curved its flight back and forth over the city, fell missiles—strange, harmless missiles, tubes of fragile glass that shattered into thousands of fragments on the streets and house-tops. But there was nothing deadly about these tubes of glass. Nothing happened. There were no explosions. It is true, three Chinese were killed by the tubes dropping on their heads from so enormous a height; but what were three Chinese against an excess birth rate of twenty millions? One tube struck perpendicularly in a fish-pond in a garden and was not broken. It was dragged ashore by the master of the house. He did not dare to open it, but, accompanied by his friends, and surrounded by an ever-increasing crowd, he carried the mysterious tube to the magistrate of the district. The latter was a brave man. With all eyes upon him, he shattered the tube with a blow from his brass-bowled pipe. Nothing happened. Of those who were very near, one or two thought they saw some mosquitoes fly out. That was all. The crowd set up a great laugh and dispersed.

As Peking was bombarded by glass tubes, so was all China. The tiny airships, dispatched from the warships, contained but two men each, and over all cities, towns, and villages they wheeled and curved, one man directing the ship, the other man throwing over the glass tubes.

Had the reader again been in Peking, six weeks later, he would have looked in vain for the eleven million inhabitants. Some few of them he would have found, a few hundred thousand, perhaps, their carcasses festering in the houses and in the deserted streets, and piled high on the abandoned death-waggons. But for the rest he would have had to seek along the highways and byways of the Empire. And not all would he have found fleeing from plague-stricken Peking, for behind them, by hundreds of thousands of unburied corpses by the wayside, he could have marked their flight. And as it was with Peking, so it was with all the cities, towns, and villages of the Empire. The plague smote them all. Nor was it one plague, nor two plagues; it was a score of plagues. Every virulent form of infectious death stalked through the land. Too late the Chinese government apprehended the meaning of the colossal preparations, the marshalling of the world-hosts, the flights of the tin airships, and the rain of the tubes of glass. The proclamations of the government were vain. They could not stop the eleven million plague-stricken wretches, fleeing from the one city of Peking to spread disease through all the land. The physicians and health officers died at their posts; and death, the all-conqueror, rode over the decrees of the Emperor and Li Tang

Fwung. It rode over them as well, for Li Tang Fwung died in the second week, and the Emperor, hidden away in the Summer Palace, died in the fourth week.

Had there been one plague, China might have coped with it. But from a score of plagues no creature was immune. The man who escaped smallpox went down before scarlet fever. The man who was immune to yellow fever was carried away by cholera; and if he were immune to that, too, the Black Death, which was the bubonic plague, swept him away. For it was these bacteria, and germs, and microbes, and bacilli, cultured in the laboratories of the West, that had come down upon China in the rain of glass.

All organization vanished. The government crumbled away. Decrees and proclamations were useless when the men who made them and signed them one moment were dead the next. Nor could the maddened millions, spurred on to flight by death, pause to heed anything. They fled from the cities to infect the country, and wherever they fled they carried the plagues with them. The hot summer was on—Jacobus Laningdale had selected the time shrewdly—and the plague festered everywhere. Much is conjectured of what occurred, and much has been learned from the stories of the few survivors. The wretched creatures stormed across the Empire in many-millioned flight. The vast armies China had collected on her frontiers melted away. The farms were ravaged for food, and no more crops were planted, while the crops already in were left unattended and never came to harvest. The most remarkable thing, perhaps, was the flights. Many millions engaged in them, charging to the bounds of the Empire to be met and turned back by the gigantic armies of the West. The slaughter of the mad hosts on the boundaries was stupendous. Time and again the guarding line was drawn back twenty or thirty miles to escape the contagion of the multitudinous dead.

Once the plague broke through and seized upon the

German and Austrian soldiers who were guarding the borders of Turkestan. Preparations had been made for such a happening, and though sixty thousand soldiers of Europe were carried off, the international corps of physicians isolated the contagion and dammed it back. It was during this struggle that it was suggested that a new plague-germ had originated, that in some way or other a sort of hybridization between plague-germs had taken place, producing a new and frightfully virulent germ. First suspected by Vomberg, who became infected with it and died, it was later isolated and studied by Stevens, Hazenfelt, Norman, and Landers.

Such was the unparalleled invasion of China. For that billion of people there was no hope. Pent in their vast and festering charnel-house, all organization and cohesion lost, they could do naught but die. They could not escape. As they were flung back from their land frontiers, so were they flung back from the sea. Seventy-five thousand vessels patrolled the coasts. By day their smoking funnels dimmed the sea-rim, and by night their flashing searchlights ploughed the dark and harrowed it for the tiniest escaping junk. The attempts of the immense fleets of junks were pitiful. Not one ever got by the guarding sea-hounds. Modern war-machinery held back the disorganized mass of China, while the plagues did the work.

But old War was made a thing of laughter. Naught remained to him but patrol duty. China had laughed at war, and war she was getting, but it was ultra-modern war, twentieth century war, the war of the scientist and the laboratory, the war of Jacobus Laningdale. Hundred-ton guns were toys compared with the micro-organic projectiles hurled from the laboratories, the messengers of death, the destroying angels that stalked through the empire of a billion souls.

During all the summer and fall of 1976 China was an inferno. There was no eluding the microscopic projectiles that sought out the remotest hiding-places. The hundreds of millions of dead remained unburied and the germs multiplied themselves, and, toward the last, millions died daily of starvation. Besides, starvation weakened the victims and destroyed their natural defences against the plagues. Cannibalism, murder, and madness reigned. And so perished China.

Not until the following February, in the coldest weather, were the first expeditions made. These expeditions were small, composed of scientists and bodies of troops; but they entered China from every side. In spite of the most elaborate precautions against infection, numbers of soldiers and a few of the physicians were stricken. But the exploration went bravely on. They found China devastated, a howling wilderness through which wandered bands of wild dogs and desperate bandits who had survived. All survivors were put to death wherever found. And then began the great task, the sanitation of China. Five years and hundreds of millions of treasure were consumed, and then the world moved in—not in zones, as was the idea of Baron Albrecht, but heterogeneously, according to the democratic American programme. It was a vast and happy intermingling of nationalities that settled down in China in 1982 and the years that followed—a tremendous and successful experiment in cross-fertilization. We know to-day the splendid mechanical, intellectual, and art output that followed.

It was in 1987, the Great Truce having been dissolved, that the ancient quarrel between France and Germany over Alsace-Lorraine recrudesced. The war-cloud grew dark and threatening in April, and on April 17 the Convention of Copenhagen was called. The representatives of the nations of the world, being present, all nations solemnly pledged themselves never to use against one another the laboratory methods of warfare they had employed in the invasion of China.

—Excerpt from Walt Mervin's "*Certain Essays in History.*"

THE VOICE IN THE NIGHT

William Hope Hodgson

It was a dark, starless night. We were becalmed in the Northern Pacific. Our exact position I do not know; for the sun had been hidden during the course of a weary, breathless week, by a thin haze which had seemed to float above us, about the height of our mastheads, at whiles descending and shrouding the surrounding sea.

With there being no wind, we had steadied the tiller, and I was the only man on deck. The crew, consisting of two men and a boy, were sleeping forward in their den, while Will—my friend, and the master of our little craft—was aft in his bunk on the port side of the little cabin.

Suddenly, from out of the surrounding darkness, there came a hail:

"Schooner, ahoy!"

The cry was so unexpected that I gave no immediate answer, because of my surprise.

It came again—a voice curiously throaty and inhuman, calling from somewhere upon the dark sea away on our port broadside:

"Schooner, ahoy!"

"Hullo!" I sung out, having gathered my wits somewhat. "What are you? What do you want?"

"You need not be afraid," answered the queer voice, having probably noticed some trace of confusion in my tone. "I am only an old—man."

The pause sounded odd, but it was only afterward that it came back to me with any significance.

"Why don't you come alongside, then?" I queried somewhat snappishly; for I liked not his hinting at my having been a trifle shaken.

"I—I—can't. It wouldn't be safe. I—" The voice broke off, and there was silence.

"What do you mean?" I asked, growing more and more astonished. "What's not safe? Where are you?"

I listened for a moment; but there came no answer. And then, a sudden indefinite suspicion, of I knew not what, coming to me, I stepped swiftly to the binnacle and took out the lighted lamp. At the same time, I knocked on the deck with my heel to waken Will. Then I was back at the side, throwing the yellow funnel of light out into the silent immensity beyond our rail. As I did so, I heard a slight muffled cry, and then the sound of a splash, as though someone had dipped oars abruptly. Yet I cannot say with certainty that I saw anything; save, it seemed to me, that with the first flash of the light there had been something upon the waters, where now there was nothing.

"Hullo, there!" I called. "What foolery is this?"

But there came only the indistinct sounds of a boat being pulled away into the night.

Then I heard Will's voice from the direction of the after scuttle:

"What's up, George?"

"Come here, Will!" I said.

"What is it?" he asked, coming across the deck.

I told him the queer thing that had happened. He put several questions; then, after a moment's silence, he raised his hands to his lips and hailed:

"Boat, ahoy!"

From a long distance away there came back to us a faint reply, and my companion repeated his call. Presently, after a short period of silence, there grew on our hearing the muffled sound of oars, at which Will hailed again.

This time there was a reply: "Put away the light."

"I'm damned if I will," I muttered; but Will told me to do as the voice bade, and I shoved it down under the bulwarks.

"Come nearer," he said, and the oar strokes continued. Then, when apparently some half dozen fathoms distant, they again ceased.

"Come alongside!" exclaimed Will. "There's nothing to be frightened of aboard here."

"Promise that you will not show the light?"

"What's to do with you," I burst out, "that you're so infernally afraid of the light?"

"Because—" began the voice, and stopped short.

"Because what?" I asked quickly.

Will put his hand on my shoulder. "Shut up a minute, old man," he said, in a low voice. "Let me tackle him."

He leaned more over the rail.

"See here, mister," he said, "this is a pretty queer business, you coming upon us like this, right out in the middle of the blessed Pacific. How are we to know what sort of a hanky-panky trick you're up to? You say there's only one of you. How are we to know, unless we get a squint at you—eh? What's your objection to the light, anyway?"

As he finished, I heard the noise of the oars again, and then the voice came; but now from a greater distance, and sounding extremely hopeless and pathetic.

"I am sorry—sorry! I would not have troubled you, only I am hungry, and—so is she."

The voice died away, and the sound of the oars, dipping irregularly, was borne to us.

"Stop!" sang out Will. "I don't want to drive you away. Come back! We'll keep the light hidden, if you don't like it."

He turned to me:

"It's a damned queer rig, this; but I think there's nothing to be afraid of?"

There was a question in his tone, and I replied.

"No, I think the poor devil's been wrecked around here, and gone crazy."

The sound of the oars drew nearer.

"Shove that lamp back in the binnacle," said Will; then he leaned over the rail and listened. I replaced the lamp and came back to his side. The dipping of the oars ceased some dozen yards distant.

"Won't you come alongside now?" asked Will in an even voice. "I have had the lamp put back in the binnacle."

"I—I cannot," replied the voice. "I dare not come nearer. I dare not even pay you for the—the provisions."

"That's all right," said Will, and hesitated. "You're welcome to as much grub as you can take—" Again he hesitated.

"You are very good!" exclaimed the voice. "May God, Who understands everything, reward you—" It broke off huskily.

"The—the lady?" said Will abruptly. "Is she—"

"I have left her behind upon the island," came the voice.

"What island?" I cut in.

"I know not its name," returned the voice. "I would to God—" it began, and checked itself as suddenly.

"Could we not send a boat for her?" asked Will at this point.

"No!" said the voice, with extraordinary emphasis. "My God! No!" There was a moment's pause; then it added, in a tone which seemed a merited reproach:

"It was because of our want I ventured—because her agony tortured me."

"I am a forgetful brute!" exclaimed Will. "Just wait a minute, whoever you are, and I will bring you up something at once."

In a couple of minutes he was back again, and his arms were full of various edibles. He paused at the rail.

"Can't you come alongside for them?" he asked.

"No—I dare not," replied the voice, and it seemed to me that in its tones I detected a note of stifled craving—as though the owner hushed a mortal desire. It came to me then in a flash that the poor old creature out there in the darkness was suffering for actual need for that which Will held in his arms; and yet, because of some unintelligible dread, refraining from dashing to the side of our schooner and receiving it. And with the lightning-like conviction there came the knowledge that the Invisible was not mad, but sanely facing some intolerable horror.

"Damn it, Will!" I said, full of many feelings, over which predominated a vast sympathy. "Get a box. We must float off the stuff to him in it."

This we did, propelling it away from the vessel, out into the darkness, by means of a boat hook. In a minute a slight cry from the Invisible came to us, and we knew that he had secured the box.

A little later he called out a farewell to us, and so heartful a blessing, that I am sure we were the better for it. Then, without more ado, we heard the ply of oars across the darkness.

"Pretty soon off," remarked Will, with perhaps just a little sense of injury.

"Wait," I replied. "I think somehow he'll come back. He must have been badly needing that food."

"And the lady," said Will. For a moment he was silent; then he continued:

"It's the queerest thing ever I've tumbled across since I've been fishing."

"Yes," I said, and fell to pondering.

And so the time slipped away—an hour, another, and still Will stayed with me; for the queer adventure had knocked all desire for sleep out of him.

The third hour was three parts through when we heard again the sound of oars across the silent ocean.

"Listen!" said Will, a low note of excitement in his voice.

"He's coming, just as I thought," I muttered.

The dipping of the oars grew nearer, and I noted that the strokes were firmer and longer. The food had been needed.

They came to a stop a little distance off the broadside, and the queer voice came again to us through the darkness:

"Schooner, ahoy!"

"That you?" asked Will.

"Yes," replied the voice. "I left you suddenly, but—but there was great need."

"The lady?" questioned Will.

"The—lady is grateful now on earth. She will be more grateful soon in—in heaven."

Will began to make some reply, in a puzzled voice; but became confused, and broke off short. I said nothing. I was wondering at the curious pauses, and, apart from my wonder, I was full of a great sympathy.

The voice continued:

"We—she and I, have talked, as we shared the result of God's tenderness and yours—"

Will interposed; but without coherence.

"I beg of you not to—to belittle your deed of Christian charity this night," said the voice. "Be sure that it has not escaped His notice."

It stopped, and there was a full minute's silence. Then it came again:

"We have spoken together upon that which—which has

befallen us. We had thought to go out, without telling anyone of the terror which has come into our—lives. She is with me in believing that tonight's happenings are under a special ruling, and that it is God's wish that we should tell to you all that we have suffered since—since—"

"Yes?" said Will softly.

"Since the sinking of the Albatross."

"Ah!" I exclaimed involuntarily. "She left Newcastle for 'Frisco some six months ago, and hasn't been heard of since."

"Yes" answered the voice. "But some few degrees to the North of the line, she was caught in a terrible storm, and dismasted. When the day came, it was found that she was leaking badly, and, presently, it falling to a calm, the sailors took to the boats, leaving—leaving a young lady—my fiancée—and myself upon the wreck.

"We were below, gathering together a few of our belongings, when they left. They were entirely callous, through fear, and when we came up upon the decks, we saw them only as small shapes afar off upon the horizon. Yet we did not despair, but set to work and constructed a small raft. Upon this we put such few matters as it would hold, including a quantity of water and some ship's biscuit. Then, the vessel being very deep in the water, we got ourselves onto the raft and pushed off.

"It was later, when I observed that we seemed to be in the way of some tide or current, which bore us from the ship at an angle; so that in the course of three hours, by my watch, her hull became invisible to our sight, her broken masts remaining in view for a somewhat longer period. Then, towards evening, it grew misty, and so through the night. The next day we were still encompassed by the mist, the weather remaining quiet.

"For four days we drifted through this strange haze, until, on the evening of the fourth day, there grew upon our ears the murmur of breakers at a distance. Gradually it became plainer, and, somewhat after midnight, it appeared to sound upon either hand at no very great space. The raft was raised upon a swell several times, and then we were in smooth water, and the noise of the breakers was behind.

"When the morning came, we found that we were in a sort of great lagoon; but of this we noticed little at the time; for close before us, through the enshrouding mist, loomed the hull of a large sailing vessel. With one accord, we fell upon our knees and thanked God, for we thought that here was an end to our perils. We had much to learn.

"The raft drew near to the ship, and we shouted on them to take us aboard; but none answered. Presently the raft touched against the side of the vessel, and seeing a rope hanging downward, I seized it and began to climb. Yet I had much ado to make my way up, because of a kind of grey, lichenous fungus that had seized upon the rope, and which blotched the side of the ship lividly.

"I reached the rail and clambered over it, onto the deck. Here I saw that the decks were covered, in great patches, with grey masses, some of them rising into nodules several feet in height; but at the time I thought less of this matter than of the possibility of there being people aboard the ship. I shouted; but none answered. Then I went to the door below the poop deck. I opened it, and peered in. There was a great smell of staleness, so that I knew in a moment that nothing living was within, and with the knowledge, I shut the door quickly; for I felt suddenly lonely.

"I went back to the side where I had scrambled up. My—my sweetheart was still sitting quietly upon the raft. Seeing me look down, she called up to know whether there were any aboard of the ship. I replied that the vessel had the appearance of having been long deserted, but that if she would wait a little I would see whether there was anything in the shape of a ladder by which she could ascend to the deck. Then we would make a search through the vessel together. A little later, on the opposite side of the decks, I found a rope side ladder. This I carried across, and a minute afterwards she was beside me.

"Together we explored the cabins and apartments in the after part of the ship; but nowhere was there any sign of life. Here and there, within the cabins themselves, we came across odd patches of that queer fungus; but this, as my sweetheart said, could be cleansed away.

"In the end, having assured ourselves that the after portion of the vessel was empty, we picked our ways to the bows, between the ugly grey nodules of that strange growth; and here we made a further search, which told us that there was indeed none aboard but ourselves.

"This being now beyond any doubt, we returned to the stern of the ship and proceeded to make ourselves as comfortable as possible. Together we cleared out and cleaned two of the cabins; and after that I made examination whether there was anything eatable in the ship. This I soon found was so, and thanked God in my heart for His goodness. In addition to this I discovered the whereabouts of the fresh-water pump, and having fixed it, I found the water drinkable, though somewhat unpleasant to the taste.

"For several days we stayed aboard the ship, without attempting to get to the shore. We were busily engaged in making the place habitable. Yet even thus early we became aware that our lot was even less to be desired than might have been imagined; for though, as a first step, we scraped away the odd patches of growth that studded the floors and walls of the cabins and saloon, yet they returned almost to their original size within the space of twenty-four hours, which not only discouraged us but gave us a feeling of vague unease.

"Still we would not admit ourselves beaten, so set to work afresh, and not only scraped away the fungus but soaked the places where it had been with carbolic, a can-full of which I had found in the pantry. Yet, by the end of the week the growth had returned in full strength, and, in addition, it had spread to other places, as though our touching it had allowed germs from it to travel elsewhere.

"On the seventh morning, my sweetheart woke to find a small patch of it growing on her pillow, close to her face. At that, she came to me, as soon as she could get her garments upon her. I was in the galley at the time lighting the fire for breakfast.

"'Come here, John,' she said, and led me aft. When I saw the thing upon her pillow I shuddered, and then and there we agreed to go right out of the ship and see whether we could not fare to make ourselves more comfortable ashore.

"Hurriedly we gathered together our few belongings, and even among these I found that the fungus had been at work, for one of her shawls had a little lump of it growing near one edge. I threw the whole thing over the side without saying anything to her.

"The raft was still alongside, but it was too clumsy to guide, and I lowered down a small boat that hung across the stern, and in this we made our way to the shore. Yet, as we drew near to it, I became gradually aware that here the vile fungus, which had driven us from the ship, was growing riot. In places it rose into horrible, fantastic mounds, which seemed almost to quiver, as with a quiet life, when the wind blew across them. Here and there it took on the forms of vast fingers, and in others it just spread out flat and smooth and treacherous. Odd places, it appeared as grotesque stunted trees, seeming extraordinarily kinked and gnarled—the whole quaking vilely at times.

"At first, it seemed to us that there was no single portion of the surrounding shore which was not hidden beneath the masses of the hideous lichen; yet, in this, I found we were mistaken; for somewhat later, coasting along the shore at a little distance, we descried a smooth white patch of what appeared to be fine sand, and there we landed. It was not sand. What it was I do not know. All that I have observed is that upon it the fungus will not grow; while everywhere else, save where the sand-like earth wanders oddly, path-wise, amid the grey desolation of the lichen, there is nothing but that loathsome greyness.

"It is difficult to make you understand how cheered we were to find one place that was absolutely free from the growth, and here we deposited our belongings. Then we went back to the ship for such things as it seemed to us we should need. Among other matters, I managed to bring ashore with me one of the ship's sails, with which I constructed two small tents, which, though exceedingly rough-shaped, served the purposes for which they were intended. In these we lived and stored our various necessities, and thus for a matter of some four weeks all went smoothly and without particular unhappiness. Indeed, I may say with much happiness—for—for we were together.

"It was on the thumb of her right hand that the growth first showed. It was only a small circular spot, much like a little grey mole. My God! how the fear leaped to my heart when she showed me the place. We cleansed it, between us, washing it with carbolic and water. In the morning of the following day she showed her hand to me again. The grey warty thing had returned. For a little while we looked at one another in silence. Then, still wordless, we started again to remove it. In the midst of the operation she spoke suddenly.

"'What's that on the side of your face, dear?' Her voice was sharp with anxiety. I put my hand up to feel.

"'There! Under the hair by your ear. A little to the front a bit.' My finger rested upon the place, and then I knew.

"'Let us get your thumb done first,' I said. And she submitted, only because she was afraid to touch me until it was cleansed. I finished washing and disinfecting her thumb, and then she turned to my face. After it was finished we sat together and talked awhile of many things; for there had come into our lives sudden, very terrible thoughts. We were, all at once, afraid of something worse than death. We spoke of loading the boat with provisions and water and making our way out onto the sea; yet we were helpless, for many causes, and—and the growth had attacked us already. We decided to stay. God would do with us what was His will. We would wait.

"A month, two months, three months passed and the places grew somewhat, and there had come others. Yet we fought so strenuously with the fear that its headway was but slow, comparatively speaking.

"Occasionally we ventured off to the ship for such stores as we needed. There we found that the fungus grew persistently. One of the nodules on the main deck soon became as high as my head.

"We had now given up all thought or hope of leaving the island. We had realized that it would be unallowable to go among healthy humans, with the things from which we were suffering.

"With this determination and knowledge in our minds we knew that we should have to husband our food and water; for we did not know, at that time, but that we should possibly live for many years.

"This reminds me that I have told you that I am an old man. Judged by years this is not so. But—but—"

He broke off; then continued somewhat abruptly:

"As I was saying, we knew that we should have to use care in the matter of food. But we had no idea then how little food there was left of which to take care. It was a week later that I made the discovery that all the other bread tanks—which I had supposed full—were empty, and that (beyond odd tins of vegetables and meat, and some other matters) we had nothing on which to depend, but the bread in the tank which I had already opened.

"After learning this I bestirred myself to do what I could, and set to work at fishing in the lagoon; but with no success. At this I was somewhat inclined to feel desperate until the thought came to me to try outside the lagoon, in the open sea.

"Here, at times, I caught odd fish, but so infrequently that they proved of but little help in keeping us from the hunger which threatened. It seemed to me that our deaths were likely to come by hunger, and not by the growth of the thing which had seized upon our bodies.

"We were in this state of mind when the fourth month wore out. Then I made a very horrible discovery. One morning, a little before midday, I came off from the ship with a portion of the biscuits which were left. In the mouth of her tent I saw my sweetheart sitting, eating something.

"'What is it, my dear?' I called out as I leaped ashore. Yet, on hearing my voice, she seemed confused, and, turning, slyly threw something toward the edge of the little clearing. It fell short, and a vague suspicion having arisen within me, I walked across and picked it up. It was a piece of the grey fungus.

"As I went to her with it in my hand, she turned deadly pale; then a rose red.

"I felt strangely dazed and frightened.

"'My dear! My dear!' I said, and could say no more. Yet at my words she broke down and cried bitterly. Gradually, as she calmed, I got from her the news that she had tried it the preceding day, and—and liked it. I got her to promise on her knees not to touch it again, however great our hunger. After she had promised, she told me that the desire for it had come suddenly, and that, until the moment of desire, she had experienced nothing toward it but the most extreme repulsion.

"Later in the day, feeling strangely restless and much shaken with the thing which I had discovered, I made my way along one of the twisted paths—formed by the white, sand-like substance—which led among the fungoid growth. I had, once before, ventured along there; but not to any great distance. This time, being involved in perplexing thought, I went much farther than hitherto.

"Suddenly I was called to myself by a queer hoarse sound on my left. Turning quickly I saw that there was movement among an extraordinarily shaped mass of fungus, close to my elbow. It was swaying uneasily, as though it possessed life of its own. Abruptly, as I stared, the thought came to me that the thing had a grotesque resemblance to the figure of a distorted human creature. Even as the fancy flashed into my brain, there was a slight, sickening noise of tearing, and I saw that one of the branchlike arms was detaching itself from the surrounding grey masses, and coming toward me. The head of the thing—a shapeless grey ball, inclined in my direction. I stood stupidly, and the vile arm brushed across my face. I gave out a frightened cry, and ran back a few paces. There was a sweetish taste upon my lips where the thing had touched me. I licked them, and was immediately filled with an inhuman desire. I turned and seized a mass of the fungus. Then more, and—more. I was insatiable. In the midst of devouring, the remembrance of the morning's discovery swept into my mazed brain. It was sent by God. I dashed the fragment I held to the ground. Then, utterly wretched and feeling a dreadful guiltiness, I made my way back to the little encampment.

"I think she knew, by some marvelous intuition which love must have given, so soon as she set eyes on me. Her quiet sympathy made it easier for me, and I told her of my sudden weakness, yet omitted to mention the extraordinary thing which had gone before. I desired to spare her all unnecessary terror.

"But, for myself, I had added an intolerable knowledge, to breed an incessant terror in my brain; for I doubted not but that I had seen the end of one of these men who had come to the island in the ship in the lagoon; and in that monstrous ending I had seen our own.

"Thereafter we kept from the abominable food, though the desire for it had entered into our blood. Yet our drear punishment was upon us; for, day by day, with monstrous rapidity, the fungoid growth took hold of our poor bodies. Nothing we could do would check it materially, and so—and so—we who had been human became—Well, it matters less each day. Only—only we had been man and maid!

"And day by day the fight is more dreadful, to withstand the hunger-lust for the terrible lichen.

"A week ago we ate the last of the biscuit, and since that time I have caught three fish. I was out here fishing tonight when your schooner drifted upon me out of the mist. I hailed you. You know the rest, and may God, out of His great heart, bless you for your goodness to a—a couple of poor outcast souls."

There was the dip of an oar—another. Then the voice came again, and for the last time, sounding through the slight surrounding mist, ghostly and mournful.

"God bless you! Good-bye!"

"Good-bye," we shouted together hoarsely, our hearts full of many emotions.

I glanced about me. I became aware that the dawn was upon us.

The sun flung a stray beam across the hidden sea; pierced the mist dully, and lit up the receding boat with a gloomy fire.

Indistinctly I saw something nodding between the oars. I thought of a sponge—a great, grey nodding sponge—The oars continued to ply. They were grey—as was the boat—and my eyes searched a moment vainly for the conjunction of hand and oar. My gaze flashed back to the—head. It nodded forward as the oars went backward for the stroke. Then the oars were dipped, the boat shot out of the patch of light, and the—the thing went nodding into the mist.

VENUS AND THE COMET

Robert Duncan Milne

THE CONDITION OF LIFE ON THE PLANET, AND THE CONSTITUTION OF THE COMET

I returned to the cabin and assisted the major to direct the rays from Venus upon the screen. While the fixed stars were passing over the screen before the expected advent of the planet, I noticed that a bright orb, presenting somewhat the appearance of a gibbous moon, suddenly made its appearance upon the field. I knew that it could not be a fixed star, since it subtended an arc of some six inches on the screen, and I felt equally confident that it was not the planet we were in search of, since Venus, though now past her western elongation, and therefore at least seventy millions of miles away, would certainly present a picture extensive as that of Mars, owing to her superior diameter. Nevertheless the gibbous aspect of the body bore a marked resemblance to what might be expected of Venus in her present relation to the sun, and I consequently hailed the major, asking him whether it was possible that any sudden accident had happened to the lenses to account for the mysterious diminution in size of the supposed celestial object.

"No," he answered presently; "everything is right out here. Nevertheless, I am at a loss to account for the body you mention. See if anything has happened to either of the concave receiving lenses. The displacement of one of them would materially affect the size of the image."

I felt for the lenses, and found that their position was unchanged, and so told the major.

"Focus your binocular upon the object," said he; "it may possibly be one of the asteroids; a new one, perhaps, and may present an interesting study."

"But," returned I, "were it one of those diminutive planets which circle round the sun, midway between Mars and Jupiter, that would not account for its gibbous appearance. In that case we should behold a perfect orb, at all events, should we not?"

"You are right," replied the major, "it is evident that this body must revolve in an orbit between ourselves and the sun."

"Is it possible," I asked, struck by a sudden idea, "that it can be a satellite of Venus?"

"That must be it," cried the major, with emphasis. "I have always thought that the moon of Venus, as seen by Cassini, by Short, by Montaigne, by Rödkier, was not wholly a myth. Examine it carefully and note what you see."

I did as desired, and kept this moon well in the field of vision. It resolved itself into an almost absolute epitome of our own moon approaching the full, and seemed to shine with two kinds of reflected light, one radiant, such as might be referred to a solar source, and one much fainter, flooding the darkened regions of the sphere with a species of twilight. I noticed that the surface was rough and mottled by volcanic action, like the surface of our own satellite, and apprised the major of the fact.

"It merely bears out the analogy of nature," said he. "There can be no good reason to suppose that a satellite of Venus should exist lander other conditions than our own. Its small size—since, by your description, it can not be more than half the diameter of our own moon—would necessitate the extinction of its internal heat long ago, and render it unfit for the sustenance of life. Still, I am glad you have discovered it, and thus put an end to the astronomical uncertainty regarding it," he added, as the orb swept slowly out of telescopic view.

It was presently succeeded by a spectacle before which the cloud-atmosphere of Jupiter, and the well-defined, though monotonous seas and continents of Mars paled into insignificance. A landscape of surpassing beauty was passing beneath my gaze, as if at the distance of five or six miles away. Green meadows, resplendent with rainbow-hued flowers in such profusion as to be distinctly visible even at this distance, seemed to pass swiftly by with the diurnal rotation of the planet. Forests of trees, whose genus I could not exactly determine, though their foliage was dense, "umbrageous, and luxuriant, stretched over vast expanses of land, beside limpid rivers and placid inland lakes, which gleamed beneath a radiant sun through a particularly translucent atmosphere. Then came a strange and interesting spectacle. A collection of dwellings of dazzling white, seemingly constructed of porcelain or alabaster, for their graceful outlines, their aerial curves, their hanging domes, seemed to preclude the idea of marble, though their glistening sheen suggested the purest Parian, reared their fronts on the shore of a lovely and island-dotted lake. There appeared to be people, clad in shining garments, moving in the streets, which were irregular, and bore rather a resemblance to the arrangement of a country town than of a business city. Elegant structures, of a size which is rarely paralleled upon our earth, and whose symmetrical proportions naturally evoked the idea of temples, lyceums, or other buildings dedicated to the higher culture of life, were not wanting to complete the pleasing picture. As the panorama passed on, the city gave place to a succession of country houses—or rather palaces," judging from their size—all built of the same dazzling white material, and surrounded by ample pleasure-grounds, stretching as far as the eye could reach. Then a serene and shining sea passed in upon the field of vision. Ships and argosies sailing upon its bosom served to convince me that the inhabitants of Venus bad acquired, among other arts, that of navigation. I was peculiarly struck with the serenity and peacefulness of everything I saw, both on the sea, which, after a few hundred miles, again gave place to land, and on the land itself. I could see no mountains, but pleasantly rounded and verdure-clad bills; no abrupt gorges, bold bluffs, stupendous water-falls, but silvery brooks threading their way through copses, or larger rivers gliding gently over smiling and peaceful plains. Many more cities and stately buildings, built upon the same symmetrical plan, passed beneath my gaze. Continents and islands glided on with the slow and majestic movement of a panorama, necessitating re-focusing of my lenses as the body of the planet gained curvature toward the horizon, till at length the pleasant landscape vanished from the screen. Greatly pleased with what I had witnessed after the unpleasant ideas suggested by the wild and abnormal conditions of Jupiter and Mars, I went out upon the roof and talked to the major.

"Yes," said he, as I referred to what I had just seen, "Venus is the beau ideal of a world in the golden or Saturnian age; and why not? Her physical conditions are exactly suited to produce and foster a race of the most perfect development Through what degrees of development her inhabitants attained their present advanced stage in arts, in luxury, in government, we have, of course, at present, no means of knowing. I shall, however, have far greater facilities when I procure my new power of eight hundred diameters, which I told you about I can then observe and study their actions almost as well as if I were among them. I do not despair even of formulating a code of signals, after I have succeeded in attracting their attention, by means of which I can open up intelligent communication with them. You need not start and look amazed, as if the idea were wild and beyond the power of human intelligence to conceive or carry out I should have supposed that what you have witnessed here on two occasions already would have rendered you somewhat diffident as to the present penetrative powers of humanity in general, and scientists in particular. Remember that George Stephenson was laughed down and hooted at by the so-called savants of his day as a maniac, because he gravely asserted that his locomotive would drag a. train of cars along a pair of rails at the rate of six miles an hour, Morse had immense difficulty in persuading the sapient legislators of his day that the transmission of signals by electricity was a practicable thing; And will you then dare to say that I can not throw a signal to the inhabitants of Venus by the converse of that method which I employ to gather their light, and approach almost within hailing distance of that planet?" And the major turned away with considerable heat.

"No, no," he went on, as, after walking half a dozen paces, he turned laughing, "I cannot blame you for being nonplussed by my remarks. Of course, you have been brought up in the old grooves, and must religiously believe, what is told you in your schools and colleges. Hut when you are old enough to think for yourself, why shouldn't you? Tell me that." And he stopped abruptly.

I confess to having felt particularly ashamed and uncomfortably abashed at this tirade of the major's, and drew several prolonged whiffs at an uncommonly good cigar before I regained sufficient composure to hazard a remark.

"Then you do not think," said I, "that the inhabitants of Venus have passed through the same chain of circumstances, through the same processes or gradations of development, that we have?"

"I do not," he replied. "I am compelled to believe, from all I have witnessed, that the conditions of that planet have been, and are, eminently favorable to the production and development of only the best and highest types of animal and vegetable life, and, per contra as eminently unfavorable to the procreation and continuance of all that is vile, depraved, and inferior in the vital scale. The conditions necessary to the development and procreation of the latter class being wanting, I am confident that, when we have fuller opportunities for observation, we shall find that Venus is not only free from all ferocious and predatory animals, noxious reptiles and insects, but also from their congeners of the human species. Imagine, if you can, a planet devoid of Bengal tigers, crocodiles, rats, scorpions, tarantulas, lying politicians, thieving officials, hypocritical religionists, ignorant teachers, cheating; merchants, criminals and desperadoes of every class, divine-right usurpers of other peoples' labor, puny and sickly beings whose only claim to manhood is the name, and you can form some conception of the condition of society in Venus. Now for the reason. First and foremost, plenty of sunlight, with the attendant heat tempered and rendered grateful by the transparency, rarity, and buoyancy of the air. Next, a surface crust whose sharp edges were all worn off by short and sharp elemental action before it became the repository of life. On a sphere such as this, the profusion and variety of vegetable forms would naturally attract the attention of those developing types of animal life, which, upon our own unfortunate, accursed, and convulsed planet, were driven, however unwillingly at first, to prey upon one another until habit became nature. Man followed suit. Elemental convulsions have, again and again, aye, for millions of years, swept him all but entirely off the surface of this earth, so that he has lost his records, and been obliged to depend upon those mountainous and nearly barbarous races which escaped, for the slight inklings of the arts and sciences by which he has again laboriously worked his way up to some poor glimmer of knowledge and comfort during the last few thousand years of dim tradition. But he still possesses within himself a possibility of higher things, a natural memory and inalienable hereditary reminiscence of those ancestral glories which illustrated this planet before the last tremendous cataclysm swept everything before it. Now," continued the major, "you see the moon is making its appearance above the horizon, as also is the comet. We shall not have much time for the examination of both. Which had you rather see, the war-worn surface of our satellite, or the strange and puzzling composition of the nucleus and shining tail of one of those bodies which have puzzled astronomers since the days of Zoroaster and Ptolemy? If you choose the former, you will see unexpected things—deep abysses opening upon hidden central seas, and other sights as fearful as grotesque; if the latter, you will have the privilege of analyzing the most mysterious body which sounds the depths of space."

"Although," I replied, after a moment's deliberation, "I am curious to learn all that can be known about the physical constitution of our satellite, whose great proximity, occupying as she does a position more than one hundred times nearer than any other of the heavenly bodies can ever attain to, renders her a desirable object for astronomical investigation, yet I am content with your assurance that our moon is absolutely destitute of all forms of life, animal or vegetable; that she is, in fact, a ruined world, and as such can awake but a scientific interest, such as one might bring to bear upon a rare geological specimen, or some primitive rock strata. I presume nothing of any great physical moment can be learned from a minute examination of the surface of our satellite."

"That," answered the major, "depends entirely on how you look at it. An inspection of its arid wastes, its interminable lands, its gigantic crater-beds, might afford a solution of the vexed problem whether the moon ever possessed large bodies of water or an atmosphere, and, if so, where I they have disappeared to. At present there is no atmosphere such as ours existing there; taj is to say, none composed of the elements nitrogen and oxygen. Water there is, but it is all subterranean, long ago drawn and sucked into central caverns left void by the cooling down of the interior of the sphere. I am merely waiting tall I procure the higher magnifying power I told you of to institute a thorough examination of this subterranean sea through an immense opening in the great crater Tycho. I then do not despair of discovering some ghastly forms of amphibious animal life, to which the octopus, the devil-fish, and the spider-crab will appear gentle and symmetrical. Some dark hints of the existence of such fearful monsters I have already got; but, perhaps, on the whole, it will be better to defer the examination, and direct our attention to the comet, which will have vanished into space before I return again from the seaside, whereas there is no fear of a like catastrophe with the moon."

I gladly assented to this proposition, and together we directed the instrument upon She comet, which bad already attained several degrees elevation in the east. It was a matter of ease to bring so large a body upon the screen, and presently I commanded a portion of the tail, through which shone several fixed stars of great brilliancy. At first I had some difficulty in bringing what seemed an extremely attenuated and nebulous mass to a focus through the binocular. The substance of the tail, with the power I employed, seemed to defy analysis or resolution into its constituent elements.

"We must remember," said the major, as I referred the matter to him, "that the comet is more than a hundred millions of miles from us at present, and therefore not seen under nearly so favorable conditions as those under which we observed Mars or Venus. I am not sanguine of being able to analyse with our present power the minute particles of which the tail is undoubtedly composed."

I persevered, however, and at length thought that I made out a congeries of countless myriads of globules moving among themselves in ever-changing gyrations and with in credible velocity. As the scene passed across the screen, there remained no doubt about the fact. The globules grew more luminous, more numerous; their involuted motion, though still surprisingly rapid, not so agile as at first, and I argued that my vision was approaching the nucleus.

I was not disappointed as, suddenly, a sea of fire burst upon the scene. An intense white light, which was almost blinding in its brilliancy, occupied the field, seemingly proceeding from a molten or vaporous mass of inconceivably high temperature. My eyes were pained by the spectacle, and I was presently compelled to remove them, having first noted, however, that this ocean of fire and light was convulsed within itself by some fierce and potent agency which I could not understand. I again turned my glass upon the tail, but found that the extreme brilliancy of the nucleus had dazzled my sight into impotency. I mechanically arose and went out.

"Well," said the major, slowly, as I detailed what I had seen, "I can not help thinking that the nucleus of a comet is composed of electrical substances of opposite polarity, whose immense speed while near the sun at perihelion excites such powerful action as to cause them to become incandescent in the highest degree. Those particles or globules which you noticed as composing the tail, are thrown off or repelled from one of the poles—in the case of some observed comets from two or more poles, according to the polarity of the substances composing the nucleus. This electrical repulsion would account for the terrific and inconceivable speed with which the end of a comet's tail moves while rounding the sun, a speed, in some cases, certainly reaching many hundreds of millions of miles per hour. As a common dynamical simile upon this point in our every-day experience, I may cite the repulsion of steel filings from the end of a magnet, or even so light an object as a pith ball; so that actually neither the small mass, gravity, or density of a body would necessarily present a bar to such electrical action as I have described. I think we have at last got upon the track of the laws which regulate these cometary bodies, but I shall study the matter more fully with my higher power. We can do nothing more now," continued he, looking at the east. "Let us go in." We left the roof.

"Come again," said the major, as I said good-bye, "when I return from the seaside, which will be in about a month's time, and we will continue our investigations if you care to do so."

WHAT WAS IT?

A Mystery

Fitz-James O'Brien

It is, I confess, with considerable diffidence that I approach the strange narrative which I am about to relate. The events which I purpose detailing are of so extraordinary and unheard-of a character that I am quite prepared to meet with an unusual amount of incredulity and scorn. I accept all such beforehand. I have, I trust, the literary courage to face unbelief. I have, after mature consideration, resolved to narrate, in as simple and straightforward a manner as I can compass, some facts that passed under my observation in the month of July last, and which, in the annals of the mysteries of physical science, are wholly unparalleled.

I live at No.—Twenty-sixth Street, in this city. The house is in some respects a curious one. It has enjoyed for the last two years the reputation of being haunted. It is a large and stately residence, surrounded by what was once a garden, but which is now only a green inclosure used for bleaching clothes. The dry basin of what has been a fountain, and a few fruit-trees, ragged and unpruned, indicate that this spot, in past days, was a pleasant, shady retreat, filled with fruits and flowers and the sweet murmur of waters.

The house is very spacious. A hall of noble size leads to a vast spiral staircase winding through its center, while the various apartments are of imposing dimensions. It was built some fifteen or twenty years since by Mr. A—, the well-known New York merchant, who five years ago threw the commercial world into convulsions by a stupendous bank fraud. Mr. A—, as every one knows, escaped to Europe, and died not long after of a broken heart. Almost immediately after the news of his decease reached this country, and was verified, the report spread in Twenty-sixth Street that No.—-was haunted. Legal measures had dispossessed the widow of its former owner, and it was inhabited merely by a care taker and his wife, placed there by the house agent into whose hands it had passed for purposes of renting or sale. These people declared that they were troubled with unnatural noises. Doors were opened without any visible agency. The remnants of furniture scattered through the various rooms were, during the night, piled one upon the other by unknown hands. Invisible feet passed up and down the stairs in broad daylight, accompanied by the rustle of unseen silk dresses, and the gliding of viewless hands along the massive balusters. The care taker and his wife declared that they would live there no longer. The house agent laughed, dismissed them, and put others in their place. The noises and supernatural manifestations continued. The neighborhood caught up the story, and the house remained untenanted for three years. Several persons negotiated for it; but somehow, always before the bargain was closed, they heard the unpleasant rumors, and declined to treat any further.

It was in this state of things that my landlady—who at that time kept a boarding-house in Bleecker Street, and who wished to move farther up town—conceived the bold idea of renting No.—-Twenty-sixth Street. Happening to have in her house rather a plucky and philosophical set of boarders, she laid down her scheme before us, stating candidly everything she had heard respecting the ghostly qualities of the establishment to which she wished to remove us. With the exception of two timid persons,—a sea captain and a returned Californian, who immediately gave notice that they would leave,—all of Mrs. Moffat's guests declared that they would accompany her in her chivalric incursion into the abode of spirits.

Our removal was effected in the month of May, and we were all charmed with our new residence. The portion of Twenty-sixth Street where our house is situated—between Seventh and Eighth Avenues—is one of the pleasantest localities in New York. The gardens back of the houses, running down nearly to the Hudson, form, in the summer time, a perfect avenue of verdure. The air is pure and invigorating, sweeping, as it does, straight across the river from the Weehawken heights, and even the ragged garden which surrounded the house on two sides, although displaying on washing days rather too much clothesline, still gave us a piece of greensward to look at, and a cool retreat in the summer evenings, where we smoked our cigars in the dusk, and watched the fireflies flashing their dark-lanterns in the long grass.

Of course we had no sooner established ourselves at No.—— than we began to expect the ghosts. We absolutely awaited their advent with eagerness. Our dinner conversation was supernatural. One of the boarders, who had purchased Mrs. Crowe's "Night Side of Nature" for his own private delectation, was regarded as a public enemy by the entire household for not having bought twenty copies. The man led a life of supreme wretchedness while he was reading this volume. A system of espionage was established, of which he was the victim. If he incautiously laid the book down for an instant and left the room, it was immediately seized and read aloud in secret places to a select few. I found myself a person of immense importance, it having leaked out that I was tolerably well versed in the history of supernaturalism, and had once written a story, entitled "The Pot of Tulips," for Harper's Monthly, the foundation of which was a ghost. If a table or a wainscot panel happened to warp when we were assembled in the large drawing-room, there was an instant silence, and every one was prepared for an immediate clanking of chains and a spectral form.

After a month of psychological excitement, it was with the utmost dissatisfaction that we were forced to acknowledge that nothing in the remotest degree approaching the supernatural had manifested itself. Once the black butler asseverated that his candle had been blown out by some invisible agency while he was undressing himself for the night; but as I had more than once discovered this colored gentleman in a condition when one candle must have appeared to him like two, I thought it possible that, by going a step farther in his potations, he might have reversed his phenomenon, and seen no candle at all where he ought to have beheld one.

Things were in this state when an incident took place so awful and inexplicable in its character that my reason fairly reels at the bare memory of the occurrence. It was the tenth of July. After dinner was over I repaired with my friend, Dr. Hammond, to the garden to smoke my evening pipe. The Doctor and myself found ourselves in an unusually metaphysical mood. We lit our large meerschaums, filled with fine Turkish tobacco; we paced to and fro, conversing. A strange perversity dominated the currents of our thought. They would not flow through the sun-lit channels into which we strove to divert them. For some unaccountable reason they constantly diverged into dark and lonesome beds, where a continual gloom brooded. It was in vain that, after our old fashion, we flung ourselves on the shores of the East, and talked of its gay bazaars, of the splendors of the time of Haroun, of harems and golden palaces. Black afreets continually arose from the depths of our talk, and expanded, like the one the fisherman released from the copper vessel, until they blotted everything bright from our vision. Insensibly, we yielded to the occult force that swayed us, and indulged in gloomy speculation. We had talked some time upon the proneness of the human mind to mysticism, and the almost universal love of the Terrible, when Hammond suddenly said to me, "What do you consider to be the greatest element of Terror?"

The question, I own, puzzled me. That many things were terrible, I knew. Stumbling over a corpse in the dark; beholding, as I once did, a woman floating down a deep and rapid river, with wildly lifted arms, and awful, upturned face, uttering, as she sank, shrieks that rent one's heart, while we, the spectators, stood frozen at a window which overhung the river at a height of sixty feet, unable to make the slightest effort to save her, but dumbly watching her last supreme agony and her disappearance. A shattered wreck, with no life visible, encountered floating listlessly on the ocean, is a terrible object, for it suggests a huge terror, the proportions of which are veiled. But it now struck me for the first time that there must be one great and ruling embodiment of fear, a King of Terrors to which all others must succumb. What might it be? To what train of circumstances would it owe its existence?

"I confess, Hammond," I replied to my friend, "I never considered the subject before. That there must be one Something more terrible than any other thing, I feel. I cannot attempt, however, even the most vague definition."

"I am somewhat like you, Harry," he answered. "I feel my capacity to experience a terror greater than anything yet conceived by the human mind,—something combining in fearful and unnatural amalgamation hitherto supposed incompatible elements. The calling of the voices in Brockden Brown's novel of 'Wieland' is awful; so is the picture of the Dweller of the Threshold, in Bulwer's 'Zanoni'; but," he added, shaking his head gloomily, "there is something more horrible still than these."

"Look here, Hammond," I rejoined, "let us drop this kind

of talk, for Heaven's sake!"

"I don't know what's the matter with me to-night," he replied, "but my brain is running upon all sorts of weird and awful thoughts. I feel as if I could write a story like Hoffman to night, if I were only master of a literary style."

"Well, if we are going to be Hoffmanesque in our talk, I'm off to bed. How sultry it is! Good night, Hammond."

"Good night, Harry. Pleasant dreams to you."

"To you, gloomy wretch, afreets, ghouls, and enchanters."

We parted, and each sought his respective chamber. I undressed quickly and got into bed, taking with me, according to my usual custom, a book, over which I generally read myself to sleep. I opened the volume as soon as I had laid my head upon the pillow, and instantly flung it to the other side of the room. It was Goudon's "History of Monsters"—a curious French work, which I had lately imported from Paris, but which, in the state of mind I had then reached, was anything but an agreeable companion. I resolved to go to sleep at once; so, turning down my gas until nothing but a little blue point of light glimmered on the top of the tube, I composed myself to rest.

The room was in total darkness. The atom of gas that still remained lighted did not illuminate a distance of three inches round the burner. I desperately drew my arm across my eyes, as if to shut out even the darkness, and tried to think of nothing. It was in vain. The confounded themes touched on by Hammond in the garden kept obtruding themselves on my brain. I battled against them. I erected ramparts of would-be blankness of intellect to keep them out. They still crowded upon me. While I was lying still as a corpse, hoping that by a perfect physical inaction I should hasten mental repose, an awful incident occurred. A Something dropped, as it seemed, from the ceiling, plumb upon my chest, and the next instant I felt two bony hands encircling my throat, endeavoring to choke me.

I am no coward, and am possessed of considerable physical strength. The suddenness of the attack, instead of stunning me, strung every nerve to its highest tension. My body acted from instinct, before my brain had time to realize the terrors of my position. In an instant I wound two muscular arms around the creature, and squeezed it, with all the strength of despair, against my chest. In a few seconds the bony hands that had fastened on my throat loosened their hold, and I was free to breathe once more. Then commenced a struggle of awful intensity. Immersed in the most profound darkness, totally ignorant of the nature of the Thing by which I was so suddenly attacked, finding my grasp slipping every moment, by reason, it seemed to me, of the entire nakedness of my assailant, bitten with sharp teeth in the shoulder, neck, and chest, having every moment to protect my throat against a pair of sinewy, agile hands, which my utmost efforts could not confine—these were a combination of circumstances to combat which required all the strength and skill and courage that I possessed.

At last, after a silent, deadly, exhausting struggle, I got my assailant under by a series of incredible efforts of strength. Once pinned, with my knee on what I made out to be its chest, I knew that I was victor. I rested for a moment to breathe. I heard the creature beneath me panting in the darkness, and felt the violent throbbing of a heart. It was apparently as exhausted as I was; that was one comfort. At this moment I remembered that I usually placed under my pillow, before going to bed, a large yellow silk pocket handkerchief, for use during the night. I felt for it instantly; it was there. In a few seconds more I had, after a fashion, pinioned the creature's arms.

I now felt tolerably secure. There was nothing more to be done but to turn on the gas, and, having first seen what my midnight assailant was like, arouse the household. I will confess to being actuated by a certain pride in not giving the alarm before; I wished to make the capture alone and unaided.

Never losing my hold for an instant, I slipped from the bed to the floor, dragging my captive with me. I had but a few steps to make to reach the gas-burner; these I made with the greatest caution, holding the creature in a grip like a vice. At last I got within arm's-length of the tiny speck of blue light which told me where the gas-burner lay. Quick as lightning I released my grasp with one hand and let on the full flood of light. Then I turned to look at my captive.

I cannot even attempt to give any definition of my sensations the instant after I turned on the gas. I suppose I must have shrieked with terror, for in less than a minute afterward my room was crowded with the inmates of the house. I shudder now as I think of that awful moment. I saw nothing! Yes; I had one arm firmly clasped round a breathing, panting, corporeal shape, my other hand gripped with all its strength a throat as warm, and apparently fleshly, as my own; and yet, with this living substance in my grasp, with its body pressed against my own, and all in the bright glare of a large jet of gas, I absolutely beheld nothing! Not even an outline,—a vapor!

I do not, even at this hour, realize the situation in which I found myself. I cannot recall the astounding incident thoroughly. Imagination in vain tries to compass the awful paradox.

It breathed. I felt its warm breath upon my cheek. It struggled fiercely. It had hands. They clutched me. Its skin was smooth, like my own. There it lay, pressed close up against me, solid as stone,—and yet utterly invisible!

I wonder that I did not faint or go mad on the instant. Some wonderful instinct must have sustained me; for, absolutely, in place of loosening my hold on the terrible Enigma, I seemed to gain an additional strength in my moment of horror, and tightened my grasp with such wonderful force that I felt the creature shivering with agony.

Just then Hammond entered my room at the head of the household. As soon as he beheld my face—which, I suppose, must have been an awful sight to look at—he hastened forward, crying, "Great heaven, Harry! what has happened?"

"Hammond! Hammond!" I cried, "come here. Oh! this is awful! I have been attacked in bed by something or other, which I have hold of; but I can't see it—I can't see it!"

Hammond, doubtless struck by the unfeigned horror expressed in my countenance, made one or two steps forward with an anxious yet puzzled expression. A very audible titter burst from the remainder of my visitors. This suppressed laughter made me furious. To laugh at a human being in my position! It was the worst species of cruelty. Now, I can understand why the appearance of a man struggling violently, as it would seem, with an airy nothing, and calling for assistance against a vision, should have appeared ludicrous. Then, so great was my rage against the mocking crowd that had I the power I would have stricken them dead where they stood.

"Hammond! Hammond!" I cried again, despairingly, "for God's sake come to me. I can hold the—the Thing but a short while longer. It is overpowering me. Help me! Help me!"

"Harry," whispered Hammond, approaching me, "you have been smoking too much."

"I swear to you, Hammond, that this is no vision," I answered, in the same low tone. "Don't you see how it shakes my whole frame with its struggles? If you don't believe me, convince yourself. Feel it,—touch it."

Hammond advanced and laid his hand on the spot I indicated. A wild cry of horror burst from him. He had felt it!

In a moment he had discovered somewhere in my room a long piece of cord, and was the next instant winding it and knotting it about the body of the unseen being that I clasped in my arms.

"Harry," he said, in a hoarse, agitated voice, for, though he preserved his presence of mind, he was deeply moved, "Harry, it's all safe now. You may let go, old fellow, if you're tired. The Thing can't move."

I was utterly exhausted, and I gladly loosed my hold.

Hammond stood holding the ends of the cord that bound the Invisible, twisted round his hand, while before him, self-supporting as it were, he beheld a rope laced and interlaced, and stretching tightly round a vacant space. I never saw a man look so thoroughly stricken with awe. Nevertheless his face expressed all the courage and determination which I knew him to possess. His lips, although white, were set firmly, and one could perceive at a glance that, although stricken with fear, he was not daunted.

The confusion that ensued among the guests of the house who were witnesses of this extraordinary scene between Hammond and myself,—who beheld the pantomime of binding this struggling Something,—who beheld me almost sinking from physical exhaustion when my task of jailer was over—the confusion and terror that took possession of the bystanders, when they saw all this, was beyond description. The weaker ones fled from the apartment. The few who remained clustered near the door, and could not be induced to approach Hammond and his Charge. Still incredulity broke out through their terror. They had not the courage to satisfy themselves, and yet they doubted. It was in vain that I begged of some of the men to come near and convince themselves by touch of the existence in that room of a living being which was invisible. They were incredulous, but did not dare to undeceive themselves. How could a solid, living, breathing body be invisible, they asked. My reply was this. I gave a sign to Hammond, and both of us—conquering our fearful repugnance to touch the invisible creature—lifted it from the ground, manacled as it was, and took it to my bed. Its weight was about that of a boy of fourteen.

"Now, my friends," I said, as Hammond and myself held the creature suspended over the bed, "I can give you self-evident proof that here is a solid, ponderable body which, nevertheless, you cannot see. Be good enough to watch the surface of the bed attentively."

I was astonished at my own courage in treating this strange event so calmly; but I had recovered from my first terror, and felt a sort of scientific pride in the affair which dominated every other feeling.

The eyes of the bystanders were immediately fixed on my bed. At a given signal Hammond and I let the creature fall. There was the dull sound of a heavy body alighting on a soft mass. The timbers of the bed creaked. A deep impression marked itself distinctly on the pillow, and on the bed itself. The crowd who witnessed this gave a sort of low, universal cry, and rushed from the room. Hammond and I were left alone with our Mystery.

We remained silent for some time, listening to the low, irregular breathing of the creature on the bed, and watching the rustle of the bedclothes as it impotently struggled to free itself from confinement. Then Hammond spoke.

"Harry, this is awful."

"Aye, awful."

"But not unaccountable."

"Not unaccountable! What do you mean? Such a thing has never occurred since the birth of the world. I know not what to think, Hammond. God grant that I am not mad, and that this is not an insane fantasy!"

"Let us reason a little, Harry. Here is a solid body which we touch, but which we cannot see. The fact is so unusual that it strikes us with terror. Is there no parallel, though, for such a phenomenon? Take a piece of pure glass. It is tangible and transparent. A certain chemical coarseness is all that prevents its being so entirely transparent as to be totally invisible. It is not theoretically impossible, mind you, to make a glass which shall not reflect a single ray of light—a glass so pure and homogeneous in its atoms that the rays from the sun shall pass through it as they do through the air, refracted but not reflected. We do not see the air, and yet we feel it."

"That's all very well, Hammond, but these are inanimate substances. Glass does not breathe, air does not breathe. This thing has a heart that palpitates,—a will that moves it—lungs that play, and inspire and respire."

"You forget the strange phenomena of which we have so often heard of late," answered the Doctor, gravely. "At the meetings called 'spirit circles,' invisible hands have been thrust into the hands of those persons round the table—warm, fleshly hands that seemed to pulsate with mortal life."

"What? Do you think, then, that this thing is—"

"I don't know what it is," was the solemn reply; "but please the gods I will, with your assistance, thoroughly investigate it."

We watched together, smoking many pipes, all night long, by the bedside of the unearthly being that tossed and panted until it was apparently wearied out. Then we learned by the low, regular breathing that it slept.

The next morning the house was all astir. The boarders congregated on the landing outside my room, and Hammond and myself were lions. We had to answer a thousand questions as to the state of our extraordinary prisoner, for as yet not one person in the house except ourselves could be induced to set foot in the apartment.

The creature was awake. This was evidenced by the convulsive manner in which the bedclothes were moved in its efforts to escape. There was something truly terrible in beholding, as it were, those second-hand indications of the terrible writhings and agonized struggles for liberty which themselves were invisible.

Hammond and myself had racked our brains during the long night to discover some means by which we might realize the shape and general appearance of the Enigma. As well as we could make out by passing our hands over the creature's form, its outlines and lineaments were human. There was a mouth; a round, smooth head without hair; a nose, which, however, was little elevated above the cheeks; and its hands and feet felt like those of a boy. At first we thought of placing the being on a smooth surface and tracing its outline with chalk, as shoemakers trace the outline of the foot. This plan was given up as being of no value. Such an outline would give not the slightest idea of its conformation.

A happy thought struck me. We would take a cast of it in plaster of Paris. This would give us the solid figure, and satisfy all our wishes. But how to do it? The movements of the creature would disturb the setting of the plastic covering, and distort the mold. Another thought. Why not give it chloroform? It had respiratory organs—that was evident by its breathing. Once reduced to a state of insensibility, we could do with it what we would. Doctor X——was sent for; and after the worthy physician had recovered from the first shock of amazement, he proceeded to administer the chloroform. In three minutes afterward we were enabled to remove the fetters from the creature's body, and a well-known modeler of this city was busily engaged in covering the invisible form with the moist clay. In five minutes more we had a mold, and before evening a rough fac simile of the mystery. It was shaped like a man,—distorted, uncouth, and horrible, but still a man. It was small, not over four feet and some inches in height, and its limbs revealed a muscular development that was unparalleled. Its face surpassed in hideousness anything I had ever seen. Gustave Doré, or Callot, or Tony Johannot, never conceived anything so horrible. There is a face in one of the latter's illustrations to "Un Voyage où il vous plaira," which somewhat approaches the countenance of this creature, but does not equal it. It was the physiognomy of what I should have fancied a ghoul to be. It looked as if it was capable of feeding on human flesh.

Having satisfied our curiosity, and bound every one in the house to secrecy, it became a question what was to be done with our Enigma. It was impossible that we should keep such a horror in our house; it was equally impossible that such an awful being should be let loose upon the world. I confess that I would have gladly voted for the creature's destruction. But who would shoulder the responsibility? Who would undertake the execution of this horrible semblance of a human being? Day after day this question was deliberated gravely. The boarders all left the house. Mrs. Moffat was in despair, and threatened Hammond and myself with all sorts of legal penalties if we did not remove the Horror. Our answer was, "We will go if you like, but we decline taking this creature with us. Remove it yourself if you please. It appeared in your house. On you the responsibility rests." To this there was, of course, no answer. Mrs. Moffat could not obtain for love or money a person who would even approach the Mystery.

The most singular part of the transaction was that we were entirely ignorant of what the creature habitually fed on. Everything in the way of nutriment that we could think of was placed before it, but was never touched. It was awful to stand by, day after day, and see the clothes toss, and hear the hard breathing, and know that it was starving.

Ten, twelve days, a fortnight passed, and it still lived. The pulsations of the heart, however, were daily growing fainter, and had now nearly ceased altogether. It was evident that the creature was dying for want of sustenance. While this terrible life struggle was going on, I felt miserable. I could not sleep of nights. Horrible as the creature was, it was pitiful to think of the pangs it was suffering.

At last it died. Hammond and I found it cold and stiff one morning in the bed. The heart had ceased to beat, the lungs to inspire. We hastened to bury it in the garden. It was a strange funeral, the dropping of that viewless corpse into the damp hole. The cast of its form I gave to Dr. X—, who keeps it in his museum in Tenth Street.

As I am on the eve of a long journey from which I may not return, I have drawn up this narrative of an event the most singular that has ever come to my knowledge.

Note: It was rumored that the proprietors of a well-known museum in this city had made arrangements with Dr. X—to exhibit to the public the singular cast which Mr. Escott deposited with him. So extraordinary a history cannot fail to attract universal attention.